GUY FRANKS

A Smell of
TIME

LIBERTY HILL PRESS

Liberty Hill Press
2301 Lucien Way #415
Maitland, FL 32751
407.339.4217
www.libertyhillpublishing.com

Unless otherwise indicated, Scripture quotations taken from the King James Version (KJV) – *public domain*.

Printed in the United States of America.

Paperback ISBN-13: 978-1-6628-0491-5
Ebook ISBN-13: 978-1-6628-0492-2

Contents

For my wife Bobbie, who smells like home.

There was a smell of Time in the air tonight. He smiled and turned the fancy in his mind. There was a thought. What did time smell like? Like dust and clocks and people. And if you wondered what Time sounded like it sounded like water running in a dark cave and voices crying and dirt dropping down upon hollow box lids, and rain.

Ray Bradbury
The Martian Chronicles

THE FIFTIES

Ozzie Nelson:
Shakespeare is the world's greatest playwright. His plays are known the world over.

Ricky Nelson:
I think he's a little corny, myself.

David Nelson:
I don't see anything corny about him.

Ricky Nelson:
Oh, no? What about that Hamlet? Guy's talkin' to himself about commitin' suicide, walkin' through graveyards pickin' up old skulls–it just isn't commercial.

The Adventures of Ozzie & Harriet

Perhaps a child who is fussed over gets a feeling of destiny; he thinks he is in the world for something important, and it gives him drive and confidence.

Dr. Benjamin Spock

The Paradise of Childhood

There's a lot to think about when you're four years old. And there's lots to do. You really don't sit around waiting for something to happen; almost always something comes up like a stray toy, a found crayon, or a loose thread in the carpet that you can turn into a game that occupies the mind. All the games back then have a beginning and an end, and they are flush with purpose. It's the same way dolphins play.

This is around 1958 and it's all in black and white—except for special parts that are tinged with color. Some people say you can't really remember things from four years old, at least not minute, detailed things like engravings or flowered wallpaper, but they're wrong. I believe you'd agree that there's a body of evidence showing that a few people can even remember vivid details from their nursery at two years old. So maybe it's a gift; maybe some people can conjure up the distant past in the same way some folks can find water with a divining rod. At least I can, though I can't always remember what I had for dinner the night before. I think it was franks and beans.

Call them first memories—the dawn of consciousness—and I have pinpointed their inception through their retelling. It's easy really. I describe to my grandmother a train set I had as a child—that it was a Lionel with a light on its black nose and how I laid on the floor and watched it go round and round, and that the black box of a transformer was warm to the touch and smelled of ozone—and she says, "How can that be, you were only four?" I recount to my mom in detail the moment I fell off the dock at the lake—how I floated softly down in the green underworld, a sudden, peaceful feeling overcoming me until I hear a muffled splash and see a white bathing cap that grabs me and pulls me up—and she says, "You remember that? You were only four."

Only four years old, and I have just two creases in the palms of my hand. It's a time redolent with the smells of weather, cinnamon toast, fresh-cut grass, and tobacco smoke. There's a bedtime.

Which reminds me of a recurring dream I have at four years old. TVs back then are big boxes with dials and buttons, and the screens flicker to life with images of Mighty Mouse and white shirts washed with Tide. But sometimes the images crack, go askew, and fade into static. It's then that an adult gets up and adjusts the antenna on top of the set, and the image comes back to life. In this recurring dream, I am standing in front of my grandmother who is sitting in front of the TV set. Next to her is an end table covered with white lace in a pattern of snowflakes. On the table sits a big, shaded lamp that puts out a yellow globe of light. I'm getting ready for bed and my grand-mother is buttoning my pajamas. Her hands are white and she looks at my chest as she moves down the row of buttons. It's then that I get this strange sensation and feel myself beginning to fade into static. I'm afraid and I call to her but she can't hear me and pretty soon I'm gone. Just like Mighty Mouse with bad reception.

I wake up when I turn to static, then look at my Popeye night-light, turn over, and go back to sleep happy that I didn't really turn into static. In real life, while I stand before my grandmother as she buttons my pj's, I worry that the strange sensation will sprout up inside me and I'll begin to fade into static. But I don't, and my grandmother finishes buttoning my pj's and whispers to me, "Den som sover syndar icke" (which is Swedish for "He who sleeps does not sin") and sends me off to bed.

My mom comes into my bedroom and tucks me and my sister in. She kisses us and tells us she loves us, and she has an air of fresh softness that lingers. She stands in the doorway, and I close one eye and then the other multiple times, seeing her jump from left to right before she flutters off.

Adult voices ring like church bells—my father and grandfather loud and sonorous; my mother and grandmother soft and melodious. The voices and hands teach lessons, some remembered, some forgotten, and the big ones stay with you and get passed on.

In a lightning storm my grandfather holds my hand and walks me into the screened-in porch out front. There we watch the lightning fracture the purple sky. I'm afraid at first—the lightning is supernatural and the thunder shakes the house—but he holds my hand and merrily treats it like a fireworks show. The thunder always follows the lightning, he explains to me. "There, see the flash... now wait, here comes the thunder... There you go—can't have lightning without thunder. Right-o, sport?" I nod and smile. I'm okay with it now.

He's there again—"Gramps," I call him—teaching me to fish out on the lake. At four I have my own cane pole and he makes me bait my hook with earthworms. He cuts them on the bench-seat in the boat and hands me a small, wiggly section of the worm, and I take it from him like a precious pearl and thread it carefully onto my hook. I can smell the can of gas he keeps near the motor and there are boat noises—the lapping of water against the side and the creaking of wood whenever he shifts positions—but no talking, just this kind of buoyant quiet. The morning light is splayed across the water and it's hard to see my bobber, but I squint out at the red and white bulb for the longest time until I see it shiver, then dip and go under. "Got one!" he calls out.

I feel a frenzied strength at the end of my line, and I watch the line go left then right, cutting the water as I pull the fish to the surface. Into the boat it comes and flops around on the ribbed bottom of the boat until my grandfather picks it up, unhooks it, and shows it to me like found money. If it's big enough he slips it onto the stringer and drops it over the side, if not he tosses it back home. There are different kinds—sunfish and crappie—but my favorite is a bluegill. They're blue and purple with tiger strips and their belly is a bright orange.

My grandmother fries our catch up for dinner and the flaky white meat tastes good. "Watch out for bones," she says.

"Gram" always watches out and warns; she's like a lighthouse built on solid rock. Sometimes she's stern, other times a warm lap to cuddle up on. Whenever she comes home from the market she stops at the corner in her car and waits for me. I have a blue, peddle-driven car with a wooden steering wheel, and I'm ready at the corner for the race. Off we go—I peddle furiously, glancing at her as I go—and she stays even with me and is laughing as we pull into the driveway at the exact same time. It's always a tie.

There are lessons learned here, too. I get boils on my leg and she lays warm bread soaked in milk on them, wraps it up, and in the morning they're gone. She knows my fake-cry better than my mom, so I have to perfect a better one. On the rug, in a game of pick-up sticks, she lies next to me and shows me how to free a stick from the pile without moving the other sticks. It's a lesson in spatial dimensions and Newtonian physics, but more importantly, it helps me to beat my sister at the game.

Everybody smokes. The sounds and smells of a four-year-old include the scratch and spark of matches, an odor of sulphur, the clicks of a pocket lighter, a whiff of butane, and the recurring burnt-paper and tobacco smell of a freshly-lit cigarette. My grandparent's house is rigged for smoking. There are ashtrays on all the tables; some are marbled glass, thick and heavy, while others are colored plastic with melted spots. On one table sits an ornate lighter studded with brass beads that looks like a miniature Aladdin's lamp. I pick it up once and drop it and get yelled at, so it becomes off-limits.

There's an indoors and there's an outdoors. Indoors is arranged and predictable and it is governed by rules, but outdoors there is endless discovery and a kind of breezy freedom. Outdoors is also filled with insects and creatures. Monarch butterflies flirt and dance across the lawn, and you have to wait till they land and carefully pinch their wings together to catch one. They have caterpillar bodies, long and fuzzy, and their wings feel like tissue paper. When I let them go they rise up in the wind like tiny kites and swoop off.

It's twilight and some older kids catch fireflies in a jar. They stop and let me look at it, and as I gaze through the glass the bugs light up and make the jar glow. I won't touch the glass because I know that lightbulbs are hot to the touch. There are also dragon flies. I don't like them very much, and the ones at the lake, which are bigger with purple-fluorescent bodies, are scary-looking. I duck out of their way and keep a safe distance.

I have a friend named Paul and we hang out and dig up earthworms together and play with squirt guns. He lives down the block. There's a girl named Penny who lives across the alley in the back. She's older than me but she lets me hang out with her; we walk down the alley and look into people's backyards and find all sorts of neat things there like hubcaps, broken bikes, and empty soda bottles. The empty bottles we collect and redeem at the drugstore. With the money I buy purple tootsie pops (my favorite) or a roll of caps for my cap gun.

Up at the lake there is no TV, so my sister and I have to figure out things to do. We fish off the dock with our cane poles, play tag, try to catch minnows in a bucket, and do other stuff to pass the day. One adventure remains unforgotten: my grandmother gives me and my sister each a basket to go pick blueberries and we follow our mom into the woods. Soon we come upon bushes thick with blueberries and we pluck off the fruit and fill our baskets, and the fruit turns our fingertips a dark purple. My grandmother bakes a blueberry pie and we have it for desert—warm and crusty and full of the blueberries—and I ask for seconds and get it. It tastes better than anything, maybe because I helped pick the blueberries. It's like a farmer eating his own corn-on-the-cob.

At one point, undoubtedly in the spring, my mother disappears. I'm told she's at the hospital but she's not sick and that in a couple days she'll be bringing home my baby brother. A four-year-old's mind reels at this miracle.

My baby brother is doughy with tiny hands and reddish hair. His crying wakes me up at night.

My father reappears—tall and lanky and full of fun—and we move away. My grandparents live in Minneapolis, a name I can't say, but we also live in Minnesota, which I can sort of say ("Minn-soda"). My mom and dad, brother and sister—all of us together—live upstairs in a small apartment. One day, I'm playing out on the second story balcony; I have a pillow case tied around my neck to make a cape and I'm convinced I can fly, but of course I fall like a brick and hurt myself. After that I don't try to fly anymore.

We move again to a place called Chicago (which I pronounce "Cog-o"). The downtown is filled with giant buildings, and from the sidewalk I can't even see the top of them. They're the kind of buildings Superman leaps out of on TV. There's also Lake Michigan. During a storm, my mom has my uncle stop the car so we can watch the big waves come rolling in, and after a while my uncle mentions something about "an undertow." What's an undertow? I ask. My uncle explains to me that an undertow is a giant monster that lives under the water and pulls little kids in and drowns them. This scares the hell out of me and my mom gets mad at him and tells him to stop but he laughs and tells me it's true. The scareder I get the more he laughs. (He never has any kids of his own.)

My dad comes and goes; he's like the moon you only see at night. Years later he becomes mean to my mom, like a bad dog that won't behave, but when I'm four he's a playmate. We play marbles on the rug together. One marble is called a cat's eye and others are called alleys and they all look like small, alien planets. We spend hours together setting up army men and having battles, and afterwards we wrestle and he tickles me. He works in a junkyard and sometimes he comes home with used toys and gives them to me and my sister. He gives me a pirate's gun—long and curved with a flared barrel—and I wear a rolled-up red scarf around my head and pretend to be a pirate. When I shoot my dad he doubles over and falls to the floor. He's good at playing dead.

One person who's always around is my mom—washing dishes, hanging clothes out to dry, rocking my baby brother, and making scrambled egg sandwiches, cinnamon toast, and chocolate milk. She's like the summer sun, warm and pervasive, full of energy and always there throughout the day.

There's this one memory indelible as an oil painting. We live in an upstairs apartment in Chicago with big, wood-framed windows. It's early morning and I watch my mom walk out of the bedroom in her nightgown and throw open the curtains on the windows. She looks out the windows, up at the sky, and says, "It's a beautiful day," in a happy voice, then unlatches the windows and pulls them up, letting the wind rush in. The apartment fills up with the wind; it blows papers off the coffee table and fills up the curtains like sails. And there in the middle of the room, with the wind blowing her hair and her nightgown, stands my mother and she reaches out her arms to embrace the morning wind and says again, full of meaning, "It's a beautiful day." I watch her and smile, and after a while she makes me some cinnamon toast and chocolate milk.

I can summon up that image of my mom standing in the middle of the room with the wind blowing in like it was yesterday. She seems to be a part of the wind. Everything—the flying papers and curtains, her nightgown and hair—all seem to be a part of the wind like some Van Gogh painting. If I had the talent I'd paint it that way from memory.

But there's one more memory from four-years-old I want to share, and a special one, too. We return to my grandparent's house for Christmas and there's a big Christmas tree by the fireplace and we get to sleep in our old room. It's Christmas Eve night and we're waiting for my mom to come and tuck us in, but when she appears she pulls me and my sister out of bed and excitedly tells us to follow her. Down we go into the kitchen where we see my grandmother standing by the swinging door that leads out to the dining and living rooms. She puts her finger to her mouth and tells us to shush and to come see, so we sneak quietly up to her and peek out at the living room. Santa Claus— the one and only, the real Santa Claus—is next to the Christmas tree with a big bag full of gifts.

We want to squeal with delight but my mom tells us to stay quiet or we'll scare him off, so we peek back out, holding our breaths in wonder, and watch the big man lay gifts under the tree and go "Ho, ho, ho." It's a funny-guilty feeling I get peeking out at Santa Claus, almost as if I'm spying on some ancient ritual, but I know it's all right because my mom and grandmother are in on it too. Suddenly my grandmother closes the door and tells us to rush out the back door so we can see Santa fly off the roof in his sleigh, and off we go, banging out the back screen door into the backyard, and search the sky. But it's too dark, we can't see him, but we hear his sleigh bells ringing and know he's on his way.

This evidence of Santa's existence is so convincing that I firmly believe he's real until I'm eleven years old. Once the facts are presented to me, the truth comes as a blow.

But this is part of the point I'm trying to make. Just imagine the effort that went into this production number. My grandfather had to dress up as Santa Claus, my mother and grandmother had to play their parts, and someone—probably my uncle—had to hide in the backyard and shake the sleigh bells, and all of this was done just to bring a little magic into the lives of these children. I mean, who does that anymore?

So here's the bigger point I'm trying to make: these memories contain a beautiful truth. It's a deep green truth, higher than the sky and wider than the ocean, and it's embedded in this rich soil of beliefs where it's nearly impossible to uproot. At four-years-old, what I remember most is not the smell of ozone or the taste of blueberries but the memory of being watched out for—of being cared for. That abides. My childhood delivers on a promise; it's a kind of small Eden, bordered by adults, where you're not even embarrassed about being naked, where food and clothes are provided, skinned elbows are mended, and the worst of the world is kept from you.

In time, of course, comes the fall. It doesn't happen all at once, but by degrees, and sooner than later for some. It's little things here and there—an adult lets you down, you catch them in a lie, a loved one dies, or you break a rule and find out it's fun—and it all adds up in time to a fall from grace and the knowledge of good and evil. And voilà, there you are, a teenager with attitude, all pissed off and ready to burn it all down. What's it Hamlet says? "That it should come to this!" But if you're lucky, you grow out of that like you grew out of childhood, find someone, fall in love, get married, have kids, and start the cycle all over again.

And that's it for the fifties, and I really only have one more thing to say: People my age take great comfort in this—in the fact that the cycle always completes itself. Even if it gets bent and rusted, or people try to throw wrenches into the mechanism, it still makes its way around. It's just like circling around the sun; it always comes back to spring, whether you're a yuppie from Yountville or a pygmy from the Ituri forest. The cycle always completes itself.

The rest of these are just made-up stories. But they're all true.

THE SIXTIES

I viewed my fellow man not as a fallen angel, but
as a risen ape.

Desmond Morris
The Naked Ape

Ah, you fake just like a woman, yes you do
You make love just like a woman, yes you do
Then you ache just like a woman
But you break just like a little girl.

Bob Dylan
Just Like a Woman

We can no longer ignore that voice within women
that says: 'I want something more than my husband and my children and my home.'

Betty Friedan
The Feminine Mystique

Day of Mourning

"Hey, Gordy!"

He was walking to the bus and he stopped and turned around. He waited for me to run up to him. Everybody was getting on the bus. Some of the girls were still crying.

"Hey, Hines," he said.

"Whatta we gonna do? There's no one home at my house. We could go there."

"Nah."

"How 'bout your house? We could box."

"Nah."

He looked out over my head and around at the others getting onto the bus. He was a little bit taller than me but that was because he was in the sixth grade and I was only in the fourth. He liked looking out over my head. He did it all the time.

"We have to do somethin' special," he said. "It's not every day you get outta school early. It's like a holiday. I'll have to think of somethin' special."

I watched him as he started to think. His eyelashes twitched. They were black and they always looked wet, and whenever they twitched it meant he was thinking. His dark eyes looked around, one way and the other, and then stared straight ahead. He ran his hand through his black hair, and his tanned face showed he was serious.

"Come on, you two," said the bus driver.

I looked up at him in the driver's seat. He was big and his big hands gripped the black steering wheel. Gordy turned into the door, his eyelashes still twitching, and I followed him up. We walked to the back of the bus and the door closed behind us. It sounded like a punctured tire when the air rushes out.

The back bench seat was empty and we took it. The bus jerked forward and took off loudly. I sat back and bounced in my seat next to Gordy. He sat against the side, scratching his name in the metal wall with his jackknife. It was quiet on the bus. It sounded weird because nobody was talking.

"What's up?" I whispered.

"Shhh," he said. He finished the y in Gordy and brushed his name off with his finger, then clicked his jackknife shut and put it back in his pocket.

"I'm still thinking," he said. His voice sounded loud. "We can let the air out of Mark's tires like we did yesterday. That was funny."

I remembered what Mark's face had looked like. He had run out of his house and jumped on his bike and started to pedal but it wouldn't go. The bike just wobbled from the two flat tires and he fell over. I had laughed with Gordy from our hiding place behind the fence. I remembered Mark's face again and I laughed out loud.

"Hey!" yelled the bus driver from up front. I could see his face in the mirror. "Show a little respect. Quiet!"

Some of the girls turned around and gave Gordy and me dirty looks. They looked at us just like the time they caught us throwing rocks at a cat. There was no way we could have hit that cat but they gave us that same dirty look anyway.

Gordy clicked his tongue and looked back at his name in the metal. I saw the bus driver's face in the mirror so I looked down at my knees. I wasn't sure how to show respect but it was probably the same as showing sadness. When the principal told our class over the intercom what had happened, our teacher fell into her chair and all the girls started crying. I had tried to remember His face but I couldn't. I watched the different girls cry and then saw the teacher looking at me like she does when you're doing something wrong. I had felt bad then for not crying, and I tried to think of sad things to make me cry but I couldn't so I had just dropped my head and looked at my desktop. After a while I lifted my head and she wasn't looking at me anymore. So I did the same thing now, and after a while the bus driver's face wasn't in the mirror anymore.

The bus came to our corner by the field and stopped. The doors opened and those of us getting off filed out. When we came up to the bus driver his big hands twisted their grip on the steering wheel and he stared at Gordy and me. We went by him and down the steps to the sidewalk. The door slammed shut behind us and the bus took off loudly. The smoke from its tail-pipe was black and smelly.

"Come on, Hines," said Gordy.

"Where we goin?'"

"My house for a while. I'm still thinking. We'll get some-thing to eat."

His eyelashes twitched again as he started off toward the apartments. We walked together and his black loafers made a neat sound on the concrete. He had steel taps on the bottom of his shoes and they clicked as he walked. I also had black loafers but without the steel taps. My feet didn't fit right into loafers—they fell off when I ran—but I wore them anyway, just like Gordy, with white socks and blue jeans. We cut into one of the drive-ways that had carports on one side and apartments on the other. His shoes sounded even better on the driveway. They echoed under the carports and off the two-story buildings as we walked on through and into the center of the complex.

Four rows of apartments surrounded a big pool and a play-ground. The pool was closed in by a tall, chain-link fence, and the playground was filled with sand, slides, and monkey-bars. A sidewalk went around the pool and playground but you weren't allowed to ride your bike on it. The bottom apartments had wooden fences, painted black, and inside there were patios and sliding glass doors. The top apartments had patios, too, but with a steel rail and colored panels to keep people from falling over. Some of the top rails already had Christmas lights on them.

The pool was out. There was nobody in it and no adults around to keep watch, and anyhow it was too cloudy and chilly to go swimming. The playground was also empty. It was bigger and better than the one at school and we had it all to ourselves. We could play civil war.

Gordy taught me how to play civil war. The first time I met him he was playing it by himself and he let me join in. We played it all the time and it was best in the sand because you could really fight and die without getting hurt. We were always the Yanks. At first we were the Rebs until Gordy found out from the library that the Rebs were really the bad guys, so we switched over to the Yanks. What we did was take a last stand in the sand against the Rebs. We even had blue hats and a Reb flag to make it more real. It was do or die. We were always outnumbered ten to one, and when our ammunition ran out we had to fight hand to hand. Sometimes we got wounded and had to fight on with only one arm or leg. Sometimes one of us got killed and the other would have to fight on by himself. But we always won. Afterwards we would lie in the sand breathing hard and sweating and feeling good.

"Let's play civil war," I said to Gordy. "There's no one in there. We can be by ourselves."

"Nah, I'm tired of that game. It's kid's stuff. Come on to my house."

I followed him past the pool and toward his house.

"Why not?"

"I told you—it's kid's stuff. No fun. We have to do something special. It's like a holiday. No one's around."

I spied along the balconies and all around the pool area. There was no one out, no adults, not even little kids on tricycles. It was kind of spooky. It made you feel like you could do anything and get away with it.

We went through the gate into Gordy's patio and then through the sliding glass doors into his apartment. Gordy lived across the pool from me on the opposite corner. Some of my other friends lived way across the complex but Gordy was real close. His home was warm and carpeted. We went into his kitchen and Gordy opened the refrigerator and took out some grapes. He tore a bunch off and handed them to me and we sat down at the kitchen table. Gordy plucked off the bad ones, threw them away, and started eating the good ones. The grapes were light green and tasted sweet.

Gordy tossed a grape up and caught it in his mouth. I tried it but the grape hit my nose.

"You know the haunted house?" said Gordy. He threw up another grape, arched back, and caught it in his mouth.

"Yeah."

"I've been in it."

"Sure."

"I have."

"But it's all boarded up. There's boards on the door and windows. How'd you get in?"

"Easy," he said. He bit off half a grape, examined the insides, and then ate the rest of it. "I got in from underneath. There's a trapdoor."

"Sure."

"I'm telling you." His dark eyes flashed at me.

"Wow! Really? What's inside? Is there anyone livin' there?"

"I'm not sure. I just poked my head up and looked around. It was dark and there were lots of rooms. I figured I'd better get you and come back. I might need your help."

"Need help for what?"

"Because." He leaned forward and checked around to make sure no one was listening. "Because there might be someone in there. I heard a groan."

"A groan? From a person?"

"It was something else. Something evil."

He leaned back and threw his naked grape stems into the garbage can. He had five left sitting on the table in front of him and he took one and cut it in half with his thumb. He licked his thumb and put the broken grape in his mouth. I was imagining the evil something.

"We better not go," I said.

"We have to."

"How come?"

"Because, stupid"—he tossed a grape at me but I blocked it before it hit my face—"it's evil and evil must be destroyed.

Haven't you learned anything? It's our duty to destroy evil. We have to go in there and get it."

"But why not call the police? The police will get it."

He jumped up out of his chair and glared at me, his eyelashes twitching. "Christ! Because, stupid, the police are part of it. They'd say they didn't see it. They'd lie. They're controlled by it, don't you know anything? Shit, don't be so stupid. It's up to us."

He stopped and softened his look. He sat back down and put his hands out on the table. His hands were tanned and the same size as mine but his palms and knuckles were callused over. My hands weren't as tough as his but they were getting there. Gordy had showed me how to get calluses by punching the stone walls of the carports. He tucked his hands back in and leaned forward.

"Listen, Hines," he said. "It's our duty—as Yanks. We're the only ones who know about it. If we don't get it nobody will and it'll spread. It'll spread and get your family and then us. It's smart, that's why it can control the police and make them lie. But it can't control us. It has no power over kids. That's why we are the only ones that can get it."

"But what's it look like? Have you ever seen it?"

"A couple times." He checked around again to make sure we were alone and scratched his head fast. His eyelashes twitched some more. "It comes from the center of the earth. That's where it used to live but it dug its way out like a worm. It's old looking, almost like a skeleton, and dark, too, with black hair and black eyes, and its breath is ice cold. It's horrible looking and it hates everything. It does evil things."

"Like what?" In my mind I had the picture of a monster, all dark and slimy, hiding somewhere in that house.

"Well, like all bad things. Like when a car crashes or a person dies. It has the power to make people do things without them knowing it. Who do ya think killed *Him*?"

"Really? But that was far away from here, in another part of America or somewhere."

"It has the power to transport itself across the world at the blink of an eye."

"But then how do we know it's in there? It could be gone."

"No, it's in there. That house is its home base. It's probably in there right now resting after what it's done. We can catch it off-guard."

"Maybe we should tell someone. We could tell our parents."

Gordy rolled his eyes away and clicked his tongue. "Don't be stupid," he said. "It would hear it all and run away before they got there. It has the power to hear people. When people talk on the phone it hears them."

"Then it must be hearing us."

"Nah. It can't hear kids."

"Why not?"

"I don't know, it just can't."

Something wasn't right about this. I was afraid. All the other times Gordy figured something out or made up a plan I got excited. But something wasn't right. The more he talked the more I got afraid.

"I don't know," I said. "It could hurt us or kill us maybe. I don't think I want to go in there."

"Nah, it can't hurt us." Gordy leaned back and folded his arms. He grinned. "It's two against one. It doesn't stand a chance. And besides, it can't hurt you unless you're soft. It can only get you if you have a soft stomach. Stand up."

He jumped out of his chair and came around to me. I stood up and faced him.

"Why do ya think we've been workin' out for?" he said, looking at my arms and stomach. "Why do ya think I taught you how to box? Not for nothin', Hines. I don't do anything for nothin'. This thing can't hurt you unless you have a soft stomach. That's why all the sit-ups. Let me see."

I set my stomach and stood still. Gordy hit it twice with the back of his hand. It sounded like a tight drum.

"Good, good," he smiled. "You see, there's no way it can hurt you. Your stomach's too tough. Let me see your hands."

He took my hands and turned them over to look at my palms, then dropped them and showed me his hands.

"Good, they're getting tough like mine. Why do ya think I made these calluses? It's because this thing has a stone face and I can hit it without cutting my skin. It's all for a reason—all this training. Just like Sonny Liston. You stay hard and it can never get you."

He took another quick look at my hands and hit my stomach again.

"Nah," he grinned. "No way. This thing don't stand a chance against us. We'll wipe it out."

He karate-chopped the air and then headed for his bedroom. I followed him. I was feeling better. I was still a little afraid but now there was a kind of happiness to go with it. Gordy couldn't be wrong. My stomach was hard all right. So that was why we were always working out. There was a reason for it. He was always teaching me to box better, and he showed me a bunch of exercises that we did every day. He always made regular things into tests—like swimming. While all the others in the pool just swam around, me and Gordy would practice holding our breath and seeing how far we could swim underwater. And while the rest of them played on the slide and the swings in the playground, me and Gordy would play civil war or the Olympics and do tricks on the bars. He didn't like to eat ice cream or any stuff that made you soft. No wonder. It all made sense now.

There were bunkbeds in Gordy's room. He slept on the top bunk in a sleeping bag instead of blankets. The bottom bunk was his big brother's but he was away in the army. There was a poster of Willie Mays over the dresser and a Giants' pennant over the bunkbeds. The room was neat as always except for a punching bag by the door and a pair of boxing gloves on the floor. There were also some bats in the corner by his closet next to his locked army chest. The army chest was where he hid his dirty magazines. Sometimes when I slept over he would take them out and we would look at them and he would say things I didn't understand.

Gordy opened the bottom drawer of his dresser and dug in under his folded clothes. He pulled out an old jackknife.

"Here, you might need this," he said.

He handed it to me and I opened it up. It wasn't as shiny as his, the blade was kind of rusty, but it was still good. I wiped the blade off on my shirt, clicked it shut, and put it in my pocket. Gordy stood up and looked around his room.

"Let's see," he said to himself. "What else do we need? Let's see, let's see."

He went into his closet and started moving things around on the top shelf. He pulled down an army belt with a canteen on it.

"We might need this. We'll be in there for a while and we might need water. Want to wear it?"

"Yeah!"

"Okay, come here."

I went over to him and he put the belt on around my waist and fastened it. It was olive green and heavy. The canteen was metal with a black cap and sat in a pouch that snapped tight.

"That's it," Gordy said. He took a quick look around the room then went over to the bunkbed and sat down. He pulled some tennis shoes out, kicked off his loafers, and put them on. He jumped back up and looked around and over at me.

"Yeah," he said, "that should do it. We're all set. Come on."

"How about my shoes?"

"Don't have time. You'll be all right. Let's go."

We headed back into the kitchen. I unsnapped the canteen and Gordy filled it up in the sink. He wiped it off and capped it and gave it to me to snap back in. It made the belt even heavier.

"All right," Gordy said with a grin. "Time to lock and load. Right?"

"Right."

"Let's go."

It was cooler than before outside. We went back the way we came, around the pool and past the playground. There was still no one out. We cut through the driveway again and back onto the sidewalk towards the bus stop. The haunted house was in the field and the field was at the end of the sidewalk on the corner. There was a big intersection where the two streets crossed.

The field was pretty big. There were plenty of other vacant lots just like it around town. They used to be orchards but were just empty fields now full of dirt and weeds and left-over stuff. This one was bigger than others I had seen around, and it had mounds of dirt that were good for hiding behind when playing army or having dirt clod fights. And there were plenty of dirt clods; they were all over the field mixed in with the rocks and weeds and glass. In the far back of the lot was a giant tree. There used to be another one next to it but they had cut it down with buzz saws. This one was the biggest tree I'd ever seen. The branches stretched way up into the sky and the trunk was so tall that no one could climb it. Some kites were stuck up in the branches and they made noise in the wind. The field went on a ways past the tree and then turned into orchards again. A fence ran along the side of the lot, separating it from the apartments, and across the street sat another vacant lot only smaller. It had an old car sitting in it with the wheels missing.

The house was close to the big tree and set up on blocks. It had been there before I moved in and even before Gordy moved in and it had always been boarded up.

We made our way through the field toward the house. You had to watch the ground as you walked because of all the broken glass and gopher holes. Besides the gophers, there was nothing living in the field except for some mice and an old snake that nobody could catch.

Gordy led us past the obstacles until we came to a dirt mound that faced the house. We dropped down behind it, peeked out at the house, and then ducked down out of site. Gordy pulled out his jackknife and checked it. I took mine out and also checked it.

"Let's have a drink," he whispered.

I unsnapped the canteen and handed it to him. He unscrewed the black cap and took a drink. The water ran down the sides of his mouth and he lowered the canteen and wiped his mouth on his sleeve. He handed it back to me. The metal opening felt cold on my lips as I took a drink, and I wiped my mouth on my sleeve, capped the canteen, and snapped it back on my belt. Gordy inched up the mound and looked over. He slid back down.

"Take a look," he whispered.

I inched up and looked out. It was an old house and kind of small. The green paint was all chipped and yellowed and some of the wood was cracked. It was only one story high with a flat roof and all the windows were boarded up. The front door was also boarded up with crisscrossing planks. The house sat up on huge bricks and it was dark underneath. I slid back down.

"Where do we get in at?" I whispered.

"Underneath," he said. He grabbed my sleeve and took us both up to look. "Right under there. There's a trapdoor that'll take us right in."

I looked underneath the house more closely. Nobody I knew of had ever been under there except for Gordy. It was dark and I was sure there were big spiders under there.

"I don't know," I said.

I started to slide back down but Gordy pulled me back up.

"Don't be chicken. Come on, Hines." His eyelashes twitched, and he looked quickly at the house and then back at me. "There's nothin' to be afraid of. Do ya think Davy Crockett would be afraid or Jim Bowie? Do ya think John Wayne would be chicken to go under there and in that house? Huh? Come on, Hines."

I tried to think of John Wayne being afraid but I couldn't.

"I tell you there's nothin' to be afraid of. Look at me, am I chicken? I've been under there plenty of times. Let's go."

He was right. He had been under there and he was still all right. I was being a baby. We had a mission to do.

"Okay," I grinned. "Let's do it."

"That's the way to think," Gordy said as he slapped me on the shoulder. He popped up on his feet and I followed him.

"Come on," he said. "Let's get that bastard."

We ran down the mound and to the house in a crouch. Gordy dropped to a knee next to the house and waited for me to do the same. He started crawling underneath on his hands and knees and I followed him in. Suddenly it was dark and I couldn't see so good, but instead of stopping I kept on and followed Gordy's shoes. The air smelled cool underneath and the ground was damp. Gordy stopped and I could hear him feeling up around the floor of the house. He stopped feeling and then punched up. A trapdoor cracked open and he pushed it up into the house. A faint light came down and I could see the back of Gordy's head.

He raised up and pulled himself into the house. I went next and pulled myself up through the trapdoor.

I came up and looked around. There were openings and rooms in every direction. Gordy was gone. I started to call his name but a hand grabbed me from behind and I felt my breath go out of me. It was Gordy and he pulled me to him. He was crouched behind a wall, and in the doorway next to him I could see the yellow tub and toilet of a bathroom.

"Shhh," he whispered. His eyes were serious. "Quiet. Listen."

We both listened. It was dead silent. There was sort of a shadowy light which creeped in through the boarded up windows that I could see things by. We had come up in a hallway that led out to a living room. Across the hall and down a ways was a bedroom, and at the opposite end of the hall was another bedroom. There was no furniture anywhere or any doors. The air was stuffy and the bare floor was dusty and left marks where we touched it with our hands and knees. The white walls were not white anymore and the plaster was chipped and cracked. Some of it lay around on the floor like spilt flour.

Gordy got up slowly and took out his jackknife and opened it. I got out mine and opened it and stood up next to him. He looked back at me with a smile on his face.

"Ready?"

"Yeah."

He stepped out into the hallway and the floorboards creaked loudly under his foot. He stopped and then took another long, soft step. I followed him. We made our way to the living room and peeked in. It was empty. The walls were bare except for the main one that had a giant mirror set on it. It wasn't really a looking glass; it was smoke-colored with black lines running through it and looked more like a picture than a mirror.

Gordy signaled me to stay put while he scouted around the corner. He was gone for a few seconds and then I saw his hand stick out and wave me on. It was the kitchen. It was empty like the living room and there was a window over the sink. The linoleum was all yellow and bubbly, and there were marks on the floor where the refrigerator and stove used to be.

"Come on," whispered Gordy.

He backtracked and we headed down the hall again and past the bathroom towards the two bedrooms. He stopped and turned to me.

"Listen, you take the first one, I'll take the second. If you see it yell out."

He opened his jackknife and rushed into the first bedroom. I got my knife out and jumped into the second bedroom, twirled around, and stopped. It was empty. It was just like the other rooms. I went back out and met Gordy.

"Well, shit," he said out loud.

"It's gone. Is it gone?"

"I guess so."

I put my jackknife away and took a deep breath of the stuffy air. It had been fun.

"Let's go then," I said.

"Nah, not yet. Let's explore around some more."

"Okay."

He headed back into the living room and I followed him. I wanted to see that mirror again and I guess he did too. We stopped in front of it and studied it. It was almost as big as the wall itself. The black lines in the glass made a design. It didn't really make a picture of anything but the black lines were all wavy in the same places and made a neat pattern. There were stars in the smoky glass. I hadn't noticed that the first time because I was too far away, but now I could see that the mirror was speckled with thousands of tiny white stars that sparkled. When you looked in the mirror the stars went into your face. It made my face look special. Gordy put his hand to it and so did I. I couldn't feel the stars in the glass but the black lines felt like smooth wires and I traced my finger along one of them. Gordy turned away to look at something else but I stayed there. I had never seen anything so pretty.

"Hey, look at this!" yelled Gordy.

I turned away from the mirror and looked at him. He was crouched down over a large stain in the floor. I went over and crouched down next to him and looked at it. It was a dark red stain.

"Whad'ya think of this?" he said, clicking his tongue. He took out his jackknife and scraped the stain with the blade. He lifted it up and showed it to me. The specks looked even redder on the shiny blade.

"You know what this is? It's blood."

"Really?"

"I'm sure of it."

His eyelashes twitched. "That's it, that's it," he said.

"What?"

"That's why it wasn't here. That's why we couldn't find it. Somebody already killed it. By the looks of it they shot it in the stomach and it bled to death right here."

"Really?"

"I'm sure of it."

"Wow!"

I looked down at the stain again as Gordy got up and moved away. I ran my hand over it and then looked at my fingertips. They were red. I glanced up and around but Gordy had left the room.

"Gordy?"

There was no answer. I went into the kitchen but he wasn't in there either.

"Hey, Gordy?"

I went down the hall past the bathroom and into the bedrooms. He wasn't anywhere.

"Hey, Gordy! Where are you?"

I was getting scared. He had just disappeared. I headed for the trapdoor, and as I started to get down into it a head came up and I jumped back. It was Gordy.

"Give me a hand," he said.

"You scared me."

"Would you give me a hand?"

He was having trouble so I grabbed his arms and helped him up.

"Where'd you go?"

He stood up and reached into his bulging pockets and dropped out some rocks. They banged on the floor.

"Take some," he said.

"Why?"

"Just take some."

I took a few and put them in my pockets. I followed Gordy into the living room and stood next to him in front of the giant mirror. He tossed a rock up and down in his hand like a baseball.

"Ready?"

"Are you going to break it?"

"Yeah. Ready?"

"But why?"

"Why not?"

I could see our faces in the smoky glass. Our faces were full of stars and fit inside the design. I saw Gordy smile at me in the mirror and then his arm go back and throw. There was a loud crack and the mirror shook. The rock fell to the floor, and where it hit there was a mark like a spider web in the glass.

"Oooh, that looks boss," said Gordy. The spider web mark was right in the center of the design. "Go ahead. You try one."

I weighed a rock out in my hand, leaned back, and threw it at the mirror. There was a loud crack again, and the mirror vibrated and the rock fell to the floor. It left another spider web mark in the left hand corner.

"Good one," said Gordy. "My turn."

He threw a rock and there was another loud crack and another spider web mark.

"This time we'll both go. Ready?"

I took out a rock and got set.

"Ready," I said.

"Now!"

We both threw our rocks and hit the mirror. There were no loud cracks, just one loud crash. The giant mirror burst in upon itself and shattered to the floor. It came down on the floor in tiny jagged pieces. The wall was white where the mirror had been.

"Wow!"

"It just exploded."

I walked up to the pieces and looked down at them. I could see my face in all the tiny pieces at the same time. It looked weird.

"Yeehah!" yelled Gordy. "Yeehah! Yeehah!"

He turned and threw a rock at a window. It smashed a hole, and he threw another rock and the window smashed apart.

"Hoowee!" I yelled. "Hoowee! Hoowee!"

I took out a rock and threw it at a window. It cracked in half, and I threw another rock and finished it off.

Gordy ran down the hall. I heard a crash and I ran to the bathroom and saw the mirror he had just shattered.

"The window, the window!" he yelled.

We both threw rocks at the bathroom window and smashed it and the glass fell into the bathtub.

"Yeehah!"

"Hoowee!"

Gordy ran to the bedrooms and I ran into the kitchen. I broke the window there, picked up some more rocks, and ran into the bedroom to help Gordy. We smashed all the windows. There was broken glass all over the floor, in the hallway and in all the rooms, and we ran through the house looking for more windows but there wasn't any left. We stopped in the living room and Gordy threw a rock at the white wall where the mirror had been. It left a black mark.

"We got 'em all," he said. He was breathing hard. We were both breathing hard.

"Let's go," I said.

"Not yet." He stepped forward and started kicking the broken pieces of glass. We had kicked up a bunch of dust and it was even stuffier to breath.

"That was fun," he said. He dug into his pocket. "Let's finish it off."

He pulled out a book of matches and tore off a match. He struck it and held it in his hand for a moment before tossing it away. It arced like a little rocket and landed on the floor. The small flame burned blue and yellow and then smoked out. Gordy struck another and tossed it, and then another. I watched them burn.

"Hey!"

Me and Gordy looked at each other. It was a man's voice.

"Hey you in there!"

Gordy jumped forward and stamped out the matches. I went up against the wall and held my breath, and Gordy came over next to me and put his finger to his lips. We listened as the man pulled himself up through the trapdoor and stepped on the broken glass. He kicked the glass as he moved down the hall.

"What in the hell? Goddammit! Where are you? Come out. You heard me, come out here now! You're trapped!"

He moved on down the hall and Gordy peeked around the corner. He looked back at me and whispered, "When I say go, run for the trapdoor, okay."

I nodded.

"Go!"

He shot around the corner and I followed him. And something happened—I felt something go wrong with my foot and I fell to the floor onto the glass. I put my hands out to fall and the glass bit into them. I looked up and saw Gordy jump down into the trapdoor and disappear. The man turned around and saw me.

"Hey you!"

He came at me.

I tried to push up but I couldn't. There was blood on the glass. Suddenly I felt hands on my shoulders and I came up into the air and onto my feet. The hands squeezed my shoulders. I looked up into the man's face. He had an old face, and his eyes were old and they stared at me.

"Have you done this?" his mouth said. "Have you?"

He shook me in his hands.

"Why? You've destroyed it. You're a vandal... nothing more. You've destroyed all of it. Why?"

I was starting to cry and I could feel my hands bleeding. He shook me again.

"Have you no respect? Is this what you do on a black day like this? A great man has died. Have you no respect? No sorrow? This is mindless."

I was crying now. It came out of my chest and I couldn't stop it. Suddenly he let go of my shoulders and took hold of my hands.

"Let me see those," he said in a different voice.

He raised my hands up and turned them over. There was blood on the palms and all down the fingers. He dropped my hands and let go of me.

"Go on, get out of here. I don't ever want to see you around here again. Go home, take care of those hands. Get!"

He stepped aside and I took off and jumped down the trap-door. I crawled through the darkness toward the gray light and came out and ran through the field away from the house. I ran out of the field and onto the sidewalk towards the apartments.

"Hines!"

I stopped and looked back. There was Gordy standing against the fence. He walked over to me.

"You all right?"

"Yes."

"What happened? What did he do to you?"

"Nothing. I fell."

I showed him my hands.

"Jeez. You better wash those off and bandage 'em. Come on." We started walking but Gordy stopped. "Where's your shoe?"

I looked down. One of my loafers was missing.

"Oh, no." I said, and I started to cry again. "It's still in there. It fell off and it's still in that house. Oh, no."

"Don't worry about it. Stop crying. I'll go back later and get it for you. Okay? Let's go wash those hands off. All right?"

"Okay."

He patted me on the shoulder. "That's the way to think."

We walked on. The blood dripped from my fingertips and left a trail on the sidewalk.

"What-he say to you?" asked Gordy. "Did he say anything to you when he caught ya?"

"Yeah."

"What?"

"Nothin'."

"What was it?"

"He just said we destroyed everything, and that we have no respect."

"No respect, huh?"

"Yeah. Because of what happened today."

"Ahh, he's full of shit."

We walked on and I put my hands up to keep them from dripping. I looked at Gordy. He was walking, looking out over my head.

"Maybe we shouldna' broke all those windows?" I said. "Maybe we shouldna' broken that mirror?"

"Hah, what's the difference," said Gordy.

The St. Christopher Affair

The movie theater on Murphy Street in downtown Sunnyvale was showing *Help!* and Gail and her two friends were going to see it for the third time. Gail's mother was driving and they picked up both Sara and Linda at Sara's house, and all three girls rode in the back of the station wagon on the way to the theater.

"Are you going to do it?" asked Sara.

"Yeah," replied Gail solemnly. "I have it right here." She reached into her purse and showed both her friends the envelope.

"But you're still wearing it," said Sara. Sara was referring to the St. Christopher medal that hung around Gail's neck. Tim had given Gail that medal six months ago and asked her to go steady and she had said yes. They'd been six-graders together at Pippin Elementary and now they were going into the seventh grade at Mango Junior High School. For six months she had worn Tim's St. Christopher medal as a sign of her devotion—they'd even made-out five times together—but now she had decided to give it back.

Gail gently touched the medal on her chest. "I know," she said with some sadness as though she were holding back a hidden pain. "But when I see him I'm going to put it in this envelope and give it to him."

Gail's mom glanced at her daughter in the rear view mirror and nodded slightly. Gail's mom was a beautiful woman and she had passed that beauty on to her daughter.

"What's the letter say?" asked Linda. She kept any excitement out of her voice. Both Linda and Sara appreciated the gravity of the moment.

Gail did not open the note in the envelope and instead recited it from memory: "Tim, please take your St. Christopher medal back. I don't want to go steady with you anymore. Love, Gail."

"Is he going to be at the movies?" asked Sara.

"He said he was."

"Are you going to give it to him there?"

"Maybe. I don't know... If I can."

The three girls pondered the different ways one might break up with a boyfriend at the movie theater before Linda changed the subject to hairdos. She had just gotten hers cut and what had been bangs swept to one side was now a forward fringe that rested just above her eyebrows. Gail's mom said it looked cute and the other two girls agreed, and the three of them chatted happily in the back seat the rest of the way to the theater.

Help! starring the Beatles was in its third week at the Sunnyvale Theater and it was a Saturday matinée. There was already a line out front when Gail's mom pulled up to let the girls out, and she reminded her daughter not to stay past five o'clock and to call when she was ready to be picked up. All three girls waved goodbye to Gail's mom and walked towards the end of the line, saying "hi" to some of their friends along the way. The age groups ran from fifth and sixth graders to high-schoolers. Most of the boys wore blue jeans or corduroy pants with t-shirts and sported either crew-cuts, shaggy surfer curls, or the hipper Beatles mop-top with their hair combed down over their foreheads. The girls were arrayed in shorts and dresses with sleeveless blouses and an occasional tight sweater, and their hairdos ranged from short bobs to longer hair that was either center-parted or back-combed into a rounded bouffant.

A few of the more daring girls, which included Gail, wore miniskirts with white go-go boots. Gail was a looker—the boys called her "a fox"—and like being born into royalty, this was something she understood from a very early age and took advantage of. She liked to dress in a way that made her stand out, and today, besides the miniskirt and go-go boots, she wore a lavender blouse with a lace collar and matching sleeves. Her face was delicately touched-up with Maybelline blush and eye-liner with a thin appliqué of pinkish lip-gloss. She wore her reddish-brown hair short with the ends flicked up towards her cheeks.

The boys in line glanced at Gail as she walked by. Sara and Linda were not as pretty as Gail, and neither of them tried to compete with her in that category, but they enjoyed the attention Gail attracted and liked pointing out the cute guys to their comely friend. And before they got to the back of the line, a couple of those cute guys they knew from school let them cut in front of them.

Once they paid and got inside, they bought candy and drinks at the concession stand and found some seats. Gail liked to sit between her two friends at the end of the row, and they found three empty seats about halfway up the aisle and settled in. Boxes of Milk Duds, Lemonheads, and Dots, along with a Sugar Daddy and a roll of Necco Wafers passed from purse to purse until everything was properly sorted out, and each girl took a sip of their soda and set it in a holder in the arm rest.

"Did you see Tim?" asked Linda.

"No, did you?"

"No."

"I didn't see him either."

"He said he was going to be here."

"Who are those cute guys over there?" interrupted Sara as she pointed with her chin to a group of boys sitting across the aisle. One of the boys was looking at Gail.

"That one's looking right at you," said Linda as she nudged Gail.

Gail didn't need to be told she was being stared at, though she liked hearing her friends point it out. She was used to boys staring at her—and this one was definitely cute—and she glanced at him and then turned away, pretending to ignore him.

The three girls leaned forward into a huddle. They all agreed that he was a hunk and that his friends were all cute. They dressed different than the boys they knew; they wore faded blue jeans and cool-looking flannel shirts with the sleeves rolled up, and instead of Keds they wore boss-looking army boots. Who was he? Gail wondered. Linda didn't know but Sara did (Sara seemed to know everybody). "I think his name's Carl," she said. "He's on my brother's baseball team. They go to Mango. I think they're going to be eighth graders."

All three girls glanced up in unison and looked at Carl. He was talking to his friends and not paying attention. They huddled back up and Sara gave them the last of her lowdown on Carl: he was a good baseball player and as far as she knew he didn't have a girlfriend.

"Here he comes," whispered Linda.

The three girls sat back up. Carl was sitting a few rows ahead of them, across the aisle, and as he got up and started walking up the carpeted aisle, he swung over towards them, caught Gail's eye, and smiled at her. Gail smiled back and blushed slightly. Her friends leaned into her and giggled.

"He's a dreamboat."

"He looks like Paul McCartney."

"He does, doesn't he?"

As they glowed in the aftermath of Carl's smile and compared him to both Paul McCartney and Paul Peterson from *The Donna Reed Show,* an excited voice broke their reverie.

"Hey, guys. Finally found you." It was Tim.

"Hi, Tim," answered Linda.

Tim was with his buddy Dave, and Dave bent down next to Linda, who was sitting in the aisle seat, and started flirting with her. Dave had a girlfriend but he and Linda always flirted with each other and the others ignored them. Tim kneeled down and scrunched in-between the back of the seat and Linda's knees to get in closer to Gail. He offered her a piece of Bit-O-Honey candy.

"Want one?" he asked her with a smile. He had curly blonde hair and green eyes.

"No, I have candy," replied Gail.

"We're gonna sneak up into the Loge. Wanna come with?"

"No. I'm here with my friends."

"We can all sneak up there together. We found a way."

"No thanks, we like these seats."

"Okay…" Tim paused. Gail had not made eye contact with him or smiled at him, and his brow furrowed as though he was suddenly confronted with a tough math problem in class. "You all right?" he asked her.

"I'm fine."

He studied her for a moment, glancing at his St. Christopher medal that rested on her chest, and brightened back up. "Okay. Cool," he said in a chipper tone. "Maybe later. I'll see you at intermission, okay?"

"Okay."

Tim backed out and stood up. Dave was still bent over whispering with Linda, and Tim nudged him with his shoulder to get his attention. His buddy was wrapped up in a secret conversation with Linda, and Tim had to nudge him again, this time harder, to get his attention. Finally Dave broke free and he and Tim walked away.

"Why didn't you break up with him now?" asked Sara.

"I couldn't," replied Gail thoughtfully. "Not in front of everybody. How embarrassing… I still like him… I have to do it in private." She lightly touched the medal on her chest as she said this.

Sara didn't comment on this and instead leaned over towards Linda. "And what were you two whispering about?" she asked Linda.

Linda looked at the two of them and filled her lungs with air as though she was holding in a big surprise. "I told Dave you wanted to break up with Tim," she said, letting out the air.

"You said what?!" replied Gail in a shocked whisper.

"That you wanted to break up with him."

"But how could you…"

"You do, don't you?"

"Yes, but…"

"Well, now he knows. Dave'll tell him. Makes it easier."

"It makes it easier," agreed Sara.

"I don't know… Why'd you have to tell him?" Gail wanted to protest this indiscretion further but her two friends cut her off at the pass, assuring her that it made things easier and accomplished what she was after, and that it wouldn't embarrass Tim because Dave would tell him in private. Gail listened intently to her friends, nodding once or twice, and finally said, "I can't believe you told him" in such a way that both Linda and Sara knew she wasn't mad about it anymore.

The lights dimmed in the theater and the three girls settled back in their seats. "Now I'll *have to* give him his St. Christopher back," sighed Gail in resignation.

"You were anyhow."

"I know... I know." And at that, Gail said no more and watched the screen. It was a *Pink Panther* cartoon but she didn't much pay attention to it. She was lost in thought. At one point she reached behind her neck to unfasten her St. Christopher medal but thought better of it and let it be.

The cartoon ended and the movie *Help!* started. Everyone in the theater started cheering including Gail and her two friends. Gail had a crush on Paul McCartney. Linda liked Paul, too, but Sara had a crush on George. They had a few friends who liked John the best but they didn't know anyone, except for Sara's older sister, who had a crush on Ringo. The Beatles appeared on screen singing the title song, and Gail forgot about her troubles as she gave her full attention to the movie.

When the movie ended and the lights came back up, the three girls remained in their seats. It was intermission, and they had twenty minutes before *Help!* started again. Gail had no intention of going to the restroom or the concession stand. She might see Tim, she said, and she was too embarrassed to face him. Linda agreed to go get them another soda but Sara stayed with Gail just in case Tim came by.

While Gail and Sara waited for Linda to return, a figure appeared next to Linda's empty seat. Gail was afraid to look.

"Hi," said a male voice. Gail looked up to see Carl. He was looking straight at her but he glanced over at Sara. "Aren't you Jeff's sister?" he asked Sara.

Sara nodded vigorously, then sputtered out, "Yeah, I am."

"Thought so. I play on his baseball team. Your brother's a cool-head."

"I know... I mean, I've seen you out there."

"Cool. Name's Carl. What's yours?"

"Sara—and this is my friend Gail.

"Hi, Gail."

"Hi."

He was no longer paying any attention to Sara as he knelt down to get a closer look at Gail. "I dig your boots," he said to her. "They're rad."

"Thanks"

His eyes roamed playfully over her face and hair, then paused momentarily on the St. Christopher medal around her neck before moving on. "What school you guys go to?"

"Pippin, but we're going to Mango in September," answered Sara.

"Cool. That's where I go. I'll probably see you there."

"Cool," agreed Sara.

Carl stood up without taking his eyes off Gail. "Nice to meet you," he said. "Say hi to your brother for me." ("I will," chirped Sara.) "Bye, Gail. Hope to see you later."

Gail answered him with a charming smile and he smiled back and rejoined his friends across the aisle. Gail and Sara sat very still and glanced at one another out of the corner of their eye before breaking into giggles. Linda arrived with their sodas and they all quickly huddled together so Sara could fill her in on what had just happened. It was a hot topic of discussion for the remainder of the intermission, and when the house lights dimmed again the three girls had to force themselves to be quiet. But before the movie started, Gail reached behind her neck and unfastened the St. Christopher medal and placed it carefully into the envelope in her purse. Her two friends watched her without saying a word.

A little ways into the film—around the part where the bumbling scientists try to remove the ring from Ringo's finger—Gail had to get up to go to the restroom. She also needed to stretch her legs and get another box of Dots. Sara went with her. When they returned, Linda wanted to know whether they had seen Tim. No, they hadn't seen him. The whispers stopped and they settled back in to watch the movie.

When the movie ended the three girls followed the crowd out into the lobby. There was already a line at the pay phone and Gail quickly got in it. She felt a hand on her shoulder and looked back to see Carl. "Nice to meet you," he said with his cute smile. "See you at Mango."

"Oh, yeah. Nice to meet you," replied Gail with her best smile and a fetching tilt of her head. "See you there." He nodded coolly then followed his friends out the front doors and onto the sidewalk.

"What he say to you?" asked Linda excitedly.

"That it was nice to meet me and he'd see me at Mango."

"Just watch—you two will probably end up going steady," said Sara.

"How do you know that?" demanded Linda.

"I just do... Come on, figure it out for yourself."

"Just 'cause he's cute? They'll be lots of cute guys at Mango."

"What do you think, Gail?"

"We'll see," said Gail philosophically. It was her turn to use the phone and she dropped a dime in the slot and called her mom to come pick them up. When she hung up, Linda jumped into her face.

"There's Tim!" she whispered frantically.

"Where?" asked Sara, equally alarmed.

"By the boy's restroom. Standing with Dave.

"Oh, I see him. Gail, don't look."

"I'm not."

The three girls gravitated as one towards the front doors pretending not to notice Tim and Dave standing by the boy's restroom across the crowded lobby. The tight knit group stopped near the entrance but stayed inside and peered out the glass doors.

"Why don't you give him the envelope," suggested Sara.

"I can't."

"Why not?"

"I can't."

"He's right over there," added Linda. "Just walk over and hand it to him."

"l can't."

Linda and Sara regarded their friend with some confusion, but as they saw her standing there holding the letter in her hand with her eyes watering up, their confusion immediately turned to compassion. Sara put her arm around Gail and hugged her gently.

"Is he still over there?" asked Gail weakly.

Sara, who was the tallest of the three, glanced across the lobby. "Yeah—no. He just went in the restroom. Dave's still there."

"Give it to me," said Linda firmly. "I'll give it to Dave." She took the envelope out of Gail's hand without a struggle and weaved her way through the crowd to Dave. She handed him the envelope containing the note and the St. Christopher medal and said something to him. He nodded and then went into the restroom after his friend.

With the deed done, Linda returned in quiet triumph to her friends. She and Sara guided Gail out the doors and onto the sidewalk to wait for Gail's mom. Within five minutes the station wagon pulled up and the three girls piled in.

"How was the movie?" asked Gail's mom cheerfully.

"Great!" replied Sara and Linda almost simultaneously. Gail's mom smiled at their response but couldn't help but notice her daughter's somber demeanor in the rear view mirror. She could tell by her daughter's body language that something was amiss.

"What's wrong?" she asked.

"She gave Tim his St. Christopher medal back," said Linda, cutting to the chase.

"Oh," sighed Gail's mom in understanding. She glanced a couple more times into the rearview mirror before adding. "It's for the best."

Sara and Linda both agreed that it was for the best. Gail nodded with her head down and played with the strap on her purse. No more was said about Tim or the St. Christopher medal, and after they dropped Sara and Linda off, Gail remained in the back seat.

"You okay, honey?" asked her mom.

Gail tried to hum an okay but started crying instead. It was a soft, gentle cry. Gail's mom watched her daughter with a sad pride and let her have her cry.

A Dead-Game Fighter

It was late and the dining room was empty except for a party of four on table seven. A busboy worked a discreet distance away methodically collecting up glass ashtrays and extinguishing the candles on the other tables. The heavy curtains had been drawn on the dining room windows, revealing the clean night outside, and all but one of the four stations had been wiped down and re-stocked, leaving the fourth one near the hallway and kitchen still active for the closing girl. In a smaller, dimly-lit dining room partitioned off from the main room sat three waitresses at a table. This was where the girls came at the end of their shift to eat a late supper, to talk, and to enjoy a cigarette and rest their legs before going home. The table was lit by two small candles which created a kind of cozy glow that was enough to eat and talk by.

The three women sat with their legs crossed, their black nylon skirts tight about their hips and thighs, and there was a flaxen steak along the seams where the candlelight reflected. Their finished dinner plates had been partly stacked aside and each woman held a cigarette in hand, using it as a wand while they talked, and occasionally flicking it into the community ashtray in the center of the table. Their talk was quiet yet incessant, broken only by a drag off a cigarette or a sip from a drink. Over the intercom an orchestra softly played, its melodic score choreographing the women's cigarette smoke as it rose gracefully above their heads and into the dark ceiling.

A fourth waitress entered the room and quickly walked to their table where she stopped and stood, counting through a wad of dollar bills in her hands. Her name was Rita. At the table sat Toni, Jean, and Carrie.

"How's seven coming?" asked Jean

"Ahh..," replied Rita, pausing in her count to glance momentarily up at the ceiling before finishing her count. "They're done with entrees, I believe," she answered as she dropped a portion of her money onto the table and pocketed the rest in her apron.

"Hmm, good," replied Jean. She took a quick drag off her cigarette and deposited it on the plate, swept a stray hair back into her slightly frayed hairdo, and rose from her chair. "Maybe I'll get out of here at a decent hour," she said.

"Are they drunk?" asked Toni.

"Of course."

Toni shook her head knowingly. "Then you'll be here all night," she said.

"Oh, don't say that," replied Jean in a tone equally knowing yet cheerful. She unbunched her skirt and left the room.

Rita remained standing and scanned the drinks on the table. "What's everyone drinking?" she inquired with a ready smile.

"Vodka."

"And a white-wine cooler," added Carrie with a nod at her own drink.

Rita turned and walked briskly out of the room, her nylon skirt cheeping softly as she moved. The two women sat silently in their chairs and listened as the kitchen door swung open and shut, which meant Rita had entered the kitchen and was on her way to the service window of the bar to get their drinks. Satisfied by the sound, Toni uncrossed her legs with a slight sigh and released another button near the top of her starched-white blouse. She gazed out the window at the night. She was older than the other girls, in her mid-forties, and looked her age. Her face was lean and tight and was weathered about the eyes and forehead with smooth wrinkles. It was still very much an attractive face, albeit hardened, that could blossom nicely whenever she laughed or smiled. Her blue eyes were tireless and marked by a playful sarcasm. She wore her hair in a short, frosted beehive, efficient yet attractive-looking, and wore no jewelry except for a gold wedding band on her finger. She was a widow and had been for many years.

Toni turned from the window and leaned forward and mashed out what was left of her cigarette on the plate. "How do you like it so far?" she asked Carrie in a sweet-gravelly voice, the kind of voice that comes from years of drinking and smoking.

"Huh?" ... Carrie looked up out of her daydream and shrugged slightly. "Oh, just fine," she answered without enthusiasm.

"Just fine?"

"Yeah, well..." She leaned forward and put out her cigarette on the plate then reached over her chair and into the pocket of her coat. "I mean it's good for now... until I can get the money to go back to school." Her arm came back holding a pack of cigarettes.

"Hmm," commented Toni. She reached for her drink and finished if off with a flick and tilt of her wrist, the ice clinking as it slid forward and back within the emptied glass.

Carrie tapped out a cigarette and placed it between her lips and pocketed the rest of the pack back in her coat. She picked up a book of matches from the table and lit her cigarette, the match flame coloring her young, unblemished face. She half-inhaled then blew out the flame and tossed the dead match onto the plate. Carrie was in her early twenties and unlike the other women wore no make-up except for a colorless lip gloss. Her brown hair was permed and styled to look naturally curly and had a bit of a mop-top appearance to it. Her uniform, as with her other clothes, did not fit quite right, being a shade too roomy in the shoulders and waist. The subtle excess tended to hide her slim figure and appeared to make her slouch whenever she sat down. This oddity, along with one or two other idiosyncrasies, combined to detract from her overall prettiness, the oddities being tactical rather than unwitting, as though she consciously worked against her prettiness by withholding the right touch here or adding the wrong touch there. Her eyes were dark beneath thick eyebrows and darted from one thing to another when she spoke.

Carrie took another half-drag off her cigarette and followed her hazy exhale as it drifted upwards. She picked up her wine cooler. "I'm going for my Masters," she said as she sipped her drink and set it back down. "And when that's over and done with I'll be able to start my career. Something *meaningful,* you know, like teaching. Something that won't put me to sleep." She shut her eyes and let go a playful snore. She awakened from her mock snooze and laughed.

"Hmm," commented Toni again as she smiled and stared back out the window. A thought came to her and she turned to speak to Carrie but paused as a stack of dinner plates were dumped noisily into the bus pan on the other side of the partition.

"Have you waitressed before?" she asked Carrie.

"Yeah, a few times."

"That's what I meant before—how do you like this place compared to the others?"

"Oh..." Carrie straightened up slightly and glanced around the dark room. "It's very nice. I like it," she answered.

Toni nodded and re-crossed her legs. "I think it's one of the better dinner houses on the peninsula myself. You won't find many better."

"How long you worked here?" Carrie asked cordially.

"Twelve years—been here twelve years. I hired on when Ben and I first moved out here. Before that I was a waitress in Oklahoma." She gazed out the window again, or rather into it, as though the window itself was a large and friendly eye. "When I first started the place was called Sabella's, then Fritz bought it out. It used to be a seafood house, which is why that neon fish is still hanging up outside. Fritz is too cheap to take it down." She laughed briefly to herself at this and turned to look at Carrie, who rested her chin upon her cigarette hand in a languid pose, appearing to listen. "Most of the girls have been here for a while. Even Jean... I think she started here when it was still Sabella's."

"Jean?" queried Carrie, her interest suddenly aroused.

"Oh, sure," replied Toni, stroking her ear in reflection. "About nine years she's been here."

"You're kidding?"

Rita entered the room carrying four drinks on a cocktail tray and came up to the table and set each drink down in its proper place on the white tablecloth. She took a seat, making nylon sounds as she quickly got situated.

"Thanks, kid," said Toni, who reached forward and stirred her fresh drink with its swizzle stick.

"I've been dying for a drink all night," greeted Rita. She held a new pack of cigarettes in her hand and began tapping it loudly against the flat of her other palm. She was a smallish woman with a sturdy-looking figure who reminded one at first glance of a ranch house cook. Her clay-dark complexion was ingrained as though she had been baked in a kiln, and her face was almost masculine-looking and marked by a permanently furrowed brow. She wore her auburn-colored hair in a short bob, bowled up like a furry cap, and always smiled close-mouthed without ever showing her teeth. But her prime feature was her nervous condition; it was a kind of stuck-valve pensiveness that released itself through the incessant jerking and shifting of her body as she sat in a chair, and one could easily mistake it as sign of constant worry or the fruit of some unresolved gripe. But she was hardly a malcontent, and after work was when she was at her best.

"How long's Jean been here?" Toni asked her.

"Hmm, let's see," replied Rita as she paused from unwrapping her pack of cigarettes to reflect. "'Bout nine years, I think." She peeled off the red seal and removed the cellophane with a crackling sound.

"That's what I thought," said Toni.

"Nine years," repeated Carrie with a shake of her head. "But how old is she?"

"Thirty-two."

"Thirty-two!" Carrie whispered in astonishment. "I thought she was more like twenty-two."

"Nope, thirty-two," Toni confirmed matter-of-factly. "She looks young for her age."

"She's been married for fifteen years," added Rita with a cigarette in her mouth.

"You're kidding!"

"I wouldn't remind her of that fact if I were you," advised Toni with a wry grin. Rita returned the same wry grin and rolled her eyes at their private joke.

"Huh!" exclaimed Carrie with another shake of her head, quickly reconciling her first impressions of Jean with these new set of facts. And just as quickly, she picked up on the meaningful exchange between the two other women. "What?" she whispered, wanting in on their private joke.

Toni regarded her momentarily then shrugged her shoulders nonchalantly. "Let's just say she has problems," she said. "But then so does everyone." Her blue eyes left Carrie and looked out the window.

"Why?" pressed Carrie, leaning in closer.

No one answered as Carrie glanced from one woman to the other. Rita, secretly fidgeting, checked the back of Toni's head and then shifted in her chair, instantly attracting Carrie's full attention.

"Well, let's just say," intoned Rita, waving her smoking hand in front of her, "that if they gave prizes for going the distance, she'd get top honors."

Toni snickered at this without turning from the window.

"Why's that?" asked Carrie, devouring this tidbit. She leaned in even farther, to the point of tautness, itching to learn more.

"Why?" repeated Rita, somewhat baffled by the question. She pondered the question a moment longer, shifted in her chair, glanced down at the tablecloth, and said somewhat out of context, "Didn't you notice her eye?"

"Her eye? Why?"

"Her *black* eye," Rita clarified. She took a drag off her cigarette and exhaled out over the candlelit table, pausing for dramatic effect... "He beat her up the other night," she said evenly.

"You're kidding!" Carrie shook her head again with a short, violent jerk, as though she had just taken a slap to the cheek.

"Yep. I think it was Sunday night," said Rita, glancing at Toni for confirmation but getting none. "You should have seen her. She was a mess."

Carrie stared at Rita's mouth as she sank back in her chair, noticeably stunned by the succession of dumbfounding blows she had just taken. Her dazed look was more a kind of concerned amazement than it was shock; it was the sort of look that comes over certain people, especially young people, after their preconceptions on a subject have been shot irreparably to hell. Her hands rested in her lap and the ash from her neglected cigarette broke off, causing her to straighten up and sweep the ashes from her nylon skirt.

A quiet filled the room. The candles on the table sizzled softly, their fingernail-shaped flames flickering yellow and illuminating the cigarette smoke as it rose upwards into the ceiling. Laughter came from the dining room. Toni turned and reached for her drink and took a long pull from it.

"Is she getting a divorce?" inquired Carrie, breaking the quiet.

Again no one answered her, and Carrie turned in expectation to Rita, who scratched her neck with a nervous shrug.

"She's afraid," Rita told her.

"Afraid? ... Afraid of what?"

"Afraid of what he'd do to her if she tried," said Rita, shrugging with the obviousness of it.

Carrie blinked, then sniggered as she glanced at either woman. "I don't get it," she declared. "Who is this creep? Why doesn't she just tell him to fuck off?"

Toni suddenly laughed and turned and eyed Carrie with amusement. "Have you ever seen her husband?" she asked her.

"No, but..."

"Well, he's about six-four and two hundred and some pounds," she stated flatly. "Earl is not exactly someone you would say 'fuck off' to." Toni laughed again and glanced to Rita who shared in her amusement.

Lorraine had entered the room, and she approached the table and stood over an empty chair next to the women. "Who are you talking about?" she asked preemptively.

"Who else?" replied Rita, looking up at Lorraine while flicking her cigarette ash on the plate with a quick jab.

"Earl, huh?" Without waiting confirmation she peered out the window for inspection—"Why, is he prowling around?"—then started into her chair. "He'd better not be if he knows what's good for him," she said, settling into her chair with a defiant look on her face.

"No. We were just filling her in on the latest," said Rita, indicating Carrie with a wave of her hand.

Lorraine nodded, regarding Carrie momentarily, and coughed into her fist without commenting. She was a rather fleshy woman in her mid-forties with the lofty air of a grand matriarch. As she did nightly, she wore a hostess' gown that somehow always succeeded in accentuating rather than cloaking her mild obesity. Her red hair was piled up on top and curled at the ends in a bouffant á la Lady Bird Johnson, while her large pink face, shiny now from perspiration, was strategically swathed in make-up that, like a Greek mask, gave her an eternally unperturbed expression. She was both hostess and supervisor, and accordingly her relationship with "her girls" was a very parental one. When she spoke it was the voice of authority, of worldly wisdom, and begged no contradiction. And whenever she deigned like now to sit and talk with the women after work, she would take immediate control, occasionally listening tolerantly to another's opinion before speaking what was meant to be the final word on the matter.

"Well, whatever you heard isn't the half of it, believe me," said Lorraine, vaguely acknowledging Carrie as she spoke. "But then"—she paused and raised an eyebrow at the candle flames—"he isn't any worse than most men."

"Why'd he beat her up?" asked Carrie quietly.

"Who knows?" Lorraine answered with a slow, indifferent blink of her eyelids. "Most men don't know why they do things. They just do them."

"Oh, I think they know all right," said Toni from across the table. "They just can't explain it in words."

Lorraine nodded tersely at this and glanced away, as was her habit before replying, but before she could speak Jean entered the room and walked swiftly to their table. "Well, on their coffee and into the homestretch," sung out Jean with a smile as she quickly sat down and got snug in her chair. The women smiled back at her, enlivened by her presence, while simultaneously studying the subject of their gossip. She reached for her cigarette pack she had left on the table, unconscious of this special attention, and began at once to tap her foot noiselessly beneath the table.

As Toni had noted to Carrie, Jean was young-looking for her age. She was thirty-two and looked twenty-two—an alluringly mature twenty-two, to be sure—and was without a doubt what one would call a beautiful woman. She was slender-figured, her body sleek and restive like a teenaged cat, with cream-colored skin that was even more fresh-looking than Carrie's. Her face, with its dark eyebrows, expressive mouth, and sculptured cheekbones, resembled the actress Loretta Young in the 1930s, but without the same dark, shoulder-length hair. Instead, her deep-brown hair was built up in a graceful beehive that made her appear more slender and rather taller than she really was. Her eyes, set within polished whites, were a prismatic hazel, the irises every so often defining themselves as blueish or greenish or an occasional turquoise depending on the light, which together in any light dominated her comely face in the same way two lucent gems dominated a gold setting.

And though Jean's stylish figure and refined beauty gave one the expectation of an appropriately suave demeanor, such was not the case. She was a woman in perpetual motion; she could not sit still without having to promptly tap out an endless beat with her foot or drum her fingers on the tablecloth or busy her hands with the texture of a napkin or the fringe of her blouse. Yet her encompassing eyes caught every small gesture or subtle cue in the room and she missed nothing. If Rita's nervousness was a sort of stuck-valve pensiveness then hers was something else; it was more a kind of wired pep that ran full time like a high-idling engine, which instead of being annoying to those around her usually proved contagious. It was a hustler's energy, fast and loose, with that irrepressible quality to it that was the mark of a good grifter or a slick pool shark. And like a good hustler, she was a talker. She bantered expertly, laughed at all jokes, and took all sides of an argument without seeming to take any, and all with that look of heartfelt sincerity which she had developed over the years from catering to the public, including her fair share of drunks and assholes. But unlike a hustler, she lacked that basic unscrupulousness; for though it seemed an act, a put-on, and the best in the house, it lacked the core indifference towards people that characterized a true hustler. Instead, what seethed out of her—out of her tapping feet, out of her drumming fingers—was a kind of boundless sympathy, an extreme sensitivity and almost compulsive responsiveness to other's moods. Just sitting next to her one could feel it—that fathomless empathy—and feel too, distinctly, it's untiring quality, that tenacity of spirit of someone who was ready to answer the bell and keep on answering it until the end.

She removed a cigarette from the pack and lit it, inhaling deeply, and looked down at the table where she noticed the fresh drink.

"Who got drinks?"

"Rita," replied Toni.

Jean smiled appreciatively at Rita and picked up her old drink. She finished off what was left, set it aside, and moved the fresh drink onto the remaining wet ring. The women secretly watched her, especially Carrie who seemed fixed on Jean's left eye which she could now see bore signs of bruising beneath the make-up.

"Did you do what I told you?" Lorraine asked suddenly, looking right at Jean.

"Huh?" uttered Jean in surprise as she glanced anxiously at Lorraine. "What?"

Lorraine shifted impatiently in her chair, her face impassive. "Did you get the restraining order like I told you?" she said.

"Oh." Jean relaxed her posture and peeked over at Toni. "No, I didn't," she confessed, instantly raising her downcast eyes up in defense. "But they don't do any good anyhow. I should know."

"I don't believe that. They serve a purpose, and you'll need it."

"But I've had them before," she explained, "and they've never helped. I think they're more trouble than they're worth, to be honest with you."

"Would you just take my advice and get one," Lorraine softly ordered.

"They're not worth the paper they're written on," declared Toni with her eyes fixed on her drink. The women looked at her. "They cost about fifty bucks and once you get one in your hot little hand they ain't worth a chicken feather for protection. Try hitting him over the head with it when he comes at you. Lots 'a luck."

"It gives her grounds for an arrest," said Carrie.

Toni laughed sarcastically, exchanging glances with Jean. "Oh sure," she replied, eyeing Lorraine askance, "and by the time the cops get there you're food for the cat and he's long gone."

Jean laughed through her nose.

"And even if they do catch him," continued Toni—"which doesn't do you much good—he'll be back out on the street in a couple hours. One quick call to his buddy, one quick trip to the bail bondsman, and zip—he's back out and more pissed off than before. He'll stoke the fire with a few drinks at the bar then head home to finish off what he started."

"And most of the time the cops won't take him in anyway," added Jean in an apologetic tone. "They'll just give him a talking-to and let him go. They rather you didn't press charges."

"Cops don't care anyhow," said Rita.

"They're men, that's why," said Carrie.

"The police can't care," preempted Lorraine as she stiffened formally in her chair. "They can't afford to get involved—emotionally. I can understand their position. They probably answer calls like that all the time, and they have to handle them the best way they can. It's understandable."

"That's true," conceded Jean.

"But I still want you to get that restraining order."

Jean nodded artificially and reached out and flicked her cigarette ash in the plate. "Well, I'll talk to my lawyer tomorrow," she promised. "See what he says."

"What I don't get," interjected Rita, her boyish face creased with concern, "is how they expect a woman to protect herself. I mean, listening to you guys talk, it sounds like the laws are all set up to protect the man. So what do they expect you to do? Huh?" She crossed her arms in a gesture of frustration and awaited an answer.

"Who makes the laws?" asked Carrie rhetorically. She paused a split second for effect then answered her own question: "Men do."

"There's only two things you can do," said Toni, disregarding Carrie's remark. "You either put up with it for the rest of your life or you shoot him. The choice is yours. If you love him you put up with it."

Rita dropped her arms with a ticked-off chuckle and shook her head. "Sometimes men are such... such..."

A busboy entered the candlelit room and Rita dropped her remark. He was dressed in street clothes with his hair freshly combed, and he stopped at the head of the table, smiled quickly around, and peered at the collection of tip-money in the center of the table. "All yours," said Jean with a smile. He smiled back and reached over the table and scooped up the money.

"Where's Tim?" asked Lorraine.

"In the dining room," he answered as he shuffled through the dollar bills in his hand. Just then the other busboy appeared at his shoulder to inspect the divvying-up process. He was dressed in dark slacks and a white frock that was spotted in front with brown food stains. His blonde hair was curled up from sweating. "Don't give me all the ones this time," he joked in his teenage voice. His partner smirked back at him and resumed his important count. A tender quiet came over the older women as they sat there and secretly admired the two young men and their sportive friendship. Without a word and with cigarettes poised, they watched as the one boy finished the divvying-up and handed the other boy his share with playful reluctance. The other boy snatched the bills up like the winnings from a bet.

"Did you stock all the stations?" asked Lorraine.

"Uh huh," replied the busboy in uniform. He shoved his share of the tips into his pants pocket and glanced at the partition and, by imagination, into the dining room beyond. He lingered with his partner near the table, their poses noticeably restless.

"Go ahead and go, sweetie" said Jean. "It's all right. No sense waiting around all night for just one table. I'll clean up."

The busboy's face lit up, and he glanced at Jean and then over at Lorraine, who remained encouragingly indifferent. "Sure?" he asked hopefully, turning back to Jean.

"Sure," answered Jean with a dimpled-up smile.

He grinned and looked to his partner and bobbed his head. "All right," he whispered cheerfully, and the two turned and started out of the room playfully bumping each other as they went. They departed swiftly, the two young men consumed with their immediate plans, unconscious of the looks of nostalgia that followed them out the door. The women listened to the kitchen door swing open and shut. The candle flames on the table contracted at the noise of the doors, releasing into the room a deeper shade of darkness that seemed to add to the wistful quiet.

"I wish they could stay that age," softly mused Jean as she waved her cigarette hand across the table, leaving a trail of rising smoke.

"That's just the problem," said Lorraine, "they do." This elicited a round of laughter from the women around the table, and Lorraine quickly masked her surprise with a sly grin. "Yeah," she continued, shaking her head, "if they'd only grow up we'd all be happier. But I don't think they ever graduate from high school— mentally. They're still playing the same games at fifty that they were at fifteen."

Toni nodded sympathetically, overcoming her laughter to speak: "Yeah, Ben was great at that."

"Earl's the same way," laughed Jean.

"Just as I said," chided Lorraine, "no matter how old they get they still remain a teenager at heart. They never stop wanting to play hooky or chase girls or throw the winning touchdown pass. And if you don't let them, if you tell them to grow up and get with it, they throw a tantrum and run off like a little boy."

"Yeah, well, I don't think they're quite that bad," chuckled Toni as she reached down into her purse for her cigarettes.

"Granted, they're still teenagers at heart, but... aren't we all?" She glanced around the table and stopped on Jean, who nodded in agreement. "And as far as always wanting to throw the winning touchdown pass, I really don't think I'd want a man who stopped trying. You know what I mean?" she added as she struck a match and lit her cigarette, ignoring Lorraine who sat frowning at her. She took a deep drag and immediately exhaled, shrugging her right shoulder. "Maybe that's just me though. But I do think you should let them have their games. I mean, if it makes them happy, what the hell?" She took another deep drag off her cigarette and held it in, then blew it out into the slightly uneasy silence.

"I believe that," said Jean, filling in the silence. She had assumed an astute manner, and she quickly flicked her cigarette ash in the plate. "You should let them have their games, but then, like I think Lorraine was saying, you have to be a mother to them all the time. It's not easy. But I can see what you're saying. You have to know when to leave them alone and when not to."

"And vice-versa," said Carrie.

The women turned their attention to Carrie, and at seeing this she quickly added, "They should give you your own space as well—as a human being. It can't be a one-sided thing. A woman has to have her freedom, too. That was the problem with my last boyfriend. He wouldn't give me enough space of my own to create a self, so I split."

"Hmm," commented Toni as she glanced around at the women and then out the window. "And he's probably happily married by now while you're living all alone... I guess you showed him," she quipped, turning back.

Rita stifled a laugh while Jean smiled and turned her face away. Lorraine brooded without expression. Carrie darted a look into the candle flames and moved to reply, but Lorraine cut her off before she could speak. "Being a mother all the time is not what I meant," Lorraine said. "I was talking more about that competitiveness—like boys. They find it so necessary to be better than you—to win all the time. They just can't leave well enough alone... Take going to bed. They make it into such an event. They're not satisfied unless you reach seventh heaven every time, and if you don't they want to know what's wrong and why they couldn't please you. They just can't leave well enough alone."

"They do have a hang-up about sex," agreed Carrie.

"Well..," breathed Rita as she shifted positions in her chair, an inscrutable smile of her face, "maybe some men do, but not Larry. He's never had any problem with it."

"Oh, really?" inquired Toni with a grin. "And what happens when Larry gets the ol' evil eye and comes for you when you're all worn out and tired? Then what do you do—pop some diet pills and spread 'em?" The women burst out laughing at Toni's bawdy humor and exchanged glances at one another. "Shhh!" ordered Lorraine with a telltale smile on her lips. The women quickly shushed, shifting their laughter into short sniffs.

"No," snickered Rita, fidgeting in her chair. She smothered her own laughter and flashed another inscrutable smile. "No, he always waits till I'm ready. He never pushes me into it at all."

"Hmm," commented Toni with an admiring nod. "Then you have him well-trained, kid." The women hummed in accord as Rita twitched her eyebrows and sat back in a prideful pose.

"You have something on him, all right," agreed Jean with a grin. "Any husband who takes his wife fishing and hunting with him and everywhere else has got to be... I don't know—something. Earl would drop dead before he took me fishing, and I'd drop dead before I'd let him take me hunting. Yech!" she exclaimed with a grimace, as though she had just stepped on a snail.

"Yeah," chorused Toni. "I mean, togetherness is one thing but sharing worms with him is another."

"It's fun," defended Rita.

"Yeah, well, to each his own, I guess," replied Toni with an ingratiating smile. "But is there anything you don't do together? Besides work."

"Not if we can help it."

Toni, ready with a quip, opened her mouth to reply but Lorraine cut her off. "I think it's admirable myself," she said, tightening her right earring. "At least you know where he is all the time." (She finished tightening her earring and set her hands back in lap.) "Good for you—you've won—and you can't have a happy marriage unless you've won. Not until he gives in to you can you have a happy marriage... And that's a fact," she added for emphasis, glancing sternly around the table.

Toni commented on Lorraine's facts by finishing off her vodka tonic with a long swallow.

Jean leaned forward and said, "Do you mean..?"

"Just what I said," replied Lorraine curtly before Jean could finish her question.

Jean's face showed hurt, recovery, and determination all within a split second, and she remained leaning forward and glanced at the other women, reading the majority opinion in their candlelit faces. "Oh..," she began diplomatically, "I don't know if I agree with that. I mean, you can't expect a man to be at your beck and call all the time—like a puppy dog. Who wants a puppy dog for a husband?" She looked to the other women for confirmation and then relaxed into her chair. "I mean, being together is good," she said confidently. "But you can't try and walk all over a man. Least that's what I think."

"You will if you want a happy marriage," maintained Lorraine.

"No, especially if you want a happy marriage," sparred Jean, shifting out of her relaxed pose. "I've always given Earl room to move."

Lorraine touched her earring again. "Is that why your marriage is such bliss then?" she asked smoothly.

"Uh, well, you got me there," smiled Jean, rolling with the punch.

Only Jean was left, sitting at the table with Carrie. She had just brought more coffee to her party of four on table seven and she was hopeful they wouldn't be much longer. Lorraine had left their backroom table to see about closing up the bar, and Toni and Rita had left for home soon after but not before making fun of Lorraine for being such a hard-ass. Toni was a little concerned about leaving Jean all alone, but Carrie had erased that concern by offering to stay and keep Jean company.

Jean lit a cigarette and took a deep drag and blew her smoke up into the cloud above. She glanced warmly at Carrie. "Thanks for staying. I feel better with someone here."

"No problem."

Jean smiled gratefully and settled back in her chair with her freshly-lit cigarette in hand. With her free hand she patted around her beehive like one would around a fragile hat and then dropped her hand into her lap. Her foot tapped out a soundless yet steady beat beneath the table. She could tell that Carrie liked her; she was used to young people, people Carrie's age, taking an instant liking to her and she enjoyed their company. She also sensed that Carrie wanted to talk to her about something.

Carrie took out a cigarette of her own and studied Jean carefully out of the corner of her eye. "Mind if I ask you a question?" she said politely. "I mean if it's not too personal?"

"Sure," replied Jean, eagerly sitting up straight.

"Did your husband really beat you up?"

Jean touched her bruised eye with a game smile. "Yeah," she answered candidly. "As you can see."

Carrie clicked her tongue in sympathetic disgust. "But why?" she asked. "I mean, what's his problem?"

"His problem?"

"Well—I take it this isn't the first time he's done this?"

"No," admitted Jean with a faraway look. She focused back on Carrie, bringing the past with her, and told her it had happened before "a few times." Without a trace of self-consciousness, she gave Carrie a blow by blow description of their fight, which had started out as a verbal confrontation and ended up with him knocking her down to the ground. This had happened last Sunday night, in front of the bowling alley, and he knocked her down more than once before "he finally stopped and ran off."

"Didn't you scream for help, or anything?"

"No. There were people across the street watching but they didn't do anything."

Carrie wrung her hand across her face. "Jesus, I can't believe this," she said angrily. "Didn't you call the police—have him arrested? You had witnesses."

"No."

"But why not? You had witnesses."

"I don't know," Jean answered innocently. "I guess I didn't think of it."

Carrie moved to further reprimand Jean but caught herself and remained quiet. She picked up her drink, sipped it thoughtfully, and regarded Jean compassionately. She'd only known Jean for little over a week and had been immediately attracted to her high energy and vivaciousness. And even though her first impressions of Jean—of being young, single, and hip—had been knocked to the ground, so to speak, she still felt a kinship towards her. People were drawn to Jean like bees to a bright-colored flower and Carrie was no exception. But there was a greater allure for Carrie than that; Jean was a women in need of help, in need of enlightenment, and that more than anything piqued Carrie's interest in this woman.

"I never imagined," said Carrie as her darting eyes rested on Jean's candlelit face. "I mean, you seem so happy all the time. So up. You know? I never imagined you had a problem like this. It's incredible, *really.*"

"It's not *that* bad," replied Jean somewhat defensively. She regarded Carrie with raised eyebrows, her cigarette hand fluttering open and shut like a waking butterfly steaming with life. "I mean, I don't feel un-happy. I guess maybe I should, but I figure it'll all work out. It always does."

"How do you mean that?" questioned Carrie. "You mean divorce, right?"

"Well...," she hedged lightly, winking at her. "I always say that at first but... you know..." She delicately placed her cigarette on the plate with a knowing smile. "We got divorced once," she confided gaily. "My parents paid for the whole thing—they figured they were finally getting rid of him. Three months after the divorce we got married again. Talk about the shit hitting the fan." She laughed and rolled her eyes at the memory of it.

"You can't be serious?" objected Carrie with a touch of disgust in her voice. "I mean, He Beat You Up. He physically *abused* and *humiliated* you. How could you possibly contemplate any alternative other than divorce? He's a wife-beater. You're married to a *wife-beater,* and the only way you'll ever get rid of him is to end it... I mean, that seems the only reasonable thing to do to me," she added curtly, "unless you want to go through life getting beat up."

"No," Jean quietly agreed. "Yeah. I see what you're saying— when you put it that way. Sure." She nodded as she picked up her drink and gazed down into the liquid with a melancholy expression on her face. But immediately she shook her head and looked back up at Carrie. "But no," she remonstrated lightly. "I wouldn't call Earl a wife-beater. Not really. At least not the way I think of it."

Carrie held back her exasperation and instead channeled it into a kind of dialectical urgency that quickened her speech pattern. "Of course he is," she stated flatly. "I did a study on this very topic in college." And with that she launched into a short summary of her finding. Wife-beaters fit a profile, she told Jean, and regardless of their background—rich, poor, white, or black, etc.— the psychological characteristics were the same. "I guarantee you, he fits the profile," she said. "By just what you've told me, I guarantee he fits the profile. Ready?" Carrie paused a moment to allow Jean to prepare herself for the test... "Okay, one," she began as she raised a finger, her unlit cigarette tucked between her knuckles like a piece of chalk. "He appears, at least ostensibly, to be extremely manly, that is authoritative, unyielding—in other words, *macho.* True or false?"

"Yeah," allowed Jean, smiling. "I guess you could call Earl 'macho.'"

"Okay, and two, he's typically chauvinistic in his attitude towards women. He adheres strictly to the barefoot and pregnant theory and employs a double standard of behavior when it comes to extra-marital sex. True?"

"Yes," she confessed impassively.

"And what would he do to you if he caught you cheating?"

"Probably kill me," she said with a laugh that completed the one-liner.

"Ha! See," replied Carrie triumphantly as she turned to point number three. Now her diction turned more formal as she quoted parts of her paper. The macho image was just a front for his basic weakness and inability to cope, she explained to Jean. In times of crisis, this artificial front crumbles and he resorts to violence to reassert his false sense of masculinity, usually by overpowering and abusing weaker victims like women. She gave Jean a couple examples to illustrate her point.

"Wait though," interrupted Jean. "I don't know about some of that," she protested mildly. "I know Earl's violent at times, but he's never abused anyone who was weaker than him."

"How about you?!" admonished Carrie.

"Well.., that's different. Earl has never hit one of the kids in anger, and I've never seen him hurt an animal, or anything like that... No," she said shaking her head hesitantly, then more vigorously as she became certain of her views on the matter. "Seems like a lot of what you're saying sounds like most men I know."

"Exactly!" replied Carrie almost shouting. She edged forward in her chair, stealing further into the candlelight, eager to press her point. "That was my whole thesis. What you're saying is exactly what I said," she added, making it sound like a compliment. She didn't wait for Jean to respond and instead continued to quote parts of her paper, stressing key words like "psychosis" and "inculcates" as though they were nails she was hammering home. "Society breeds wife-beaters," she said coming to her conclusion. "It breeds psychotic behavior. Men's perverted image of themselves—as hunter, provider, master, and all that crap—eats away at their natural humanness. That's why they lash out in times of crisis. They lash out the way society has taught them—violently. You see?"

"Hmm...Yeah. I'm not sure if I followed all that," Jean admitted in bewildered admiration, "but it sounds possible. Earl does have his problems, I can't deny that."

"Has he ever seen a psychiatrist?"

"No. He doesn't believe in them."

Carrie snorted out an exasperated laugh. "That's a rather primitive attitude in this day and age," she opined, finally lighting her cigarette. "I was in analysis for two years and it worked wonders. I can vouch for its validity, but then *only* if you open up to it... It sounds as though he's afraid of it, of what it might reveal. Part of solving the problem is in admitting you have one."

"That's true. Earl doesn't like admitting his problems."

"Well, see? It's obvious then. If he won't seek help for his problem then your only alternative is to get out. If you don't it'll just get worse and go on and on until he ends up killing you one day."

"No.., he'd never kill me," said Jean as she picked up her cigarette and took a contemplative drag. "I'm his sanity," she added, breathing out the words with her smoke. She leaned forward and mashed her cigarette out in the plate and eyed Carrie. She had a secret to tell and it showed on her face, and Carrie recognized the look and sat quietly and listened.

"Let me tell you about Earl," said Jean softly as she leaned back in her chair, fanning the smoke from her face, and glanced out the window and back. The restiveness was gone from her demeanor, the high-idling engine having suddenly throttled back, and her lemon-colored face showed the calm intensity of a soothsayer in the candlelight. "I've lived with him for fifteen years," she started out, "and even I'm not sure that I really know him. But you have to try and understand him, his upbringing, and all that—what he wanted to be and what he turned out to be."

For the next ten minutes Jean unburdened herself. And Carrie, in analyst mode, listened without interrupting once, finding herself seductively drawn into Jean's intimate story. Her husband Earl had had a terrible childhood—alcoholic father and hardscrabble life punctuated by violence and abuse—and been in and out of trouble as a teenager. He fought in Korea, lost good friends there, and seen "terrible things" that still gave him nightmares. At one time he wanted to be a priest, even enrolled in Seminary school, but nothing came of it. He'd been a promising athlete in high school and later on had wanted to go into coaching. But like everything else it never worked out, partly because he was a trouble-maker and partly because of other things. "Jesus," sighed Jean. "When I first met him he was always getting into trouble. He had a criminal record, for crying out loud. Even drugs. But crazy as it sounds, I must have seen something in him or we wouldn't be together today."

Jean had hit her stride and the words tumbled out like coins from an uncorked bottle. He was a good father, she told Carrie—not the greatest maybe but their kids loved him. And as a husband, well, there were good and bad times, and she loved him and he, "in his own crazy way," loved her. All in all, he was a man—and here Jean had to pause in order to find the right word—he was a man of "contradictions." On the one hand, Korea screwed him up but he loved war movies; he acted dumb when really he was smart; he drank too much even though he hated drunks; and despite going to jail a few times and being in trouble with the law he was still a die-hard patriot. He said he didn't deserve her and couldn't live without her, then he turned around and did this to her (she said this pointing to her black eye). But the biggest contradiction of all, if it really was a contradiction, was his talent for blowing things apart. Just when things were going great—everybody happy, money coming in, no bills, he's not drinking—he had to blow it all apart. Every time. It was like he couldn't help it. It was almost like he didn't trust the world, knew it was going to screw him over eventually, so he'd blow it apart himself and beat it to the punch. Every time.

"You realize what kind of life that makes for?" she asked without waiting for an answer. "It's like living in a boxing ring, or something. You spend all your time faking and dodging and just trying to stay on your feet until the bell rings so you can take a quick rest before the next round."

Jean breathed in deeply, exhaled evenly, and tapped her fist against her chest three times. Carrie sat looking at her with one eyebrow raised, and Jean met her eyes for a brief moment. "I'm not trying to justify anything," said Jean rather defensively. "Most of it is nobody's fault but his own. I mean, upbringing and all that—you can't blame anyone but yourself, right? But still you have to try and understand him and why he does what he does. He has all this ambition but he sees himself as a failure... and, I don't know, I'm not a man, but that must be a terrible thing to live with."

Jean arched her back and felt along her smooth neck, appearing to collect her thoughts. "But... I'm his sanity," she said, coming back to her beginning. "Home and family—all that's normal. It's how his mind works. And that's why he'll be back, that's why he'll come after me again. You can bet your bottom dollar on it." She paused and peered out the window at the lurking night, envisioning it, then turned back to Carrie and smiled reassuringly. "But don't worry about it, he'll wait till I'm alone, when he thinks it's safe... But he'll be back, and then it will start all over again, just like always." And now Jean became more animated, using her hands and upper body to emphasize her words, as she let loose with her feelings. "But maybe you're right," she said to Carrie. Maybe it was time to throw in the towel. She had grown up believing love could conquer all, but maybe love wasn't enough. She was foolish to think she could change him— people didn't change—and she knew very well what kind of man he was when she married him. Part of this was her own damn fault, and only she could change it for the better. She had to think of the kids and what it was doing to them. But it wouldn't be easy. She'd run away before and he had always found her— always— and he would again.

"I'm afraid of him," Jean said in a harsh whisper. "But I also love him. Jesus! It sounds crazy but it's true. I love him but I'm afraid of him. Does that make any sense whatsoever? I mean, that's what it finally comes down to. I haven't any more answers... None... You tell me." She reached for her drink and clasped her hand around the cold wet glass, staring at it thoughtfully.

Carrie studied her expectantly, like a doctor does a patient after having probed the inflamed area, waiting for the tears to come. But they didn't. Moments passed away in the darkened room as Carrie waited, but the tears didn't come. Jean finally raised her head and smiled. "Well, there's my life story," she said cheerfully, bringing her drink to her lips.

"His, you mean," replied Carrie.

"Mmm," she agreed with a long sip before setting her drink back down. "That's what I meant." She smiled again as she patted gently around her hairdo, glancing out the window then back again to stare hypnotically at her candlelit drink, losing herself in it as though it were a crystal ball or a thing invested with all the secrets of the world. A vacuous silence filled the flickering room. The intercom had died, its music gone, leaving the cigarette smoke to spiral aimlessly upwards into the soundless air. Murmuring from the dining room creeped in and faded out; outside a car passed by with a muffled hiss. Carrie sat frozen, self-conscious of her rigidity. Jean suddenly popped out of her fixed stare, twisted right then left at her waist, and savored the deep breath of an athlete after a grueling event. Her foot started tapping again.

"Whew," she sighed pleasantly. "That felt good—getting it all out like that. I should do that more often. That's better than a psychiatrist any old day. And cheaper." She smiled jokingly and reached for a cigarette.

"Maybe cheaper," said Carrie, smiling back.

Jean lit her cigarette, took a quick drag, and dropped it in the plate. "Be right back," she said as she left her chair and hustled out into the dining room. Carrie listened to plates being bussed, the kitchen door swinging open and shut—then open and shut again—as Jean returned, sat back down, and pulled tip money out of her apron. "They're gone," she said counting the cash in her hand. "Let's finish our drinks and blow this pop stand."

"Okay," mumbled Carrie, her mind elsewhere, or rather consumed with the problem of Jean.

Jean finished her count and glanced at Carrie. "You look lost in thought there," she commented.

"Yeah," replied Carrie, swimming to the surface. She fixed her eye on Jean's person, studying it like a specimen. "I've been thinking about it."

"About what?"

"About your story," replied Carrie, slightly taken aback by the question. "About your marriage... Do you mind some advice? I mean, if you'd like to hear my opinion?"

"Sure."

"Well.., I know it sounds rather pretentious of me to offer you advice, seeing as you're older than me and been through a lot more. Nevertheless, I feel somewhat qualified to speak given I have a degree in Sociology and plan on getting a Masters, plus I minored in Psychology. I have an I.Q. of 137."

"137... Is that good?"

Carrie secretly cringed at Jean's naiveté. "Well, the norm is about 110," she answered cordially.

"Oh yeah?" Then my I.Q. must be about 20," she laughed. "I'm not too smart when it comes to school—English and History, and all that... But that's really good. An education is really important. My oldest son is planning to go to college." And on the topic of her kids, Jean brightened up and began to give Carrie a glowing profile of each one of her three kids, but she suddenly checked herself and smiled self-consciously when she noticed the look of impatience on Carrie's face. "Oh, don't mind me," she apologized. "If I don't stop now I'll just keep going. I'm terrible when I start talking about my kids. I'm sorry. What were you going to say?"

"That's all right," pardoned Carrie as she sat up straight, readying herself to pour forth. "I was just going to offer some advice, my opinion, if you don't mind... It's just that... well, to be frank, it's apparent that your husband doesn't *deserve you*. He doesn't *respect you* nor does he treat you like a *human being*." With sincere passion, Carrie talked about "potential" and the importance of "realizing one's potential." Everyone one had talents, she impressed upon Jean. Everyone had potential; it was just a matter of discovering those talents and realizing that potential. "For all you know," she said rapidly while nodding at Jean's chest and to her soul within, "there may be an artist or writer in there, but you'll never know unless you give yourself a chance. I mean, didn't you have dreams as a kid? What did you want to be when you grew up?"

"A wife and mother," replied Jean.

Carrie's shoulders sagged slightly as she sighed impatiently. "Let me put it to you in a different way," she said in a hopeful tone. "Women everywhere are waking up to the emptiness of their lives and demanding more, demanding their own identities. A revolution is coming. The liberation of women *is* the revolution." And here Carrie delivered a verbal flurry that described the makings of this revolution and its goals, eventually bringing the theme back to Jean. "The revolution starts with you," she told her. "I know it's a big step—the biggest step of your life—but it has to be taken if you're going to find your *true self.* The only question left is, are you ready to take that step?"

Jean gazed absent-mindedly out the window, oblivious of the question. Her attention had wondered off somewhere along the line, and she sat somewhat like a parishioner during a boring sermon, her mind preoccupied with unspiritual things. "Are you ready to take that next step?" repeated Carrie loudly. "Hmm?" mumbled Jean, coming out of her daydream. "Oh, yes.., I am," she answered.

"Good!" replied a pleased Carrie. "At least that'll get the wheel rolling in the right direction. Momentum will take it from there."

"Oh, I will," promised Jean as she flicked her cigarette ash in the plate. She took a drag then watched her exhale rise and mix with the cloud above her. "I definitely will."

Carrie nodded triumphantly. "Excellent," she said. "You're too smart to be left behind. The future is coming fast, and we have to prepare ourselves for the shock now."

"The shock?"

"The *shock* of the future," said Carrie, pausing for effect. "I don't want to get too heavy with you, but the changes are happening now. Even the most basic institutions like marriage and family will be nonexistent in the near future."

"Really?" asked a surprised Jean.

"Oh sure," replied Carrie, ready to deliver her knock-out blow. Marriage was a dying institution, she explained to Jean. Statistics were bearing this out. The nuclear family was kaput. In the future, surrogate mothers and state-run day-care would free women from child-bearing and marriage, allowing them realize their potential and assume positions of power. And when the right to an abortion came (and it was coming any day), then women would finally own their own bodies and true freedom would come. It will be a new world, one where people's natural instincts will flourish, where everyone's native bisexuality can express itself, where sex will no longer have the guilt and commitment attached to it that it does now. "Can you imagine it," she asked Jean rhetorically.

Jean stirred slightly as she confronted Carrie's eyes across the candlelit space (those eyes buttery with belief) and smiled and nodded at her sympathetically. She studied the lit end of her cigarette, lost in thought, then took a deep drag. "Yeah," she drawled heavily, breathing out the ethereal smoke. "I admire your imagination." When she noticed Carrie' shoulders sag at this comment she quickly added, "But it's fascinating," and smiled buoyantly. "You could be right. Twenty years from now, who knows? I'm too busy worrying about paying bills from last year to think about the future." (A hopeless laugh escaped her.) "But you're probably right—what you're saying... I don't think Earl would go for some of it, though," she said with an ironic smile.

"Men like him will be dinosaurs in twenty years," replied Carrie.

"Ha!—Earl the dinosaur," quipped Jean. The two of them shared a laugh at this, Carrie cutting hers short in order to recapture the somber mood. Jean finished the rest of her laughter alone and cheerfully flicked her cigarette ash into the plate. She glanced merrily at Carrie and then out the window, immediately fidgeting in place as Carrie's discordant attitude seeped quickly into that heightened sensitivity of hers like liquid into a sponge. "Well," she said in a serious tone, responding to Carrie's somber look, "you know, I wouldn't mind being one of those professional moms someday."

Carrie's shoulders sagged again. "You don't get it," she sighed impatiently "You're missing the point... You can't"—But before Carrie could set her straight they both heard a sound and turned to look. It was Lorraine walking by the kitchen door.

"You two still here?" said Lorraine, more as a statement than a question.

Jean and Carrie looked at each other like two schoolgirls caught in the hallway by the principal after the bell. "We were just leaving," called out Jean. Both her and Carrie stood up and watched Lorraine pass by on her way to the dining room to make final inspections.

Jean quickly stacked the dinner plates, picking up wrappers and brushing off ashes, as Carrie stood and watched her quiet precision without speaking. Jean took one last drag off her cigarette and mashed it in the plate along with the other lipstick-marked butts. "You grab the glasses," she said to Carrie while balancing the plates on her arm. Carrie collected up the glasses and followed Jean into the kitchen where they laid the plates and glasses into an empty bus pan next to the dishwasher.

Carrie followed Jean back to their table and waited for the right opportunity to speak. She watched as Jean gathered up her coat and purse. "Are you going to do it?" she asked abruptly.

"Do what?" asked Jean with a bewildered expression. She regarded Carrie thoughtfully, her arm frozen halfway into her coat sleeve, and made the connection. "Oh," she acknowledged, resuming with her coat.

"You can't go on like this... You have to do it *now*, for your own sake, or else it will go on forever... At least get a legal separation. Start with that and build from there. Huh? Will you do it?"

Jean slung her purse over her shoulder—"I will," she said in a sincere voice—and fixed its strap snug to her shoulder.

"Promise?"

"I promise."

"Good," said Carrie with a victorious sigh of relief. She beheld Jean's candlelit face warmly. "You owe it to yourself."

"I know," replied Jean with emotion as she met Carrie's eyes.

They smiled tenderly at one another for a long moment. "Ready?" said Jean, breaking the spell. She leaned over the table and blew out the candles. Darkness swooped over them, and they remained still and waited for the nightlight to quickly filter through the open window. Jean led the way into the hallway where she paused to make sure Carrie was following behind, then continued on past the kitchen door and through another door into a large banquet hall. They walked abreast across the empty hall, their shoes squeaking on the linoleum floor, and came to the exit door. Jean pushed against the horizontal bar, breaking the door open, and the two of them emerged into the open air.

The night was clear and cool. Somewhere far off a dog was barking. They stood next to each other in an empty parking lot. Jean hitched up her coat against the coolness and glanced at Carrie who was in short sleeves.

"Where's your coat?" she asked. "You're going to freeze."

Carrie waved off her concern. "I'm fine... Where you parked?"

"Out there," Jean answered, indicating the street with a nod.

They stepped in unison and headed for the sidewalk, gliding swiftly over the hard blacktop like women do when they walk late at night. They came onto the sidewalk near Jean's station wagon and turned to one another.

"Thanks for keeping me company," smiled Jean. "I really appreciate it, kid. Really."

"Sure," said Carrie, smiling back. She abruptly dropped the smile and looked seriously into Jean's face. "You promised now," she warmly-yet-sternly reminded her.

"I know... I will," replied Jean as she looked away from Carrie's exacting stare and into the dark street... "It's time I did something"—she reached into her purse and fished unconsciously about for her car keys—"for myself... You're right."

"Exactly!" exclaimed Carrie with a big smile. "And if you need help, any one to talk to, or whatever, just get a hold of me. Don't hesitate... If you need any help at all. I'm here. Just call. Okay?"

"I will."

"Promise?"

"I promise."

Carrie stepped in and hugged Jean, whispering in her ear, "Okay. Now take care of yourself, all right?" She stepped back, her hands on Jean's shoulders, then dropped them, taking her leave like a mother from her child on its first day of school. "I'll see you later."

"Bye, bye," chirped Jean.

Carrie saw him as she turned away.

Jean bolted upright as Carrie jumped back to her side, the two of them keyed on the large man who had suddenly appeared from behind the station wagon. The sight of him sucked the air out of their lungs.

"Earl!" gasped Jean.

He stood motionless on the sidewalk, some ten yards away, with one shoulder lowered as though set to charge, scowling at Jean.

"Get over here!" he commanded.

The women were silent, frozen.

"Now!"

The two women stood shoulder to shoulder, terrified but firm. The night, with all its peculiar sounds, became suddenly mute like the inside of a dark cell. A moment passed away in dread silence as he stood waiting. Impulsively Jean's body twitched, trembling awake as though from a coma, and she struggled to steady her stance, assuming finally a posture of defense. "Go away, Earl," she said in a surprisingly calm voice... "Please, just go away."

"Did you hear me? Get over here!"

"I won't... Just go away."

His face went scarlet, his eyes wide in their sockets. "Goddammit, get over here!" he snarled.

"Go away or we'll call the police," threatened Carrie in a quavering voice. "Want me to call the police?" she whispered urgently in Jean's ear. "I'll call them, okay?" She looked back at Jean's husband. "I'm going to call the police," she declared out loud again. She turned to run but Jean grabbed her arm and pulled her back.

His burning stare remained riveted on Jean, oblivious to Carrie's existence. "Move!" he hissed through clenched teeth.

Jean stood her ground, her hand gripping Carrie's arm firmly as another tense moment passed. He started towards her.

"No!" yelled Jean.

He stopped suddenly, then straightened up and staggered back a step as though he had been caught on the chin by a stiff blow. His eyes blinked once, and again, as the scowl vanished from his face, and he shuddered through the shoulders and fell into a dazed stare. The metamorphosis was instant and spellbinding, as it always is when a man breaks. Nothing stirred; the mute night, the women—all waited tensely for his next move. He mumbled something to himself, then slapped his hand to his forehead and squeezed hard, rising his head slowly up to look at Jean with his hurt-filled eyes.

"I..," he moved to speak but choked, and he struggled to try again, his face knotting-up with the effort... "Help me," he pleaded in a desolate voice. "I need you, baby. Please... Help me."

Carrie laughed.

"Don't, Earl," Jean answered coolly. "Please don't."

"I need you... Please, baby. I can't make it without you... Let me come home... I need you."

"Please, Earl."

He opened his arms to her in a gesture of desperate yearning, but she remained still. "I nee—" His voice suddenly broke, his eyes welling with tears, and he stopped and looked upwards into the dark sky. His head swayed there, traversing the infinite emptiness, and then dropped back down as his torso convulsed in a sudden heave. A sob burst from his chest, fracturing the night like a fragile shell, and he looked to Jean with a twisted face.

Jean's shoulders melted as something let go inside her, and a shocked cry contracted in her throat and escaped out her mouth. Carrie cut short another laugh as she recognized what was happening. It was unmistakable; it was a sign of relinquishment, of surrender, and seeing it, knowing it for what it was, Carrie felt her outrage towards it rise swiftly up through her body. As Jean wavered towards him, Carrie grabbed hold and pulled her back.

"Don't listen to him!" she begged in Jean's ear, trying to rally her courage. "It's a trick. A trick... Think! Think what you're doing. Don't lose it now. Jean!"

He wept openly on the sidewalk—an alien and wretched sound—and fought to get his words out: "I... can't... I ... Help me... Baby... Let me come home..." He lost it and hunched forwards, pounding his fist against his forehead.

Jean reached out to him but Carrie yanked her back.

"No! Jean!" she seethed. "You can't. Remember what we talked about. Remember what you promised. Remember! Think of yourself. Remember? You promised. Don't let it start all over again. Stop it now... Hear me? Jean!"

She pulled at Jean's transfixed body, shook it in a panic to awake it from its stupor, plying her argument into Jean's ear like a corner man into his fighter's ear. But Jean stared straight at her husband, oblivious to Carrie's appeals.

He backed off the curb and against the car like an injured man. "I want to go home... Jeanie... I want to go home."

"Don't listen to him."

"Jeanie."

"You promised."

"Baby."

"NO!"

Jean twisted gently out of Carrie's grip and confronted her quickly, her hazel eyes clear and lucid in the darkness. "I'm sorry," she said with a smile, touching Carrie's sallow cheek. "I'll be all right." She squeezed Carrie's hand perfunctorily and spun away.

She flew into her husband's arms and they clinched against the station wagon.

The night exhaled suddenly; the nocturnal sounds of rustling leaves, insects, and distant traffic blended with passionate whispers to pour forth into the night like a sigh of relief. But Carrie stood in stunned silence, paralyzed like someone who has just witnessed a bad accident or seen some miraculous feat. The gut-wrenching jolt of failure weighed her body down, but she quickly came to as the sight before her—the desperate clinch, the rapid whispers, the entire betrayal of her ideals—finally registered and sparked her back to life. She turned away from it and walked quickly to her car, fighting back the hot urge to cry.

Carrie came to her car door and shoved her key into the lock, livid with disgust. She opened the door to her Volkswagen, jumped in, and slammed the door shut, her eyes darting about for something to strike. She found it—a stack of books on the seat next to her, and she swept them off in a violent jerk of her arm, and they smashed against the dashboard and flopped awkwardly to the floor. She hit her palms against the steering wheel. "Jesus!" she exclaimed shaking her head. Her hands gripped and twisted the steering wheel as she worked to calm herself down, and she abruptly looked up into the rearview mirror. They were inside their car now, their figures iridescent against the dark interior, sitting close together, wiping tears away, and stroking each other's face.

Carrie suddenly laughed. She plopped back against her seat, thoroughly amused, then sat straight again and shot a scornful glance back into the rearview mirror. There they were, clinched and pawing each other like teenagers, and the entire vulgar farce of it all, so laughably trite, was comically apparent to her. She laughed again—a laugh colored with sarcasm and condescension, with a mastery over the situation—and flicked the mirror aside as though it were an affront to her intelligence. She leaned over and carefully collected up her books and stacked them neatly back on the seat. Her keys were in her lap, and she picked them up and inserted the correct one into the ignition.

She fired the engine up, its sound exploding out across the night, and pulled and released the hand break. She eased her hand over the ball of the stick shift, paused and shook her head in a final gesture of disgust, then pushed it into gear and took off, laying a scratch out of the cement gutter as she shifted quickly and sped away. She came to the intersection and without stopping turned right against the red light and disappeared.

THE SEVENTIES

There's got to be more to life than just screwing around.

Linda Lovelace
Deep Throat

Who was that lost lad? What was his name? Without knowing it, he was playing the xylophone in a boneyard. He was the unique new creature of the 1970s. He was Candide in reverse.

Tom Wolfe
The Intelligent Coed's Guide to America

Don't let me hear you say life's taking you nowhere
Angel
Come get up, my baby
Look at that sky, life's begun
Nights are warm and the days are young

David Bowie
Golden Years

Movie Night

What does one wear to a porno flick? Trish stood inside her walk-in closet and thought it through. There would be people her own age there—mid-twenties—but more importantly there would be people *just like her* there—college-educated, hip, well-to-do, and tuned-in to what was chic for events like this—and all this had to be taken into consideration. There were different elements involved. There was the freak-show element, and certainly a raunchy component as well, yet there remained this over-riding sophistication, this slumming of the illuminati that had to be taken into account.

In the end she went with a peasant blouse that showed-off her neck and chest without revealing any cleavage, and for pants she choose a comfortable pair of flared blue jeans. Shoes were another matter and she spent a good ten minutes perusing her ample collection before settling on faux-suede booties. At her jewelry stand she picked out a Chanel rhinestone necklace with burgundy stones that went well with her autumn-colored blouse and dark auburn hair, and then affixed the matching earrings. The final touch was a brass bracelet, engraved with Native American symbols, that she slipped onto her wrist as she walked over to the full length mirror to inspect the finished product.

At the mirror she bent a knee to the left and then to the right, raised her head and turned her chin, and inspected her "look" with a discerning eye. She brushed her hair off her shoulders. It was long and parted in the middle like Ali McGraw in *Love Story,* and she appeared satisfied with what she saw. Before leaving, she glanced over at her favorite picture hanging on the wall. It was a framed black and white photo of Audrey Hepburn, taken by Richard Avedon, and in the picture the famous actress is looking out through a rain-swept window. She's holding a cat and has a far-away look in her eyes.

Trish walked into the living room where she found her husband Alan sitting on the divan watching a news program on PBS. When he saw her, he used the remote to click off the TV and turned around to look at her. He liked what he saw without saying so.

"I called Trent and told him we'd pick them up in the Volvo," he said. "Thought it'd be easier that way."

"Sure," she replied as she walked around to give him the full picture. She waited a moment and then said, "Well... How do I look? Is this what they're wearing to X-rated movies nowadays?"

He nodded and smiled. "You look very nice—and I wouldn't know."

"You never watched a stag film in college—you and your buddies?"

"Well, yes... But it was on Super 8 and we had to sneak the projector in under someone's coat. We watched it in the dorm room under cover of darkness. It played to a packed house."

Trish sniffed a short laugh. The divan was a corner group and she sat down at a right angle to her husband and quickly reviewed his attire to make sure they didn't clash. He also wore a pair of blue jeans but they were pressed and not flared, and for shoes he sported a pair of canvas deck shoes. His long sleeve, turtle-neck sweater was light green and next to him on the divan lay his brown, corduroy sports coat with patches on the elbows. He had decided to wear his wire-rim bifocals instead of his turtle shells (which she was glad to see), and his light brown hair, which was slightly graying, was long without being too long and beginning to flip up behind his ears. In the few seconds it took Trish to complete her inspection, she had assimilated his color scheme, mixed and matched against her own, and come to a favorable opinion. She even smiled to herself at the thought that he looked clean and business-like even when he went casual.

"What time we leaving?" she asked.

"Ten minutes or so."

She thought he might say something more but when he didn't she surveyed the top of the coffee table. It was neatly arrayed with magazines—Time, Life, Cosmo, National Geographic—and she picked up a copy of Vogue, flipped it open and leafed through the pictures. Alan clicked the TV back on to catch the end of his news program.

Alan and Trish Harding had been married for two years. They had met in his law office when she was twenty-two, fresh out of college, and working there as a secretary. That was four years ago, and since then they had married, honeymooned in Barbados, moved in and then out of a one-bedroom apartment in the City, and had recently settled into a spacious house in Los Altos Hills. He was nearly ten years older than her but the age difference appealed to the both of them; she found him nice-looking in a scholarly sort of way and was especially attracted to his intellect and success (he was someone she could learn from), while he found her young and beautiful and attentive to his needs.

In their social circle, which included other well-to-do couples like themselves, they were admired and liked for their friendliness, he for his wit, she for her stylishness, and were considered "in" and politically with-it, which meant left of center with a world-view that was not confined by either ethnic prejudice or old-fashioned ideologies. Alan and Trish were a boon to anyone's dinner party; Alan could hold forth on a variety of topics, from soap box derbies to Bobby Fischer, and his witty insights and one-liners kept his listeners entertained. Trish had an astute eye for décor and fashion, as well as a good ear for what was clever versus trite, and her opinions were appreciated.

Despite only two years of marriage, they had settled into a comfortable routine. Alan worked Monday through Friday in the law offices of Nye, Freidman, and Harding in San Francisco. Trish worked at getting their new home to look just the way she wanted it, a task that included trips to art and antique stores, fine rug merchants, and assorted knickknack stores in downtown Los Altos and the Stanford Shopping Center. She cooked dinner five nights a week, usually from a recipe pulled from a gourmet magazine, dishes like herb-encrusted halibut and pork chops with raspberry sauce, and occasionally she went with Chinese take-out from their favorite restaurant Chef Chu's. They ate at the dinner table while listening to soft jazz and talked about current events, which, for the most part, entailed Trish listening to Alan expound on topics like the growing Watergate scandal, Nixon, or the abolition of the death penalty. After dinner they played backgammon or watched TV—shows like *Great Performances* and *Upstairs, Downstairs*—strictly eschewing popular sitcoms and detective shows. They both read in bed before falling asleep. On Saturday they got dressed-up and went out to a nice restaurant, or met up with friends for dinner, and on Sunday they both did yard work and later in the evening heated up left-overs for dinner.

And tonight—Friday night—was usually movie night.

Artsy or foreign films were their preference, films by Bergman, Kurosawa, or Felinni, which could always be found in college towns like Palo Alto or in the more bohemian parts of the City such as the Castro District. Occasionally they took in a major Hollywood production. Just last week they had gone to the Century Theater in San Jose to see *The Candidate*, a film they both enjoyed, Alan for its cynical view of modern politics and Trish for its main star Robert Redford. After a film—such as *Cries and Whispers* by Ingmar Bergman—they would sit and enjoy an espresso at their favorite coffee house where Alan would explain the intricacies and subtle symbolism of the film while Trish listened attentively, nodding her understanding and venturing a comment of her own on occasion.

The film on tonight's fare was a little different—the X-rated movie *Deep Throat*. It had been the talk of their social circle for a couple weeks, a cause célèbre, and even The New York Times had reviewed it. Everyone wanted to see it, including Alan and Trish. It was a novelty, a little bit naughty, and the fact that religious leaders and right-wing pundits were decrying it as a sign of the apocalypse made it even more appealing. But like their enlightened friends, Alan and Trish understood the game at hand. This was not a movie to be taken seriously; this was to be taken as a hip excursion filled with witty epigrams and a few horse laughs. They were looking forward to it.

After leafing through her magazine, Trish looked up at the clock and saw that it was time to go. "Should I put Mel out?" she asked.

Alan clicked off the TV and they both looked over at their cat who sat curled up on the recliner across from them with its eyes half shut. They had no kids yet (that was somewhere in their future), and for pets they owned, or sort of owned, this one calico tomcat that came and went as it pleased. His name was Melvin Belli—Mel for short.

"No... He looks too comfortable. Does he have food?"

"Yeah."

"Well then," he said, getting up and grabbing his sports coat, "let's not keep the Nelsons waiting."

Trish smiled at his joke—it was a reference to *Ozzie and Harriet* and meant as a sly dig at the make-believe families of the fifties. She enjoyed his sense of humor; it was partly a lawyer's humor, dry and cynical, but colored with a kind of broad-mindedness that made it seem more cultured than the jaded wit of your ordinary, run-of-the-mill lawyer.

Trish picked up her purse—a small buckskin model with a long strap—and slung it over her right shoulder. At the front door, Alan turned on the safety alarm, shut the door behind them, and they walked over to Trish's yellow Volvo. His Porsche 911 was in the garage and only seated two. The Volvo, with its four doors and roomy back seat, was the better choice for tonight.

Alan drove and they wound their way through the upscale confines of Los Altos Hills, which consisted of mostly narrow roads that curled through wooded foothills, until they reached the driveway of Trent and Judy Weston. It was a long, sloping driveway, and at the end of it Alan pulled up in front of a magnificent, Tudor-style mansion complete with multiple steeped roofs, cross gables, and patterned brickwork.

"Wow," said Trish looking out the window.

"What'd you expect, an igloo?" replied Alan. "He's an architect."

"I know... but wow."

They sat with the car idling, admiring the Weston home.

"Look at those chimney designs," marveled Trish.

"Hmm, I guess it pays to be a bricklayer these days."

"Should I go get them?"

Alan craned his neck to look out the passenger window. "No, here they come."

Trent and Judy walked hand in hand down the flagstone path smiling the whole way. "Hi's" were exchanged all around as they jumped into the back seat.

"Quite a house," said Alan. "Tudor-style, right?"

"For the most part," replied Trent. "I took a few liberties with the Dormer windows and I went with slate tile on the roof to give it that thatched look."

"It's beautiful," said Trish.

"And so are you," replied Trent with a wink. "You'll have to see the inside when we get back."

"I'd love to."

"It's settled then," said Trent cheerfully. "James," he added, pretending Alan to be his chauffeur, "to the Pussycat Theatre if you please." Everyone laughed as Alan pulled the car around and drove up the driveway.

Trent and Judy were new friends. Alan had met Trent only a month before at a gym in San Francisco where they both played handball. They struck up a conversation and quickly learned that they both had offices in the City, both owned homes in Los Alto Hills, and were both married to younger women. In addition to these coincidences, they found they shared similar viewpoints and were simpatico when it came to things like favorite foods and the Vietnam War. Plans were made to get together for dinner, and two weeks later the four of them met at a trendy restaurant in Menlo Park. The dinner featured garlic-butter escargot, three bottles of Napa Valley's finest cabernet, and sparkling conversation that lasted well into the evening. The four of them hit it off, and somewhere between strawberry soufflés and a round of espressos, the film *Deep Throat* was mentioned, triggering an animated discussion that ended up with the four of them agreeing, somewhat jauntily, to get together and go see the film.

Deep Throat was playing at the Pussycat Theater in downtown San Jose and was about a twenty minute drive. Trish turned sideways in her seat and talked to Judy, surreptitiously checking out her outfit. Judy wore a black tube top with white hip huggers that were secured by a wide black-leather belt decorated with silver studs. She wore her hair in a shag like Jane Fonda in the movie *Klute* and her earrings were mid-sized silver hoops. Around her neck was a narrow, black-leather choker with sliver studs to match her belt. The whole ensemble suggested to Trish something a little too daring—quasi bondage, perhaps—and she didn't really care for it.

"So anyone know what the plot of this movie is?" asked Trent.

"Is there a plot?" added Judy.

"Well, as I understand it," replied Alan as he sped up onto the freeway on-ramp, "the heroine finds out that she was born with her clitoris in her throat. An unfortunate birth defect—which leads her to have to satisfy her desires by... well, you can guess the rest."

"Lucky for her it wasn't the lower colon."

"Who stars in it?

"Some gal named Linda Lovelace."

"Of the Boston Lovelaces?"

"Precisely."

"Not Doris Day then?

"No—but there's also a guy named Harry Reems."

"That conjures up an image."

"Probably the brother of Dick."

And so the banter continued until they reached their destination, found a parking spot, and walked a block to the theatre. There was a crowd already forming out front and Alan got in line to buy tickets. The four of them stood tightly together and surveyed the scene with an amused grace, taking in the assortment of hip party-goers, curious college kids, and colorful characters. There were young professionals like themselves, similarly dressed, out for kicks, who stood around waiting for the doors to open with a casual coolness that confirmed their member-ship to the select club. Mixed in with the potpourri of poly-ester knit jackets, crushed velvet pantsuits, granny dresses and stylish jumpsuits, were a couple Hell's Angels in their leather vests, looking like Viking raiders, each one holding hands with his elegantly-dressed and surprisingly beautiful wife.

A theatre employee wearing a t-shirt with the Pussycat logo on it weaved his way through the crowd selling boxes of pop-corn. "Popcorn!" he yelled cheerfully. "Fifty cents! Popcorn here!" Off to the left of the main crowd stood a scruffily dressed man on top of a wooden crate. He held a black bible above his head and extolled the crowd to listen to his words. "Are you ready to stand before God!" he shouted. "Are you ready to stand before Him in Christ! The only way to be born again is through faith and repentance—not through filth and smut!"

"Sounds like we're all damned," joked Trent.

"Damned happy to be here," quipped Alan.

Judy chuckled at this exchange as she surveyed the crowd. "Well dressed crowd for a blue movie," she observed.

"You're right," agreed Trish, who glanced about, mainly at the women, many of whom sported the same haute hippie look she wore. "I was expecting old men in trench coats," she added.

"You might—only it'll be cashmere."

Just as Alan was paying for tickets, the theatre doors opened and the large, talkative crowd funneled towards the entrance. Alan handed everyone their ticket.

"Is that Harry Edwards?" said Trent in surprise as he looked over the heads of the crowd.

"Who?"

"Dr. Harry Edwards. You know—the black power guy. Thought I saw the back of his head."

"I can't see him."

"Wonder what he's doing here?"

"Field trip no doubt."

The other three could not confirm Trent's sighting, but with their tickets now in hand they stepped into the crowd flow and entered the theatre lobby. There they found a bit of a surprise.

Instead of a nondescript theatre lobby they found plush carpeting, velvet ropes and sashes, as well as chandeliers hanging from the ceiling and beveled glass windows. Murals and colorful oil paintings adorned the walls. Trent, in particular, was captivated by the décor, and he and Alan, along with Trish and Judy and all the other dilettantes of porno chic, soaked in their surroundings with an amused eye.

They found four seats together towards the back and settled in for a good time. It was a raucous crowd in a playful mood. Once the movie started, wisecracks were shouted from the crowd at opportune moments: "Things go better with Coke!" grabbed the biggest laugh next to "The closest thing to a closer shave!" Alan and Trent were on top of their game; the witticisms came fast and furious, and even the people sitting around them laughed happily at their one-liners. When the movie ended they filed out with the rest of the crowd. "And to think I missed *Hickey & Boggs* for this," said Alan loudly. This elicited general laughter from everyone within earshot, and the four of them walked out of the theatre in a buoyant mood.

They got into the Volvo, only this time Trent sat behind Alan instead of Trish. Alan noted the switch and went to move his seat up. "Need more room back there?" he asked Trent.

"I'm only four inches away from happiness," he replied dryly.

This quip—a line from the movie—caused Trish and Judy to break out laughing. As Trish laughed she glanced over at Alan to confirm he wasn't laughing. He wasn't. She'd never seen him laugh out loud. At a particularly funny joke, a joke that would make anyone else laugh out loud, he would dip his head, smile, and sometimes nod his head in amusement. But in all their time together she had never seen him throw his head back and just laugh out loud.

They returned to the Weston's Tudor-style mansion and Trent gave Alan and Trish the grand tour. Trish was especially blown away by the ornately-carved, wooden staircases as well as the inglenook fireplaces. Their tour guide provided them insights to his architectural decisions, pointing out the differences between Tudor, mock Tudor, and Renaissance revival motifs. The tour ended in a spacious living room where Judy awaited them wearing a floral kaftan with a v'd neckline and extravagant butterfly sleeves. She handed Trish a glass a white wine, Alan a cold Heineken, her husband a Harvey Wallbanger, and invited everyone to sit down.

They sat and joked about the movie for a while and then moved on to other topics. An hour flew by, and in that hour Judy replenished drinks, set out hors d'oeuvres, and lit up a joint that everyone passed around. In the second hour Alan noticed that his wife was bothered by something—what, he wasn't sure, but her body language was unmistakable. She had stopped talking for the most part and sat quietly nursing her glass of white wine. Pot could make her that way, he knew, but she had stopped taking hits after the first couple rounds so this quiet was due to something else. At eleven-thirty he checked his watch, made their excuses, and together they said their goodbyes to the Westons.

Once in the car he asked her what was wrong, waited for the obligatory "Nothing," then pressed harder. "Come on, Trish. I know better. What's wrong?"

She regarded him for a moment and then shook her head. "I can't believe you didn't pick up on it," she said reproachfully.

"Pick up on what?"

"They're swingers."

"What!"

"Swingers—and I can't believe you didn't pick up on it. He kept dropping hints. I mean, what was that whole thing about *Bob, Carol, Ted, and Alice* being his favorite movie? And her giving you a neck massage? What was that all about? Trent couldn't keep his eyes off me. He kept throwing out compliments—like how hot I'd look in a bikini—and other stuff like that.

"Well, he's an architect. He appreciates beautiful curves and arches.

"Funny."

"Okay," replied Alan as he started the car up, "but I think you misread it."

"I don't think so... and it was all kind of creepy."

"Okay, but let me just try to explain something," he said in a parental tone that she was very familiar with. She listened politely to his explanation—about the Weston's "avant-garde sensibility" and how it could be "misinterpreted"—but she knew what she knew. She knew what it meant when a man looked at her in a certain way. So she listened politely and thought about how her husband always had to be the Great Explainer and rode along in silence.

He was winding down his closing argument when they pulled into their driveway and saw the jeep. It was owned by Teresa's boyfriend. Teresa was Trish's younger sister and she was staying with them while she went to community college.

"What's he doing here?" commented Alan.

"It's her boyfriend," said Trish, stating the obvious.

"It's a little late," he added, but he let it drop from there as he parked the Volvo and they went inside. He took off his sport coat and laid it carefully on one of the chairs in the front room. "Want to catch the end of Carson?" he asked.

"Sure."

"Let's check on them first."

"Okay."

Together they walked down the long hallway of closed bedroom and bathroom doors until they came to the last door on the right. Trish knocked softly on the door.

"Come in," came the reply.

Trish opened the door and both she and Alan stuck their heads in. Teresa lay on her bed in a robe reading a book. She'd recently taken a shower and her hair was wet and combed back. Her boyfriend sat in a wicker, fan-back chair. He was also reading a book.

"What you guys up to?" asked Trish cheerfully.

"Just reading," replied Teresa. She showed Trish the cover of her book—*The French Lieutenant's Woman*—and laid it down on her chest.

Trish looked over at her sister's boyfriend. He had shaggy blonde hair and wore a t-shirt with cut-off blue jeans. He was bare-footed. "What you reading?" she asked him.

He held up the cover so they could read it. It was a book by Faulkner.

"For school?"

"No."

Trish waited for more to come from him but what followed instead was a brief and awkward silence.

"How was the movie?" asked Teresa. "What you go see?"

Trish and Alan glanced at each other like mischievous kids and Trish giggled and told her. Her sister laughed in surprise and wanted to know more, and Trish quickly filled her in—how they went with friends, about the crowd, how Alan kept everyone in stitches with his one-liners—and Alan capped her summary off with the observation that the movie was not in the running for an Academy Award. Teresa found the whole story amusing.

"We went to the movies," said her boyfriend.

"Oh... what you go see?"

"*Sounder,*" replied Teresa.

"Was it any good?"

"*We loved it,*" breathed out Teresa as she looked over at her boyfriend. He looked intently back at her, nodded and smiled.

Trish had heard it was a good movie and wanted to see it herself. There was a little more chit-chat between the sisters that quickly wrapped up as Trish began to back out of the doorway. Alan pushed slightly forward. "We're going to catch the end of Carson," he said. "Why don't you two come out and join us?"

"Maybe," answered Teresa, glancing over at her boyfriend. "I'd have to get dressed first."

"Okay, sweetie," said Trish. "Maybe we'll see you in a bit." And with that she backed herself and Alan out of the doorway and closed the door. They went into the living room where they kicked off their shoes, put the cat out, got a couple drinks, and turned the TV on to Johnny Carson. It was past midnight. They watched the rest of *The Tonight Show* and Teresa and her boyfriend never came out to join them. Alan clicked off the TV and let the cat back in. Trish quickly cleaned up and went off to bed where she found Alan waiting for her at the door.

"I don't like him here this late," he said. "He needs to go home."

Trish nodded. She could see he was annoyed. "I'll go talk to her," she said and quickly left. Alan went into their master bedroom and began to undress. Trish returned in less than five minutes.

"Well?"

"He already left."

"Good."

"You know, he doesn't much like you."

"The feelings mutual... I don't understand what she sees in him."

Trish smiled knowingly to herself as she unfastened her necklace. "She loves him," she said with some emotion. "We talk—sisters talk—and she tells me everything... They have a *very* passionate relationship."

"Two hamsters rutting around in a cage isn't the same as passion."

Now it was Trish's turn to be annoyed. "Are you calling my sister a hamster?" she replied sharply.

"No... Well, you know what I'm trying to say... They have enough sense, I hope, to use protection?"

"So now you're calling my sister stupid?"

"I didn't say that," he replied calmly while holding up his palm like a traffic cop. "I just don't want to see her get pregnant. You know there's an epidemic of unwanted pregnancies in this country? Right? I don't want to see her become another statistic."

Trish stood and regarded her husband for a moment. He started to speak again but she cut him off. "She's not a hamster, she's not stupid, and she's not a statistic," she answered back, and then added, "And you're wrong about the Westons" before spinning around and disappearing into the bathroom.

Alan could see that she was upset. After the movie, there had been a certain sexual charge in the air between them but now, with this, he wasn't sure what to expect. He got undressed and thought about it, neatly folding his clothes and setting them on a chair by the bed. Next he slipped into bed in just his boxers, took off his watch and laid it on the nightstand, then picked up the book he was reading (*Soul on Ice* by Eldridge Cleaver), thought better of it, and set it back down on the nightstand along with his glasses. He'd have to smooth things out with her, he knew. And maybe she was right about the Westons. He'd tell her so when she came back in. He was sure he could smooth things over with her.

Trish removed her jewelry and hung up her clothes in her walk-in closet. She stood in only her panties, glanced momentarily at the see-through teddy that she had laid out earlier in the evening, then opted instead to put on a cut off t-shirt that said San Jose State. At the sink she brushed her long dark hair and thought about expectations and obligations. When she finished, she went back into the closet and changed into the see-through teddy and examined the finished product in the full-length mirror. She turned her head slightly and looked at the photo of Audrey Hepburn holding her cat behind the rain-swept window. The woman looked so sad, thought Trish. And with that thought she realized for the first time that she had never been in love.

Attack of the Ladybugs

Wedged in the bushy foothills above the Berkeley campus sits Strawberry canyon, green and steeped and a bit rustic-looking, with a pleasant view of the bay. It's more of a gorge really than it is a canyon—to be topographically correct, that is—but to have called it Strawberry Gorge would have sounded rather gluttonous, I suppose. Strawberry Canyon sounded much better, all pastoral and all, like something out of an Ingmar Bergman film. Why it was named Strawberry of all things I'll never know, unless it was for an abundance of strawberries somewhere (though in my two years there as a student, I don't recall ever seeing a strawberry patch or a strawberry stand anywhere around). Perhaps at one time long ago the canyon had been stuffed full of strawberries, its succulent treasure the feast of early settlers, but through time had been ravaged by famine and pestilence, by the ROTC and student riots. All I know is that's what they called it.

I mention all this about Strawberry Canyon because that's where the pool was. Actually, on a plateau just above the football stadium was where it sat and probably still does, in a "multi-purpose" park that featured, besides the pool, a large field good for softball, soccer, track, and Frisbee-throwing. I used to jog up there on Saturdays during home games. I liked it best then because I'd be all alone with the cheers from the football crowd reverberating through the canyon around me. I'd pretend to be in the Olympics, leading in the home stretch of the marathon, the crowd wildly cheering me on to victory. Of course there was a lot of cheering back then because we had such a good team. Joe Roth was our quarterback, a natural, fearless in the pocket, with a quick release and a gutsy style. He died his senior year of cancer. It was a damn shame too because he was one hell of a quarterback.

On warm days the pool was a hang-out of sorts for students like myself looking to take a quick dip and lay in the sun before going back to class. On hot days—and Berkeley, when the wind left it, could become unbearably hot—the pool became a mecca for human beings seeking to beat the heat, reminding one of that scene from *Gone with the Wind* where all the bodies are sprawled out shoulder to shoulder in the railroad yard. Making your way through that mass to an empty piece of real estate was an experience all its own; one had to step over heads and in-between crotches, past the odors of sweat and coconut oil, through the din of small talk and radios, past the glint of mirrored sunglasses, white smiles, and shaved and oiled legs. Swimming at these times was an impossibility, unless you enjoyed wiggling underwater through a forest of legs. The best one could hope for was a short wade, a refreshment short-lived because of the drying heat, but appreciated nevertheless.

It was early fall and a Monday. I remember it was early fall and a Monday simply because classes had recently started and because the Raiders were playing the Steelers on *Monday Night Football.* The latter was foremost in my mind as I walked out of English Lit class and into the sun. It was a warm day but not too hot. I hated hot days (always have) and will do anything short of felonious assault to avoid them. But this day wasn't too bad, a shorts and t-shirt type day, and the best kind of day for girl-watching.

Now before you dismiss me for a fraternity-type lout for thinking this, let me tell you right now you're wrong. First off, I didn't belong to a fraternity but instead shared an apartment with two other guys, and second, I was but one of a couple thousand male students there at the time who shared the exact same thought—Girls, Women, "Female pulchritude" (as Howard Cosell would say). Despite the image you may have of Berkeley as a den of radicals and revolutionaries, when it came right down to it Cal wasn't any different than Kalamazoo Community College. Take my word for it. The real pastime at Bezerkley wasn't political activism or drugs or philosophizing in expresso shops. The real pastime for every red-blooded American boy, or every red-blooded Marxist boy, for that matter, was girl-watching, girl-chasing, and girl—if you were lucky—catching. Of course, just like Kalamazoo Community College, the girls weren't any easier to catch here than there. You can take my word for that, too.

So, standing there, books in hand, sun on face, and with three hours before kick-off, I thought on how best to pursue the local pastime. Sproul plaza was an idea. I could sit there on a bench and watch the girls enter and leave the campus, walking briskly with their knapsacks slung over a shoulder, their hair swept to one side or in ponytails to keep their necks cool. Only at this time of day all the freaks would be out, the holy-rollers, the burnt-out hippies, and every assorted space cadet known to man. The best choice was the pool in Strawberry Canyon. There I would be alone and undistracted. There, behind my sunglasses, I could closely study the nuances of the female body as it lay about me in skimpy bikini, enjoying the freckled cleavage, the smooth stomach, the glistening line of perspiration down the column of the back, and all without interruption or distraction, just like an astronomer at midnight admiring a heaven full of celestial bodies.

I calculated quickly that by stopping off at the apartment to change into trunks I could be up there in twenty minutes. Since it wasn't my turn tonight to cook or clean dishes, that gave me more than two hours at poolside. By the time I got back home, dinner would be ready and Frank, Dandy Don, and Howard would be at the mic. Perfect. I smiled at the divine order of things and took off.

The walk to Strawberry Canyon was all uphill, and by the time I got there I was sweating pretty good. I showed my card to the guy at the turnstile and he let me pass. The pool was free with a student body card. Without one it cost a buck, a fee presumably levied to keep out the riff-raff. I walked up the cement ramp and entered the pool area and stopped to check it out. It wasn't too crowded, so I decided on the grass. The grass was across on the other side of the pool and I strode evenly over to it where I snapped my towel out and sat down.

The pool was your typical public job, L-shaped and big, with a shallow section and a diving section. A turquoise spring board sat at the head of the deep end next to a cement tower used for high-diving. The high dive was for the skilled and fearless, of which I was neither, though not many others were either. Occasionally someone, coaxed on by his buddies, would make it up there only to stand warily by the edge until finally, after an embarrassing interlude, they either climbed back down in humiliation or took a deep breath and jumped feet first and landed with a noisy splash. The guys from the diving team used it once in a while, showing off with twists and summer-saults, but I always thought they looked kind of silly in those bikini trunks with the bulge in the crotch. But the girls didn't seem to think so.

I decided to kick things off with a quick dip (give them a taste of the killer physique). I pulled off my shirt and walked over to the edge, flexed my back muscles, and dove in. Like most public pools the water was over-chlorinated, which killed my eyes, so I kept them closed as I swam along the bottom. The water was cool and nice. I came up for air and then continued underwater into the deep end. I let my body sink to the deepest part of the pool then pushed off when I felt bottom and came to the surface. I enjoyed that sensation of drifting downwards in silence, and as I repeated it I imagined a woman swimming towards me, naked, her hair full and flowing like chestnut fire as she came against me and we embraced, kissed passionately, and drifted downwards into oblivion. But I touched bottom and the image disappeared, so I pushed off and came back up to the surface and swam over to the edge, popped my head up, and looked around.

There wasn't much action girl-wise. A couple of sorority sisters in Dodger-blue bikinis were laying out on the cement in front of me (you know the type, blonde, perfect suntans, perfect bodies, from San Fernando Valley or somewhere silver-spoonish like that). Other than that there wasn't much going on, just a few C-plusses here and there, but that was it.

I pushed off and swam back towards the grass, got to the edge, and pulled myself up and out. As I did, I suddenly noticed what had just sat down next to my towel.

One luscious female.

I quickly wiped my face with my hand, braced myself, and walked towards her. She was sitting on a towel directly in front of my own and, as I passed her, she glanced up, smiled, and said "Hi."

Somewhat startled, I said "Hi" back without smiling and stumbled past her to my towel.

Dammit! I thought to myself as I stood there toweling off— say something, start a conversation, anything. But nothing came out; my mind was twisted in a knot. She picked up a book and opened it and I tried to catch its title but failed. She lay over on her side and began to read. I stood there awkwardly, leaning forwards as though set to pounce, yet held back by an invisible rope, the towel hanging from my hand like a dead rabbit. My chance had come and gone. I sat back down on my towel, put my sunglasses on, and sulked. I had choked in the clutch.

Why did I always do that? I wondered. I'd get my chance and then blow it. The problem, you see, was that I was quite shy, not pathologically shy or anti-social, or anything like that, but just shy. Shy with women. Why that was I didn't know, and I didn't consider it a problem, necessarily, just an inconvenience, sort of like being a big league pitcher without a good fastball. But the game wasn't over yet. I just had to work harder, concentrate, and I would come up with something. She was definitely worth another try.

And worth it she was. A solid B-plus. When I say B-plus I don't mean A or B, which are two different creatures, but rather *B-plus.* This, of course, was according to the rating system devised by my roommates and me: A for Adorable all the way to F for Forget it. Most attractive girls fell into the B to B-plus range. I had never seen an A, and an A-plus didn't exist or, if she did, they kept her locked up in a vault with all the other fabulous treasures of the world. Now a woman with a high grade point average usually came with a degree, either a B.A. (Beautiful Ass) or an M.A. (Magnificent Ass) or, if so endowed, a P.H.D. (Perfectly Heavenly Derriere—or, as my roommate Neal would say, women of this stature gave him a Perfectly Hard Dick).

This particular beauty was definitely a B-plus with a B.A., working hard on her M.A. She had that Berkeley look about her, natural, without make-up, with brown hair that was neither curled nor styled but rather long and slightly frizzy. She wore a black one-piece bathing suit that high-lighted her fair skin and gave her a sensually sinister look. All the attributes of a B-plus were there—the long smooth legs, curved hips, and tightly v'd bust line. But her face was the topper. It was oval with big round eyes underneath dark eyebrows, and her mouth was slightly wide with full lips. She was a cross between a model and a rock star and kind of looked like Grace Slick.

She was so close I could almost touch her. If I reached out I could tap her head with my foot. I imagined it for a moment, tapping her head with my foot, and wondered what she'd do. Scream? Tell me to fuck off? Or maybe she would laugh, then grab my foot and lick it erotically between the toes. Was it possible?

I started to reach out my leg but stopped myself in time.

Her body was bewitching me; it lay there smooth and cool, gently rising and subsiding with each breath she took, evenly, rhythmically, chanting to me like sirens offshore, beckoning me to join her, to crash against her hips and die in her arms. I felt an irresistible urge to run my hand over her hip and down her white leg. I wanted to lie next to her, fit my body into hers, and kiss the back of her neck. Her alabaster skin was almost translucent (It was a known fact that nymphomaniacs were all fair-skinned.). It was the sort of skin that produced rose-colored marks when you handled it. And I wanted nothing more than to handle it. I wanted to devour it, ravish it until her whole body was left rose-colored. I saw myself pouncing on her, she submitting instantly to my will, clawing-moaning in ecstasy as I stripped her naked and had my way with her right there on the lawn.

I leaned towards her in pouncing position but came to and sat back down.

I was losing my mind. I was in that dangerous zone between fantasy and reality, and if I didn't resolve it quickly I could not be held accountable for any acts perpetrated by my lust-ridden mind. Not that I was a sex maniac, or anything. Far from it. You have to understand that it had been a long day, in fact a long couple of weeks, what with lectures and notes, homework, studying, concentrating, all of which was part of the general grind of discipline and self-denial necessary for the achievement of scholarly excellence. Not that that was such a tough thing in itself, but add on to that the stress of warm weather and women—women in halter tops, in short and skirts, sitting cross-legged next to you in class or bouncing past you in the hall—one almost needed the self-control of a Trappist monk to stay on track. No wonder then that my sanity was slipping. It had all come to a head (pardon the crude pun), right here and right now, what with my swollen gonads, this warm weather, and this bona fide B-plus in front of me. It was enough to make even the most decent and upstanding gentleman waver. And take it on account that I was one of those very gentlemen. My intentions toward this young lady were nothing but honorable.

You probably find this hard to believe considering the rather graphic nature of the sexual fantasies now splashing around in my head, but these were tame compared to most males, especially my roommates, that is if they were any representation of the normal male mind, which I sometimes doubted. If you had sat up nights with those two like I had, listening to them recount in lurid detail the sexual fancies they harbored for some unsuspecting coed (some of it going beyond just plain pornography and into the realm of the depraved), you would have given my reveries a modest PG-rating in comparison.

Like I said, my intentions toward this beauty were strictly kosher. Sure, I wanted to ravish her, but in the style of a 13th century troubadour, with passion and élan. I wanted romance. I wanted love. I wanted to leave that white body rose-colored for a candlelit eternity. I wanted her soul, to fuse it with my own like two suns that join together and burn with ferocious desire before exploding. Then I wanted to fall to earth charred and devastated, and rise from the ashes like Phoenix and write a book of magnificent poetry in her honor.

So you see, you couldn't accuse me of being a sex maniac. A hopeless romantic, perhaps, but certainly not a sex maniac.

Just then she rolled onto her back and I caught the title of the book she was reading: *Emily Dickinson's Poems.* A stroke of luck, I thought. Being an English Major I had read some of her stuff, and I plunged into my mental filing cabinet to find what I remembered about Emily Dickinson. There was not much, only snippets of verse here and there. One stuck out, and without preparing myself I suddenly said it out loud: "Hope is a thing with feathers that perches in the soul."

Startled by my brazenness, I sat very still. She stopped reading and an awkward silence ensued.

"What did you say?" she asked.

Keeping my cool, I repeated myself: "Hope is a thing with feathers that perches in the soul."

She sat up and spun around to face me. "That's incredible," she said, her dark eyes flashing. "I was just reading that very poem. Either you've got great eyesight, or you're psychic."

"I'm psychic."

She laughed at this, studying me intently. "Really?"

"Really" I assured her, scooting forwards. She was even better-looking up close. Her eyes were brown and she had great tits. "You like Dickinson?" I asked quickly. I couldn't let up now, I was on a roll.

"Oh yes," she crooned. "She's a genius."

I agreed with her, following up with the standard stuff about Emily Dickinson being such a neglected poet, and all. She agreed whole-heartedly and asked what it was exactly that I liked about her as a poet. "Basically," I said (It was always proper in collegiate-talk to preface one's remarks with a "Basically" or an "Essentially" as it gave notice that you were cutting through the bull and going directly to the root of the matter.)—"Basically, it's her dynamic quality that fascinates me, that juxtaposition or struggle within each of her poems between her devout spirituality on the one hand and her existential despair on the other." What that meant, I hadn't the slightest, but it sounded good.

"Oh, yes," she crooned again. "Definitely." (She said "Oh yes" in the most marvelous way, as though we were in the throes of passionate love-making and she was excitedly whispering her approval, "Oh yes, oh yes.") "I'm fascinated by that very quality myself," she continued. "But more so, I think, because her passionate verse—this just so, really, prodigious depth of thought—is coming from a woman. I mean, all this time we've been led to believe that all great poets are men, that only they are capable of such, you know, profundity, but it isn't so. Not at all." She held the book up for emphasis.

That was a good point, I told her. I had never considered it myself, but now that I had, her point was well taken. She smiled when I said this and bowed her head. The effect of my flattery on her pleased me to no end and I lost my train of thought. Before I could recover it, an embarrassing lull had taken over. Usually what happened when this occurred was that I immediately started muttering, inane stuff like "Yeah" "Uh huh", "Well, that's great," which just worsened the situation. Luckily, I suddenly remembered old Emily and took off again.

"Why I'm so interested," I said, "is because you don't see many people reading Emily Dickinson these days, or any poetry for that matter, unless they're English Majors. Is that your major?

She said it wasn't, she just enjoyed it. Her major was Political Science, at least for the time being.

"For the time being?" I asked.

"Yes, at least until we can establish our Feminist Studies program."

"Feminist Studies? Never heard of it."

"Exactly," she replied with an ironic sort of laugh. "That's because there isn't such a thing, which is a disgrace, you know, considering we have major studies programs for Blacks and Hispanics, et cetera, but absolutely nothing for women—their heritage, their political struggle, really, *their everything*."

"Unbelievable," I said, sounding sympathetic.

"I know, but it's quite true. They're afraid to acknowledge us, really, it's that simple.

I was sympathetic again, commenting on the whole injustice of it all. This brought on another "Oh yes" from her (God, how I loved the way she said that.), and I asked her how she was going about this noble effort. This question excited her, and she straightened up, pushing her tits out, and began to explain it to me in that erudite tone of hers. As I listened, I quickly appraised the situation: she liked me, there was no doubt about it. I had caught her secretly checking me out with those big brown eyes of hers. Just her manner, her whole body language, revealed a definite attraction towards me. Don't ask me to explain this precisely, I just knew, that's all. She wanted it and I planned on giving it to her. I just had to be careful not to press it too soon or I'd scare her off—just keep the conversation rolling along and delicately work it around towards a date, find out what she liked in music or movies and go from there. But I knew I had it. I knew I had it the same way a team with momentum knew it was going to score. Everything was falling into place and I was executing perfectly.

"Wouldn't you agree?" she asked.

"Certainly," I said instantly, not knowing what I was agreeing with exactly. But it didn't matter as she nodded and said, "But of course," and continued her saga. I concentrated again on listening to her, fighting the distraction of her deep cleavage and the wonderful image in my head of me kissing down and around it once I got her in bed. Luckily she was nearing the end—something about prevailing and having their day—and finished with a shrug and a raised eyebrow.

"Amazing." I said dramatically, paying tribute to her struggle. "But I know, just from listening to you, that you'll succeed. I hear both dedication and eloquence—a rare combination—and with those qualities you can't fail."

"Are you being psychic again?"

"Yes, you can't fail."

She smiled and bowed her head, the same way she did before when I had complimented her. This time, however, she raised her arm up to scratch her head, and as she did, I saw something I hadn't noticed before. She had hairy armpits.

Now call me narrow-minded if you want, but there was just something about hairy armpits on a woman that turned me off. I couldn't help it; it was a matter of poor aesthetics, like catsup on a filet mignon or throwing back silk sheets and finding a spider in your bed. It just gave me the willies, that's all. And, as I glanced away startled by this rather seedy revelation, I stared into the grass and desperately struggled with my williness.

I had a choice to make, either quickly overcome my aversion, or get up and walk away, walk away from those big brown eyes, those great tits, those long white legs, and walk away from any chance of ever man-handling that B-plus with a B.A. body into a rose-colored ecstasy. Without further ado, I chose the former—to quickly overcome my aversion. It was remarkable what sacrifices one was capable of making when poised on the precipice of a great sexual adventure. (Personally, I was a moral relativist in matters like this: one didn't screw the armpits, afterall, which is the very point my roommates would have impressed upon me had I returned home empty handed.) Of course, it wasn't going to be easy from hereon, considering every time she raised an arm or turned a certain way my eyes would shoot to the spot for a glimpse of her hairiness. Not on purpose, mind you, but simply out of the perverse fascination one has for any blemish on an otherwise perfect specimen. I could manage it though. At least she didn't have hairy legs.

Had she noticed my dilemma, I wondered. Since the sighting, the conversation had stopped for a good thirty seconds or so (an eternity). If she had noticed, I was done for; she'd become defensive and withdraw, and I'd be left with nothing but an image of her hairy armpits to remember her by. If she hadn't noticed, then it was up to me to quickly end this lull before she did. Regain momentum. Break the huddle and throw a pass.

Again I was lucky. Nature intervened.

As I looked up at her, smiling dumbly, a bug flew into her hair. "Hold still," I said and instantly leaned over and plucked the bug from her hair. "What is it?" she asked, her body frozen stiff.

Nothing, I told her, just a ladybug that had flown into her hair. The ladybug stayed on my finger where I scrutinized it closely, admiring its enameled shell painted red with black spots, before flicking it off and watching it fly away.

"There," I said, proud of my deed. I then asked her the first thing that popped into my head: "See the game Saturday?"

She looked bewildered by my question. "The game?" she asked.

(The game, she asked—what other game was there? We had beaten USC. Really put it to them.) "The Cal game," I said.

"The Cal game," she repeated, thinking for a moment. "Oh, you mean football, the football game... No, I didn't, sorry. I don't care much for football."

"Don't be sorry. I don't care much for it either," I lied. "I was just making conversation, I guess." I gave her a sheepish grin and rolled my eyes as though I had just told a corny joke.

She reached out and touched my leg. "You don't need to do that," she said in a rather seductive tone. "It's obvious we're attracted to each other. I want you, you want me—so just let it happen. Know what I mean? Just let it happen by itself. Silence is all right. Really. I'm not going anywhere." She touched my leg again and smiled a warm, come-hither smile.

Stunned, I managed to be witty nevertheless. "Sure you're not a Psych Major," I said.

We both laughed.

My roommates were not going to believe this, I thought. I mean, it was one thing for a girl to come on to you, to smile, drop a few hints, and all that, but it was quite another for a girl to step up and grab you in the crotch with a statement like "I want you." Not that it bothered me any. Au contraire. Aggressive women appealed to me in a way no other kind of woman did, especially if I was looking to get my rocks off. They made things easier, and quicker too, sort of like a zipper compared to laces. I thought it was great. I felt just like a poker player who goes in big and then watches everyone fold—you know, wonderfully smug.

My worries over keeping this little tête-à-tête alive were over. The conversation took off like a quarter horse (the bell had rung, the gate shot open, and she—the jockey of this horse—had taken its reins and stung its ass with her whip). It was enough just to keep up with her. She joked, confessed, and asked me personal questions in the manner of a lifelong buddy. She bore in on me with an irresistibly intimate style, those dark eyes flashing, that bosom sighing, her words stroking me, crooning to me, and drawing me in like some dumb hick at his first carnival.

But this dumb hick had an excuse—she was good. Real good. A regular gourmet. I was being tenderized, dressed, and basted like a prime cut of beef for her consumption, and she had a hearty appetite. But I didn't mind, because in just a short while the tables would be turned. In a short while I would have her in bed and then *my feast* would begin. I would stuff her like a plump chicken and cook her until she fell apart, then devour her succulent meat until only her bones were left. Then would come her surrender, the very same trembling surrender that came from a woman at the point of ecstasy when she gave it all up and was completely, irrevocably yours. Then we would be more than even. I would be the victor.

Still, it was a pleasant conversation. The sky was blue, the sun warm, the grass green, her legs were long and smooth, and this kind of verbal foreplay, tinged as it was with sexual anticipation, seemed to accentuate the qualities of sight and sound for me. I don't remember exactly what we talked about, only its sensual character, though I do recall her telling me she was a vegetarian, that she liked Fellini films, and listened to Joni Mitchell. It didn't matter that I was neither a vegetarian nor a Fellini fan, and I could have cared less about Joni Mitchell, what mattered was the sound of her voice, the look of her body, and the erection in my swim trunks. I also remember we even disagreed once about a very pregnant woman in a bikini who had laid down near us to sunbathe. I commented that I thought it rather "tacky," while she maintained it was "natural" (I stood by my "tacky" despite her efforts to dissuade me.). But even this minor spat fed the boiler on the steam engine we were riding. We were at full throttle with the tunnel just ahead. Nothing on earth was going to stop me from entering that tunnel. I was beyond stopping; I was in the karmic realm of the destined. Nirvana was mine and only a catastrophe of epic proportions was going to derail my joyful fate.

I hadn't noticed the ladybugs. I had plucked a couple more out of her hair during our conversation but they hadn't registered. I mean, considering the mystical-sexual state I was in it was understandable. I was preoccupied in the same way, I assume, a movie star was when his name got called for the academy award, his body going weightless and the world turning surreal. Maybe there were a few more ladybugs than usual flying about, and a few more than that, but like I said, I didn't notice—until it was too late.

The conversation had peaked and I figured it was time to make my move. I was hoping she had her own place; if not my roommates would just have to vamoose. (They'd understand, of course, being the considerate deviants that they were.) So, as we discussed the merits of pass/non-pass courses and the sensuality of Van Gogh, I waited for the right moment, the moment when I could nonchalantly ask her to share a bottle of wine with me, perhaps at her place if she happened to live alone. I'd leave the rest unsaid, for we'd both know what I really meant.

The moment came but she beat me to the punch.

"I have a bottle of wine at home," she said casually. "Why don't you come over and..."

But she never finished, because just then two things happened almost simultaneously. The first thing was I noticed a shadow come over the sun and instinctively looked up at the sky. What I saw puzzled me—I thought someone was shaking out a dusty blanket behind me—for the sky was filled with flying particles. But they weren't particles at all, I realized, but bugs—ladybugs—thousands of them, descending upon us from the hill above, and in their vanguard ran people with towels and radios in hand, heading for cover.

"Look at that," I said in amazement, turning back to her. And then the second thing happened, for as I turned back, I saw one of the bugs land on her chest. Startled, she glanced at the approaching horde and then looked down at her chest where she watched helplessly as the ladybug crawled down her cleavage and into her swimsuit. She sat for a moment in astonishment, then erupted, screaming "Get it, get it!" while picking madly at her cleavage. I leaned towards her to comply but she jumped up and began shaking and hopping about with her arms flailing at her chest. "Get it, get it!" she continued screaming, her body convulsing about with her eyes popped out, her frizzy hair shaking. It struck me that she looked like Larry from the Three Stooges pretending to be electrocuted, and I, of course, did the only thing a normal person could do in a situation like that. I laughed.

If looks could kill I'd have been murdered right then and there, but I was too busy laughing to care. "Get away!" she screeched, either at me or the bugs swarming about her head, and she swatted at the air, frantically brushing her swimsuit to rid herself of the beasties. But it was useless, they were all about her now, en masse, as though the entire ladybug nation had singled her out for attack. They enveloped her like static fuzz envelops a person on a television with bad reception, nesting in her hair, landing on her neck, and she hopped and shuddered and slapped crazily in defense. (I remember thinking at the time, why is she getting so hysterical? Ladybugs don't bite, don't sting; they don't even fly very well. They're harmless.) But it was all too much for her. I could see that the bugs, my laughter, her humiliating position—it was all too much for her to contend with, and she grabbed her towel and book hissing "No more!" and fled her attackers. For a second I considered chasing after her but thought better of it. She was gone.

I stopped laughing. It suddenly occurred to me what had happened. She was gone. Those long legs, those great tits, that inviting bottle of wine—it was all gone. It had been right there in my hands, and now nothing. I felt like I had just dropped an easy pass in the end zone.

Dammit, I thought to myself. *Damn it all.* I looked dejectedly down at the grass and there was a ladybug. I put out my finger and let it crawl on and brought it up to my nose. There was the culprit, sitting there on my finger, staring at me so innocently. It ruffled its wings once then walked off to explore some more of my finger. I could have crushed it but I didn't. Instead

I laughed. I couldn't help it, I could see her there again hopping and bouncing about screaming "Get it, get it!" as though a deadly snake had crawled down her cleavage instead of this little ladybug, and the more I thought about it the more I had to chuckle to myself. Wasn't that just my luck?

In a short time the ladybugs had passed and I had the pool all to myself. I took another swim, pretending I was Mark Spitz on the last leg of the hundred meter breaststroke, then went on home. The evening wasn't a total loss. I had a nice dinner and watched a good game (the Raiders won), and even did a little homework before going to bed. I refrained from telling my roommates about my episode and instead kept it to myself. They would have just ribbed me about it anyway.

The rest of my college days passed uneventfully. I managed to graduate and go on to become a normal person, spending the succeeding years forgetting everything I had learned at Cal. I also got married—to a pretty gal (I'd say a solid B with an M.A.) who keeps a clean house, cries when we fight, and adores me with an unquenchable passion. I love her dearly. As for the girl at the pool on that fall day in Strawberry Canyon, I never saw her again. I never even tried to look her up (I had somehow neglected to get her name). But once in a great while I think about her and wonder what it would have been like. What kind of life would we have had together, she with her Feminist Studies and hairy armpits, and me with my Monday Night Football? How would we have fared? But I'll never know. The ladybugs took care of that.

The Batting Cage

Chiqui took payment from the dad for a round of miniature golf and returned his change. She handed out four putters—one each to the mom and dad, and the other two for their kids—then set four golf balls on the counter. They were colored red, blue, yellow, and green, and she waited for the inevitable argument to end as to who got what color ball before handing out their score cards. Chiqui reminded them to take pencils with them, which sat in a cup on the counter, then said "Have fun" with a big smile.

This was Chiqui's third summer working at Karts & Golf. It was a part-time gig that paid a little over minimum wage and her hours were Sunday through Thursday from 5:00 to 10 pm. That was cool with her because it gave her Friday and Saturday off and enough spending money to have fun with her friends. She preferred working in the arcade. It had a counter on one side where she sold soda and candy, and on the other side was a sliding window where she rented out putters for miniature golf along with bats and helmets for the batting cages.

Employees were supposed to rotate between the go-karts, golf course, batting cages, and the arcade. The golf course and batting cages were kind of boring; all you did was retrieve stuck balls or re-set the pitching machines, and she didn't like working the go-karts because they were always breaking down. But things had a way of sorting themselves out. None of her co-workers liked working in the arcade, and her boss said she had an outgoing personality and a great smile (plus she was bilingual), so he pretty much let her have the arcade all to herself.

From the window, Chiqui could see the entrance and parking lot. She also had a good view of the batting cages. There was no one in the batting cages at the moment, so she leaned out and looked left to check the go-karts. There was no line for the go-karts but it was still early, only 6 o'clock, and it would probably get busier later on. The heat felt heavy on her face so she leaned back in and slid the window shut.

It was another warm evening in Chula Vista. Karts & Golf sat on Industrial Blvd overlooking Highway 5 and in the summertime, especially around July and August, it could get hot and stay hot into the evening. This was another reason she preferred working in the arcade, it had an air conditioner. It didn't work all that great but it was still cooler in the arcade than it was outside.

Chiqui walked over to the counter and surveyed the scene. There were about a dozen kids and teenagers playing assorted games, which included pinball machines, Pong, Space Invaders, Anti-aircraft, and an air hockey table. At the moment, no one was interested in a soda or candy, so Chiqui turned her radio up and listened to music. That was another perk that came with working in the arcade, she could listen to her small boom box. She kept it tuned to her favorite radio station KGB-FM, which played rock and roll and none of that disco crap.

There was a tap on the window and Chiqui went over, slid open the window, and retrieved golf clubs from a guy and a girl who had just finished their game.

"Don't you go to Hilltop High?" asked the guy.

"Yeah—well, I graduated this year," replied Chiqui. "You go there?"

"Yeah, we'll be juniors," he said, indicating both he and the girl next to him.

"My brother graduated with you," said the girl. "Class of '78, right?"

"Right. What's his name?"

"Tony Alvarez."

"Sure, I know him," replied Chiqui with a smile.

"Right on... You going to college?"

"Not sure yet. Probably Grossmont."

"Cool."

There was a momentary lull in the conversation and Chiqui filled it with, "Nice to meet you guys. Come by again."

"Will do," replied the guy. "Keep it real."

"You, too," said Chiqui as she watched them walk away. "Say hi to your brother," she added. The girl waved back at her while replying, "I will."

Chiqui slid the window shut, grabbed her soda cup, and added more ice to her Dr. Pepper. Everyone was always asking her about college. Her parents, her friends—even strangers— all wanted to know if she was going to college. It annoyed her. She might go to college, but she wasn't sure yet. She had other options; she could keep doing what she was doing or get a full-time job, travel, or even go into the Navy. She wasn't sure yet and she wished people would stop bugging her about it.

A couple kids appeared at the counter and ordered sodas. She set her own drink down, filled their order, and then went back to listening to her radio. Things picked up around 7 o'clock and Chiqui got busy handing out golf clubs, filling soda orders, and re-stocking the change machine in the arcade. At 7:30 three guys her own age came up to the window and asked for batting tokens. She didn't know them but one of them wore a Spartan baseball cap from Chula Vista High School. She handed them each a bat and a helmet then watched them set up in one of the fast-pitch cages and take their swings. Chiqui figured that they were jocks from a local baseball team, and she watched them for a while before she had to turn around and take a drink order.

More golfers came in as well as a small group of little leaguers eager to use the batting cages. The three baseball jocks came back after a half-hour to turn in their bats and helmets. They were all sweaty. The one in the Spartan baseball cap tried flirting with her but she ignored him. She'd just broken up with her boy-friend and wasn't in the market for a new one. They left and she continued to work the arcade counter for the next hour and a half until she looked up and noticed it was 9 o'clock.

The hour triggered a memory, and she walked over to the window, slid it open, and looked out. Funny, she thought, she'd been working there almost a month now and this was the first time she had remembered Monty. It was Tuesday at 9 pm and there was no Monty. She looked out at the entrance and beyond into the parking lot—but no Monty.

She retreated back inside and thoughtfully sipped her Dr. Pepper. Monty had been a fixture in the batting cage every Tuesday and Thursday night for the last two summers she'd worked there. Her co-worker Dan, who was full-time and had worked at Karts & Golf for five years, said that Monty had been coming there for as long as he could remember and always on Tuesday and Thursday nights at exactly 9 pm.

Chiqui remembered the first time she met Monty. Dan was training her in the arcade when he appeared at the window at 9 o'clock. She slid the window open and took his order for five tokens (a hundred pitches) while Dan stood behind her.

"Hey, Monty," called out Dan.

Monty looked behind Chiqui and answered back, "Daniel—how's your Pods doing?"

"Same ol' same," answered Dan. "They're losing 5-2." Dan was a San Diego Padres fan and always wore a beat-up Padres cap. He kept a transistor radio in his pocket with an ear piece so he could listen to the games.

"Pitching," said Monty. "It's all about pitching."

"Tell me about it."

"And who's this young lady?" asked Monty with a smile. Dan introduced her to Monty and they said "hi" to each other. She guessed him to be in his late fifties and retired military. Chula Vista was filled with retired military and they all had the same look about them—tidily dressed, clean-shaven, with their white or silver hair cut neat and trim.

Monty studied her face for a moment then asked, "Cómo estás?"

"Bien, y usted?"

"I'll tell you in about forty minutes," he replied quickly. "Give me the blue bat there." (She handed it to him.) "And the number three helmet." (She handed that to him as well.) He took his tokens and gear, spun around, said "Hasta la vista," and marched towards the batting cages.

"Watch this," said Dan with a grin. They both watched as Monty went straight to the cage on the end—the fast-pitch, hardball cage—and fed in his token. He took a slightly open stance and got ready, fouling off the first couple pitches before finding his groove and making solid contact thereafter.

"Wow, he's pretty good for an old guy," said Chiqui.

"And check it out," said Dan. "He doesn't stride to the ball. You know what I mean? Big leaguers always step forward when they swing... Well, anyhow, he doesn't stride. He just stands there like his feet are stuck in cement and swings from his waist—and makes contact every time. He sets it at ninety miles per hour and hits line shots every time. The guy's amazing."

"Who is he?"

Dan filled her in on what he knew, and she'd guessed right, he was ex-military. Dan was pretty sure it was the Marines but wasn't positive. The old guy had the same routine, every Tuesday and Thursday at 9 o'clock, always five tokens, and after he was done he always ordered a medium Pepsi and drank it at the picnic table next to the entrance. He always finished his drink right before closing time at 10 o'clock.

After that she got used to seeing Monty and he became a fixture. He always had something nice to say to her and had different nick-names for her. One was "Chick-a-dee," another was 'Brown-eyes," and sometimes he called her 'Lancer" because he noticed her wearing a green and black Hilltop High shirt and their mascot was the Lancers. She'd greet him with a big smile, say, "Hola, Monty," hand him his tokens, bat, and helmet (always in that order), and have his medium Pepsi waiting for him when he returned.

They never really talked except for once. It was towards the end of last summer. She and Dan had closed up the arcade, had gotten a couple of sodas, and were walking out to the entrance when they saw Monty still sitting at the picnic table. They plopped down next to him and started talking. He asked her about school and she told him how it was going. Dan asked him if he was an ex-Marine and whether he had fought in World War Two. He answered yes to both questions but didn't say any more about it.

"How do you know Spanish?" she asked him. She was half gringo but he was all gringo and she was curious.

"My wife's Mexican," he replied with a mischievous grin forming on his face. "She's a fiery Latina. I like 'em that way... Me and John Wayne."

"Why John Wayne?"

"He only marries Latin women. Crazy Latinas. It's his particular poison—same as me."

She and Dan laughed at that and then Dan asked him if he had ever played baseball. Yes he had, he said as he finished off his Pepsi, got up, and wished them "Buenas noches." And that was the end of their conversation.

Now it was a whole summer later and there was no Monty. At closing time, she asked Dan about Monty but Dan had no clue. He hadn't seen him in over six months and thought he had probably moved away. Too bad, thought Chiqui. She liked old Monty and was going to miss him.

Two and a half weeks later Chiqui found out she was pregnant. She hadn't told anybody, not her mom, not her big sister, not even her best friend. Her ex-boyfriend had gone into the Army but she had no intention of writing him a letter to let him know either. She continued to go to work and hang out with her friends, just as though nothing was wrong, and she kept the secret to herself.

Two more weeks passed and September was creeping up, and she knew that in another month she'd start showing. She had until then to make a decision but her choices were limited. She could tell her mom, but she knew her mom would totally freak out and she dreaded the whole scene. Or she could have an abortion. She'd been to the clinic and they'd explained everything to her and had promised to keep her secret safe. But she didn't like the whole vibe there or the lady who interviewed her, so Chiqui had put her off and left the place in a bit of a sour mood.

A week later, in September, Chiqui was behind the counter in the arcade. Her manager came by to check on her and Chiqui asked if he had a few minutes to talk. He did. She was looking for a full-time job, she told him, and wondered if, after summer vacation was over, she could come on as full-time. She wasn't going to college this year and was looking for a full-time job.

"Shouldn't be a problem," he said. "Glad to have you... But where's that big smile of yours. I haven't seen it for a while."

She gave him the big smile.

"There it is," he replied. He turned away to go off on his rounds but called back over his shoulder, "We'll talk later."

She nodded and then turned her radio up to listen to a David Bowie song. She was lost in thought when she heard a tap on the glass and looked over at the window. It was an old man.

She slid open the window and looked at him without much interest.

"Hey, brown eyes."

"Huh?" she replied, startled. She looked closer and saw Monty—but it wasn't Monty. This was a frail, old man. He wore a baseball cap that looked too big for him and his cheeks were drawn in from loss of weight. It was obvious he'd been sick, badly sick, but she quickly recovered from the shock at his appearance and smiled at him. "Monty!" she said cheerfully.

"That smile makes my day," he said. His voice was raspy.

"Where you been?"

"Busy," he answered simply. There was a moment of awkward silence before he handed her a five dollar bill and glanced over her shoulder. "Got a bat in there for me?" he asked.

"Sure do." She took his five dollar bill, counted out five tokens, and then handed him his blue bat and his number 3 helmet.

"Keep a cold one for me, Chick-a-dee. I won't be long."

"Will do." She watched him as he turned around and started walking towards the batting cages. He walked slowly, using the bat as a cane. He still wore long track pants and high top sneakers but instead of a tight-fitting tank top he now wore a long-sleeve t-shirt. That and the hat, along with the weight loss, made him look totally different. She guessed that he'd lost at least twenty pounds. And as she watched him make that slow trek to his favorite batting cage a feeling—call it a premonition—came over her.

She went over to the intercom system and buzzed Jerry. Jerry was working in the batting cages and he quickly answered her. She tried to tell him to look out for Monty but he didn't understand her (Jerry was a bit of a space-case and she knew for a fact that he smoked a joint before and after work), so she changed her tactic and just asked him to come up and replace her so she could take a break. He said okay and was on his way.

Chiqui left the arcade and passed Jerry on the sidewalk that led to the batting cages. He glanced in some confusion at her but she waved him off saying, "Give me fifteen minutes," and kept walking.

When she arrived, Monty was just getting into the fast-pitch cage, and she stood back and watched as he put on his helmet and took a couple practice swings. The bat seemed big and heavy in his hands, like a sledgehammer, and he stopped for a moment, choked up on the handle, and took a couple more swings. Satisfied, he fed a token into the slot and adjusted the speed dial. He got himself set and waited for the first pitch. Chiqui remembered that he always hit 90mph fastballs, but the first pitch was slower than that, maybe 70mph, and he let it go by without swinging. He swung at the next pitch but missed badly.

Monty swung again and then again, missing both times. Chiqui wanted to stop him but she checked the urge when she saw his face. It was frozen in a fierce determination. That look acted as a warning and she stayed back. Five more times he swung and missed but he was able to foul off the next pitch. By the time his token ran out, he had managed to hit two grounders and a soft line drive.

He leaned on his bat and walked a couple steps over to the control box and picked up another token, but as he went to feed his token into the slot his arm began to tremble. He dropped his arm to his side and fought against the trembling that now seemed to spread through his body. Chiqui opened the cage door and came up next to him as he dropped to a knee.

"You okay, Monty," she asked gently. She had her arm around his shoulder and could feel his whole body shaking.

"Just gotta catch my breath," he managed to say between rasping breaths. He raised his head and tried to take a deep breath, coughed, and tried again. The effort weakened him and he dropped his head and took quicker, shorter breaths.

"It's okay. Take your time," she said in a reassuring voice. "I got ya."

They knelt there together for over three minutes as Monty worked to control his shaking. All the while Chiqui held him across the shoulders and reassured him in a calm voice that it was okay. Finally his trembling subsided and he was able to take a deep breath without coughing.

"Wanna sit on the bench?" she asked him.

"Yeah."

She slipped her arm around his waist and helped him stand up. He carefully arched his back and leaned on his bat. "Gracias, muchacha," he said weakly. She led him over to the bench outside the batting cage and they sat down together. He bent over with his elbows on his knees while she rubbed his back.

Her manager suddenly appeared. "What happened?" he asked in a panic. "Is he okay? Do I need to call 911?"

"No!" answered Monty in a strong voice. He raised up and looked at the manager. "I'll be okay. Just give me a minute."

"You sure? How 'bout your family? Can we call your family?"

"Want me to call your wife?" added Chiqui.

"No," replied Monty. "She thinks I'm at the VFW... Just give me a few minutes... Let me catch my breath. I'll be okay."

"You sure?" pressed the manager.

"Yeah. I got Chiqui here. She'll take care of me."

"Okay, if you're sure then," said the manager obviously relieved that he didn't need to call 911. "You got him, Chiqui?"

"Yeah, I got him. He'll be all right."

"Okay then. I'll tell Jerry to stay in the arcade until further notice." And with that, her manager left them alone. Monty took his batting helmet off, plucked his ball cap out, wiped the sweat off his head, and put his cap back on. Chiqui could see that his hair was gone.

After a while she could feel his strength beginning to return as he took deeper breaths and sat up straight. He glanced at the batting cage. "Whew. Bit off more than I can chew," he said more to himself than to her.

"Ready?" he said as he started to get up.

"Ready." She stood up with him, grabbed his helmet, and linked arms with him as they slowly walked back up the path to the arcade. She sat him down at the picnic table next to the entrance. "Want a Pepsi?"

"Love one."

She left him the bat in case he needed it as a cane and went into the arcade. Jerry wanted to know what was up and she quickly told him as she poured out a medium Pepsi with ice. She filled up a Dr. Pepper for herself and went back out and sat down opposite Monty at the picnic table. He took a long sip of his soda.

"Ahh, much better," he said. "Thank you, brown eyes."

"You're welcome." She studied him carefully for a moment and then added, "You gonna be okay to drive home? Sure you don't want me to call your wife?"

"No, I'll be fine," he said, taking another sip of his soda which seemed to be rejuvenating him. "I lied to her—told her I was going to the VFW... If she found out she'd kick my ass." He chuckled to himself at that.

Chiqui nodded slightly and tried a chuckle of her own but it didn't come out right. Monty was studying her face.

"You don't need to worry about me," he said as he reached over and patted her hand. "You worry too much, Chick-a-dee. I can see it right there—that crease above your nose—you're worrying. Life's too short to worry. Right?" He grinned at her then stopped, reading something in her face and eyes that made him pause.

"Are you all right?" he asked her.

And suddenly, for reasons she could never explain, it all came loose inside her and she burst out crying. Monty gripped her hand, alarmed, but waited patiently for her to calm down before asking her softly, "What? What is it, hija? Tell me."

"I'm pregnant."

"Por Dios... Okay. There now... Look at me... Come on, look at me—there you go... And where's the father?"

"Gone."

"And you're afraid to tell your parents?"

"It's just my mom—but, yes." She had managed to stop sobbing but the tears were still heavy in her eyes. She wiped her cheeks with the palm of her hand. "There's another option," she said weakly. She hiccupped twice, caught herself from sobbing again, and then added, "But I have to do it pretty soon."

"I see."

Monty reached into his pocket and pulled out a white handkerchief and handed it to her. She took it and wiped the tears from her face. "Blow your nose," he said, and she blew her nose, folded the handkerchief over, and dabbed her eyes while she studied him for a moment.

"What should I do?" she asked.

"Take a sip of your drink," he ordered in a kind voice. "You'll feel better... Go on... Better?" (She nodded yes.) "Bueno... Now listen to me—'cause this is all I can tell you... Life is precious... La vida es preciosa. Si'? Life is precious and everything in it. I learned that in '42 and never forgot it... Just look around you. It's all precious—even this dingy park and that beat-up batting cage. All of it, comprende?

She managed a smile and replied, "I think so."

"Don't think so, know so," he said in a stern voice, but softened it by adding, "Hear me, hija?" An adult couple on their way out of the park hesitated and glanced over at them. Monty regarded them for a moment. "Have a good evening," he called out to them in a voice that sounded more like a command than a greeting. They took the cue and kept walking.

"The whole goddam thing is precious—even what's in there," he said, nodding at her belly. He stared into her eyes and she met his stare without looking away. He smiled and nodded, then shook the ice in his empty soda cup.

"Wanna another one?" she asked. The tears were gone and there was relief in her voice.

"No, gotta go home—before my wife calls the VFW and finds out I lied to her." He lifted himself up using the table top as a brace and came up straight.

"Are you going to tell her the truth?"

"Always," he replied with a wry grin. "I just have to wait for the right moment." He handed her the bat and steadied himself to walk again.

"I'm going with you," she said, placing the bat on the table. She came around, linked arms with him, and walked with him out to his car. They didn't speak. After he opened his car door he turned to her and said, "Give me a hug." She hugged him gently, feeling the ribs beneath his shirt, and kissed him on the cheek. She still held his hanky in her hand, and she offered it back to him but he told her to keep it.

"Take care, Monty," she said.

He shut the door and winked up at her. She stepped back and watched him pull out onto Industrial Blvd and drive away. He never returned.

Nearly a year later Chiqui brought her two cousins, along with her mom, to Karts & Golf. Her cousins were visiting from Phoenix and looking for something to do so she suggested a round of miniature golf. As they came up to the arcade window, Chiqui parked her stroller and leaned down to lock the back wheels. Within minutes, a number of her old co-workers including the manager came up to say hi.

There was a buzz of talk and activity around the stroller. Chiqui's old manager half-kiddingly asked her if she wanted her old job back but she said, no, she wasn't interested because she was starting at Grossmont College in a couple weeks. Dan came by and gave Chiqui a hug.

"Check this out," he said confidentially. He steered her off to the side and pulled out his wallet. He plucked a newspaper article out and began to unfold it. "Remember Monty?" he asked her.

"'Course. What's that?" she asked, feeling a sudden foreboding.

"His obituary. He died last April." Dan handed her the article and immediately pointed to a paragraph he wanted her to read. "See that there," he said. "He lost both his feet in World War Two. That's why he never stepped towards the ball. No wonder. It also says that he designed his own artificial feet and made a fortune off the patent."

Chiqui didn't want to hear any more—she wanted to read—and she put her hand up to shush Dan and turned her back to him. Thoughts and emotions swirled around inside her and she tried to settle them down so she could focus and read Monty's obituary.

He died at age sixty, leaving a wife, three daughters, and four grandchildren. Montgomery Brooks was born and raised in Bakersfield, later going to UCLA where he played baseball. He was drafted by the Cardinals but instead joined the Marines right after Pearl Harbor, serving as a Lieutenant with the 1st Raider Battalion under Lieutenant Colonel Merritt A. Edson (Edson's Raiders). He was wounded at the Battle of Tulagi in 1942, designed his own artificial feet so he could walk again, sold the patent, and settled down and started his own business in Chula Vista where he met and married Dolores Soto and raised a family.

There was more to the obituary but Chiqui couldn't read it any longer. She folded it up and turned back to Dan. "Can I have this?" she asked."

"Sure."

She thanked him, placed the folded-up obituary into her purse, and rejoined her family. One of her cousins asked if she was okay and she said yes in a way that meant she didn't want to talk about it. Her mom rented four putters and handed her one. Chiqui waited patiently while her two cousins argued over who got the red ball. When they were done, she took the green ball and reminded everyone to grab a pencil for scorekeeping. With that, she leaned down to unlock the stroller, said "Let's go," and led the way down the path.

THE EIGHTIES

I can only answer the question 'What am I to do?' if I can answer the prior question 'Of what story or stories do I find myself a part?'

Alasdair MacIntyre
After Virtue

Sam:
Have you noticed that, uh... somebody in this bar is getting a little loony?

Frasier:
Sam, everyone in this bar is on a connecting flight to beyond loony.

Cheers

Life is one grand sweet song so start the music.

Ronald Reagan

The Day the Cat Died

It was Sunday afternoon before they finally let him take her home. She dozed off next to him as they drove home in the rain. It wasn't very far and traffic was light, and he let the radio play softly in the background as they drifted along the wet streets. He lightly shook her awake when they pulled into the driveway and helped her out and brought her inside. He quickly turned on the heater and started a fire in the fireplace, then he got her robe out of her bag and carried it into the bedroom for her. She sat on the edge of the bed slowly undressing, and when she had finished he helped her on with the robe and she lay down on the bed. He pulled the covers over her and leaned down and kissed her cheek.

"Get me Maudie," she said weakly.

"Sure."

Maudie was their cat. It was marmalade-colored with white paws. They had argued when she first brought the kitten home, but that was a year ago and now he cared for it as much as she did. He opened the front door and whistled. It was a special whistle that never failed to bring Maudie running, but this time she didn't appear. He whistled again and waited, then went over and whistled out the back door. She didn't come. He closed the door and went back into the bedroom.

At first he thought she was asleep and he stopped, not wanting to disturb her, but she rolled off her back and looked over at him.

"Where's Maudie?"

He kneeled down beside her. "She won't come," he said softly.

"But I want her... Please get her. She'll get all wet." She pressed her dry lips against his forearm and closed her eyes.

He kissed her temple. "Sure. Don't worry," he said and got up and left the room.

She listened as he put on his coat and went out the front door. The telephone rang. God, she didn't feel like talking to anyone, not now. But it rang again and then again, relentlessly, so she reached over to the nightstand and picked up the receiver just to stop it. It was her mother. She wanted to know how she felt, how she was doing, and she told her in a drowsy voice. Her mother gave her some well-meaning advice and she listened patiently until her mom finished, then she hung up and lay over on her back. It felt worse there, so she rolled onto her side again and curled up. That was a little better, but the emptiness was still there.

She had taken her medication a half hour before and now, at last, she began to feel its effects. She closed her eyes and waited for the numbing warmth to spread over her. It came in waves like the sea and filled the abyss in the pit of her soul, then receded and left her alone with the terrible emptiness until it returned again. Please come, she pleaded silently, but the emptiness was all she felt, a nauseating hollowness, as though her living parts had been sucked out by a machine. She had been the center of attention for the first time in her life, the most important thing, and now there was nothing. Just this emptiness. She squeezed her eyes against the hot tears but the wave came then, warm and liberating, and she let go, weeping into it as it picked her up and carried her gently out to sea. It was a deep, lifeless sea but she didn't care. Just as long as it was warm and never brought her back.

It was gray and drizzling out as he walked up the street. He looked under cars and on top of fences, whistling for Maudie as he went, but without any luck. He just had to find her, he thought, he just had to. He turned back towards the house and searched the other way. He was going to stay out as long as it took, he didn't care, because he had to find her. "Here, Maudie," he called and whistled again, but still she didn't appear. The intersection was before him and as he passed it he caught something out of the corner of his eye. A bad feeling came over him and he stopped.

He looked up the side street and saw it. At first he thought it might be a wet towel left in the road but he couldn't tell for sure. He walked towards it and stopped again. Then he knew because he could see it plainly. A car had hit Maudie and she lay dead in the street.

He walked over and kneeled down beside her. She was soaked from the rain, and he ran his hand over her wet fur. He thought he would cry for a second but it didn't come so he just shook his head. Who would do this, he wondered. Who would do a thing like this? But he knew it was probably just an accident. Nobody's fault. That's what they said—nobody's fault. He picked Maudie up, cradling her in his arms, and carried her back to the house. He brought her around the side and placed her in a garbage can and set the lid on tight so she'd stay dry. He would bury her in the backyard in the morning.

She couldn't find out, he thought. Not now. She wouldn't be able to take it. He'd tell her tomorrow, or the next day, when she was stronger, and until then he'd have to stall somehow. He stood for a while in the drizzling rain and thought it out and then went in.

He kicked off his shoes and put away his coat and went over and poked the fire. He added a log to it and watched as it smoked and then slowly caught fire. It was time, he knew, and he walked into the bedroom and lay down next to her on the bed. He put his arm around her and she touched his hand lightly and held it. He could tell she had been crying.

"She won't come," he whispered to her. She curled up tighter and dropped his hand. "But I saw her," he added. "She was under a car with that tomcat, the one you like, the one with the red collar. I tried to get her to come out but she wouldn't. She's being a brat." He snuggled up closer to her and said playfully, "She's in love. Let her have some fun. When she gets hungry enough she'll come home. Huh?"

She smiled weakly and picked up his hand again. "Now rest," he said, and he kissed her neck and hugged her gently. "Don't go," she said. "I'm not," he assured her. "I'm here... now rest," and he settled his head on the pillow next to hers and laid still. He lay without moving for a long time, until he felt her body go to sleep, and then quietly got out of bed and went into the living room. The fire was dead but he let it go and put on his shoes and went out the kitchen door into the garage.

The garage floor was under an inch of water. They lived on the downside of a hill and whenever it rained the garage flooded. He stepped down into it and tip-toed over to the mail basket. He noticed the baby crib sitting on the workbench and made a mental note to put it back up in the rafters. The mail basket was full and he pulled out the letters and leafed through them. Most were bills and he skipped those and came to a pink envelope which he pulled out and examined. It was from their landlord. An uneasy feeling crept over him as he held it, and instead of going back in he opened it right there and read it. It said they were selling the house. He had ninety days to move.

He held the open letter in his hand and waited for some reaction, but there wasn't any. He was numb to it. It was just one more thing, and he could call it unfair and get upset but what would be the point? All that was left was the worry of it. This would kill her, he realized. In her state, what with Maudie and now this, it was just too much for her. She loved this house. It would kill her. And he stared down into the dark water at his feet and tried to slip the worry of it, but it was too heavy and it bent him over. Dammit, he thought. God dammit. He rose up, took a deep breath, and raised his arms above his head and stretched.

Without realizing it he had gone flat-footed, and the water seeped into his shoes. He looked down at his wet shoes and wet pant legs and sniffed a short laugh, and then tip-toed through the water and back into the kitchen, closing the door behind him. He opened the pantry and stuck the bills in a wooden holder along with all the other bills, then he folded the landlord's letter, shoved it in his back pocket, and slowly closed the door. He stopped when he noticed the bottle of tequila on the top shelf. He started to reach for it but thought better of it and let it go. He closed the pantry door and went into the living room.

He took off his wet shoes and socks and started the fire again. The room was cold but he dared not turn up the heater any farther. Their utility bill had more than doubled the month before and they'd agreed not to use the heater as much anymore. He stoked the fire until it was going good and stood in front of it, drying his pant legs. He saw he'd have to get more wood in a while.

The fire felt warm on his legs, and he leaned over and let it warm his face and chest. He took the letter out of his back pocket and threw it into the fire and watched it burn. He'd tell her about Maudie in a day or so when she was stronger. As for the house— he would find another place, and when he had already found a new place he would tell her then. It would be easier that way. Yes, whatever it took. He'd find another house to rent, some place nice, and tell her then. He stared into the fire, his mind set, and swallowed decisively. His throat felt funny, like it did when he was about to get a cold. *Perfect,* he thought to himself.

She dreams she is in a cold desert. It is night and she walks along a road waiting for a car, her arms folded to keep her warm. Headlights appear in the distance and she stands anxiously by the side of the road. Suddenly she hears a cat cry, and she looks behind her and sees its fluorescent eyes in the darkness. It's Maudie. She calls to her cat but Maudie only cries again and stays where she is. "Here, Maudie," she pleads softly. "It's all right, come on. Come on, Maudie." But Maudie won't come. She glances up the road at the approaching headlights and then looks back into the darkness at Maudie's eyes. She can't leave without her, and she calls to her again but Maudie only cries. She has no choice but to go and get her. She walks away from the road and into the darkness. As she nears her fluorescent eyes she reaches out to take her but the eyes blink shut and disappear. "No—Maudie—come here!" she whispers frantically, but it's too late, Maudie is gone. She glances back at the road and sees the car speed past. She screams at it to stop but the scream gets caught in her throat and comes out distorted.

"You all right?" she heard him say. She awoke from her dream and felt him next to her. "You all right," he asked again.

"Is it time for a pill yet?"

"Sure, hold on," he said. She listened as he left the room and got the pill, filled up a glass of water, and came back in. She raised up and took the pill then lay back down and curled up. He lay down next to her and stroked her temple with his hand. His hand felt good. It was warm and gentle, and she closed her eyes to its caressing rhythm and listened to his soft voice. "It's all right... Everything is all right... Shhh... It's all right." The wave would come soon and she waited for it. It would start in her stomach, at the center of the emptiness, growing warm there, and gradually spread through her body. And she waited for it, nestling in tighter, feeling his soothing hand and voice caress over her like the purring of a cat. "I love you... It's all right now... Shhh... I love you." And the wave came, warm and strong, and picked her up, and she let go and easily went with it as it carried her out to sea. It was a warm and fathomless sea, just as she remembered it, and she smiled and assented and let the sea do as it pleased with her. She asked only one thing of it. She asked only that it never bring her back.

"Shhh, now," he whispered, stroking her temple gently. "It's all right... Everything's all right."

A World of Mikes

I have a friend named Mike—Mike Agostino to be exact. He's third generation Italian-American, short and stocky, olive-skinned with dark hair, brown eyes and a deep baritone voice. He exudes self-confidence in the same way large, masculine dogs exude virility. He also considers himself God's gift to women.

Now why do all Italian-American men consider themselves God's gift to women? It has to be some sort of Fabio-Latin-lover-machismo thing going on with their genes. Just look at history: there's Romeo, Casanova, Valentio, and those guys from the sixties—Frank and Dino. Players one and all. I mean, even Tony Carbone, one of the homeliest guys I know, acts the same way. It's rampant. Check it out for yourself.

Anyhow, back to Mike Agostino. He's a fellow of interesting qualities who probably sits high on my ranking of Mikes in my life. And there are a ton of them. Somehow I've become a veritable Mike-magnet. Over my lifetime of twenty-seven years, they have popped up and collected around me like lint on suede. There are Jims in my life, a few Johns and Joes, and even a Scott here and there, but nothing equaling the mountain of Mikes that shadow my space. They are legion. It's a Cat-in-the-Hat, Dr. Seuss parade of Michaels, Mikes, Mikeys, big Mikes, little Mikes, and Mikes on bikes of every shape, color, size, and sexual orientation. There's Agostino, Flores, Murphy and McGuire, Bergman, Dupree, Wong and Woo, Sakamoto, Ragnarson, Nickovitch and Petrovitch, Capuyan, Savoor, Pamintuan and Patel. It's an American crockpot of steaming Mike stew.

As I said, the Agostino of Mikes probably sits near the top of my Mike List, which is a new list I'm compiling. Rating and ranking is something I've been doing for years. As a kid, I used to rank things like soda pop and candy bars. In college, my roommates and I had a rating system for girls. Where this habit developed, I can't say, though my dad ranked all sorts of things from baseball players to cars to brands of beer. All I can say is that I'm not alone in this pursuit. Just look around you—it's the national pastime. Whether it's college teams or the Fortune 500, it's the very expression of Yankee competitiveness. I mean, really, who can pass up an edition of People Magazine ranking the 10 Sexiest Women of the Year?

Over the years, I have honed my talents for rating and ranking into an art form. Some folks have a talent for playing the piano, others for cooking up gourmet meals; I have a talent for sifting through the unpackaged bit-stream of life, rating it and ranking it, and creating order out of chaos. And not unlike a tortured artist, *I have to rank,* I have no choice. Rating and ranking feeds my soul, nourishes it like spiritual milk, and helps keep this low-fat, high-in-fiber, data-rich world in perspective. Take, for instance, the best break-up lines: "I need space" lacks all originality and goes immediately to the bottom of the list. On the other hand, "I love you but I'm not *in love* with you" is a topper for its Yogi Berra-like quality alone. Then there's "I'm involved with someone else" or "We have nothing in common" which round out the top of my list. They contain a certain visceral truth that "I need space" sorely lacks.

It's how my mind works. Garry Kasparov sees chess moves in the designs of the carpet. I see lists.

But back to my List of Mikes. It's a big one. There are twenty-two of them in all. It might seem a daunting task to rate and rank all twenty-two, from dumpy Mikes to middle-class Mikes to top-drawer Mikes, but it's necessary. Character traits are the main criteria for a list of this kind with a dash of physical traits mixed in. I'm not going to give a Mike of admirable inner qualities top billing if he looks like Freddy Krueger. There has to be a balance of mind and body.

When it comes to character traits, I like to go with the Boy Scouts. If you recall your Boy Scout Law: a Scout is Trustworthy, Loyal, etc., etc., ending with Clean and Reverent. It's as good a guidepost as any and better than most. Given all that, my model Mike is trustworthy, friendly, clean in mind and body, as well as kind and brave by nature. An unattainable ideal, you say? Perhaps. But you have to set the bar somewhere, and by setting it high you almost always get a nice bell curve. I call it the "The 10-80-10 Rule for Homo Sapiens." Place a set of rigorous standards before a group of people and 10% will inevitably rise like cream to the surface, 10% will just as surely settle like undissolved sugar to the bottom, and the rest will mix in the middle. Mike Agostino is cream. Trustworthy? You bet. Clean in mind and body? Absolutely. Even with his annoying trait of viewing himself as God's gift to women, he's still a candidate for the top spot.

In large lists like these, I find it easier to nail the top and bottom first before dealing with the middle. Number twenty-two is a no-brainer: Mike Petrovich, my next door neighbor. Trustworthy? No way. Clean in mind and body? Nyet. Petrovich is a fifty-ish, ratty old hippie, who is a poster child for welfare abuse. Trapped in the sixties and reeking permanently of too many doobies, this Mike sits last on my coveted Mike List. Next up from the bottom is a little tougher. In the vast scheme of Mikes, it is probably one of the five Mikes who stand around me warming up for the Friday Night Softball Game.

Left field is my position and Jack's Bar & Grill is the name of my team. Jack's serves up beer and wine and burgers to the young and restless. Jack's is neither owned by Jack or run by Jack but rather owned and operated by—you guessed it—Mike. Mike Dupree is a thick, swarthy, Fred Flintstone-looking character who holds court daily from behind the bar overlooking three pool tables, a shuffle board, numerous pin-ball machines, and two flat-screen TVs dedicated to sports. It's an all-around nice joint. Jack's Bar & Grill sponsors our softball team, which is made up of twenty and thirty-something patrons like myself and managed by Big Mike Dupree.

The moniker of "Big Mike" is key here. A softball team with five Mikes can lead to confusion and untimely errors: "Throw it to Mike!" (OK, but which Mike?) "Next inning, go in for Mike." (Swell, take your pick.) "Hey, Mike, get your head in the game!" (Fine, but whose head we talking about?) You can see the dilemma. Shortstop, second base and first base are all Mikes, so a 6-4-3 double play is Mike to Mike to Mike.

To solve this dilemma, we did what all good ball players did: we created nicknames.

The manager Mike Dupree is Big Mike, which fits since his son the shortstop is a feisty, five-foot-seven lad nicknamed Little Mike (or Mikey). Second baseman Mike Sakamoto, another diminutive but sure-handed fielder, is simply called Sako. The first baseman Mike Simpson, who is the only black guy on the team and easily our best player, has the distinct honor of being called Mike, probably because no one has the guts to mess with his name. And finally there is Mike Murphy, or Murph as we call him, our pitcher. Murph is pushing forty, the elder of the tribe, an Irish-American who plays a little too hard on and off the field. He favors bottled beer, meat and potatoes, and has an irksome habit of losing his cool and getting into fights, especially when he's been drinking.

Now why do all Irish-American men want to fight, especially when they've had too much to drink? Notre Dame doesn't call themselves the "Loving Irish" or even the "Friendly Irish." Nope. They're the "Fighting Irish" and for good reason. It has to be some sort of IRA, Jimmy Cagney, permanent-chip-on-your-shoulder thing going on with their genes. Check it out for yourself.

So there you go—the five Mikes. Each one a credit to his gender. And where they fit, exactly, on my Mike List is yet to be determined. I'm still working on it and it takes time to get it right. Just like no wine before it's time, there will be no list before its time. So, while I harvest and crush the grapes for my bottle of Mikes, let me give you a recap of the game.

It didn't go well.

Though it started out just fine.

It was a cool summer evening, fresh and clear, just perfect for a softball game. The stands were lightly populated with wives, girlfriends, and a smattering of kids. We took the field at 8pm, and in the first inning we set them down one-two-three with three infield grounders—Mikey to Mike twice and Sako to Mike once. Both teams played good defense, and when we came to the fifth inning the score was tied 1 to 1. That's when the wheels came off. Our pitcher Murph walked the first batter and then another. That was followed by three consecutive hits, and after a grand slam that cleared the bases, the score was suddenly 7 to 1.

I stood in left field, hands on knees in the ready position, and shouted encouragement at Murph. He walked the next batter on four straight pitches. A couple of the pitches looked like strikes from where I was standing and our coach in the dugout—Big Mike—certainly thought so. He started yelling at the umpire. Big Mike was joined by a group of his cronies in the stands. These were professional beer-drinkers who hung out at Jack's every day, shot the bull with Big Mike, and considered it their patriotic duty to get drunk and come out to the games so they could loudly razz the umpire and opposing players. The umpire quickly took umbrage and stopped the game to warn Big Mike and his cronies to pipe down. They did, but it was only a momentary lull.

Meanwhile, Murph's Irish blood was beginning to boil. He walked another batter, and with two on and no outs, he got a grounder to shortstop. It was a tailor-made double play ball, but Sako dropped the feed from Mikey and everybody was safe. Murph snapped the throw back from Sako and stared daggers at him for a moment before stepping back on the mound. A hulking left-hander with a big smirk on his face settled into the box and Murph leaned forward and got ready to pitch.

(In case you're not familiar with slow-pitch softball, pitching a softball under-handed is similar to pitching horseshoes. You stand feet together, hands out in front of you, and step forward swinging your pitching hand back then forwards. Done properly, the ball rises in a slow arc, peaking at about eight to ten feet, and drops right behind home plate with hollow, cork-like sound.

After that, it's up to the umpire to call it a strike depending on his eyesight and mood.)

As described, Murph strode forward and lofted a pitch that landed squarely behind home plate. "Ball!" called the umpire. This was immediately followed by loud complaints from Big Mike and our fans in the stands (even some of the wives joined in): "Where'd that miss, Blue?"—"Terrible call!"—"Come on, ump!"—"Jeez Christ, wan-him to put it onna tee?"—"For crying out loud!" But the umpire ignored the catcalls and exchanged smirks with the batter. Murph took the throw back and glared at the umpire, glared at the batter, and glared up at the unfair gods in the heavens.

From the outfield I could see Murph's jaw muscles tightening. He was about to go tilt, but to my surprise he composed himself, stepped back on the mound, and lofted another pitch. "Ball two!" called the umpire. This triggered more complaints from Big Mike and our fans, but louder this time and bordering on lewd and crude, and even our first baseman Mike Simpson (who hardly ever showed emotion) raised both his arms up and dropped them in disgust. Murph walked halfway to home plate demanding to know where the pitch missed. Big Mike came out of the dugout and demanded the same. The umpire stood in a regal pose and ordered Murph back to the mound and Big Mike back to the dugout. "Outside!" he yelled, gesturing with his hand that the pitch had been outside. "Now play ball!"

Murph regarded the umpire with a look of disgust. Our catcher lobbed the ball back to Murph but he ignored it and let in roll past him as though it were a rotten apple. The players in the other dugout laughed at this and Murph shot them a menacing glance, then he looked straight at the hulking left-hander standing in the batter's box and said, "You got a six run lead— swing the fucking bat!" The hulkster, bat on shoulder, unfazed and still smirking, replied "Just pitch it over, little man, and I'll swing at it." At that, howls erupted from his teammates in the other dugout, and they came up against the chain link fence and yelled out at Murph: "Whoaaa!"—"Look out, Jerry, he's gonna bean you!"—"Come on, Pitch, give him somethin' to hit."—"Yeah, Pitch, get one over—then duck and run!"

The umpire shouted over at their dugout to "Hold it down!" and they did so, snickering and mumbling as they sat back down. "Play ball!" yelled the ump again, and he looked out at Murph like a cop waiting on an errant pedestrian, gesturing for him to return to the mound. Murph picked up the rotten apple of a softball and stepped mechanically backwards to the mound. I'd seen this before—he'd gone into RoboCop mode, the part where ED-209 malfunctions, stops taking orders, and starts indiscriminately shooting up people—and his next step was predictable. In his utter disdain for the umpire and all that umpires stood for in this world, Murph swung his arm back like an erector set and tossed a flat and oh-so-fat pitch to the plate. The hulkster, bent in his stance and smirking at Murph, crushed it for another grand slam.

The four baserunners laughed as they circled the bases, and their cheering teammates in the dugout rubbed it in with extra chili powder by taunting Murph. This had all the makings of a bench-clearing brawl, and I watched all the parts unfold from the outfield. Murph stared down each baserunner as they crossed home plate while our shortstop Little Mike shouted angrily at the opposing dugout. Big Mike went on a tirade and joined his son in yelling at the other team. Big Mike's cronies, now totally drunk and beyond repair, spit insults at the umpire and opposing team. The field umpire, who up to this point had kept a low profile, stuck his hands in his pockets and looked around nervously. Some of the wives in the stands gathered up their kids and hurried off.

Amidst the storm, the next batter strolled merrily to the plate. Somehow Murph had gotten the ball back and he watched the batter approach the plate, but before the batter reached the box, Murph launched a ridiculously high pitch—18 feet or more—that landed behind the umpire. "Time!" yelled the umpire, raising his hands. "No pitch!" Big Mike laughed at Murph's antics and sat back down in the dugout to see what happened next. We all waited to see what happened next. Murph took the return throw back from our catcher and glared over at the opposing dugout. They were taunting and baiting him. Something was said and he suddenly spun sideways and fired the ball at the chain link fence in front of their bench.

The players behind the fence jumped up and down like excited monkeys in a cage. The taunts and insults flew back and forth. I could only pick up tidbits, but Murph was yelling stuff at them like "Wanna piece of me!"—"Chickenshit!"—"Come on, let's go!" The field ump hustled over to their dugout to block their exit, but they were content to stay inside their cage and gleefully toss verbal turds back at Murph.

It was at this point, the point where peace and world order teetered on the brink, that I decided to do what any red-blooded American would do: I intervened. I walked towards the infield, towards the center of the strife where Mike Murphy stood hurling verbal hand grenades at the opposition, and attempted to quell the conflict. Afterall, Murph was a friend of mine—not at the top of my Mike List, or even at the bottom, but in the middle, a solid eighty-percenter—and maybe he'd listen to me.

"Hey, Murph!" I shouted as I neared the infield. "Murph, Murph, Murph! Shut up! ... Murph!" There was no response; he was too busy going ballistic. I walked in closer. "Murph! Murph!" I shouted at the top of my voice. There was still no response. I stepped in even closer and tried again. "Hey, Mike, shut the hell up!" The three Mikes in the infield jerked their heads towards me. Mike Simpson—the big and powerful Mike Simpson—yelled from first base, "Who ya tellin' to shut up?" I quickly backed up, pointing at Murph, and lamely replied, "I meant Mike—Murph... Someone needs to calm him down."

Simpson dismissed me with a wave of his hand and I retreated back to the outfield, my little Operation Urgent Fury a failure. I took a knee and glanced over at Scott in left-center field. He sat in the semi-darkness with his arms around his knees and returned my glance, shaking his head like a guy waiting for the powder keg to blow. He'd resigned himself to fate. I did the same and took a knee to watch what happened next.

In short order, the umpires ejected Big Mike and Murph from the game. In a rage, Big Mike threw a bat onto the field that almost hit our third baseman. Murph remained on the mound calling out the entire opposing team, but he was getting no takers. One of Big Mike's cronies threw an empty beer bottle onto the field. Both umps quickly consulted, threw up their hands, and called the game a forfeit. At that, Sako-Mike picked up second base and tossed it into center field, while Mikey launched his glove past third base and over the dugout (easily his best throw of the night).

Scott and I exchanged glances, got up, and slowly walked in. By the time we reached our dugout, park security had arrived and it was announced that our entire team—Jack's Bar & Grill, players, coach, and cronies—had been ejected from the park.

Let me repeat this so it fully sinks in: *our entire team was ejected from the park*.

I have never been ejected from a game in my life let alone been on a team—a team deemed so rotten—that it needed to be ejected from a park. It was a first for me. I looked around in disbelief (and a growing disgust). Murph had picked up the thrown bat and brandished it like a battle sword. Big Mike chased after the umpires who were fortunately faster than he was. And the other Mikes—Sako, Mikey, and even Simpson—were out for blood and looked like they wanted to fight someone.

I calmly walked into the dugout and began to change my shoes. I wasn't sure if there'd be a fight or not. As a teammate, I was morally obligated to back my Mikes up in any fracas, but as far as I was concerned, all my Mikes could burn in hell. This was an embarrassment, an utter embarrassment, like getting evicted from your apartment for being a deadbeat. But I waited to see. One of the security people yelled out that he'd just called the police. This had an immediate sobering affect. Everybody associated with Jack's Bar & Grill—players, wives, girlfriends, cronies, even all the Mikes—quickly began gathering up their belongings.

We followed security out the gate. Big Mike led the fool's parade like a martyred hero. Scott and I brought up the rear, scanning the parking lot for squad cars. I figured we were now, probably, suspended from the league. No more Friday Night Softball. I shook my head in disgust.

"Going over to Jack's for a beer?" asked Scott.

It was the voice of reason. It was tradition to go to Jack's after the game to celebrate victory or drown our sorrows with a few beers. It was why we picked the Friday Night League in the first place, to play a game and afterwards drink beer, hang out, chew the fat, and let the eagle fly. And Jack's was a great place to be on a Friday night girl-wise.

"Sure, why not," I replied.

"Cool," said Scott. "A regular goat rodeo out there, huh. Cops'll probably be here any second. Better jam." I agreed and we hurried off to our cars.

Jack's was in full swing. There was a growing crowd that pressed against the bar and filled a number of tables. Two of the pool tables were in use and a game of shuffleboard was underway. A rock song played on the jukebox while the two TVs carried the Giants game with the sound turned down. I breathed in the familiar aroma of beer, burgers, fries, and pool chalk and smiled. *My people.* There's nothing like the warm feeling you get when you walk into a friendly, crowded bar.

I spied Scott and our right fielder Billy at a table already drinking beer. I caught Scott's eye, giving him the point and two-fingered hand salute for "do you want another beer?" and he nodded yes. I squeezed in-between two regulars at the bar and attempted to get Patty's attention. Patty was Big Mike's wife, a short, stout, penny-pinching, earth-mother type, who worked the bar on game nights until her husband came back. She saw me and headed over, throwing her hand up in a stop sign before she reached me, and said, "I already heard the story, don't want to hear no more. What'll it be? A Bud?" I threw up three fingers for three Buds, and she spun around to work my order. I paid for the beers and sat down with Scott and Billy, placing a fresh beer in front of each.

They were talking about the game and I let them talk, commenting here and there with a shake of the head, a grunt, or a one-word reply.

"That ump was brutal," said Billy.

"Uh huh."

"Can you believe Murph throwing the ball at their dugout?" said Scott.

"Unbelievable."

There was a commotion at the doorway and we turned around to see what it was. Big Mike entered to great fanfare, yelling, "Banned in Boston!" at the top of his voice, which elicited cheers and laughter from the Faithful. "Are they gonna kick you outta the league?" shouted someone at the bar. "Over my dead body!" boomed Big Mike. "If they do they'll owe me five hundred dollars. The crooks! Give us our money back. We'll go play in Mountain View. Sunnyvale can kiss my ass!" Big Mike's retinue included the rest of the Mikes—Little Mike, Murph-Mike, Sako-Mike, and Simpson-Mike—and they filed in from behind like conquering heroes, soaking up the cheers.

I tuned them out. (That's it—my list of Mikes requires re-visiting. I'm tempted to create a sub-category of Mikes. The Sioux have their Contraries, the Hindu their Untouchables, and even the Klingon Empire has a dishonored caste that's shunned by respectable Klingon warriors. I'll have a Mutant-Mike category, Mikes unfit for normal commerce, Mikes unworthy of fortune and glory, and these Mikes coming through the door will be its charter members.)

But soon there was something better to think about. Three women sat at a nearby table—two brunettes and one blonde, mid-twenties, attractive, career types—and one of the brunettes, the gem of the lot, made eye contact with me. The game was afoot. Scott and I started playing pool, which brought us into closer proximity to their table. I lined up a shot just across from Miss Eye Contact and glanced up right before I stroked the cue ball. She watched me. I missed the shot and walked over to my beer, took a long drink, and looked back at her. We made eye contact again and smiled at each other. That made it official: she was interested. Somehow, in this sweaty, noisy bar filled with male animals of all stripes, this raven-haired beauty had singled me out.

Now why do all attractive women get to call the shots? It has to be some sort of Kathleen Turner-femme-fatale thing going on with their genes. They instinctively know they have the power. Just look at Delilah and Cleopatra—both great beauties in their day. And I bet not once—not once—did they ever sit at home waiting for a guy to call. Nope, they simply gave some dude of their choosing *the look* and, voilà, he was theirs. It's widespread. Check it out for yourself.

Scott, my trusty wingman, struck up a conversation with the blonde and soon we were playing partners against the blonde and my brunette. In-between shots, the two stood together and watched us, occasionally chatting with their friend at the table. At close quarters like this, I was able to make a full assessment of My Brunette. She was fair-skinned with dark eyebrows and a sprinkling of freckles across her nose. A Debra Winger type. She wore tight-in-the-hips slacks that accentuated her curved bottom and slim waist, and her short-sleeved blouse exposed her smooth, slightly tanned arms. Her attire was attractive but professional, and all of them had probably gone bar-hopping right from work. Her blouse had an extra button unfastened, one that probably stayed buttoned at work, which revealed more of her smooth skin and caused the eye to run from her neck to her inviting cleavage, especially when she bent over to shoot pool.

Without a doubt, she had a legitimate shot at cracking the top five of my Dark-haired Beauty List which, from first to last, went Kelly LeBrock, a young Liz Taylor (circa 1952), Val at work, Debra Winger, and Eva Bomb (a.k.a. Sarah Feingold) who fronted for a local punk band called Raven Cloud.

Scott and I handily won the pool game and we quickly started another one. In a quick tête-à-tête between Scott and the Blonde, a bet was proposed—losers would buy the drinks—and we all agreed to the stakes while I got ready to break. Their friend at the table got up, announcing she had to leave (she had work in the morning), and she hugged her friends and wished them "good luck." That settled the math and left us to our game (and the game within the game).

About halfway through the game, I missed my shot and the Brunette, anxious to take her turn, brushed up against me as I turned around. I breathed in her aroma, a spring breeze with a hint of vanilla, and rubbed against her smooth, warm arm. She shot and made her ball. Standing behind her, admiring her form, I said, "Nice shot." While still leaning over her shot, her shoulder-length hair swept to one side, she smiled back at me and replied, "Thanks" (a husky-purr kind of "Thanks").

A cheer went up from around the bar (the Giants must have scored) but I ignored it and watched from behind as she scoped out her next shot. Her weight shifted nicely within her wonderfully tight slacks, and she settled on her shot and leaned over in front of me to line it up. I held my breath in admiration. She shot and missed, stood up and turned around, and stuck her lower lip out in a mock pout. It was warm inside the bar and I pulled out my tucked-in jersey, giving her a sympathetic shrug in return.

It was a perfectly messy game with lots of missed shots, but finally only the 8-ball remained for the win. The Brunette got first crack at the 8-ball—a long rail shot—but missed. "Almost," I said, oozing compassion. That left a cross-pocket shot on the 8-ball for the win and Scott chalked up his cue and took aim. It was a medium-difficult shot but one that I'd seen Scott make many times before, but Scott—a man after my own heart, a man who understood the big picture—slyly tanked the shot, leaving the Blonde an easy shot for the win. She sank it and did a quick shimmy-dance of celebration while the Brunette clapped with her fingertips.

"White wine coolers, right?" I asked. They nodded triumphantly. I glanced at Scott, arching my brow in knowing amusement. "Bud?" He tipped his ball cap back on his head. "Yep." Orders taken, I headed for the bar on a sweet mission from god.

The bar was packed two deep. Patty was still the bartender and I scanned for Big Mike. He was at the end of the bar in loud conversation with his sect of cronies including all the Mikes from the team. The topic of conversation was the game. They huddled closely together, beers in hand, gesticulating up and down, east and west, talking over one another in heated agreement. I had no desire to get sucked into this beer-soaked vortex but the closest opening was right next to them, so I worked in stealthily, like a Navy SEAL, and squeezed in covertly between two patrons. I flagged down a harried-looking Patty, who was obviously pissed-off at her husband's dereliction of duty, and gave her my order.

While I waited for my order, I glanced up at the TV (the Giants led 6 to 2 in the top of the ninth) and tried to ignore The Big Mike Show. But it was impossible. Accusations and recriminations bombarded my air space" "Sunnyvale can kiss my ass!" (He was still on the kiss-my-ass theme.)—"They're after us ever since we won league last year."—"That's right!"—"That one asshole ump was friends with their team!"—"That's right!"—"They're not getting away with this!"—"No way."—"I'm a business man in this city and they can't screw us over like that."—"That's right!"

Patty finally appeared, balancing two beers and two wine coolers in her hands, and I paid and moved to make my getaway.

"Isn't that right, Tim" yelled Big Mike. My cover was blown.

"That's right!" I yelled back. But before he could rope me in, I corralled my drinks and made my escape. Their nonsense had degenerated into victimhood. Set upon by the Man, martyrs for the Cause, they had battled the System—they, the happy few—and in noble strife fought the good fight against tyranny and injustice. It was a regular Democratic Convention filled with downtrodden Mikes, the discriminated-against Mikes, and the workers-of-the-world-unite Mikes. Screw them all. A pox on the House of Mikes.

I blocked all Mikes from my thoughts and headed for warmer climates. There she sat at the table, a vision in dark hair, waiting for her drink—and for me. I stopped to deliver drinks to Scott and the Blonde, who had started their own pool game. That left Debra and an empty seat. I sat down opposite her and pushed the wine cooler across to her waiting hand. I lifted my bottled beer, clicked her glass in a salute, and took a drink. I removed my baseball cap and tousled my hair, then set the cap back on my head in a happy-go-lucky pose.

She said thanks in that same husky-purr and smiled grandly, showing off her perfect white teeth. It was a disarming smile that changed her face the way sunlight changed the shape and color of an orchid. Her chin dimpled slightly with her smile and her green eyes sparkled. (Was it eyes or smile? What was more captivating? I know some guys are struck first by a woman's legs, others by her breasts. But above the shoulders, what are the chart-topping features? Probably the eyes and eyebrows followed by the lips and smile. Next was the hair, especially if it's a lush peppercorn like hers...)

"Did you guys play a game today?" she asked, pointing at my jersey that read "Jack's Bar & Grill."

"Yeah," I replied. She raised her eyebrows to hear more but a play-by-play of this evening's debacle was not in my game plan. "Wasn't pretty," I tossed off... "Did you guys come from work?"

"Yes. Came over from H.P."

"In Palo Alto?" (She nodded yes.) "I work at Sun."

"Sun? Really?" She leaned forward and I caught another hint of vanilla in the air. "I know some folks over at Sun," she said. "Do you know Cindy Ferrin in Sales?" (I shook my head.) "Or Cheryl Hawes?—I think she's also in Marketing." (Nope, didn't know them.) "I also have a cousin who works over there. Larry Parker."

That name rang a bell and I racked my brain to place it. "Larry Parker? I think so... Does he work off San Antonio?"

"Yes!" she exclaimed, jumping slightly from her chair. "Shaves his head and wears a goatee."

"Yeah, I know him. Works in Shipping." (I knew her cousin. We were practically family.) I leaned forward and offered her my hand. "My name is Tim, by the way."

She extended her hand and we shook. Her hand was warm and pleasantly moist. "Hi, Tim... I'm Michelle."

Michelle. What a wonderful name. Musical. European. Michelle my Belle. Michelle my dark-haired beauty. A loud, piercing cackle erupted from across the room, breaking my reverie. It was Big Mike and his cronies, and it was followed by their annoying laughter. I closed my eyes to block them out and opened them again upon Michelle, upon the green eyes, the freckled nose, and the tanned smooth arms. *Michelle.* It fit her.

"What a beautiful name."

"Thank you," she smiled, showing her perfect teeth and her slightly dimpled chin… "But my friends call me Mike."

An Old Song

The music exploded—a beat by itself, forceful and steady, like the hammering of a well-oiled machine.

Schhhump—Schhhump!

The women cheered wildly and clapped to the methodical beat.

Schhhump—Schhhump!

The male stripper marched across the stage moving his arms and hips to the beat.

Schhhump—Schhhump!

The women cheered and clapped. The dancer worked the beat. An electric guitar flipped in and out like machine gun fire. Then came a singer, high-pitched and raunchy—

Now everybody
Have you heard
If you're in the game
Then the stroke's the word
(Da-da-da-da-da, shot a guitar)
Don't take no rhythm
(Da-da-da-da-da)
Don't take no style
(Da-da-da-da-da)
Got a thirst for killin'
Grab your vile

The male stripper spun and gyrated across the stage, and when the chorus came he thrust out his pelvis with the lyrics:

Stroke me—Stroke me!

"Stroke—stroke!" shouted the women in unison.

Stroke me—Stroke me!

"Stroke—stroke!" they shouted, throwing up their hands.

With legs apart the dancer thrust forward, then thrust again as though he were trying to mount a horse. He wore black bikini trunks that bulged in the crotch, and his tanned skin was sprinkled with dots that sparkled under the lights. He dropped to his knees at the front of the stage, facing the audience, and worked the beat, moving his arm piston-like from his crotch to his chin. In the front row of tables, women leaned out towards him holding dollar bills in their hands, screaming to get his attention. One of the women jumped out of her chair and stuck a bill in his bikini trunks. He leaned down and kissed her.

Stroke me—Stroke me!

"Stroke—stroke!" cheered the women.

Others quickly followed her up. Each stuck a bill into his bikini trunks and got their kiss. One heavy-set woman shoved her dollar bill into his trunks and tried to slip her whole hand in, but the dancer spun away in time and got to his feet. He shook his finger at her, playfully scolding her for being naughty.

Stroke me—Stroke me!

"Stroke—stroke!" shouted the women, cheering and laughing.

At a table farther back sat three young women and an older woman. One of the younger women—Jackie—turned and looked at her grandmother. Her grandmother was seventy-seven today, and she sat in her chair holding her purse, still wearing the sweater that had been her birthday present, with a look of dismay on her face. Jackie nudged her girlfriend Elly and had her glance over at her grandmother. They looked at each other and shared a laugh.

"Stroke—stroke!" they shouted with all the other women.

The male stripper lay prone on the stage doing push-ups to the beat. The muscles along his arms rippled as he worked—Schhhump-Schhhump!—his back glistening with sweat—Stroke-stroke!—his pelvis thrusting deeply into the invisible body beneath him. The crowd of women swayed and clapped—they were that body—and shouted ecstatically as he thrust down upon them.

Abruptly it stopped—the beat, the song—and the stripper dropped to his chest exhausted and smiled up at his audience.

The women went crazy. Their cheers thundered out and shook the room. They wanted more. "More! More!" they chanted.

The M.C. broke in loudly over his microphone. More was coming, he assured them, but first he wanted to know whether they were having a good time. ("Yes!" screamed the crowd.) Were they feeling all right, he asked. ("Yes!" they shouted.) Were they ready for more? ("Yes!" they cheered.) How much more, he wanted to know, and he spread his hands a foot apart. "This much more?" he asked. ("No!") He spread them farther—"This much more?" ("No!") He spread them even farther—"This much more?" ("No!") He flapped his arms out as far as they would go and threw his head back—"THIS MUCH MORE!" ("Yes!") The women screamed raucously and whooped it up ("Yesss!—Woohoo!")

On cue, the music started and the next stripper suddenly appeared on stage.

It was Wednesday night at Orphan Annie's. Male Stripper Night. For the rest of the week the night club was a dance spot for couples and cruising singles. Except on Wednesday. Wednesday was Male Stripper Night and Orphan Annie's closed the doors and raised the cover charge and brought out more tables and created an extra woman's restroom. And tonight, just like every Wednesday night, it was first come first serve for the tables with a waiting line outside the door. The place was packed.

"Having a good time, Gram?" Jackie asked her grandmother.

Her grandmother couldn't hear over the music. She sat in her chair watching the stage with that same look of dismay on her face, which was more a grimace than it was a look of bemusement or even disgust. It was subtler than that; it was a grimace lightly fixed and creased with chagrin, the sort of look one might give to a particularly silly-acting child up past its bedtime or to a bad movie one had paid good money to see.

"Hey, Gram!"

But again she didn't hear. The music was too loud.

Jackie nudged Elly who, in turn, nudged their friend Fredricka, who was nicknamed Fred. Fred leaned close-in to Jackie's grandmother and yelled, "Hey, Bea!" and got her attention. She directed Bea's eyes over to Jackie.

"Are you having a good time?" Jackie asked again, this time mouthing the words so her grandmother could read her lips.

Bea smiled sarcastically. She raised her hand off her purse and twirled her finger.

The girls laughed. They laughed affectionately, with a hip pre-eminence, as young women will at a much older woman whom they are fond of but who is also hopelessly, wonderfully out of it. Bea smiled back good-naturedly.

"Why don't you take your sweater off and relax?" Fred asked her.

"I'm fine," Bea assured her. She took a sip of her Bloody Mary and set it back down. It was a weak drink.

It had been Jackie's idea to bring her grandmother to Orphan Annie's for her birthday. Elly and Fred had helped her carry out the plan. They told Bea they were taking her to "see a show" and not to worry—she'd love it. But Bea was reluctant at first; she didn't particularly like shows, and just a quiet evening spent with her granddaughter at home was more her idea of entertainment. The girls had finally persuaded her with gentle yet persistent pleas which, as Jackie knew, never failed to work on her grandmother. They loaded up in Bea's four door sedan, with Elly following in her car, and drove up the peninsula. It was a good half hour drive and fifteen minutes into the trip Bea complained, "If I'd known it was this far..." But the girls kidded her—"It's too late now," said Jackie. "You're committed." So Bea sat back, stoically concurring, and rode on with a bemused expression. She had no idea what they were up to but she didn't want to ruin their surprise, so she accepted the situation, reminding herself that there was no sense in shutting the barn door after the horse had bolted. She could see they were excited; Jackie seemed on the verge of a giggling fit, and Fred, whose husband was home baby-sitting their two kids for the evening, fidgeted next to her like someone who'd just been let out of prison.

"Want another drink?" Bea was asked. She looked over at the girls. One of the dancers stood next to Jackie. He wore nothing more than a leather vest and tight-fitting bikini trunks, and he stood waiting for their order with a drink tray in his hand. No thanks, she said, she was fine.

The girls ordered for themselves then had the dancer lean down so they could whisper in his ear.

Bea looked back up at the stage. The dancer there had stripped down to his trunks. Just like the first one, she thought. It was old hat now. What wasn't old hat was the incredibly loud music. It hurt her head.

The music stopped and the male stripper bowed to the wild cheers. Abruptly there was a kind of quiet and Bea sighed at the sudden reprieve.

A face stared into hers. She leaned back and focused on it. It was the dancer who had taken their order and he leaned in closer to her, smiling. He looked the same age as her grandson.

"Yes?"

He smiled professionally, like a car salesman. "I hear it's your birthday, little lady," he said.

"Yes, it is."

"Well, you know"—he winked momentarily at the girls—"we give out a special present on birthdays. It's called a Whopper Kiss."

"I don't..."

"Now a Whopper Kiss is a kiss that lasts as many seconds as you are old—thirty years, thirty seconds, like that. How old are you?" ("Seventy-seven," said Jackie.) "Seventy-seven!" he cried, staggering back in animated shock. The girls laughed. "That means seventy-seven seconds. Jeez! What a kiss. You ready there, little lady?" And he leaned in even closer towards her, smiling professionally.

"That's all right, young man," she said, putting up her hand. "I'd rather not."

"Come on, Gram," said Jackie. "Yeah, come on, Bea," appealed the others. "You have to—come on."

The dancer shook his head fatefully. "You heard 'em, Bea. How 'bout it?" He smiled and winked at her. "If you don't, I'll have to tell everyone here it's your birthday and you won't kiss me. I will."

Bea looked at the girls. "Come on, come on," they kept saying. She looked back at the dancer. He smiled that professional smile and waited. She raised an eyebrow and frowned, telling herself that it was easier sometimes just to plow around a stump instead of fighting it.

"Okay," she said in surrender. "But wait—just a short, nice kiss. I'm not up to seventy-seven seconds. Just a short, nice kiss and we'll call it even."

"A deal," said the dancer, smiling. He leaned down to her and she offered up her puckered lips coolly. They kissed perfunctorily and parted. The dancer raised back up and smiled. "All right," he said, bobbing his head. "Happy birthday, little lady. Hope you have many more." He winked at the girls and shimmied off with his tray to take more orders.

The girls cheered and applauded her, laughing together. Bea managed a sporting smile.

A new song started and another dancer began his striptease, and Bea waited until it was done to leave. She sat and waited, her head aching fully now from the music, holding her purse firmly in her lap with the sweater she had gotten for her birthday still wrapped around her shoulders and that same lightly-fixed grimace on her face. The crowd of women cheered and clapped, her granddaughter among them, and Bea waited. And when that sudden and brief reprieve finally came between songs she leaned over to the girls.

"I have to get going," she said. "It's way past my bedtime. You can all get home in Elly's car, right?"

"What?" objected Jackie. "You're not going?" The others joined in, entreating her to stay. But Bea was firm—she had to go, it was past her bedtime. She thanked them for her birthday party and kissed her granddaughter on the cheek. "Don't stay out too late now," she reminded them, and she patted Fred warmly on the shoulder and left. The girls called out "Happy birthday!" to her and watched her walk out.

"I don't think she liked it too much," said Elly with a chuckle. Jackie agreed, "Yeah... well, you know, she's kind of old-fashioned." They all nodded knowingly then turned quickly back to the stage as the music started again.

It was brisk out. Bea crossed her arms and walked swiftly to her car and got in. After starting the car up, she turned on the heat, buckled up, and drove off. She'd take 280 home, she decided. It was longer but she liked the drive much better than she did the Bayshore Freeway which was just a straight line of asphalt.

She sat erect with both hands on the wheel until she was through the city and onto the freeway. Once on 280, she relaxed and sat back. It was a wide, expansive highway that curled through the foothills and she felt safe on it. The hills were dark on both sides and the road empty, and she accelerated up to sixty and kept it there. She turned her hearing-aid back up and listened to the quiet.

Her head felt better already. She clicked off the heater and partially opened the vents to allow the outside air to filter in. It smelled of nightfall and green hills, and she breathed in the smell as one would the aroma of a homemade pie, and smiled. It reminded her of the Midwest—that smell—of the farm she lived on as a kid and of the lake where her and her husband once owned a cabin. And like an old melody that pops into your head years later, her mind hummed along with this deep-rooted memory:

The lake... In the morning it possessed a fragrance, a fragrance of clear water and trees, of dew on the ground and early sunlight. Especially in the summertime. But it was autumn there now. Back home, autumn had its own smell to it, not like here— not like California. It was a scent separate unto itself and distinct from the other seasons, a tindery, brash kind of smell, pungent with the odors of burning leaves and cooked cranberries. Here in California the seasons all blended together, but there was no snow to shovel or stifling humidity or mosquitoes to contend with and she liked it here. It was pleasant. But occasionally, like now for instance, she missed the turning-over of the seasons and the unique set of virtues each one brought with it. Like winter, skating on frozen ponds, and the way ice crystallized on the windows in the morning. Or summer and the smell after a surprise rainfall and the taste of walleye. And in spring that sort of special satisfaction you got for the order of things when you saw the first blossom.

Len...

She is home. She wipes her hands on her apron—a yellow apron embroidered with blue flowers—and steps back from the stove to listen. Her son is practicing the piano in the front room, her daughter is setting the dinner table, and there—the garage door just closed. She hears Rowdy barking playfully at her husband as he walks across the backyard and opens the screen door. It slams noisily behind him. "Hey, Jo, I'm home," he calls out in that voice of his, gravelly and robust. "In here," she answers. And he appears instantly and stands before her, a once lean frame turning handsomely stout, tucked in faded work clothes with a fedora pushed back on his head and a smile, that ingratiating, affable smile, creasing his tired face. "How was work?" she asks. "Good day today. Good day," he replies with a wink. "Made lots of money, lots of money. Your ship's coming in, Jo. I saw it today. It's coming in." She soaks up his affectionate teasing with a smile—"Oh, Len." He comes up next to her and gives her a short kiss, and she smells the pleasant mix of beer and tobacco on his breath and the heavy masculine odor of dried sweat beneath his clothes. "What's cookin'?" She opens a pot and shows him—"Chicken and dumplings," she says. "Mmm, my favorite," he tells her with a hug. "I'll wash up"—he starts out of the kitchen—"I heard a good one today, but not for the kids. I'll tell you later"—and the "I'll tell you later" trails out the swinging door with him as he heads for the bathroom. She sets the lid back on the pot and steps back from the stove. The kitchen is empty but alive at the same time. Her son is practicing the piano in the front room, her daughter is setting the dinner table, and she can hear the sound of running water in the bathroom where Len is washing up...

The image ended, as though clipped suddenly, and she sat in dazed silence.

The vividness stunned her. She had not experienced an image like that, so clear and precise, for years and it overwhelmed her, yet she continued to drive on, steadily, mechanically, like someone who continues to brush their teeth after witnessing an apparition in the sink bowl. It was as if a jolt of electricity had popped on an old projector in her brain, bringing its brittle reel to life before shorting out again. How marvelous, she thought. How completely wonderful. She savored the magically eerie feeling that had come over her, tingling at the vibrant air and the fluorescent quality of things within the car. She felt blessed.

The memory of Len—his face, his fedora, even his pet name for her ("Jo")—was still fresh in her mind, and like a firefly cupped in her hands she was reluctant to let it go. To think of Len was to think of back home, she realized. They embodied each other, like a president and his era, and she couldn't think of one without the other. *Back home... Len...* And when he died she left. When he died there was only an empty house and an empty bed, a chair he used to sit in, a fireplace he once stoked. And outdoors there was a country redolent with him, whose harshness and beauty, whose robust and varied temperament only served to remind her of her loss, and it was all too much for her so she went away. She went away and came to California, to her children and grandchildren, and started a new life, lighting a candle instead of cursing the darkness.

She stretched her back and refocused on the highway in front of her and lost her train of thought for a moment. But she found it again, that same old melody, once forgotten, and hummed it back to life as she sailed between the dark foothills, pushing a tape cartridge into the cassette player to help her along. She hit rewind and waited. It was her one and only cassette tape in the car. Her grandson had recorded all her favorite music (Lawrence Welk, Dick Contino, Don Ho, Ray Conniff) and put it on this one tape for her, and she always rewound it to the beginning whenever she played it because the first song was her special favorite.

The tape ended its rewind and she hit play. The volume, as always, was set low, sufficient to appreciate the music. She didn't believe you had to blast music to enjoy it; instead it should be subtle and enhancing like a fresh-brewed cup of coffee with your morning paper. And when the music began—an orchestra of violins accompanied by a chorus of voices in pleasant harmony— she listened with a kind of effortless care, allowing it to mingle unobtrusively with her thoughts.

Somewhere, my love
There will be songs to sing
Although the snow
Covers the hope of spring

She smiled to herself, glad that she was miles away from that loud music and that roomful of screaming women. Kids today— it was all about sex. Just listen to their music (music tells you everything). Nowadays, love meant sex, a good love life meant a good sex life, and when the sex life fizzled out and dried up, so it seemed did the love. If anything had changed it was that. And she found that sad.

Someday, we'll meet again, my love
Someday, whenever the spring breaks through

Sex (or love-making, as she preferred to call it) had been a part of her love life, but just a part, just one savory ingredient in a long list of ingredients that went into a flavorful relationship. Love-making could be a slice of heaven but it certainly wasn't the be-all and end-all of existence. There was so much more to a happy love life. She used to comb Len's curly hair and go fishing with him, or drink and play cards together, or lie in bed at night with one another and just talk about everything and anything. Marriage back then simply meant one thing: that you were willing to carry on with the business of society, to work and raise a family and prepare for the next generation. A pleasant, inevitable task, she believed, and you took the bitter with the sweet. But today kids expected too much out of love; they expected it to be the sun and the moon, the answer to all their problems, not knowing that reaping is more difficult than sowing. And how unforgiving they were when it didn't work out that way—almost brutally unforgiving. She saw it with her own grandchildren and it made her sad. They built it up and tore it down, wore it out like a new fashion then went on to something different, acting like people with an incurable disease who try and cram a whole lifetime into the few years they have left.

She crinkled her nose as if to say, "What nonsense," and laughed at herself. She was just being an old fuddy-duddy, that's all. Kids weren't any different today than they had always been. Whenever she reminisced about the past too much it always happened, she became a hard old fuddy-duddy. You had to roll with the punches, she knew that. Kids were kids. One generation might be a little crazier than the next, but it always came around again and got back to normal. It all came out in the wash.

She nodded in agreement with herself and listened to Don Ho:

Someday, I know
You'll come back again to me
Till then my heart will be
Beyond the reef

An off-ramp sign, luminous green in the night, passed her by and she just caught its name. It was the exit she used to take when she visited her friend Helen, and the exit sign triggered a flood of memories. Helen had been the same age as she, but an invalid, and she would visit Helen twice a week and spend the day and sometimes the entire evening talking with her and playing dice and word games. Helen was a good friend, they had known each other a long time, and it had come as a shock to her when she died last summer. She'd been traveling, and when she got home she called Helen only to find out that she had died the week before. The week before... For a week Helen had been gone and she hadn't even known. Damn.

She sighed. It depressed her to think about that. It seemed like all her friends were dying off, especially the men. Sometimes she almost felt like the sole survivor of a shipwreck. And it wasn't just friends but her whole generation, her contemporaries, people like actors and politicians whom she had grown up with. Each day it was somebody else, somebody who had faded into retirement years ago, and she'd wonder what had become of them, and then one day she would pick up the paper and find out by reading their obituary. Just the other day it was Bennie Goodman. Jeez, it seemed like only yesterday she danced to his music in her black, patent-leather pumps. And now he was gone. It wasn't sad so much as it was simply unsettling. It was unsettling because this person was *her age*, but even more so because this person was part of an era, *her era,* whose allotted time was ending. That became more and more indisputable with each passing day. It was an irrefutable fact she could no longer argue with anymore, nor cared to. It simply unsettled her.

But it wasn't in her make-up to brood about things like that for long (afterall, you can't unscramble an egg), and her thoughts turned to other matters. She had a busy day tomorrow with lots to do. And the prospect of a busy day tomorrow pleased her. That was the key, she knew—keeping busy. Too many of her friends got old, retired, and withered on the wine from lack of—what?— from pure lack of staying busy, that's what. She played golf three times a week, worked in her yard, entertained friends, travelled, and even dated on occasion when she was lucky enough to meet a man her own age who wasn't already married or on life support (she chuckled to herself at this)... Things even got a bit harried at times, especially when it came to her grandkids, but she liked it that way. And strangely enough it paid off (she was sure of it); people told her she looked young for her age, and she felt young too. That wasn't to say she hadn't changed because she had. She needed more sleep nowadays, and her memory wasn't very good about some things, and then there was her back (but she had a wizard of a chiropractor for that).

Thinking about golf just now reminded her that she had a tee-time of 9:30 tomorrow morning.

Golf... what a wonderfully frustrating game, she mused as she drove through the quiet night. She loved it. Her second husband Martin had been a golf nut... *Martin...* Not only did he put love and romance back into her life but he had given her the gift of golf as well. It sounded silly to put it that way, she thought, but it was true. To Martin, golf had been like a religion of sorts, a creed of discipline and precision that he practiced daily and found great joy in. He approached golf the same way he approached everything he loved, with a devout exuberance. And when they met and fell in love ("Mom's autumn romance," her daughter called it), she was swept up in that exuberance like a country girl who's swept up and carried away by the zeal and mellifluousness of a gifted evangelist.

Martin had taught her the game of golf and they played together regularly (even when his health was failing they played). They would walk the golf course holding hands and flirting, and he would take time to explain to her the intricacies of the game, why she should use this club or that club, and cheer her when she did well or lend her support when she shot poorly, and it would be so beautiful out there, so green and well-groomed and quiet, and after the game they would go into the clubhouse feeling pleasantly exhausted and have a drink while Martin talked to the pros he always seemed to know, and he would tell them about his wife here and how pretty soon if he didn't watch out she'd be able to beat him. That was why she still played golf, not because it brought back Martin or their days together but because when she was out there in the early morning, as she gripped her club and stepped up to the tee and looked down the dew-covered fareway, that feeling would come over her, that exuberance and zest for living that Martin had brought back to her. That was why.

Her turn-off. She'd almost missed it with her daydreaming, and she quickly signaled and pulled onto it. She slowed for the stop sign, and with the letdown in speed she felt the past leave her as she came to a stop. There was traffic and she sat erect with both hands on the wheel and turned out into it. Within minutes she was home, and she turned into the mobile home park and drove slowly over the speed bumps and eased into her driveway.

She owned a mobile home, one of those long, house-like models with an awning-covered driveway, and she climbed the front steps and went inside. She turned on the lights and looked around. Years ago, before she bought the place, her family had tried to persuade her to stay in an apartment and save her money. But she bought it anyway and it turned out beautifully. It was perfect for her; it was quiet and roomy, and most of her neighbors were people her own age. And she liked living alone, she enjoyed it, though it always seemed like one of her grandchildren was staying with her. But not tonight, and satisfied that there was a place for everything and everything was in its place, she locked the door behind her and lay down her purse and went into the bedroom.

She took out her nightgown and quickly prepared for bed. It was late, way past her bedtime, and she had a golf date in the morning. She completed her rituals of washing up, removing her glasses and hearing-aid, checking the doors, turning off the lights, and setting the thermostat before slipping into bed where she lay with the nightlight on. Usually she read a book before falling off to sleep, but she was too tired tonight, so she just set her clock and turned out the nightlight and closed her eyes to the darkness.

But sleep never came easy to her, and she sighed and rolled onto her back and waited for it. She hoped she wasn't going to lie awake for hours like she did some nights. She deserved a good night's sleep, after all it was her birthday. She was seventy-seven years old today... "Seventy-seven," she slowly repeated to herself in disbelief as though she were reading an unexpected telegram in the dead of night... "Seventy-seven" My God, where had the years gone, she wondered. One day you were a gangly teenager all impatient to grow up and the next day you were seventy-seven years old. My God. Time brings all things to pass. But she wasn't doing too badly for an old gal of seventy-seven, not bad at all considering she had buried two husbands and raised two children, including three grandkids. Not bad at all. And the way she figured it, she damned well deserved a good night's sleep.

The phone rang and she picked up the receiver off the nightstand. It was her granddaughter.

"Hi, Gram, were you sleeping?"

"No."

"I just called to make sure you got home okay."

"Thank you, dear."

"Okay... well, I'll talk to you later. Happy birthday."

"Okay now—don't stay out too late, you have work in the morning."

"We won't. Bye, Gram."

"Bye."

She hung up the phone and lay back. It was going to make her worry. She could hear the sounds of the bar in the background; it was late and they were still there and still drinking and she was probably going to lie awake worrying about it. But no, she decided. They were adults now and she wasn't going to worry, and she cleared her mind, flushing it clean with a bedtime prayer, and remembered an old proverb her Swedish grandmother used to whisper to her each night before bedtime: "Den som sover syndar icke" (He who sleeps does not sin.). She smiled at that and relaxed into thoughtlessness. She lay with her eyes closed and waited for sleep. And it came quickly for a change, swooping down on her with dark-feathered wings and carrying her off to unconsciousness, to that resonant twilight of remembered faces and familiar voices where old souls dwell.

"Did your Gram get home okay," asked Elly as Jackie sat back down. Jackie nodded and took a sip of her drink.

Fred sat holding a dime she had just plucked from her purse. "What time is it?" she asked. Jackie told her. "I should call home," she said, "But I know Steve's gonna be mad."

"So don't," said Elly. "He's just gonna give you a bunch of crap—so don't."

"But I should be going."

"Why? Come on, Fred, you deserve a night out," argued Elly. Jackie agreed and quickly made the following points: Didn't he stay out late nights? Didn't he leave her home with the kids and go out with his friends? Wasn't she entitled to do the same?

"I guess so," replied Fred.

"Damn right," said Elly. "And since he's gonna be mad at you anyway, you might as well sit back and enjoy yourself."

"Maybe..."

The music started, smothering Fred's reply. It was an upbeat, disco number and a male stripper jumped onto the stage, bouncing to the rhythm. "It's Randy again!" shouted Jackie in excitement. They cheered. Fred dropped the dime back into her purse and leaned out to see better. Randy was her favorite.

> *I don't want an everlasting thing*
> *I don't care if I see you again*
> *So grab your coat and, honey, tell your friends*
> *You won't be home*
> *You won't be home*
> *You won't be home*

The dancer leaped to the edge of the stage and stood spread-eagled like Elvis, pointing out at the audience as he mouthed the words:

> *Tonight I'm yours*
> *Do anything that you want to*

"Don't hurt me—don't hurt me," the women sang in chorus.

> *Tonight I'm yours*
> *Do anything cause I want you to*

"Don't hurt me—don't hurt me!"

The dancer spun away, throwing his vest off as he did, and bumped and swiveled to the beat. The women loved it, and they screamed and shouted, stomped and cheered, and sang "Don't hurt me—don't hurt me!" right on cue. Within the roar, piercing out like calls from a burning house, the women yelled shrilly for his attention. "Randy! Here, Randy!" Others were bolder; over the din came their piped voices, the obscene offers, the promises and invitations, each one pleading, begging, demanding, trying anything in their shrill attempts to get his attention. Back at their table, Fred joined them. She jumped up and down next to her chair shouting, "Randy! Randy!—Me!"

Jackie and Elly joined her. They chanted together, calling out his name, their fists thrown in the air, and in the riot of sight and sound they caught each other's eye and glanced as one back at Fred. There she was standing and shouting and having a good time, and they looked back at each other and out of the corner of their mouths smiled in satisfaction.

THE NINETIES

Every instinct I have, in every aspect of life, be it something to wear, something to eat— it's all been wrong.

George Costanza
Seinfeld

Natural male aggressiveness today is treated like sex in Victorian England.

George Gilder
Men and Marriage

I'll take the varmint's path
Oh, and I must refuse your test
Push me and I will resist
This behavior's not unique.

Pearl Jam
Corduroy

The Pumpkin Hour

He shifted positions again and glanced at the clock. It was ten-thirty.

She was late.

He turned back to the TV and stared at the screen. He was thinking.

She wasn't really late, he reminded himself—just partially late. Afterall, ten-thirty was not absolute; it wasn't the hour her carriage turned back into pumpkin; it wasn't the same nor did it have the same irrefutable quality to it if it were, say, eleven-thirty. Which it wasn't. It was only ten-thirty.

But still...

But still last week she had come home at ten, and the week before that at ten—on the button. And here it was past ten. It was Tuesday night, bowling night, and it was past ten and she wasn't home. That made her late. Right? A precedent had been set and now broken, a precedent maybe not as steadfast as seventy-six years was to Halley's Comet or as precise as March Nineteenth was to the swallows and San Juan Capistrano, but it was a precedent nevertheless. There was every reason to believe that she had intended to make ten-o'clock a habit, and one she had further intended he should become accustomed to. She was dependable in that way.

He knew that was the kicker: she was dependable. It was in her make-up the same way it was in the make-up of the swallows to get their asses back to the Mission by March Nineteenth. The facts were all there, he thought. For instance, she always kissed him in the morning upon waking and always shopped on Saturday, always made her salads with beets on top of carrots on top on onions on top of avocados on top of tomatoes on top of lettuce without variation or the occasional crouton. She always watched *I Love Lucy* reruns at six-thirty and read before going to sleep, and always and irresistibly wore the same see-through nightgown whenever she was feeling frisky. There was the additional fact that this was a work night and, as long as he had known her, she had always been conscientious about getting a good night's sleep before work the next day. And there was one more thing (and this was key)—she was madly in love with him and they'd only been living together for a short time. It wasn't like they were an old married couple who couldn't stand the sight of one another.

The facts were all there, he knew. Hers was a habitual nature, reliable and inveterate. In that simple and silent way of hers, she always assumed a practice, established a routine, and ever after adhered to it. Which was why he had this gut feeling, he figured. There was just something wrong about ten-thirty. The reasons were a hundredfold, all subtle, all little things, but when added up explained this gnawing worry in the pit of his stomach.

How long did it take to bowl three games, anyway? Not that long. Something could have gone wrong. Maybe her car broke down. Maybe...

But this was silly, he chided himself. It was ridiculous to worry; he was acting as though twenty-two hundred hours was H-hour or something. Everybody fudged a little, it was only human. She probably decided to enjoy a few more drinks with friends before leaving and was on her way home now. No doubt. No sweat. Afterall, it was only ten-thirty and ten-thirty was still within the realm of ten, or thereabouts. It wasn't like it was eleven-thirty. Eleven-thirty was a whole different story; there was no rationalizing eleven-thirty. Eleven-thirty was unarguable; it was "le point de non-retour." It was irrevocable and unjustifiable. Eleven-thirty was H-hour.

He stretched comfortably back against the sofa and laughed to himself. Without really trying he had just made eleven-thirty the deadline, thus eliminating any reason for premature worry. He wasn't going to worry anymore, he decided, and that was that. At least not until eleven-thirty.

There was a living room clock in his peripheral vision and he dismissed its existence as though it were a panhandler on the sidewalk where he was walking. Instead he concentrated on the television set in front of him with a revitalized interest. His decision not to worry anymore had a cleansing affect, and he poured his new-found attention into the colorful image before him.

Where had he left off? What was going on? Without much effort, he quickly picked up the simple storyline: The beautiful heroine reporter, on track of the villain, soon found herself in peril. With the heroine in dire straits, the commercial came on and he automatically got up from the sofa and walked into the kitchen. He opened the refrigerator and peered inside at its sparse contents, waiting for something to jump out at him. When nothing did he picked out some left-over cheese, unwrapped it, and tore off a piece. He replaced the cheese back in the fridge and confronted the kitchen clock.

It was a quarter to eleven.

He frowned and turned away from the clock. Just what the hell was holding her up, he wondered. The possibilities paraded through his head as he chewed the soft cheese. Some of the possibilities were darker than others, some vicious and terrible. He quickly blocked those out and concentrated on the lighter ones, the ones that made more sense.

He walked back into the living room while carefully working it out in his head: Okay, let's say that she started at six since they always started at six, and it took one hour to bowl one game. That meant three hours to bowl three games, which meant that they finished at nine-o'clock. Nine-o'clock—make it nine-fifteen, better yet nine-thirty, considering they may have started late or had problems with the lanes or any number of things. Nine-thirty it was then. Afterwards, no doubt, they went into the bar for a few drinks to celebrate, or whatever. Two wine-coolers at fifteen—no, twenty minutes apiece—made forty minutes for her to drink—no, to nurse—two wine-coolers in the bar. Make it three. Perhaps they met a friend or got to talking or someone bought her an extra drink which she felt obliged to finish. Okay, that was three drinks at twenty minutes apiece which made one hour, along with three and half hours to bowl made a grand total of four and a half hours. That meant she had left for home— that's with every benefit of the doubt given her and even a few thrown in—at approximately ten-thirty. Considering the border- line nature of the time, she had decided not to call and instead had just left, hopped in her car, and taken off for home. An easy ten minute drive. Give her an extra five minutes for, let's say, a cold start or a couple of long lights and, barring any unforeseen delays like a flat tire or a speeding ticket, she should be getting home just about...

He looked at the clock and swiftly re-checked his calcula- tions to make sure.

... Now.

Just then he heard the sound of a car pulling into the car- ports outside. He stood up, stepped over to the TV and turned it down, and stood very still, listening. There it was, the sound of a car door slamming shut, and he quietly listened as the foot- steps started their lengthy walk toward the front door. It sud- denly struck him that he'd look ridiculous standing there like this when she came in, so he turned the TV back up and quickly sat back down on the sofa. As the footsteps neared the door, he folded his arms, then thought better of it and unfolded them again. He wasn't going to be mad, he decided. He was going to give her the benefit of the doubt.

The footsteps passed by and entered the apartment next door. His heart sank. Well hell, he thought, leaning back into the sofa. He threw his legs up on the coffee table, popped the last of the cheese into his mouth, and chewed in vigorously. What the hell?

His thoughts grew darker. Each car door that slammed shut, each set of footsteps that passed by his door, and each glance at the clock sucked at his brain and dragged him little by little like a reluctant child into the house of horrors. But he fought against it. He sat without moving and thought of prisoners of war. He remembered how, to survive their misery, they taught themselves not to think. That took true strength. So he fought against it. He sat without moving in his mental sweatbox and tried not to think. But without success.

He could see it plainly:

A fiery crash, the night street filled with shattered glass and twisted metal, with whooping sirens and flashing lights, her body burned beyond recognition. They'd have to cut her out of the charred wreckage. A Jane Doe. It would take them hours, probably days before they got a make on her. They'd call him— no, instead come to the door in the evening. A soft knock. He'd answer it sick with the knowledge inside him, and two men in gray suits, somber and official-looking, would stand there and tell him the awful truth. He'd take it valiantly and go on with his life, hiding the pain inside him. His friends would try and help him. Women would pity him; they'd throw themselves at him in a vain attempt to revive his dead soul. He'd go from one woman to another, unfulfilled, an island unto himself.

Or... A quiet parking lot, the somber night fractured by the sound of gunshots, her body slumped over the steering wheel as a deformed figure lopes from her car and disappears into the darkness. D.O.A. Front page news. Another victim of a psycho-path. No clues, no motive, just a dead body and his devastated heart. A storm would rage over the land the night of her funeral. A wild storm. And he saw himself in it, bursting in on the hushed assembly, looking as wild as the wild night outside, his eyes black with grief, his hair dripping from the storm as he walks to her casket and flings it open, wrenching her body to him in a des-perate and unyielding embrace. Then they would know the true depth of his passion, of the utter profundity of his sorrow.

Or... A muffled scream, the soft night assaulted by the sound of quick scuffling and desperate grunts, her body shoved into the back seat at knifepoint as two dark figures take control of the car and speed off unseen. Abducted into the hills. Into the black woods. Beaten and raped, they dump her semi-nude body off the road, found alive but without a mind, stripped of her sanity, left to vegetate the rest of her life in a catatonic daze. And the rapists? – They'd be picked up, brought to court, and released on a technicality. And he? – Deprived of his Beloved, with his soul ripped apart like a valley in an earthquake, he'd track them down one by one and cut their throats with quick jerks, leaving their carcasses to rot in the rancid-smelling back alleys of the big city. He'd go to prison, of course, but he'd become a martyr for justice, a cause célèbre. Bob Dylan would write a song about him. His face would be on the cover of Time.

"Arrrhhh!" he sighed, shaking his head. This was nuts, he scolded himself. She'd be the first to accuse him of having an overactive imagination. He folded his arms and smiled. And for a moment his mind was empty, and he felt warm and cozy because of it. He gazed pleasantly at the television.

The Eleven-O'clock News was starting.

Unfazed, he grabbed the remote and changed channels. He needed something light, he figured, something light and engaging to maintain this comfortable state of mind he was in. He found a rerun of *Seinfeld* and settled back to watch it. The trick was to stay cool, and so he turned his attention to the images on the screen. He sat through it all without once getting up, even laughing out loud a couple times, and when it was over he smiled to himself and stretched out to embrace the comfiest of feelings. In reflex he glanced at the clock.

It was eleven-thirty.

A blast of artic wind blew into his brain and his thoughts let loose. Dammit! God damn it! What the God-damn hell was going on? He stood up and began pacing. Whenever he worried he paced, and he paced now, into the dining area and back into the living room, back and forth like a caged bobcat, his mind racing as his body sought to keep up.

This was it. H-hour. He knew it. There was no getting around it. No faking or dodging it. Something had happened, *really happened,* or else she would have called by now, and because she hadn't called meant only one thing. He knew it. And pacing there, his mind locked in a muddy tug-of-war with itself, the dark thoughts seeped back into his consciousness, dark-terrible thoughts, without the day-dreaminess they had had before. They were suddenly real and horrible. He saw her dying. He saw those same dark figures pawing her as she cried out, as she screamed out to him, as she pleaded...

He stopped and squeezed his eyes shut in an attempt to block the image.

He walked mechanically into the bathroom and brushed his teeth, the mundane routine of it momentarily clearing his head. He washed out his mouth and looked up at himself in the mirror. His face startled him. As he stared at it, studying his face intently as though it were the face of a worried stranger, the absurdity of the whole thing struck him.

Why was he worrying, he thought. He was totally overreacting. His imagination had gotten the better of him as usual, and here he was in the middle of a crisis that didn't exist except in his own head. Boy, he saw it clearly now. What he had to do was look at this thing properly, in a clear and clinical way. Face it, he admitted to himself, she was just out drinking and having such a good time that she'd lost all track of time. The fact that she was having such a good time without him chinked his armor a bit, but he could handle it, no problem. What the heck, everyone was entitled to a blow-out and a slip-up once in a while. He was the last person who should criticize that. And the fact that this behavior exhibited a bit of inconsideration on her part didn't bother him either, even though she was supposed to be in love with him, her mind consumed at all times with the thought of him. What was inconsideration in a woman anyway? It was the same as... what? ... the same as indifference.

He frowned at himself and turned away from the mirror. He began worrying again.

In his renewed pacing, the delicacy of the crisis became painfully apparent. Something had to be done, that was certain. But what? If he acted too soon and his worries proved groundless he'd be made a fool of, yet if he acted too late and it was true she was in trouble then he'd have to live the rest of his life knowing he might have helped her but didn't. It was the worst kind of dilemma, with a feeling of nauseous weightlessness at the center of it. Should he act or not? Should he admit the worst and go from there, or hold out? Should he cut away and pull his reserve chute or hope his main chute untangled itself in time. He didn't know, and because he didn't know it frustrated him. It frustrated him with a prickly sweat at his temples and under his arms; it frustrated him because he knew full well its meaning. It was cowardice.

He was a coward, no different than a witness to a murder who remains hidden in the dark. The circumstances were different, sure, but at the heart of it, it was all the same and he felt ashamed because of it. It was abject cowardice, pure and simple; the inability to act in a crisis, to make a quick and accurate decision. And it was plain to see what he was. What he was, he knew, was some kind of simpering, over-educated wimp, who was paralyzed like a cripple from the neck up.

He opened the refrigerator door and stared inside. Enough, he commanded himself. Crisis or no crisis, wimp or not, he had to decide on a course of action and now. A fresh determination seized him. And as he stared into the cool white light of the fridge, he went over his alternatives, examining each one carefully as though it were a piece of food he was about to eat.

Calling the cops was out of the question at this point. She wasn't a missing person until twenty-four hours, and they were useless until then.

Her parents were out for obvious reasons. By calling them he'd just start a minor panic.

One thing was certain, though—he had to stay put, at least for the time being. If he went off looking for her he'd miss her call or, worse yet, miss her on the road as she was coming home.

He could call the bowling alley. It was just a matter of picking up the phone and dialing the number...

He closed the refrigerator door and walked away. No, he wasn't going to call anyone, he decided. He wasn't going to act the fool any longer. He was going to wait it out. He was pissed off now, and he clenched his fists and punched the air and walked angrily about. How dare she pull this, he fumed. Who in the hell did she think she was staying out late like this and not calling? He'd teach her a thing or two about inconsideration. Just wait.

He gritted his teeth and growled, reveling in his new-found anger. Each moment that passed without her fed the red flame between his ears. The flame warmed him, filling the icy void of worry, and he worked to sustain it. But it was no good. The void was too great, too foreboding, and it snuffed out the flame. He tried to stoke it back to life but without success, and he soon found himself next to the phone.

What the hell, he sighed to himself in surrender.

He found the number in the small book next to the phone, picked up the receiver, and dialed up the bowling alley. It began ringing, and as he held the receiver in his slightly shaking hand he suddenly realized how anxious he was. He took a deep breath and waited. It rang and rang with no answer, and finally on the seventh ring a man answered. "Yeah?" He gave the man her name and asked him to page her. "Sure. Hold on." The man placed the receiver down and the sounds of the bowling alley filled his ear—the roll of balls, the crash of pins, laughter, the sound of her name over the intercom—and as he listened to it an image abruptly flashed in his mind of her sitting there at the bar with another man, the two of them nestled together whispering and giggling ("What? Someone paging me? Pretend I'm not here," she says as she winks at him and they giggle again.). He quickly shook his head and cleared the image from his mind. After what seemed like an eternity, the man returned—"Sorry, no answer"—and hung up. He stared at the receiver in his hand. Son-of-a-bitch.

And with that he slammed the phone down.

He turned off all the lights except the one near the door and went into the bedroom where he quickly undressed and slipped into bed. He glanced at the illuminated clock on the nightstand. It was almost midnight. He lay quietly in the dark and confronted it. Instead of feeling better at having finally acted he felt worse. It was a sick, panicky feeling like the time he'd lost his little brother at the fair and couldn't find him.

Alone in the quiet darkness, he worked to stay calm and think things through, casting off into the whirlpool of explanations and reeling each one in for examination... Maybe she was mad at him? Could it be, he wondered. Maybe she was mad at him and paying him back by staying out late. But the more he thought about it and analyzed the past day or so for something he might have said or done, the more he knew it wasn't possible. No way, none whatsoever. So maybe... or maybe... Each maybe fell under his scrutiny, some for a longer period than others, but eventually like the rest they were let go. Soon the obvious maybes ran out and he had to wait patiently for new ones to strike, and when they did he eagerly reeled them in and examined them.

Somewhere along the line in this agonizing game it occurred to him, vaguely, in a dim image at first, that she was already here, in her car, parked just outside, but unable to come inside because she was unconscious or wounded or, worse yet, under attack. He let it go like the rest but it kept coming back, each time more vivid and real than the last time. (*She was just outside in her car, under attack, in the sealed silence of her car, fighting off her attacker, calling out to him as he lay here in bed like a complete idiot doing nothing.*) It was too much to stand. He fought against the image but it tugged and tugged against him until it snagged in his brain, thrashing there violently.

He jumped out of bed and threw his clothes on, the adrenalin pumping through his body. There wasn't a minute to lose, he knew, groping awkwardly in the dark to find his shoes. Every second could mean the difference between life or death. He grabbed his shirt and rushed out of the bedroom, banging his knee against the wall. He stopped in the hallway. There was no time for pain, he commanded himself, stifling the bright ache in his knee. No time—no time. Once the pain cleared, he remembered something and hurried back into the bedroom where he opened a dresser drawer and felt around until he found it— his switchblade (A Tijuana special, smuggled over the border for just this kind of emergency.). He slipped the knife into his pocket, pausing for a moment as a feeling of elation passed over him, then rushed from the bedroom, banging his knee again on the way.

He limped down the hallway, silently cursing his stupid knee. With his hand on the switchblade, he quickly went over his moves in his mind: He'd have to strike first, by surprise, cut him before he cut her, and hope for some luck. There wasn't time to plan; he'd have to rely on intuition, on his animal instincts. He reached the front door and turned the knob, at the same time placing his thumb over the switchblade's button. He burst out into the night and ran crouching towards the carport.

Her space was empty.

Of course it was, he admitted to himself. What had he been thinking? But his stomach turned over at the sight of her vacant parking place nevertheless. A feeling of letdown came over him, but it was quickly replaced by a greater feeling of silliness as he caught the picture of himself standing there set to do battle with the phantom boogey-man. It was cold outside without a jacket and he shivered, and with that shiver came an emptying out of all feeling in him. All that remained in him was the unspent adrenalin, which, like a kind of lust, begged for an outlet no matter how cheap.

It occurred to him then that perhaps she was parked out on the street. The thought excited him and he went off in pursuit, walking the length of the street and back along the line of parked cars. But the obvious soon sank in; her car was not there. And this sobering fact, along with his brisk walk, served to evaporate the adrenalin from his system. He stopped, dog-tired, but quickly jumped behind a telephone pole to avoid the headlights of an approaching car. If it were her and she saw him, he'd look like a complete fool. He couldn't have that, so he hid and waited, peeking out at the car as it passed by. Not her. What a stroke of luck, he thought. He took one last glance about then jogged back to his apartment. Once there, he reached into his pocket for his key.

He'd forgotten his key. He stood for a second in disbelief, then searched his pockets again. He didn't have it anywhere, and the shock of it started to blossom. "No!" he hissed at himself—"unbelievable!"—and he slapped his forehead with his open palm. Panic began to set in, and he searched again and again, but it was true. What an idiot! What an unbelievable jerk! And with that he slapped his forehead again.

He tried to calm down but the more he thought about it the more the panic grew, the panic of a mountain climber caught on a ledge without an out. The manager's was closed so he couldn't go there, he knew. If he waited around much longer she'd show up and catch him. The utter embarrassment of that would be too much to bear. And, worse yet, stuck out here like this meant he could be missing her phone call—her call for help. That was the coup-de-grâce, the slip and fall of his panic, and the jolt of it sent a fresh flow of adrenalin into his system. There was only one alternative, he decided, and that was to break in through his bedroom window.

He went around the walk, gliding silently as a cat burglar, and carefully cut through the ivy to his bedroom window. He crouched there and caught his breath. As luck would have it, the window was cracked open slightly which meant all he had to do was pop off the screen and work the window open. He took out his switchblade, clicked it open, and looked around. Crouching there, dressed in dark clothes and wielding a knife, the insanity of his situation struck him head-on. If a security guard, or anyone for that matter, saw him like this he'd be a dead duck. A skittish cop might just shoot first and ask questions later. He could see it now, wounded, killed even, for breaking into his own apartment, and it would all be her fault. Damn her.

He cleared his mind of that and set to work. With the knife as a pry bar, he leaned in towards the screen to pop it loose. Instantly the blade broke off in his hand. He threw the handle away in disgust. Using his fingers, he clawed along the edges for a leverage hold, found it, and pulled until the screen popped off and fell noisily to the ground. He ducked down and held his breath, waiting for a light to come on in one of the apartments or a voice to yell out. But nothing stirred. When he was sure it was safe, he leaned back to the window, slipped his hand into the crack, and worked in open till it was far enough to get his body through. Almost home, he thought, and he took one last look around before slipping through the opening and plopping down into his bedroom.

He closed the window and locked it, threw off his clothes, and jumped into bed. Safe, he sighed, and he glanced at the clock. Twelve-thirty.

He was suddenly very tired—tired from the humiliation, tired from the worry, and tired from the late hour. She was overdue, something had happened, but he didn't care. All he wanted to do was sleep. He was tired of the whole damned thing, but as he closed his eyes to allow the tiredness to take over and usher him into sleep, his mind kept it from him. Even in exhaustion, it persisted, like a faucet dripping. It dripped "what-ifs", "could-bes", and "maybes"; it dripped steadily and annoyingly. He turned on his side for a new perspective but the what-ifs dripped on, so he tossed over to his other side but they dripped there as well. He flopped onto his back again, angry with himself.

Screw this, he thought, starting out of bed. But with a force of will he laid back down. He remembered then about the yogis. In order to clear their minds before meditation, they thought of a white wall. If they could do it he could do it, he decided, so he conjured up the whitest wall he could imagine and concentrated on it. He thought on it and thought on it, immersing himself, struggling to achieve total whiteness. But it eluded him. He doubled his efforts, slowing his breathing, relaxing his muscles, and reabsorbed himself into the white wall. Then—just as he was about to succeed, just as he was on the verge of achieving total, pure, blessed whiteness—a thought struck him, a thought so new and vigorous that it awakened his whole body and crumbled the white wall from his mind.

What if she was testing him?

What if, he wondered, she was doing all this on purpose? What if staying out late and not calling was all part of a test she had devised to see whether he would worry or not?

He smiled to himself. That sounded just like her, he knew, and that's what made this "maybe" so much more compelling than the others, because it was just like her. A Lucy-like antic. A kooky scheme. If he worried it meant he cared; if he worried it meant he loved her. It was so obvious this was the answer, and it amazed him that he hadn't thought of it before.

Finally, he could rest now (he'd passed the test), but the feeling of relief that filled him was promptly swept aside by anger—an anger at having been manipulated. How dare she pull this on him, he thought as he glanced at the clock and slugged his pillow all in one fluid motion. How dare she drive him crazy with worry like this? He wasn't going to stand for it. Two could play at this game. He simply wouldn't give her the satisfaction. When she returned home, he wasn't going to ask her where she'd been or what the big idea was for staying out so late, or in any way betray a hint of worry. That would teach her. And with that he picked his pillow up, tossed it over, and slammed it down as though it were a midget wrestler.

Furthermore, he decided, he wasn't going to worry any longer. He was through with debating in a vacuum, with maybes and could-bes. As of—he turned and looked at the clock—twelve-thirty-eight he was through with it. His revenge would start now.

He closed his eyes and glued them there. Consciousness, just like hunger or pain, was a state of mind and, to him, it had become a weakness as well. As he saw it, the longer he remained conscious the longer he played the dupe. So, as payback and by an act of sheer will power, he would overcome consciousness. He would smother it, blow it out like a match light, and terminate its existence. Consciousness was his villain, it mocked and humiliated him, but final victory would be his. He willed it.

But victory wasn't his. Restlessness and worry kept him awake. He could no sooner will sleep than a starving man could will a full belly, and he knew it. He was beaten, and the full and terrible profundity of that—of the fact that he loved her, dearly loved her, and couldn't live without her—hit him like a heavyweight's punch. His solar plexus caved inwards, and he lost his breath inside a sudden sickness. How could he survive if she were gone—*really gone?* How could he live? He couldn't, he realized. It was as horribly plain as that. And laying there, sick with emptiness, adrift in the utter nothingness a life without her would mean, he stared into the dark ceiling, into its infinitude and the presence beyond, and struck up a deal.

He would believe in Him, he promised, if He would make her safe. Just make her safe, that's all. Bring her home safe and sound, nothing more. If He could do that he promised to believe in Him forever. No more doubting, no more smart remarks; he would return as the Prodigal Son returned, a sheep back to the fold. Was it a deal? he asked... Was it? ... But when no answer came from above, he took a swift inventory of his self and found the reason. His sincerity wasn't total. Somewhere in the fiber of his being there remained a speck of skepticism. It was a small percentage, perhaps five percent at the most, but it was a five percent that was definitely delinquent and unaccounted for. With that five percent there could be no deal, he knew. And God knew it, too. So he excused himself from His presence and purged himself, flushing out the heretical five percent in a dark corner of his mind and tackling it to the ground where he wrestled with it until it cried uncle. He returned to His presence, ready now, imbued with a new strength, and made ready his covenant.

He promised, upon his honor and with total and perfect commitment, that if He made her safe and brought her home, he would forever, with pure heart and unmatched fervor, always and everywhere believe in...

Just then he heard the jingle of keys and the lock turn. The door opened.

She was home.

Finally! he sighed to himself. His body went light, unbelievably light, as a warm shower of relief poured down his neck and filled his belly. He wanted to go run and hug her, scream at her, hit her, anything, but he remained put. Calm and steady was what he'd be, like a man who has just inherited a fortune and knows he has all the time in the world to spend it. Cool reason returned to his brain. He glanced at the clock—twelve-forty-five—and turned over with a relaxed roll onto his side and pretended to be asleep.

He listened as she laid her purse down, removed her jacket, and finally strolled into the bedroom. She came over and sat down on the edge of the bed. He moaned slightly and rolled towards her as though rustled out of a peaceful slumber. Her cold hand touched his cheek.

"Asleep?" she whispered.

He took a deep, yawning breath. "Hmm," he answered. "What time is it?" he asked groggily.

"Ah"—she turned and looked at the clock and the nightstand— "twelve-thirty." ("Hmm," he said again.) "I didn't realize it was so late," she explained in a whisper. "I went out for a drink with Cathy and them and I guess I lost track of time... Are you mad?"

"Huh?" he uttered, pretending not to understand.

She leaned over and nestled against him. "Are you mad?" she asked again, her cool lips touching his cheek. He could smell the scent of lime from the wine-coolers on her breath.

He lay quietly for a moment then answered. "I'm sleeping," he mumbled.

She stayed nestled against him and softly kissed his cheek. "I love you," she purred tenderly. When he didn't react, she kissed him again and slid her moist tongue along his cheek and into his ear. He groaned and rolled away from her. She sat back up and waited a moment, then sighed and got up and walked into the bathroom.

Everything was all right now, he knew. He didn't even need to think about it anymore. A nice and snug satisfaction seeped into him, gradually growing nicer and snugger as he listened to her prepare for bed. Each sound—the unfastening of clothes, the brushing of teeth, the opening of closets—covered him with a new layer of blanket, with a new extra layer of snugness. Sleep came quickly to him then, without a fight. It was dark green and fathomless, and it had hovered elusively above him for so long. But now it swooped down, engulfing him like a surgeon's anesthetic, sucking him into its starless universe without a struggle. He slept hard and deep and wonderfully. He slept without thought or dream.

His mind was emptied.

Outdoors

This year it was going to be fun. Real fun. Nothing they had done before would compare to it. No river they had run, no rapids they had shot would equal this one. That was a promise. The brochure said it was for experienced rafters only and "experienced" was underlined in red. No beginners, no sightseers or picnickers, just seasoned rafters who knew what the hell they were doing. That's the kind of river it was going to be—class three, maybe class four rapids, with no let-up—and that meant you had to be damned strong and agile to cut it.

"It's gonna be great," said Blake when he showed them the brochure. "This is major league stuff. We're talking Deliverance here."

The other three men looked over the brochure with their wives. For the past three years it was the same—Blake would show them the brochure and then, at an impromptu barbecue with plenty of beer, they would plan their trip out and give Blake the go-ahead to make the arrangements. It was a chance to get out of the valley. The valley was where they all worked, in electronics, day in and day out, and the yearly raft trip gave them a chance to get out of it, to get outdoors and have some fun and unwind. And when that Friday finally came, the three married couples along with Blake and his girlfriend would pack up and drive away to some far-off river for a three-day weekend of rafting, beer-drinking, horseplay, and love-making under the stars.

But this year it was going to be different in another way. This year the women refused to raft.

"I'm not going on that river," said Lori. She turned to her husband Jim. "You can go," she said, "but no way am I."

"You sure?" Jim asked her. There wasn't much conviction in his voice. He had read the brochure and realized at once that it was probably too dangerous for her.

"I'm sure," she replied. "I'll find a nice sandy beach to lay out on and get a suntan. I'll wave to you as you go by."

"I'll join you," said Blake's girlfriend. "We'll bring a bottle of wine and some suntan lotion and be set for the day."

Denny's wife thought that was a good idea, too. All the women were agreed then not to raft—all except for Wendy. Wendy was Mark's wife. She was a tall blonde with large shoulders, and she sat in a chair with those shoulders hunched forwards and a look of disappointment on her face.

"What's wrong?" asked Mark. "You can go if you want."

"What's the point," she replied. "No one else wants to."

"You can still go if you want," he said.

"No, forget it. That's all right," she said in resignation. She shrugged it off with a smile but it was apparent she wasn't happy about it.

Blake spoke up. "Hey gals, it's up to you. It's your choice. I don't want you to think we're forcing you not to go, but you've read the brochure. It's not going to be like the times before. It's going to be a lot different—a little dangerous and a lot of work. So... It's up to you."

The men all laughed. The sticky part was over. Like Jim, each of them had quickly calculated the danger quotient: It was high—injury, even drowning was a real possibility—and each one silently understood this as a men-only excursion. But none of them could have flatly told their wife or girlfriend not to go, or even suggested it, without raising the battle flag. They knew better than that. Instead they sought to make the women appreciate the danger involved through their excitement of that danger. They fidgeted in their chairs and read the vivid details of the brochure out loud, listening to Blake's theatrics and exchanging tense smiles all around. "All right!" each one said emphatically—"Sounds great! All right!" And this unspoken conspiracy, carried out at an intuitive level, had finally struck pay dirt. Lori, God bless her, had finally appreciated the situation.

So the men laughed because the sticky part was over. But they also laughed, a special masculine laugh, because now it was just them.

Soon the party split into two groups. The men sat at the table drinking beer and talking about the trip, while the women gathered around the sofa sipping wine. The talk at the table was loud. The conversation around the sofa was quieter. Occasionally one of the women would glance over at her loud partner and then turn away, shake her head, and smile. The men traded stories, mostly about rafting, and each took his turn fantasizing about their upcoming adventure (fearlessly, in a beer-loud voice, detailing the ferociousness of the river, the river of no return, a river like no other, and their chances of surviving it). The women discussed their friends and work, half-listening to their husbands in the background, and enjoyed each other's company. All the women, that is, except Wendy.

"Son of a bitch!" cried Blake. He was disgusted and he was letting everyone know about it. He took a beer from the cooler, popped it open, and sat down at the picnic table. "Shit!" he said angrily.

The others milled around the campsite not saying much. They had gotten in an hour before and had just finished setting up camp. The road into the campgrounds ran along the river and they had all seen it for themselves—seen the river for what it was. A bust.

The other men avoided each other's eyes and tried to ignore Blake's tantrum, but they agreed with him. The brochure had lied. Instead of being a river of whitewater thrills, they had discovered just the opposite; a meandering, lazy sort of river good for nothing except maybe catfishing or canoeing. The disappointment was great but they were quiet and kept their disappointment to themselves. They each felt like the kid who'd saved up his money and sent away for a cool-looking battleship only to receive a cheap plastic thing in return. You pretended it was okay. Too much had been invested not to.

Blake's girlfriend nestled up next to him and mussed his hair. "Oh, Blake, come on," she said playfully, but he ignored her.

Mark took a beer out of the cooler and popped it open and took a drink. "Screw it," he said. I came up here to have a good time." He walked over to Blake and slapped him on the shoulder. "I plan on getting a good heat-on tonight, son. Play some games, drink some beer, and have a good time. Whaddya say?"

"Sounds good to me," said Denny. Jim agreed.

Blake looked up and shrugged his shoulders. He smiled. "Might as well," he said. He downed the rest of his beer and crunched the empty can in his hand.

There was a collective sigh of relief. Things were better—not great, but better. They had decided to make the best of it. Denny and Jim opened beers, tossed a fresh one to Blake, and the four of them huddled up and quickly chose teams for horseshoes. They filled a small cooler with beers and headed out through the trees toward a meadow where the horseshoe pits were dug. But before they left, Wendy spoke up.

"Does this mean we can go now?" she asked.

Sure, said Mark, only there was one problem, they had reservations for four, not eight. Wendy replied that they had seen people rent rafts at the last second before, so why couldn't they? Mark reminded her it would cost more, but Wendy said they all had plenty of money. "Well, it's up to you," he said, and the four men left for the horseshoe pits.

Wendy turned to the other women and smiled triumphantly. But they didn't share her enthusiasm. They had decided long before not to go, and getting them to change their minds now was like convincing them to go out to dinner after they had already cooked a complete meal at home. But Wendy pressed her case. She reasoned and kidded them and appealed to their spirit of fun with the determination of a head cheerleader. By the time the men returned from horseshoes they were all agreed. They were going.

That evening they feasted on barbecued steaks and corn-on-the-cob, and afterwards they sat down to games of Scrabble and dice. Later they cleared a space by the campfire for dancing and turned up the cassette player. The beer and wine flowed, and the four couples danced together in the glow of the fire and the Coleman lanterns. They bumped together and laughed, sometimes singing, and threw their arms around each other to form a dancing circle. Somewhere during the night, Blake and his girlfriend snuck off to their tent. Jim passed out from too much beer and Lori shook him awake and helped him to bed. Denny and his wife tried to keep up with Mark and Wendy but they, too, finally tired and went to bed. Only Mark and Wendy were left. They danced in the glow of the dying fire, stopping briefly between songs before starting again. They danced without slowing, relentlessly, with the intensity of a contest. At last Mark stopped and turned the cassette player off and took Wendy's hand. She pulled her hand away and turned the cassette player back on. They argued for a moment, and then Mark lowered the volume on the music and went off to bed alone. Wendy sat down at the picnic table and pulled a broken potato chip out of a bag and ate it. There was a lantern next to her and she watched the moths swirling about it. They beat against the glass to get to the flame inside.

Saturday came and went. They obtained a second raft and guide without a hitch and ran the river in four hours. It was a pleasant ride. The sky was clear and the weather warm and sunny, and everyone got a little sun-burned. There was only one set of rapids, through a narrow part of the river clogged with rocks, and Mark talked the guide into letting him jump out of the raft and run it in his life preserver. He shot the rapids feet first then backstroked once he cleared them and waited for the raft to pick him up. Everyone thought that looked like fun, so they beached the rafts and hiked upriver and shot the rapids together. That was the highlight of the day. That evening, after dinner, everybody sat around the campfire roasting marshmallows and talking quietly, then turned in early.

Sunday morning the women cooked up a big breakfast of bacon and sausage, with eggs fried in their grease, and grilled toast and flapjacks. Everyone was stuffed afterwards and sat around in lawn chairs not wanting to do much. Finally they all agreed to go swimming, so they mustered the energy to load up the coolers, put on swimsuits, and head out in their cars. They drove a ways until they came to a section of the river that was blocked off from the raft trips. They hiked down to the bank and found a beach.

Here the river was different. Downstream lay a spillway to a dam, and here the river, narrowing and rushing to greet the spillway, roared past them in brutal splendor. At the center of the river the whitewater leaped and gushed, sending up a spray, and in the air above the mist refracted the sunlight into an array of small rainbows. The beach they had found sat between two giant boulders, and in-between, close to shore, ran a barrier of tules and rocks that protected the beach from the force of the river. The result was a calm pool of water that sat right in front of them. It was perfect, and they quickly set out their towels feeling good inside for having found the place. In the background they could hear the dull thunder of the spillway. It had a relaxing sound.

Some of the men went swimming in the pool of river water. It was cold and clear and deep enough that they could dive into it from one of the big rocks. Denny blew up his inflatable raft and floated on it with a beer between his legs. The women stayed on the beach with their fronts and backs bared to the sun. Blake went exploring upriver and found a set of mini-rapids that fed into the pool.

Everyone felt at ease. It was a slow and tranquil day in a slow and tranquil place. Only the tumultuous river seemed out of place. It was the kind of day one could give into and simply enjoy by doing nothing. The men quickly got bored.

Somehow a game started. How it started or who started it would have been hard to say, but the men had rapidly perfected it into a contest of skill and speed.

"Seventeen seconds!" yelled Denny. He was working the watch.

Mark jumped out of the water with the inflatable raft and shot his fist into the air. He gave a victory cry.

Mark had just set a new record. The new record—nineteen seconds—had been set by Blake only minutes before. It was now Jim's turn. Mark scrambled to the top of the boulder where Blake and Jim stood waiting. "Asshole," Blake said with a grin. Mark laughed, handed the raft off to Jim, and watched him jump down and run up the bank to the starting line.

The rules of the game were simple: make it from start to finish in the quickest time. The course started from a point upriver and ran through the tules and between rocks and ended at the rock in the middle of the pool. At the word "go," the racer lept onto the raft, caught the swift-moving eddy, then swept through a patch of tules, maneuvering between rocks and flopping down a small waterfall before shooting into the pool where he stroked with his arms to pick up speed for the finish line.

"Twenty seconds!" yelled Denny.

Jim came out of the water with the raft under his arm. "Shit! I would'a had it only I got hung up in those fricken' tules. See." He showed Denny the scratch on his shoulder where a tule had caught him. Denny laughed and took the raft from Jim, handing him the watch in return, then ran up to the top of the boulder where he stopped to take a high five from Mark for good luck before jumping down and running upstream to the starting line.

So the game went. Even the women became interested, sitting up on their towels to watch and root for their guy. The men waited eagerly for their turn to race, running a bit faster and leaping farther in order to speed up the rotation. A kind of pep filled them. It made them tight in the chest, and their arms and legs felt charged with energy. They stood upon rocks and along the bank bare-chested and smiling, hardly touching their beers, whooping at the finish times and slapping one another on the back as they passed each other in rotation.

During the game, Wendy got up from her towel and walked down to the river. Mark had just completed his run and, as he gave the raft to Denny, she stepped in.

"Can I try it?" she asked.

Mark and Denny glanced at each other. "Sure," said Mark with a shrug, and Denny handed her the raft.

She took it and started up the bank. "Go get 'em, Wendy!" yelled the women. "Show 'em how it's done!" She smiled back at them. Blake watched her approach from atop the boulder and put his hands on his hips. "Wendy's going to try it once!" Mark shouted up at him. Blake nodded and sat down and picked up his beer.

They waited for Wendy to walk up the bank to the starting line, then waited again for her to run the course. She shot into the pool clinging to the raft and floated over the finish line with the women cheering her on. Denny announced her time. She was ten seconds off the pace.

"Can I go again?" she asked as she came out of the water.

Mark took the raft from her and handed it to Denny. "You'll have to wait your turn," he said. He watched Denny jog off and then turned back to her. "You're after me."

The game slowed down. Time was taken to realign the rotation to fit Wendy in and the course was altered slightly to make it a little easier for her. The men sat down and drank beer and waited for their turn. There wasn't much else to do; their rotation had been like a well-practiced fire drill, a perfect blend of enthusiasm and order, but now it had changed and there wasn't much point in trying to recapture it. So they sat around and waited for their turn. The game continued at a leisurely pace. The women lay back down on their towels and snoozed in the sun. Wendy took her turns, but when she found she wasn't able to improve on her time, she quit and joined the other women in sunbathing. The men tightened their rotation back up and continued playing but somehow that pep from before was gone. After a while they stopped and gathered by the boulder.

The sun felt good on Lori's body and she nestled under it. The warmth made her sleepy as did the thundering of the spillway in the distance. She faded in and out, floating in a pleasant sort of semi-consciousness. The sharp sound and excited laughter roused her and she propped herself up on her elbow to take a look.

The men were standing together down by the river. Her husband and Mark were throwing stones out into the water and when one of the stones hit a rock they all stopped and pointed at it. They talked vigorously among themselves, nodding to one another and laughing. She couldn't hear what they were saying so she looked out at the rock they were pointing at. It sat on the boundary between the tamer shoreline on one side and the wild whitewater on the other side. A crude, surging eddy ran in front of the rock, at times boiling over it and spilling into the tumultuous mainstream. The rock was surrounded by a few tules. She looked at the rock, and at the men, then back at the rock again and got a bad feeling.

"What are they up to now," she said aloud.

"Huh?" mumbled Blake's girlfriend. She awakened from her nap and looked over at Lori. So did the other women.

"They better not be doing what I think," she said.

And what was that, the women asked as they came fully awake and sat up. Lori pointed out at the rock and told them and they quickly understood. They looked at the men but the men had already split up and were running to their positions. Blake ran towards the women with a grin on his face.

He stopped in front of them. "Check this out," he said excitedly. "This ought'a be good."

"You're not going out by that rock, are you?" asked Lori.

"Yep. It's going to be hairy. Just watch."

"You're nuts," said his girlfriend. "What happens if you miss the rock?"

"Then it's adios, amigo," he laughed.

"That's not funny," said Lori, standing up. "Your little game is over. Jim's not doing that—no way." She started into a brisk walk towards her husband upriver.

"Calm down, would you," Blake called after her. "Don't make such a big thing out of it. Jim's not up yet anyhow. Mark's first."

Wendy jumped up from her towel and started running.

"Jesus Christ," sighed Blake. "What's the big deal?" Denny's wife ignored him and followed Lori and Wendy. His girlfriend came up next to him and put her hand on his arm. He looked at her in bewilderment. "Can't we have any fun around here?"

Wendy ran past Lori and scaled the boulder. She paused at the top and looked down at Mark. He was holding the raft, knee-deep in water, ready to push out.

"Mark!"

Mark glanced up at her.

She jumped down from the boulder and ran towards him, stopping at the edge of the water. "Don't you dare!" she shouted.

"What the hell are you talking about?" he yelled over the roar of the river.

"You're not going out by that rock."

He looked out at the rock and at the swift-moving eddy which swept past it. He'd have to paddle hard to stay inside the rock and kick off toward shore to avoid flipping over and into the raging current, and he contemplated this danger for a moment before looking back at his wife. "Just watch me," he said.

"No, you're not!"

Mark glanced at Jim who stood staring down at his feet. "Yes, I am," he answered back. A sly grin crossed over his face. "You can go next if you want."

"I don't wanna go!"

"You can be one of the boys."

"No—now stop it!" But Mark remained in the water. She stared at him, then raised her hand and swept her hair back in anger. "Is this supposed to be macho!" she yelled. "Do you think you're being macho?"

Mark glanced at Jim again (who still stared down at his feet). "No!" he yelled back at her. "I'm just having fun... Get off my back!" He turned from her and readied the raft.

"Mark!"

He turned back and gazed at her.

"Did you hear me?" she screamed. "Don't you dare! ... I'll call the ranger!"

"Go ahead," he said, and with that he lay down on the raft and pushed out.

"Mark!—damn you..." The rest caught in her throat as she stood and watched.

Everyone else crowded together near the shoreline to watch.

Mark guided the raft out until he caught a side current and rode with it through some rocks and tules. A swifter current picked him up and he went with it until he reached a junction of converging streams. There he paddled hard, veering right toward the river, and broke through into a fast-moving eddy that circled out to the rock. He tucked his arms in and held on. The eddy swept him toward the rock. As he neared it, he threw his arms out and back-peddled to slow himself. But he was going too fast. He kicked out and took the rock sideways, slamming into it hard, and froze there for a moment. Abruptly, the surging current boiled up and tossed him backwards onto the rock. The raft flew out of his hands. The river grabbed it, flipping it into the air like a toy balloon, and carried it on towards the spillway. Mark clung to the rock.

On shore everyone held their breath and watched. Wendy was bent over at the waist with her hands on her knees.

Mark fought to hold on, but the rock was slippery with algae. He grabbed a tule but it broke in his hand. The river pulled at him, it sucked at him with mindless determination, and he slid towards its drag. The other men on shore were yelling at him to grab this and grab that but he couldn't hear them. His grip was slipping. Suddenly he looked over his shoulder at the raging whitewater and seemed to contemplate it for a moment. He looked back and let go of the rock with one of his hands and reached beneath the surface. He went under.

The men on shore went silent. One of the women screamed.

There was nothing, just the rock, the seething river beyond, and the dull thunder of the spillway in the distance. The next instant, Mark's head popped up ten feet from the rock heading towards shore. He was clear.

Jim gave a victory cry.

"Holy balls!" yelled Blake. This was a saying he used for special occasions and he yelled it again. "Holy balls!"

All of them stood at the shoreline and waited for Mark. He half-rode, half-swam the eddies inward, taking a bit of a beating on the rocks. He had a grin on his face.

"Hey, you jerk!" shouted Denny. "That raft was a Sears special. It cost me nine bucks."

Everyone laughed.

Mark slipped into the pool and swam towards them and came out of the water. His chest and arms were covered with scratches. He bent over to catch his breath, then rose up and smiled at them sheepishly.

"You okay?" asked Jim.

Sure he was, he said, but he needed a beer. Denny ran off to get him one. The women wanted to know what had happened— what had happened when he went under?—and he told them. He had found a handle beneath the rock and grabbed it, and when he went under he had pulled himself around the rock and away from the whitewater. No problem.

There was more laughter. Already it was a good story. In time it would be a classic.

The women walked back to their towels, talking rapidly among themselves. Denny and Jim followed their wives then ran off to see if they could find the raft. Blake slapped Mark on the shoulder. "That was frickin' great," he said. "I'm going to have to try and top that one before we leave tomorrow." He laughed and walked over to his girlfriend. Mark took a long drink of his beer and turned around and looked out at the river.

Wendy came up close behind him and studied his figure for a time. She reached out and touched one of the scratches on his back. He didn't move. She came around in front of him and hugged him lightly.

"You scared me," she said softly.

"Really?" he said. He glanced out past her at the rainbow-studded mist above the river, then looked back into her eyes and smiled.

"Did I really scare you?" he asked.

Skiing with the Family

"So, what happened?"

"Well, I guess I was going too fast and caught an edge."

"Where, on the back-side?"

"No, on Claimjumper. Black diamond... Anyhow, I go down and the next thing I know there's people standing around me and the Ski Patrol shows up."

"You got knocked out? Holy shit."

"I must have. Anyhow I sit there on the slopes with these Ski Patrol guys around me until I get the cobwebs out and I can stand up."

"Did they have the sled?"

"Yeah, but I told them I didn't need it. I didn't tell them about my shoulder. They would'a made me ride down in that stupid sled if they thought my shoulder was separated."

"That would'a been embarrassing."

"I know. Anyway, two of them shadowed me down to the lodge and we took it nice and easy—and I found El and the kids and we took off for home. My shoulder was killing me but I took a couple Advils before I went to bed, but the next morning it was still killing me and I couldn't lift it so I went to the doctor and they x-rayed it. It was separated so they popped it back in, and I gotta wear this sling for another week."

"Did you tell him you almost got in a fight?"

"A fight?"

"Yeah, in the lodge with some kid—tell him about it."

"What happened?"

"Yeah, just some J.D. Probably a snowboarder. He was wearing a t-shirt that said 'Fuck off and die' and I took exception to it. We're in a ski lodge, for cryin' out loud, with kids and families, and he's wearing this t-shirt as big as day as though he's advertising for Geno's Pizza."

"So what did you do?"

"I took exception to it and confronted him on it—the little grunged-out, Generation-X dick-wad—and we got into it. No punches were thrown, but there was yelling and pushing, and he kept saying, 'It's a free country, dude. I got my rights, dude.'"

"Hey, that's pretty good. How'd he say it again?"

"'It's a free country, *duuude.*' That was his favorite word—'*duuude.*' He also called me a 'fascist.'"

"A fascist? He should'a looked in the mirror."

"Exactly. Anyhow, some guys who worked there came over to break it up but they were worthless. They were his age and refused to make him cover his shirt up, and this dick-wad says, 'See, dude, I have my rights, so get outta my face.' But finally the owner or manager comes over—some guy our age—and he yells at his employees to get back to work, tells this kid to cover his shirt up or go home, and apologizes to me and even comes over to our table and apologizes to El and the kids."

"And what did this 'grunged-out dick-wad' do?"

"Oh, he turned his shirt inside-out and kicked his stuff around a bit and finally left with his buddies. And that was it."

"You didn't run into him later, I take it?"

"Nope."

They got up to Dodge Ridge to go skiing once, maybe twice a year and always stayed at The Christmas Tree Inn in Mi Wuk Village. It was inexpensive, and you could get a room with two queen beds which was plenty big for the four of them. It also had the added feature of being close to a pizzeria and only a few miles from the ski slopes.

Tim loaded his skis and boots in the back, added in the packed cooler, and closed the rear door of the minivan. Everyone was in their seats—his wife Ellen (who he called "El"), his ten-year old son Zach, and his seven-year-old daughter Cara—and he slid into the driver's seat, buckled up and started the van.

"Everyone ready?" he asked cheerfully.

Yep, everyone was ready.

It was a cold, crisp morning and looked like a perfect day for skiing. The lifts didn't open for another forty minutes but Tim wanted to get there early so he could get his wife and kids outfitted in the rental shop by the time the lifts opened at 9:00. It was mid-week—a Thursday—and the traffic was light driving up to the lodge. By the time they parked, got everyone outfitted in skis, boots, and poles, bought lift tickets, went to the bathroom, and got out to the beginner slope it was five minutes to nine. Perfect timing.

They had a routine down. In the morning, leading up to their lunch break, Tim skied with the family on the beginner and intermediate slopes. After lunch, Tim headed up the mountain to the expert slopes, leaving El and the kids on the easier runs, and spent the rest of the day skiing on his own.

The first two hours they all spent on Clementine, which was a beginner lift that ran slowly up the side of a hill and deposited everyone at the top of a long, gently sloping hill. It was here that Tim had taught his wife and kids to ski, and today he was working with his daughter on improving her turns. After two hours, and feeling confident, they all agreed to move over to Gentle Ben, which was a blue diamond run for intermediate skiers. It was a steeper run and here Tim continued to work with his daughter while his wife and son skied together. After about an hour, El skied down to the lodge to secure a table and get everything ready for lunch. Tim took one more run with the kids and then skied down to join her.

The three of them unbuckled their bindings, stuck their skis in the snow, tramped up the metal stairs, and pushed through the large doors into the lodge where they found El camped out at one of the tables. She had the cooler open and there was food and drinks laid out on the table.

"All the tables by the window were taken," she said as they plopped down next to her and started taking off their gloves and beanies.

"This is fine," replied Tim.

The warm, intimate small-talk of a family broke out as everyone got comfortable, grabbed their favorite sandwich to eat ("No, the salami's Dad's, the peanut butter and jelly is yours."), popped open sodas ("Where's my Pepsi—give Cara her Sunny-D."), and divvied-up the bags of chips ("What, I thought you liked Cheetos—then, here, take the Doritos instead."). They had hearty appetites, and the lunch tasted especially good because they had been skiing all morning in the frosty weather.

"Did you see Cara on her turns?" asked Tim. "She's getting them down."

"Yeah, I'm getting them down. Did you see me, Mom?"

"I did. You're a fast learner."

"I know," agreed Cara happily.

"And how about Zacharoni here," added Tim. "He's lookin' good. Pretty soon you'll be skiing black diamonds with me."

Zach smiled at the compliment, but he had something else on his mind: "When can I snowboard, Dad? You said I could snowboard once I got good at skiing."

What followed was a one-sided discussion on the finer points of skiing as Tim tried to explain to his son how skiing was an art steeped in heroic tradition while snowboarding was a passing fad meant for the likes of heathens and delinquents. But as he made his argument, Tim knew that he would eventually lose out and his son would take up snowboarding.

After Tim finished his appeal, he took a bite of his sandwich and noticed his wife's face. Something was bothering her, and when he caught her eye he saw she was staring at something behind him with a disapproving frown. Tim turned around to look and saw three young men standing around a nearby table. They had the baggy gear and laced boots of snowboarders. One of them had tossed off his coat and stood facing them, revealing a black t-shirt with bold orange lettering that said "Fuck-off and Die."

Tim turned back and looked at his wife, shaking his head in shared disapproval. He glanced at both his kids but they were too busy eating at the moment to notice. He thought about letting it go but El said, "Unbelievable. The guy's a jerk."

"Who's a jerk?" asked Cara, and with that both kids looked around to find the jerk. They quickly found him—there, standing not too far away, facing them with his offending t-shirt. "Oh," said Cara, returning to her sandwich. Zach snickered, glanced at his dad, and then turned back to his food with a look of amusement.

"Isn't there a dress code here?" wondered El out loud. "There's families here with small kids."

"I would imagine... I'm sure a manager will make him cover it up." But as Tim said this he knew better. No one would confront this kid. He would boldly flaunt his colors, getting nods and smirks from kids his own age, and take a rebel's pleasure at the frowns and hard looks he got from parents and adults. No, no one would call him out. That only happened in Westerns.

El nodded at her husband's reassurance, said "I hope so," and watched as the kid in the t-shirt disappeared with his buddies into the cafeteria to buy their lunch. She ate quietly, waiting, and when the kid returned to his table with his tray of food she saw that his t-shirt was still on and still broadcasting its obscene message to the world. "I knew it," she said to her husband. "They didn't do anything. He went into the cafeteria and none of the employees said a word—I guarantee it. They just let it go. Everybody just let it go."

"Why don't you let it go, mom," said Cara. This from an seven year-old.

Her older brother snickered at her comment without looking up from his food. Tim tread more carefully; he looked at his wife and raised both eyebrows as if to say, "That's our daughter for you—what can I say?"

"I know that sounds like good advice, dear," El said to her daughter in a soft yet parental tone, "but you just can't always let things go. Sometimes you gotta speak out. That kid is being very rude and we shouldn't have to put up with it. Right? Sometimes you have to speak up."

Cara shrugged her shoulders slightly and nodded in agreement with her mother. El glanced back at her husband for support and he, too, nodded in agreement. But what Tim knew, as he nodded in agreement with her, was that this gesture of endorsement wasn't going to be enough. More was being asked of him; more was being expected of him. He knew this as well as he knew anything, at a gut level, without really needing to ponder it. She was calling for him to kill a spider in the bathroom and his choice was clear—kill the spider or wuss out.

"What do you want dad to do—go over there and beat him up?" suddenly asked their son.

Tim's thoughts had been wandering in that same direction and his son's honest faux pas almost caused him to laugh out loud.

"Nooo," replied El, dismissing the question as silly. "I'm not saying that... But something should be done."

"Want me to go talk to the manager?" asked Tim.

"Would you?"

"Sure."

And with that Tim stood up tall and looked around the large room for someone in charge. After a moment, he spied two employees in blue vests standing over by one of the trash stations and walked over to them. They were two young men in their late teens or early twenties and one of them was replacing a trash bag while the other watched and talked to him.

"Where can I find the manager?" asked Tim as he came up to them. The one stopped talking and they both looked at him.

"Ahh, the manager... I don't know," said the one not working. "I think he's downstairs in the gift shop. Do you need him?"

"I'd like to talk to him."

"Want me to go get him?"

Before Tim could answer that question, the second employee stood up with his twisted and tied-off trash bag and asked, "Whaddya need him for? Can we help you with something?"

"Well, yeah. Maybe you can. Do you have a dress code here?"

"A dress code? Whaddya mean?"

"I'm talkin' about that guy over there—there—see him?—eating at the table, facing you with the t-shirt that says 'Fuck-off and Die.'"

"Yeah, I saw him earlier," said the one with the trash bag.

"Did you say anything to him, like ask him to cover it up?" Tim only got a blank stare in response to this question, so he tried a different tack. "It's a little offensive, don't you think? I mean this is a G-rated family setting here with kids and all."

"More like PG-13," said the one with the trash bag. His partner sniffed a laugh at that.

"Even so," pressed Tim in a polite and diplomatic tone. "You don't get to say the F-word in a PG-13 movie, right? So it would be nice if we could get this guy to change his shirt, or at least cover it up. Wouldn't you agree?"

The two young men quickly exchanged glances with one another. Tim read those glances and the rest of their body language and knew at once they wouldn't be any help. It was the attitude, part bemusement, part sarcastic, which told him all he needed to know. He pressed once more, rather half-heartedly, and only got blank looks and shoulder shrugs in return. The one with the trash bag finally summed it up with this credo: "There's really not much we can do about it, sir."

"Understood... Can you do this for me?" Tim asked, wrapping up his wasted time. "When you see your supervisor, let him know I'd like to talk to him. I'm sitting right over there. Okay?"

"Sure."

Tim gave them each a perfunctory smile and returned to his table where he briefed El on his fruitless mission.

"Should we wait around to see if the manager comes by?" she asked. She still held out hope that right would prevail.

Tim glanced around the table and saw that everyone was done eating lunch. "Nah, let's go skiing," he replied cheerfully. "Whaddya say, Twinkie. Ready to hit the slopes?"

His daughter smiled and said, "I'm ready."

"Good... Zach—ready? Dear—you ready?"

Yep, everyone was ready.

Tim collected up all the wrappers and plastic bottles and walked over to the nearest trash station. As he put the last bottle into the recycle bin he looked up and saw the kid with the t-shirt standing next to him. He was waiting to empty his tray into the same garbage can. The kid looked to be eighteen or nineteen and was slightly shorter than Tim but stockier in his build. Tim had played football in high school and this kid had middle linebacker written all over him—the same thickset body, large forearms, and thick unruly hair—and this assessment was reaffirmed when the kid glanced up and caught Tim's eye. There it was, the same piercing and slightly crazy eyes of a middle linebacker.

And for whatever reason, be it out of parental concern, good citizenship, or perhaps a perverse desire to rattle the cage, Tim asked him point blank, "What's with that shirt?"

The kid regarded him for a moment with a vacant stare, suddenly hummed "I don't know," and responded with his own question, "Why?"

"Don't you think it's a little over-the-top for a place like this? There are small kids around."

"So what?"

"So, it's offensive."

"Big deal."

"It's a big deal to me and to most of the parents around here—so, please, if you would, do us a favor and change your shirt or cover it up."

The kid had squared off and faced Tim directly, giving him the full force of his half-crazy linebacker eyes. "No," he said, and as he did he brushed past Tim, making body contact, and emptied his tray into the garbage.

"No, huh?"

"No, dude."

After emptying his tray the kid had backed up, but now Tim took a step closer to him and stared straight into the kid's face. "Look," he said calmly. "I'll ask you politely one more time. Please remove that shirt, or at least cover it up, and we can all have a nice day."

"Fuck off, dude."

"Really? How did I know that was coming," replied Tim. "Is that the extent of your vocabulary?" He was getting angry, recognized he was getting angry, checked it for the moment, and quickly added, "Come on, now. Do us a favor. Let's not make a big deal out of this. Just cover the shirt and be done with it."

"You're the one making a big deal out of it. This is a free country, dude. I can do what I want."

"Well, that's where you're wrong," Tim said, and he thought about relaying to him the example of someone yelling "fire!" in a crowded theatre as proof to the limits of free speech, but he knew the distinction would be lost on this kid, so he finished off with this: "Livin' in a free country doesn't give you the right to be a jerk."

At that, the kid's shoulders hunched up as though he were about to take on a running back. "You're the jerk, dude!" he shot back. "Get outta my face!"

And what quickly ensued—a thing that could have been avoided, should have been avoided, but in its own aboriginal way couldn't be avoided—was a shouting and pushing match that grabbed the attention of the whole ski lodge.

El was bagging up their left over lunch when she heard the yelling. Before she could find where it was coming from she heard her son say, "It's dad." She looked to where her son pointed and saw her husband and the kid in the t-shirt squared-off yelling at one another. The whole lunch crowd was drawn to the commotion and people were converging on the spot to break it up. Her daughter slid over next to her and El put her arm around her. The yelling got louder and suddenly the kid in the t-shirt stuck his finger into her husband's chest and she watched as Tim slapped it away. This led to pushing. People now jumped in to break it up.

In short order, things had gone from a verbal confrontation to pushing, and Tim could feel a hand on his sleeve pulling him back. Across from him, the kid's two buddies made attempts to restrain their friend. Triggered by the release of adrenalin Tim's mind raced, bracing for a rush, watching for a fist, looking for a weapon, registering the faces around him. He glanced over at his family. His wife was wide-eyed, his daughter curled up next to her with a frightened look on her face, and his son stood poised in a crouched position.

"Whoa, whoa, whoa! Break it up, break it up!" yelled a voice. "Come on now!"

The voice came from a young man in a blue vest—the same one Tim had spoken to earlier—the one with the trash bag. His blue-vested co-worker was with him and they both worked to restore order.

"Everyone just calm down," he added. "What's going on here?" He looked at Tim when he asked this question.

Tim struggled to rein in his anger so he could talk clearly. "This is the guy I pointed out to you before," he said breathlessly. "I politely asked him to cover up his shirt and he went Hannibal Lecter on me."

"You got in my face, dude!" hissed the kid in the t-shirt. "I got my rights!"

"I remember," replied the blue-vested trash guy. "But I..."

"And now we got this," interrupted Tim, pointing to the kid in the t-shirt as exhibit A. "He wants to fight me—make a scene— instead of covering the shirt up."

"This is a free country," repeated the kid in the t-shirt.

The blue-vested trash guy put his hand up, signaling he had something important to say, and looked at Tim as he did so. "But as I said before, sir, there's nothing we can do about it. He's right, it's a free country."

"See, I told you," taunted the kid in the t-shirt. "You're a fascist."

Tim sniffed a derisive laugh, told the kid he wouldn't know a fascist if he tripped over one, and glanced around him taking quick inventory. He found that he had wandered into the back-woods and picked a fight with a bunch of hillbillies who were all related. The kid in the t-shirt stood triumphant in his free country, flanked by his two buddies who stood like smirking statues. The blue vests had done their job and restored order; it all smelled like teen spirit to them.

Tim saw his chances for justice dwindling quickly, but like Ali on the ropes he wasn't quite done yet. "Where's your manager?"

he asked. "Did you tell him like I asked?" This put the blue vests on defensive and they hemmed and hawed an answer. "Get him!" Tim demanded, "'cause this idiot's not leaving here until he covers the damn shirt."

"Fuck you, dude. It's a free country!"

"I'll get Ray."

"Yeah, get Ray."

"Yeah, I'll go get him—wait, here he comes now."

A neatly dressed gentleman in his early forties arrived on the scene and in short order and with military efficiency sorted things out. What was going on, he wanted to know, and he addressed the question directly to Tim while ignoring his two employees. Tim gave him a brief, unvarnished synopsis. "Is that right?" replied the manager. He glanced momentarily at the kid in the t-shirt, giving him the once-over with his eyes, and then looked at his two employees. "Do you have anything to add?" he asked them. They did not. "Fine, then go back to work," he ordered.

The manager quickly surveyed the lodge to confirm that everyone had gone back to eating their lunch. Satisfied, he regarded the kid in the t-shirt with a stern eye. "Do you have a day-pass or a season pass?" he asked the kid. The kid stammered slightly—the air had gone out of his balloon—and replied that he had a day pass.

"Fine," said the manager. "You have five minutes to change that shirt or cover it up or I'm pulling your pass. Understood?"

The kid understood and turned away with his buddies.

The manager faced Tim and grinned slightly. "Sorry about that," he said. "You okay?"

"Sure."

"The name's Ray Purdy. I'm the manager here."

"Nice to meet you Ray," replied Tim, shaking his hand warmly. "Name's Tim."

"Tim, it's a pleasure—and again, sorry about all this. My employees should have handled that better. Here by yourself or with your family?"

"My family. There right over there."

Tim pointed with his eyes over to El and the kids, and Ray walked with him over to their table. Tim introduced everybody and Ray shook hands all around with a charming smile. He was sorry this all had to happen and hoped it hadn't ruined their day. El assured him with a charming smile of her own that it hadn't. They exchanged more pleasantries and after a couple minutes Ray glanced over at the table behind him to check on the kid in the t-shirt. The kid had flung his shirt off and stood facing them, his linebacker eyes piercing Tim, his bare chest covered in thick, dark hair. The kid turned away, kicking his glove that was on the floor, and started putting on his jacket.

"I think I prefer him in the shirt," said Ray with a chuckle. Tim and El shared his chuckle. "I see you already ate lunch," he added. "Here's a coupon for a free lunch—next trip up. No, please take it. My pleasure. And next time, Tim, if you see an idiot like that making trouble, don't go John Wayne on him— come get me. Deal?"

"Deal."

They all shared another chuckle together before Ray said his goodbye and left them.

"Great guy," said El. Tim agreed and they locked eyes for a moment in shared relief. "I'll take the stuff back to the van and meet you out there," she added. And with balance once again restored to the universe, El took the cooler and headed out to the parking lot while Tim followed the kids outside to their skis.

Tim grabbed his and El's skis and poles and walked up the snowy bank towards the lift. He stopped and waited for his wife to return, handing her gear to her when she walked up. Their kids were already getting into the lift line.

"Would you have fought him?" El asked her husband. "You looked like you were ready to punch him out. It was kind of scary."

"I don't know. Maybe."

El grimaced and shook her head. "That was crazy," she said.

"Yep," he replied. She grimaced and shook her head again but he noticed there was a smile in her eyes.

They rode up on the lift together, their kids two chairs ahead of them, and collected together at the top of Gentle Ben. There

Tim kissed his wife, reminded his daughter to work on her turns, cautioned his son not to ski too fast, and then pushed off and veered off to the right towards another lift that would take him higher up the mountain. Once at the top he skied across on a trail that led to another chair lift which took him even higher with access to a number of black diamond runs.

There was hardly anyone in line at the chair lift and Tim got right on. There were more shadows on this side of the mountain and the ride up was colder. The chair deposited him out on a snowy plateau where Tim skied over and headed down a long, wide run known as Stampmill that went along the ridge of the mountain. Branching off from this main run where shorter, much steeper runs that took you back down to the chair lift. These were the runs Tim wanted and he pulled up at the one named Jackpot and looked down the challenging slope. It was empty of people. He smiled at that because it meant he could go balls-to-the-wall, get his Bode Miller on, and not have to worry about obstacles. Tim tested his baseball cap to make sure it was snug, re-gripped his ski poles and pushed off.

In less than a minute the run was over and he was back at the chair lift. He'd get a least a dozen or more runs like this in before the day was over. Next time up he took on Bobby's Freedom Run, another black diamond run, but he had to slow down to navigate past a group of black-clad snowboarders who had stopped in the middle of the slope to palaver. He came back to it again and this time it was clear and he had a good, fast run.

Tim came up to the chair lift and got ready to load. He glanced at the young man who managed the lift. The young man had ignored him the first three times but this time he glanced up and gave Tim a nod. Behind him, in a booth, a CD player blared out a Pearl Jam song. Tim nodded back, slid on to the moving chair, and lifted off. To Tim the kid looked like every other kid who worked the chair lifts here, with the same baggy, grunged-out look and the same bored disdain that marked their generation.

It was a long, slow ride up and Tim's thoughts wandered. He chuckled to himself at the characterization he just given that young man at the chair lift, and that in turn triggered a replay of the events in the lodge. He had to admit he was fortunate the whole thing hadn't turned into a fight. That would have been a disaster, he knew. Someone might have been hurt, the police called, arrests made—who knows what. But luckily Ray had showed up in the nick of time. He thought some more about what he might have said or done better to avoid the conflict, decided in the end that it probably couldn't have gone any differently, and slid off the chair lift at the top mountain with a sure feeling that justice had prevailed.

Tim skied along Stamphill until he reached his favorite black diamond run—Claimjumper—and he pulled up and looked down. It was in two parts with a steep, fast run at the top that leveled off and then went steep and fast again, emptying out into a bowl that led back to the chair lift. The run was clear of skiers, and Tim glanced behind him and saw some snowboarders quickly approaching. Tim checked his gear, felt a rush of adrenalin, and pushed off before they arrived.

He made quick, sharp turns at first, carving up the snow, and then opened up to longer, faster turns like a downhill racer. The speed was exhilarating and he pushed it right to the edge of his abilities, but he caught an edge, nearly ate it, found his balance again, and came to a stop at the level part right before the second half of the run.

"Whoa!" he said to himself, laughing at the near disaster. He waited a moment to collect himself, took a deep breath, and pushed off again. He made a sharp turn right, planted his pole for a left turn—

There were people around him talking and he found the whole thing confusing. He held a ski glove in his hand but wasn't sure what it was for. Someone brought him a ski and set it next to him. Tim sat in the snow and tried to figure it all out, and after a while guys in red vests appeared and asked him questions. It dawned on him that they were Ski Patrol. They had a sled with them. He listened politely to their questions, sorting through them like a jumbled deck of cards, while becoming conscious of a dull ache in his left shoulder. He remembered his name—yes, he was here with his family—no, he didn't think anything was broken—no, he didn't want to ride down in the sled.

They helped him up and assisted with his bindings. Once his skis were on they handed him his poles. He reached up and felt his head. "I lost my hat," he said. No, here it was and they handed it to him. They told him in calm voices to take it easy, they would shadow him down—"pizza wedge the whole way"—and two of them stayed beside him as they carefully made their way back down to the lodge.

El stood on her skis at the bottom of the chair lift and admired her daughter's turns. Cara planted her inside pole each time before she turned, just as she had been taught, and made it cleanly down to the chair lift where she slid to a stop in front of her mother.

"Very nice," said El. "Ready to go again?"

"Yeah. Where's Zach."

"He went to the restroom. He'll catch up with us later."

They pushed off with their poles towards the lift line but stopped abruptly when they heard someone call out "Ellen!" El turned around and saw a man in a Ski Patrol uniform approaching her. "Yes," she answered.

"Are you Ellen Hines," he asked her.

"Yes," she replied and immediately she felt a wave of panic as her face flushed and became warm. The Ski Patrol calling her name meant only one thing—her husband was hurt or her son was hurt, but something bad had happened. "What's wrong?" she managed to ask in her growing panic.

"Your husband had a bit of a spill," he said calmly. He was older with white hair and a kind face. "But he's okay," he assured her with a slight grin. He pointed to a picnic table about twenty yards away where El saw her husband sitting next to another Ski Patroller. "He might have a slight concussion," he explained to her, adding that he should probably go see a doctor and have it checked out. El listened intently, nodded her understanding, and thanked him for his help.

"Go find your brother and meet us over there," she said to her daughter. With that she unbuckled her skis and walked with the

Ski Patroller over to her husband. She knelt down next to her husband and looked into his eyes, saw what she needed to see, and then thanked the Ski Patrol again for their help. Both patrollers made a couple jokes to ease the situation before making their official hand-off to El. Their kids arrived in a breathless rush.

The family huddled around dad and the kids peppered him with questions. "I guess I was going too fast and crashed. I think I got knocked out for a little bit," he said rather sheepishly. El held his hand and looked into his eyes, telling the kids to shush for now, and then announced that they were all going home. No one argued with her.

The dull ache in Tim's shoulder had become raw and constant and he had some difficulty loading the skis into the van. "I messed my shoulder up," he said to El. She took the car keys from him and ordered him to get in the passenger's seat and he did as he was told. El started up the van and looked around to make sure everyone was buckled up.

"Everyone ready?" she asked

Yep, everyone was ready.

That night Tim had difficulty sleeping. The pain in his shoulder was nonstop and even three Advils didn't help much. Dream images, brief and sharp, punctuated his restless sleep and seemed to work in concert with the pain in his shoulder. In one, he is following his son along Stamphill. His son is on a snowboard and getting farther and farther away from him. He can't raise his arm up to signal his son to wait up, so he tries to speed up but his skis don't work right. In another, he's on a steep slope and his daughter goes flying by him out of control. She's not turning like he taught her. He yells at her to turn, to stop, but she continues on and crashes into thick netting. Heartsick, he skis down and tries frantically to untangle her but his left arm is useless and it seems to take forever. Now he is in the ski lodge searching for his wife. She's lost and he's worried about her. He comes to a door—she may be behind it—but he can't open it with his bad arm. The manager Ray appears and Tim asks him if he's seen his wife. Ray says no but he's pretty sure he's lying. And just as suddenly he is on Claimjumper, stopped at the midway point, and everything is clear and bright. He pushes off, turns, and is hit from behind, side-swiped by a dark figure. He feels a sharp pain in his shoulder, and as he goes down he glimpses three snowboarders flashing by him. They look familiar and they're laughing. One of them is the kid in the shirt, the one with the crazy linebacker eyes, and he yells back at Tim. "Fuck off and die, dude!"

Tim awoke from this image and lay still for a moment. He reached his hand over and touched his wife's hip. She was sound asleep. He rolled off his back onto his right shoulder and tried to get comfortable but it was useless. He got up, put his robe on, and went into the living room where he watched old black and white movies until the sun came up.

THE MILLENNIUM

(The Two-thousands)

If the battle for civilization comes down to the wimps versus the barbarians, the barbarians are going to win.

Thomas Sowell

The question isn't, 'What do we want to know about people?' It's, 'What do people want to tell about themselves?'

Mark Zuckerberg

Behind the ritual, behind the ritual
You find the spiritual, you find the spiritual
Behind the ritual in the days gone by

Van Morrison
Behind the Ritual

Dean and Frank

" **N** ice shot," said Dean.

Frank lifted up his racquet and saluted his opponent, politely acknowledging the compliment. It also signaled the end of their game as well as the end of their hour inside the racquetball court. Frank opened the door and stepped out into the hallway where he bent down and picked up a small towel. He was sweating profusely and he removed his drenched sweatband, flipped off his goggles, and wiped down his face. Dean joined him and did the same.

They both unscrewed the caps on their power drinks and rehydrated, simultaneously closing the caps on their drinks before picking up their gym bags and walking into the locker room. They showered down and changed into their street clothes, keeping up a sophisticated chatter that included witty observations, puns, and an ongoing political discourse filled with dry sarcasm and educated criticisms of current events. Given it was 2002 going on 2003, there was much to be critical of—President Bush, a rush to war with Iraq, child abuse scandals in the Catholic Church. The list was endless. They finished dressing and stood ready to leave. Each was attired in business casual, with a studious finish, that befitted their rank as members of the Napa Valley College faculty.

"Good for Thursday?" asked Frank.

"Yeah," answered Dean.

Dean and Frank played racquetball together every Tuesday and Thursday right after their last class at 3:30. Dean Tan was a professor of Sociology and taught *Introduction to Sociology* along with two other courses that focused on social problems and human sexuality. Frank Navarro was a professor of Anthropology and taught *Biological Anthropology* along with a course on cultural anthropology and one on sex, gender, and sexuality. Both men had been at their post for over five years and were in their early thirties.

They walked out to the parking lot, said goodbye, and each got into their car and drove home to Yountville. The fact that they both lived in Yountville was just one of many coincidences between them. Besides age and tenure both men were married to academicians (who kept their maiden names), had no kids, and were published authors in their fields of expertise. Both men were dedicated to physical fitness—Dean to mountain-biking, Frank to jogging—and they both enjoyed playing racquetball. Dean Tan was half Chinese, half Caucasian, but looked more Asian than white, while Frank Navarro was Hispanic and claimed to be part Yaqui Indian. This gave them both official minority status and enhanced their credibility with their students and colleagues. The biggest difference between the two men was physical stature: Dean was short and stocky while Frank was tall and lean.

Despite all these similarities and despite sharing a world view shaped by an adulthood spent in Liberal Arts and the Humanities, they did not socialize with one another outside of work. Their connection was strictly racquetball. Dean had come looking for a game a few years back and found Frank sitting on a bench outside one of the courts waiting for a game. They struck up a conversation, tallying up their similarities, and remarked along the way that they were each looking for a reliable playing partner. They grabbed a court and played a few games, quickly finding out that they were evenly matched, not overly competitive, and played the game with a genteel sort of sportsmanship that each man, being themselves cultured and reputable, recognized at once in the other. That sealed the deal.

They were fortunate even to have a racquetball court on campus. The racquetball boom had ended years ago and many courts across the country had closed or been converted into gyms that featured aerobics and weightlifting. Napa Valley College still had a multi-court facility dedicated to racquetball, one of the few around, and Dean and Frank rarely had a problem finding an open court.

They usually played for an hour with a match consisting of two games to fifteen and a tie-breaker, if needed, to eleven. If they went over an hour it was because they started a match that went to a tie-breaker, and they both viewed it as bad form not to play a game to its final end.

As noted earlier, their game was characterized by a genteel sportsmanship. Neither man argued a point or inwardly fumed over a missed opportunity (or at least didn't show it). On a disputed call, like a double bounce close to the wall, one would say, "Was that good?" while the other would reply, "Yeah, I think so," or "No, don't think so," and that would be the end of it. They were both solid intermediate players with hard shots but they went out of their way to avoid hitting the other even if it meant passing up a sure winner. On the rare occasion that happened—a shot to the back of the leg or off the shoulder—both men would apologize profusely, one for making the shot, the other for being in his way, and mutually agree to a replay. Theirs was a gentleman's game, played hard but played fair, and neither sought victory for victory's sake, thinking such a thing to be uncouth and beneath their better nature.

But that all changed one day in May.

"I got some new balls," said Frank as he lifted up the plastic container with two blue balls inside to show Dean.

"Oh, good. We need 'em," replied Dean.

They were in the locker room changing into their gym clothes. Dean unzipped his racquet from its cover, took it out, and examined the edges like a hunter checking his trusty spear. This image must have triggered a comparison in the Professor of Anthropology's mind because Frank said, "Did you abstain from sexual activity last night?"

"From what?" asked Dean a bit surprised by the question, but he noticed the wry grin on Frank's face.

"Sexual relations. It's universal among primitive peoples for the hunter to abstain from sex the night before the hunting expedition. They also note their dreams, cleanse themselves, avoid certain foods, and usually paint or adorn themselves to get in good with the spirits. It's done to evoke the mystic powers they need for a successful hunt."

"I see," replied Dean. He was used to Frank citing primitive customs and practices to make a point or crack a joke and he went along with this one. "Fortunately, I did abstain, not necessarily by choice, and I did take a shower this morning and avoided eating animal flesh. So I think I'm in good with the spirits."

"You can never be too sure—hence the power necklace," said Frank, referring to the braided necklace that Dean placed around his neck before playing racquetball. It was currently popular with professional athletes and featured an Auqu-Titanium technology which claimed to promote stable energy flow throughout the body. Dean was convinced of its powers but Frank remained skeptical.

Dean tied off the braided cord behind his neck and adjusted it until it sat just right. "I can't say it acts as a talisman," replied Dean. "But I'm open to the possibility that it taps into a universal energy flow, something akin to what I think the Sioux call 'wakonda.'"

"Ahh, yes, 'wakonda.' The Melanesians call it 'mana' and the Hindus 'shakti.' And then we have the Christians and Muslims who would call it 'the power of god.'"

Dean nodded at this insight and said with a smile, "Nothing wrong with tapping into a little shakti if I can. You should really try it. I think you'd find it lessens your fatigue and shortens your recovery time."

"Do you have any case studies to back that up?"

"No," replied Dean with a short laugh. "But that's an idea. We'll see if we can't get one of our departments to fund a cross-functional study to support or refute the power of the necklace."

"Good luck with that."

"You wouldn't be open to pitching such a study to your department?"

Frank knew that Dean was in jest and he replied in kind: "Hell, Dean, I can't even get them to fund a model of homo erectus."

Both men sniffed a laugh at this as they gathered up their bags and racquets and headed out of the locker room. They set their bags down on a bench in the main lobby and assessed the scene. The main lobby acted as a viewing area. There were two courts on prominent display, both made of durable, see-through glass, that at one time had hosted tournament championships. To the left and down a hallway were a number of other courts that were closed-in boxes of concrete. In these courts a game could only be viewed from a loft above that ran the length of the hall. Both men preferred to play in a glass court, and today they were in luck. One was available.

The other glass court had a game going on, and as they approached their eyes couldn't help but take in the sight. Two women were playing. Dean and Frank dropped their bags next to the door outside the empty court and watched them for a moment. Two things were immediately apparent: both women were exceptionally attractive and neither of them was very good at racquetball. There was poor footwork, missed shots, shouting, laughing, and a lot of unnecessary movement that could only be described as elegant bedlam. They looked to be having a grand time.

Dean and Frank, racquets in hand—Frank with two new balls bulging out of his front pocket—entered their court and began to stretch out. There was a glass wall between the two courts and the two men and the two women could clearly see each other. One of the women chasing the ball suddenly banged into the wall next to Frank and her ample breasts pressed up against the glass. Frank, stretching out, glanced up at her. She came off the glass, smiled, and waved at him. Frank waved back.

"Hi, guys!" she called out through the glass, waving again. She signaled her partner and her partner waved back as well.

Both men stood up and waved back, a bit comically, and said "hi" in return. The women flashed friendly smiles, nodded to each other as if to say. "Hmm—cute guys," and resumed their game.

"You know them?" asked Dean, his hand frozen in a wave position.

"No, do you?"

"Don't think so." The two men stood for a moment and studied their next door neighbors. Both women looked to be in their early twenties. One was a blonde and the other was a redhead, and their shoulder length hair was tied up in ponytails. The blonde, the one who had come up against the glass, looked a bit like the actress Cameron Diaz, and she wore a sleeveless, low-cut top that showed off her cleavage and caused her breasts to bounce as she ran. Her trunks were short, tight on her butt, and the two men's eyes ran easily down her dancer-like legs. The redhead instantly reminded one of a star of a work-out video. Along with being pretty, she was trim and fit and wore black spandex shorts along with a green t-shirt, cut above her navel, which hung off one shoulder.

"No, never seen them," confirmed Dean. "But that's quite an outfit." He was referring to the blonde. Besides wearing an outfit that accentuated her voluptuous form, the matching top and bottom were a canary yellow highlighted with a black trim.

"Yes, very bright," deadpanned Frank. He cocked his head to one side and gave both women another thorough glance. "It could be the Reed Dance of Swaziland," he commented in his professor's voice.

Dean caught the gist of the analogy—women brightly dressed in a mating dance—and sniffed a short laugh before bouncing a ball and taking a practice shot. Frank joined him and the two men practiced for a few minutes and then lagged for serve, got in their ready positions, and started their game.

Their first game was a swift, nicely played game that Frank won 15-13. Frank had his low, line-drive shot working and hit at least five un-returnable shots into the front right corner that proved to be the difference-maker. After the game, they popped out the door to grab their towels and wipe off their sweaty faces. The two women exited their court at the same time, their faces flush, their bodies moist with perspiration, and met up with Dean and Frank.

"Wow, you guys are good!" enthused the blonde. "We could take some lessons from you."

"Thanks," replied Dean—"but you two seemed to be doing just fine. It's the work-out that counts, right?"

"Right," agreed the redhead with a big smile.

"You two students here?" asked Frank.

"Yeah, no, well I was last year, for a short time," explained the redhead, "but I'm taking this year off to make some money." When asked by Dean where she worked she replied cheerily, "Carpe Diem Wine Bar, downtown."

"Never been there," said Dean. "Nice place?"

"You'd love it. You should come by some time."

They continued to chit-chat for another minute or so, and in that brief time Dean and Frank learned that Brittany the blonde was up from L.A. visiting her friend Kat (short for Kathy) the redhead. Both women wiped their moist arms and legs down with a dry towel as they talked, while Brittany took the extra step of raising each arm up and drying off her underarms as though she had just stepped out of a shower. Both were duly impressed upon learning that Dean and Frank were professors at Napa Valley College.

There was a lull in the chit-chat and Frank said, "Nice to meet you."

"Nice to meet you!" they both chimed back. "Mind if we watch you for a while?" asked Brittany. "Yeah, we could use some pointers," added Kat.

Dean glanced at Frank and shrugged good-naturedly. "Sure," he said.

"But don't blame us if you get bored to death," said Frank.

"That won't happen—guaranteed!" replied Brittany with a laugh. And with that, both women picked up their bags and sat down on a bench nearby to get comfortable. They had front row seats.

As winner, Frank had the serve, and a little self-conscious at being watched, he lobbed an easy serve back to Dean who immediately slammed it home, catching Frank flat-footed. Dean retrieved the rolling ball and quickly took his place in the service zone. With his left foot forward in a ready position, Dean bounced the ball and hit a sharp serve that skipped past Frank for the first point of the game.

"One zip," called out Dean

Calling out the score like that was a slight breach of protocol. Usually the two men kept score in their heads, validating the score along the way by saying things like "Six-four, right?" ("Right.") or "For the game, right?" ("Yeah, for the game.") but never, at any time, loudly calling out the score after a winning shot. Yes, it was a slight breach of protocol and it irritated Frank just a little bit.

Dean reeled off five straight points, and when he won the rally for the fifth point he called out again, "Five-zip."

"I know the score," said Frank. He crouched in the ready position with his racket out in front of him and waited for Dean's serve. His earlier funk was gone and he was freshly focused. Dean's serve was a line shot to his right which Frank anticipated nicely and his return shot, about a foot off the ground, was to Dean's backhand. Dean lunged at it and was able to get his racket on it but it was a weak return shot, high and slow, that Frank lined up and hit back for a winner. The women cheered his shot. Frank smiled to himself as he retrieved the ball and took over serve.

Frank scored two points before losing serve. Dean switched his serve to a lob to the back corner. Done right, the ball would die in one of the back corners and make a return nearly impossible. It was a tough serve to keep up but Dean had it going and scored another five points to make the score 10-2. On the tenth point, Frank had tried to curl his racket into the back corner to scoop the ball back but failed and, upon failing once again, banged his racket against the wall in frustration. This show of frustration was uncharacteristic of Frank and it caught Dean's attention.

"That serve won't last," said Dean. Frank ignored the platitude and got ready for the next serve. Dean shrugged one shoulder and got ready to serve, but having said his serve wouldn't last that possibility was now ripe in his head, and he hit his lob shot too long, off the back wall, causing him to lose the serve.

An invigorating intensity had been slowly building throughout the game. It could be seen in the effort each man was putting forth to reach the ball, place a shot, or jockey for best position. These growing efforts sometimes caused one of them to bang into the wall or brush into the other as they leaped after the ball. This burgeoning effort was rewarded by the two women in the front row. They punctuated the game with shouts of encouragement, rewarding winning shots with a "Wow!" or a "Nice shot!" and recognizing extra effort, even if it resulted in a losing shot, with "Almost, almost! Nice try!"

When the score hit 12-4, a victory for Dean seemed a sure thing, but Frank rallied to make it 12-10 before Dean got his killer serve back and finished out the game 15 to 10. The women applauded their effort as the two men came out the door to towel off and re-hydrate. Both men were breathing heavily, and Dean acknowledged their applause with a quick wave.

"You gotta teach me that serve, Dean" said Kat.

"Mmm," replied Dean between sips of his lemon-lime Powerade. "I got lucky."

"I doubt it's luck," complimented Kat.

"What's the score now?" asked Brittany, quickly adding—"It's a game apiece, right? This is for the championship."

Frank nodded and replied, "Yeah," somewhat laconically as he kneeled down next to his bag and began to dig around inside.

"Great!" exclaimed Brittany. "We're staying for the championship. Right, Kat?"

"Wouldn't miss it."

Frank found what he was looking for—his good luck charm, an eagle's feather—and he carefully pulled it out of his bag. With his back to the women, he fastened the feather to the side of his trunks and stood up sideways so they couldn't see it. But Dean saw it, and in response he too fished into his bag and pulled out his I-Ching coin, rubbed it for good luck, and stuck it into his front pocket. Both men eyed the other as they put their goggles back on.

"I got my money on you, Dean," sang out Kat.

"I'm betting on Frank," countered Brittany cheerfully.

Dean and Frank re-entered the court and closed the door behind them. Game three, the tie-breaker, was to eleven and Dean quickly took up his position in the service zone. Their demeanor was no-nonsense, as though they had stepped into an examination room, and a grim alertness accentuated their movements. Dean tried his lob serve again but it was less than perfect and Frank dug it out of the back corner. They exchanged shots back and forth for nearly a minute before Frank finally prevailed and took over serve.

With the score 4-1 in Dean's favor, Frank again won back the serve and looked fiercely determined to change the momentum in his favor. He quickly scored a point, then another, and looked to tie it on the next serve. It was a long rally, hard fought, and the court was filled with the sound of grunts, squeaking sneakers, and the ball careening off the walls. After a weak shot by Dean, Frank sprang into position to hit the winner, but as he swung his racquet at the ball Dean jumped in front of him and his shot hit Dean square in the back.

There were sympathetic yells from the women in the front row. "Ow! That had to hurt. You okay, Dean?"

Dean arched his back but didn't rub the spot. He picked up the ball and tossed it back to Frank. "Replay," he said.

"Why?" retorted Frank. "You jumped in front of my shot. That should be my point."

"It's always a replay."

"In a tournament, that'd be ruled my point."

"This isn't a tournament."

"You jumped in front of my shot."

"The hell I did. I was trying to get into position for the next shot. It's a replay."

The two men faced one another, each making eye contact with the other's chin, but kept a polite distance apart. Frank glanced at the ball in his hand, squeezed it tightly, thought better of it, suddenly said "Fine!" and got into position to re-serve. Dean barely got back in position before the serve came flying back at him, but he was able to put a good return on it and the rally was on.

Deep into the rally, Dean made a shot, quickly glanced back to see where Frank was, and moved to his left to avoid his return shot. Despite this maneuver, Frank's shot ricocheted off of Dean's right shoulder and the game stopped. To anyone watching, including the two women, it almost seemed intentional, and the two women remained quiet as they looked on intently.

"Sorry," said Frank. "Bad shot. Replay, right."

Dean stood without speaking and gave Frank the evil eye— what the Sicilians would have called jettatura—and Frank recognized it immediately. "Sure," replied Dean in a stone-cold voice. Frank nodded and took up his position in the service zone, but before he served he turned his head slightly back towards Dean and dry-spit three times as though he were trying to get something off his tongue. Done, he bounced the ball and hit his serve.

The game resumed with an anger-fueled intensity and this catalyst, like some magic spell, boosted their efforts; both men were now a step faster than before, both men now hitting shots harder than before, each man now selling out like never before. A break came with the scored tied at 9-9 and Dean and Frank paused a moment to catch their breath. Their shirts were drenched with sweat and they used their sleeves to wipe their faces. This was a pivotal moment in the game and they both knew it. It was Dean's serve and he got into position, and as he waited for Frank to get ready, he reached quickly into his pocket and rubbed his lucky coin. Frank stroked his eagle feather with the back of his finger.

The serve went to the back right corner but Frank backhanded it before it dropped to the floor, hitting a strong return shot that Dean had to short-hop. The shots went back and forth until Frank, caught out of position, looped a weak shot to the front wall that Dean, seeing his opportunity, quickly lined up for a sure winner. Seeing what was about to happen, Frank raced to the only spot where he had a chance to return the shot, shoving Dean out of the way as he dove for the ball. Despite his effort, Frank missed the ball and lay sprawled on the floor.

"Ten-nine," said Dean.

As Frank slowly gathered himself up, a growl deep and primordial issued from his throat. Dean heard it and it struck a chord.

"That was interference," said Frank. "It should be a replay."

"The hell it was."

"I'm telling you it was. Obvious interference."

"No way. Since when do we call interference?"

"Since now—since you blocked my chance. Cause and effect."

"*Cause and effect.* Bullshit!"

The two men drew menacingly close to one another, their voices rising to a yell. Suddenly there was banging on the glass and the two men looked over to see Brittany trying to get their attention. "Boys, boys!" she shouted out. "Play nice now!"

Properly chastised, Dean and Frank stepped back from one another and dropped their heads to gather themselves. Still upset, Frank approached Brittany and asked her if she'd seen the shot and whether she thought it was interference or not. Yes, she'd seen the shot but she didn't know the rules for interference, so she really couldn't say. How about Kat, Frank wanted to know. What did she think? But when he glanced over Brittany's shoulder he saw Kat deep in conversation with one of the young men who worked at the facility.

"I guess it was good," offered Brittany. "It looked good to me." She shrugged her shoulders as if to say, "That's the best I can do," and hastily retreated back to the bench where she quickly joined in the conversation with Kat and the young man.

Frank shook his head in disgust, turned back to Dean, and threw his hands up in a sign of forced resignation. "Go ahead... Serve," he said simply.

After a short rally, Dean scored the winning point and the game ended and both men exited the court, leaving it smelling of male sweat and burnt rubber. They grabbed their towels and glanced over at the women. The two women were no longer paying any attention to them. Instead, they were caught up in their conversation with the young man and appeared to be talking about some concert at the Mondavi Theatre. Without speaking to the other, both men toweled off, rehydrated, and gathered up their gear to head to the locker room.

"Hey, guys, thanks for the show," Brittany called out.

"Yeah, nice game, guys," added Kat.

Dean raised his racquet up in acknowledgement and smiled. In the locker room, they both showered and changed back into esteemed members of the Napa Valley College faculty. No mention was made of next Tuesday.

When Tuesday rolled around they each showed up to play as usual. There were no puns or witty observations about current events nor sarcastic jokes about President Bush. Instead, a quiet decorum prevailed. Each man felt slightly embarrassed, soiled in a way, as though they had thrown back a curtain and seen something obscene, and both of them were reluctant to speak about it. They entered one of the glass courts and started stretching out.

Dean broke the ice. "Hey, Frank. Sorry about the other day," he said in a diplomatic tone. "Things got a little out of hand."

"No need to apologize, Dean," replied Frank. "It takes two to tango. Let's just put it behind us, shall we?"

"By all means."

"We can smoke a peace pipe on it. I have one from the Keetoowah Cherokees back in my office."

"Put a little hashish in it and I'm in."

"That can be arranged."

They smiled at one another and went back to warming up. Their first game was a tentative affair but by the second game that genteel sportsmanship of the past had returned, albeit somewhat exaggerated, as though they were still a little self-conscious of past sins. Over the following few weeks, their racquetball relationship settled back in, though something was missing. They could both feel it—the loss of something—but neither could articulate it. Instead, what they recognized, both of them in fact, was that their games had become rather ordinary and, quite frankly, boring. But good form dictated that they carry on.

The two women did not come back to the courts and Frank never saw them again. But Dean did. He started hitting happy hour at the Carpe Diem Wine Bar before going home, every Wednesday and Friday from four to six. There he kept to a small table where Kat waited on him.

The Saga of Roy and Dora

The engineering offices of PacCom sat off highway 101 in Redwood City. It was a quick jaunt off the freeway to Twin Dolphin Business Park where two stylish four-story office buildings stood. They were grayish-blue in color, with large tinted windows that looked out over an expansive parking lot. The two buildings, A and B, sat at an oblique angle to the other, and PacCom leased all four floors of building A. The first three floors were populated with clerks, admins, planners and office managers performing their tasks in an open work environment filled with work-stations (each with its own phone and computer), multiple shared printers, fax machines, rows of filing cabinets, and a potpourri of indoor plants, motivational signs, message boards, coolers and coffee stations.

On the fourth floor, alone in their loft, resided the engineers. These were primarily first and second-level managers of all stripes and sizes, both male and female, ranging in age from mid-twenties to late fifties. Each one had either hired out of college or out of the military or matriculated over time to the coveted title of "Manager-Engineering". They performed their job within a honeycomb of cubicles, talking on the phone, clearing emails, working their CAD program, or just plain shooting the bull with a co-worker in their private space. A low white noise, used to mask the ambient din, hummed out from speakers in the plenum ceiling while occasionally a head popped up from behind a cubicle to check the clock or to see if their boss was in.

There were large windows on both sides of the long room and if you were lucky enough or had seniority you sat in a cubicle along the windows with a view. The east side, by far the more preferred view, looked out over the Redwood City Yacht Harbor and the San Francisco Bay. The west side looked out over a vast parking lot, with the freeway just beyond, and the Santa Cruz Mountains beyond that with houses dotting its foothills. It was there on the west side, in a cubicle against the window, that Mary Conley, an engineer responsible for facilities in Palo Alto and Menlo Park, first spied Roy and Dora.

The parking lot was in the shape of a catcher's mitt and contained rows and rows of white-painted parking stalls. It seemed over-built, better sized for a concert venue than a modest business park, and the fact that Building B was empty caused the parking lot on any given weekday to be less than half-full. That left large empty spaces where one could park out-of-the-way and not be bothered.

Mary Conley noticed the two cars parked next to each other on a Thursday. They were parked out towards the lonely edge of the parking lot, there by Mary's end of the building, and she merely noted it as an odd curiosity and went about her work. Next Thursday the same two cars reappeared, and she was walking back to her cubicle from the copy machine when she caught sight of them. Her interest—piqued by the coincidence—caused her to stop and study the two cars. One was an old blue minivan and the other was a white sedan—maybe a Corolla—that was in need of a wash. It was a good hundred yards from her spot at the window but she looked closer and thought she saw two people sitting in the front seat of the sedan. A drug deal she guessed. She was in a hurry to get on a conference call, so she made a mental note to check throughout the week, especially next Thursday, to see if the cars came back.

She checked Friday and periodically throughout the following week but there were no cars. When she came into her cubicle at 7:30 am on Thursday she checked again (no cars) and sat down at her computer to go to work. She usually lost herself in work but today she had a slight distraction, a bubbling anticipation, as one might get at the possibility of uncovering a nefarious plot. Every so often she rolled her chair out to the opening of her cubicle, lifted up slightly to see, and checked for the cars. At exactly 10:00 am, the unwashed sedan appeared. Mary got up out of her seat and watched closely.

"Hey, Sandy," said Mary to the woman in the cubicle next to her. "Check this out."

Sandy was working on her CAD program but looked up when she heard Mary's voice. "What's up?" she replied.

Mary popped her head around the cubicle opening so Sandy could see her and repeated, "Check this out." Mary and Sandy were not particularly friends. Sandy was in her early thirties and single while Mary was in her mid-forties and already a grand-mother. Mary's cubicle was decorated with pictures of kids and school drawings while Sandy's cubicle had pictures pinned up of Hawaii and Europe, places she'd been or planned to go. They didn't have much in common but they were work colleagues and on professionally friendly terms. Sandy got up and joined Mary at the window.

"See that car down there?" said Mary pointing to the white sedan. "Every Thursday that same car pulls up and parks right there. In a minute a blue minivan will join it."

"The same two cars?" asked Sandy. "Every Thursday?"

"Yep. The same two."

"What are they up to?"

"Not sure," replied Mary, leaning towards Sandy in a conspir-atorial manner. "But it might be drugs. I haven't seen the people get out of their cars yet, but it might be a drug deal."

"Think so?" replied Sandy with a smile. "Maybe we should go down there and score some. Might be good stuff."

Mary ignored her and kept watch out the window. An awk-ward minute passed where neither of them spoke. "Did you say it was a blue minivan?" asked Sandy, breaking the silence.

"Yeah," confirmed Mary. Another awkward minute of silence ensued as they both stood staring out the window. Finally Sandy said, "Let me know if it shows up. I got to finish my fiber job," and turned back towards her cubicle. But before she could turn-around, Mary sang out, "There it is!"

Sure enough, a blue mini-van cautiously approached the white sedan and parked next to it. Both women were now riveted to the view outside their window. A man got out of the unwashed sedan. He was in his forties or maybe early fifties, tall, balding, with sloping shoulders. He wore a short-sleeved shirt with a tie. The man waited patiently as the other person—a woman—exited the minivan and walked around to him. She was slightly chubby with big blonde hair and also looked to be in her forties. She wore a lemon-colored dress that was cut below the knee caps. As she approached, the man looked around before taking her into his arms in a tight embrace.

"Whoa!" laughed Sandy. "There we go. Ah ha. A little lover's rendezvous."

"Hmm," agreed Mary. It was obviously not a drug deal but this was even more intriguing. Forbidden passion. Back-street lovers. She watched as the two kissed. They then paused and spoke a few words to each other and kissed again. The man led the woman around to the passenger's side of his car and let her in then went back around and got in the driver's side and closed the door.

"Now what are they up to?" wondered Sandy out loud. "The Easy-8 motel? His place? Why don't they just use the minivan?" she asked, laughing again. Her laughter caught the attention of Leon who was in the cubicle on the other side of Sandy's.

"What you two laughin' at?" he asked, sliding up to them and following their gaze out the window. Leon was gay and loud and proud about it. He had LGBT and Rainbow signage pinned up in his cubicle and prominently displayed a picture of his boyfriend on his desk. He made Mary uncomfortable.

Sandy quickly filled him in—the same two cars every Thursday, "a little lover's rendezvous", now sitting in the car together—and Leon gulped down the juicy gossip. He rubbed shoulders with Sandy as she explained the situation. The two were buds, often joking and making racy remarks to the other over their shared cubicle wall, and almost always took each other's side in staff meetings.

"Bad, bad boys and girls," he mockingly sighed then sang—"*Me and Mrs Jones, we got a thing goin' on*"—as he peered more closely out the window. "What they doin' now. She givin' him a blow job?"

"Really?" reproved Mary. "You really got to go there?"

"He goes there all the time," snickered Sandy.

"You know it, girl," replied Leon with a wink. He turned his attention back to Mary. "Sorry, Mary—Mary, Mary, quite contrary. If she's not going to perform 'an act of oral sex' then what are they doing? Goin' to a motel? What's wrong with the minivan?"

"That's what I said," chimed in Sandy.

"Looks like they're just holding hands and talking," commented Mary.

"BORING," breathed out Leon. "What are they, Mormons cheating on other Mormons? We want some action, honey. Let's get that van rockin'. You hear what I'm sayin'? Rockin'."

Sandy laughed just as Leon's phone rang. "Oh, gotta get that," he chirped, "but keep me posted. If the van starts a rockin' call me. You hear? Promise? Call me, I don't want to miss it." He scooted back into his cubicle to answer his phone.

"We will," replied Sandy laughing.

"You will," whispered Mary to herself.

The man and woman sat talking together in the unwashed sedan and an uneventful minute or two passed before Sandy said, "Well, I got to get back to my fiber job."

"Me, too," said Mary, backing into her cubicle. "If I notice anything I'll let you know," she added. She sat back down at her workstation and answered a couple new emails. After she was done she rolled her chair away and lifted up to look out the window. They were still parked there, and from what she could see they were still talking together. Mary opened her CAD program and started working on a job, lost track of time, and finally looked back out the window at around eleven. They were gone.

Word spread throughout the fourth floor and come next Thursday there were eight people standing by the window at

10:00 am. When the white sedan appeared the group of eight hummed or chuckled in satisfaction. Then the banter began.

"So he always shows up first?"

"Yep. Exactly at ten—in the same white car."

"It needs a wash. The guy's probably a slob."

"A slob with a woody."

"Ha. He's getting out.

"He looks like a church deacon."

"He does."

"What's a church deacon look like?"

"Like him."

"You'd think a church deacon would wash his car. Nah, he looks like he sells insurance."

"You're in good hands with Allstate."

"Like a good neighbor, State Farm is there."

"Yeah, he's a good neighbor all right—wait, here she comes."

"No shit. In a minivan."

"I knew it. She's a soccer mom. A horny soccer mom."

"Wait till you see her."

"Here she comes…"

"Ha, she looks like my Aunt Dora. Where'd she get that dress?"

"It's strictly out of the sixties."

There was a collective "Whoa!" when the two embraced and kissed. The banter continued as the two kissed again and got into the sedan.

"Now what?"

"That's it. They sit and talk."

"What? That's it? That's all? They just sit and talk?"

"That's it."

"What's wrong with the van? They got a perfectly good minivan going to waste."

"That's what we said."

"I was all keyed up for action and that's it? No Porn Hub? They're just going to yak?"

"Not even a hand job."

"Nope."

"It's un-American."

Out of the eight, four were doing most of the talking—Leon, Sandy, Chad and Larry. Chad was two years out of college and had an opinion about everything. Some of the old-timers didn't like him. He was on a mission to get promoted and was always signing up for leadership classes. His cubicle walls were sparse—just a pennant of his alma-mater and a cycling poster—and gave the impression of being the temporary abode of someone on a fast track. Larry, on the other hand, was the office cut-up. He'd been an engineer for eight years, knew the ropes, was slightly cynical and had a one-liner to meet every occasion. There were Dilbert cartoons pinned up in his cubicle along with off-beat posters that said things like, "If at first you don't succeed, then skydiving definitely isn't for you". He was well-liked.

When it became apparent that this was the end of the show for now, the group began to break up.

"I'm telling you he looks like a church deacon," said Chad.

"Nah," replied Larry. "He looks more like my insurance agent Roy."

"No, church deacon for sure, or a pastor of some sort, and he's cheating on his wife with the church admin. I tell you, I got it all figured out."

"Hey, no one post this on Facebook," called out Larry. "Someone might know them and scare them off and I wanna see where this goes... Who's keeping look-out?"

"Mary is."

"OK, Mare, keep an eye on Roy and Dora for us. Let us know if anything changes."

"Will do," laughed Mary.

In the ensuing weeks the interest in the two lovers peaked. A growing number of engineers collected along the window to spy out at the couple. News of the Thursday rendezvous leaked down to the lower floors and on one Thursday a total of twenty-one people peered out at the couple from behind the tinted windows. As for the man and the woman, they continued to stick to their routine. They met every Thursday at 10:00, hugged and kissed, then disappeared into the sedan to talk until exactly 10:55 when they kissed, parted, and drove away oblivious to the fact that they had become the main attraction to the employees in building A.

Larry's moniker for the two—Roy and Dora—stuck and intra-office conversation invariably came around to the topic of Roy and Dora. Who were they and what were they up to? Did anyone recognize them? Were they just going to sit in that car and talk and do nothing else? A mythos developed around the two that included theories as to who they were. Tall tales sprouted up concerning their pasts as well as fanciful predictions regarding their futures. In terms of theories, there were four main ones that the engineers on the fourth floor subscribed to in one way or the other.

The first one, heard before, belonged to Chad who steadfastly maintained that Roy was a deacon and Dora a church admin. Over time he flushed his theory out and embellished it. Roy was an ordained minister, married with no kids, with a small congregation and a paltry salary that explained his unwashed sedan. Dora was married with three kids—hence the minivan—but they were older kids and maybe out of the house and her husband traveled on business. Roy and Dora worked in the same church and had known each other for years. She told him about her problems and he told her about his, and over time they fell in love despite each knowing it was a sin. They were in love but it weighed heavily on their conscience. This was why they met in secret and *never did anything.* To Chad's satisfaction, a number of engineers on the fourth floor bought into this theory.

The second theory came from Leon, who added salacious detail to it every time he told it to the delight and entertainment of some of the younger engineers. Roy and Dora were right-wing, white-bread fuddy-duddies. I mean, just look at them, he would say as proof of his claims. The shirt and tie, the frumpy dress, the pro-life bumper sticker on the minivan (one of the engineers had picked that up using binoculars)—it was all proof positive that they were uptight rednecks and probably members of the Tea Party ('tea-baggers' he called them). This explained why they *never did anything,* but eventually their lust would win out; they'd overcome their hang-ups, and when that happened look out. There'd be mondo bondage, sex with other couples, and probably bestiality. Bet on it, he'd say. That was typical of hypocrites like them.

Larry owned the third theory and it was colored with his characteristic cynicism. If Roy wasn't an insurance salesman then he sold tires down at Big O. Dora was a stay-at-home mom bored out of her mind who watched too many soap operas. They lived on the same street, were probably next door neighbors, and Roy was friends with her husband. Both were in unhappy marriages, that was obvious, and a combination of boredom and mutual angst brought them together. But they were paranoid of getting caught (he couldn't afford the alimony and she didn't want to lose her kids), and so they were afraid to take it to the next level. This explained why they *never did anything.* Eventually she would see he was neither Bold nor Beautiful and he would realize that she was neither Young nor Restless and the whole thing would fizzle out.

The fourth theory evolved from conversations between some of the older, female engineers like Mary and was more romantic in tone. Roy and Dora were high school sweethearts. Married to someone else now, they had met again at their 25th high school reunion. In high school they were the perfect couple and everyone was sure they'd get married, but after graduation they somehow drifted apart (or were torn apart by evil forces). When they met again at the reunion they realized the spark was still there, and that electricity was too powerful for them to ignore. So they met every Thursday in the parking lot for an hour just to feel that electricity once more. But their love was platonic, spiritual, and would never be consummated with something as ordinary as sex (which is why they *never did anything*). Theirs was a greater love, tragic in nature, like Heathcliff and Catherine.

Debates raged as to which of the four theories was closer to the truth and bets were placed on who was right. There was a pool going on that was up to thirty-six dollars but winning it, everyone admitted, would require deep investigative work that no one was willing to undertake. So the pool remained at thirty-six dollars and after a couple of months of the same-old-same—the same unwashed sedan, the same hug and kiss, the same endless talking—the debates began to peter out and interest waned. Roy and Dora became just another fixture in the parking lot along with the birds nesting in the trees.

This changed in the third month, in late fall, when something *different did happen*. This time it was Letty who caught it and not Mary. Letty was a petite woman full of energy and talk. She had a large family back in the Philippines and almost every day could be heard talking on the phone in Tagalog, in a high-pitched voice, to one of her relatives. Her cubicle was filled with family pictures and inspirational posters that said things like 'I'm too blessed to be stressed'.

Letty had taken a special interest in Roy and Dora and made a conscious effort every Thursday to walk past the window at 10:00 am and check on the couple and make sure they were still at it. There was no one else at the window when she stopped to watch them park, kiss, and get into his car. Letty lingered a moment before turning away but stopped abruptly when she noticed the back-up lights on the sedan come on. The car swung out and began to drive away.

"Mary!" she whispered loudly. "They're leaving together!"

"What!" exclaimed Mary as she popped up out of her cubicle.

"Look," said Letty pointing down at the unwashed sedan. "They're driving off together."

"No way! Really? Hey, Sandy, check this out."

Sandy quickly came out to witness the momentous event and called to Leon to join them. The four of them watched as the sedan carrying both Roy and Dora drove out of the parking lot. It appeared to get on the freeway but they lost track of it. Within minutes, news of the event spread across the fourth floor. Letty and Leon popped into cubicles to spread the news like bees pollinating flowers, while Mary and Sandy took to their laptops to instant-message their co-workers. Quickly a group of excited engineers gathered together along the window to confirm the news and take part in the lively discussion. There was an array of speculation as to where the two had gone off to. Some were sure it was to a motel while others guessed that they had finally decided to run off together. Others, like Larry, doubted all that and figured they'd be back at the usual time to part ways and return to their separate lives.

Larry was right. At exactly 10:55 the sedan returned and parked next to the minivan and everyone behind the big tinted window on the fourth floor were waiting for them. Roy and Dora got out of the sedan. She was holding a small shopping bag. They hugged and kissed as usual. The fact that Dora was holding a small shopping bag caused a stir behind the window.

"Letty, did she have that shopping bag before?"

"No, not that I saw."

"They went shopping then. He took her shopping."

"For what, I wonder?"

"Her prescription IUD."

"Or maybe a pack of Trojans."

"Ribbed for her pleasure."

"What's the bag say? Can anyone one read it from here? Art, did you bring your binoculars?"

"No, forgot 'em."

"It might be 'Zales'. Does it look like it says 'Zales' to you?"

"He bought her a diamond. How sweet."

"No way. He can't even afford to wash his damn car."

"Yeah, let alone buy a diamond."

"Exactly."

Roy and Dora drove off in their separate cars leaving their audience to sort out this new development. Being engineers with logical minds, they quickly came to some reasonable conclusions. Obviously, if the two went shopping together, they weren't afraid of being seen. That could only mean that they weren't from around here. Maybe they came over the bridge from the Easy Bay or from down on the peninsula in San Jose. Either way, this was a new dynamic and upped the ante.

By next Thursday the pool was up to fifty dollars, which motivated Leon to declare that if they drove off again he was going to follow them to see where they went. At the appointed time, Leon sat in his car amongst a cluster of parked cars, far from Roy and Dora's rendezvous point, and waited. And waited.

He finally got a text from Sandy saying the two were just talking like always, so he gave up his stake-out and went back inside. But the following Thursday his vigilance paid off. Roy and Dora drove off again in the unwashed sedan and Leon followed them. The entire fourth floor watched as the two cars drove out of the parking lot and disappeared.

At 10:55, the sedan returned with Leon following discretely behind. The posted lookouts sent out the alarm and people rushed from their cubicles to get a good spot along the windows. Leon pulled into his usual spot and got out of his car. He waved up at the fourth floor. Everyone up there waved back, even though they knew he couldn't see them, and had a good laugh at his antics. Roy and Dora parted and Dora was the first to drive away. Leon stood next to his car and waited for the blue minivan to approach. Timing it perfectly, he raised up his hand and stepped in front of her path. Dora braked to let him walk by. Everyone on the fourth floor got a kick out of that.

When Leon came up in the elevator, he was mobbed like a celebrity. He soaked up the attention, ignoring the many questions thrown at him, and took his time (and had his fun) telling his tale. Roy and Dora had driven over to Hillsdale Mall and gone inside. He—Leon—acting like "a private dick" (which he meant as a double entendre), tailed them into See's Candy. Roy bought Dora a bag of candy, and there they sat for the next half hour eating candy and talking. Leon had kept his distance but spied on them the whole time. He even took a picture of them with his iPhone.

"No way!" exclaimed Sandy in disbelief.

"Yep," replied Leon proudly. "And it came out great. Check it out." He lifted his phone up as everyone gathered closely around him. He tapped his screen, brought up the picture, and expanded the image so everyone could clearly see. There they were—Roy and Dora—sitting at a small table with their heads bent towards each other like two high school sweethearts.

"It's Jack and Diane!"

"They're going to the Soph-Hop!"

"Text me that picture."

"Me, too."

Within days, the picture of Roy and Dora had been texted and shared throughout the building. Teri Wentz, an Administrative Assistant on the second floor, was the first to post the picture on Facebook. She was a large woman and a bit of a busy-body. Her low-walled cubicle looked out over the entire floor and she could see everything that was going on. She wanted very badly to be an engineer and spent a lot of her time on the fourth floor. Her crowded desk was chockful of pictures of her three daughters and Lucille Ball (she was a big "I Love Lucy" fan), along with a woman-empowerment plaque, prominently displayed, that read "Well-behaved women seldom make history."

Teri let it be known that she had posted the picture of Roy and Dora on her Facebook page with an appeal to others to do the same. "It's time to 'out' these two," she said, and no one argued with her. Like wildfire, the picture spread across social media in an attempt to gain their identity. But after a week there were no hits. This only deepened the mystery around Roy and Dora.

Normally this deepening mystery would have presented a challenge to the more persistent types, causing them to double their efforts to "out" the couple, but a harsh reality intervened. A department-wide downsizing was declared and everyone's attention in Building A turned elsewhere. The general stress level rose as the PacCom employees awaited the numbers (Would it be 10% this time? Some had heard it would be as high as 15 %.). People went into hunker-down mode and waited for the axe to fall. Roy and Dora were forgotten.

The process ground along to its inexorable end. Within a month, rating and rankings had been completed, low-performers identified, meetings fixed, assurances made, letters sent, and the names of the chosen (like the low-vote-getters in a talent contest) were made known to one and all. Two engineers on the fourth floor were tapped. One was old enough, with enough service, to take the severance package. The younger one luckily found a job in another department. The losses meant that the remaining engineers would have to absorb the additional workload but, all in all, the general opinion was it could have been a lot worse. There was a collective sigh of relief.

During this month of time—four Thursdays to be exact—Roy and Dora rendezvoused in the parking lot, hugged and kissed, and sat talking in the unwashed sedan without a single pair of eyes to spy on them. That quickly changed. With the black cloud lifted and things back to normal, the folks on the fourth floor resumed their surveillance. More than that, and in the light-hearted afterglow that sometimes follows high stress, a renewed interest was kindled in Roy and Dora. The office pool shot up to $76. Art, one of the engineers on the fourth floor and kind of a techno-geek, swapped his binoculars out for a high-powered lens and camera. The pictures he took of Roy and Dora through the fourth floor window were closer and clearer than Leon's famous iPhone picture. Art posted them to a share drive for everyone to see, and Teri and others wasted no time in posting them on Facebook to their network of friends.

But another week passed with no hits. There was general disbelief that, in this day and age, with the vast tentacles of social media, no one—not one person out of the hundreds on Facebook who had viewed the pictures of Roy and Dora—no one knew who they were. Letty was sure that meant they were both from out-of-state but Larry reminded her that both vehicles had California license plates. Leon and Sandy were sure (and Chad now tended to agree with them) that this was evidence that Roy and Dora were members of some fundamentalist religious sect, like the Amish or the Neo-Luddites, who spurned technology. Mary thought it could be possible that they were sixties radicals, on the run, and living underground, but she was quickly shot down. Roy and Dora were too square-looking for that to be the case.

Two more weeks passed with no hits on social media. The office pool stood at $76 and the general frustration grew. Leon, seeking to break the case open and regain the limelight, decided to follow Dora home but he lost her in traffic and returned back to the fourth floor with nothing to show for his efforts. Delicate inquiries were made as to whether anyone had a friend in law enforcement or at the DMV who could track them down using their license plate numbers, but nothing came of it.

Roy and Dora remained a mystery. They continued to meet every Thursday at 10:00 am in the same corner of the parking lot. They always hugged and kissed. Most times they sat in Roy's unwashed sedan and talked. Occasionally they drove off to the See's Candy Store but returned and parted at exactly 10:55. They were punctual, predictable, and boring. And to the engineers on the fourth floor, the saga of Ray and Dora, with all its boring predictability, began to lose its entertainment value. As the weeks passed and the same tiresome routine played out, the spying crowd along the tinted windows dwindled in size and most folks remained working at their desk between 10:00 and 11:00 on Thursdays.

Teri came into Larry's cubicle one day and found him counting out a wad a cash. It was the Roy and Dora pool, he explained, and it still stood at $76. Since the mystery couldn't be solved, they had decided to use the money for a luncheon at The Cheesecake Factory. Teri made sure she was invited to this luncheon before sitting down in the chair she always sat in when she came upstairs to shoot the breeze with Larry. He didn't mind the interruption because she usually had juicy office gossip to share.

"Why don't we end this nonsense with those two?" she said. "Shake things up."

"What do you mean?" he asked, but he quickly realized she was talking about Roy and Dora. "How?"

And she proceeded to tell him her simple plot. They could print out a picture of the two—one of Art's clearer photos—and place it on one of their windshields with a note on the back that read, "We know who you are." At first, Larry treated her idea as a joke and made wisecracks about it, but the more they talked and the more she pressed the more intrigued he became by the idea. He promised to bring the idea up with his colleagues to see what they thought about it.

On Monday morning in the big conference room, before the start of their staff meeting, Larry floated the idea to his engineering colleagues. Most were for it, especially Leon and Sandy, but Mary and Letty were against it and preferred to leave Roy and Dora alone. But there was one sentiment everyone in that room shared—they were all more or less weary of the whole subject. It was like an endless rerun of a PG-rated movie. The idea quickly gained momentum and size, like a trending video on YouTube, and even Mary and Letty were swept up in its energy. Chad swiftly mapped out the proper tactics for success: the picture and note could not be delivered here in their parking lot (that would give them away); it had to be slipped under the windshield wiper of the white sedan when the two were in See's Candy together. All they needed was for someone to carry out the plan and Leon happily volunteered.

That very Thursday, the plan went off without a hitch. With cool, engineering logic, all of Art's photos had been rejected since the angle of the shots gave away their location. Instead, Leon's See's Candy shot was chosen and Chad wrote the note on the back of an 8 ½ by 11 copy in non-descript printing. Everyone on the fourth floor was sworn to secrecy and not a word of the plot was leaked down to the lower floors. All except Teri. As author of the plot, and to her infinite delight, she was allowed to join the engineers along the window on the fourth floor to await the outcome of their scheme.

At 10:45, Leon drove into the parking lot and hustled up to the fourth floor where he was greeted by his giddy co-conspirators with handshakes and slaps on the back. At 10:55, nearly every engineer waited in eager anticipation along the long, tinted window that overlooked Roy and Dora's parking spots. It was raining lightly, which made it a little more difficult to see out the window, and the spectators pressed in closer to the glass. 11:00 came and went but no unwashed sedan appeared. Speculation swirled amongst the crowd.

"Maybe they got stuck in traffic."

"Maybe—or maybe they lit out. On the run."

"Not those two. They're predictable as the mail."

"Yeah, but something's off. We stirred the shit for sure."

For the next ten minutes, the group of men and women wondered out loud and in hushed tones what had become of Roy and Dora. They had certainly stirred up the shit. This was something new. This was something unprecedented. No one moved from their spot along the window. Ringing phones went unanswered while the fourth floor held its collective breath. At 11:10 the unwashed sedan drove slowly into the parking lot.

"Here they are!"

"No shit, here we go!"

"Oh yeah, here we go."

"Who's got the popcorn?"

"Milk Duds for me."

"Someone turn up the sound."

The sedan came to a stop and the man got out and walked around to the passenger's door. He opened the door and extended his hand but the woman did not emerge. The man dropped his arm. He didn't wear a jacket and stood waiting in the rain. He reached out again and finally, like a frightened animal reluctant to leave its cage, the woman took his hand and came out of the car. She came into his arms and buried her face in his chest. He held her tightly with his chin on top of her hair.

Even from a distance, and even through the light rain, everybody watching from the fourth floor could see that the woman was crying. There were no comments from the crowd, instead they remained riveted to the scene as it played itself out. The woman suddenly twisted out of the man's hug and hurried towards her minivan, her head down, crying. The man followed, caught her arm, and turned her back into his arms. She had her hands to her face and appeared to be sobbing. They remained like that for a moment—a seemingly long, exquisite moment—until she broke the spell and raised her hands up to the man's face and cradled it like a fragile vase. She spoke to him and he nodded, and she brought his head down and kissed him before breaking away.

The entire scene took no more than a couple minutes. The woman got into her minivan, started it up, and backed away as the man stood in the rain and watched her. She swung out and drove off but the spectators on the fourth floor kept their eyes on the man. He looked drenched from the rain, but he did not move from his spot as he watched the minivan drive away. Once it was gone, the man leaned back against his car with his head down

"He's getting wet," said Letty to no one in particular.

"How sad," murmured Sandy.

"At least he's getting a free car wash," said Larry.

There were a couple chuckles at this crack but it mostly fell flat as everyone's attention remained on Roy. The rain had picked up and it was harder to see, but after a minute spent watching in silence they saw him break out of his trance and get into his car. There he sat without moving. His once unwashed sedan now had brown rain-streaks along the side. Minutes passed, the rain fell, and Roy remained in his parked car.

"What's he up to?"

"He's not going to do anything crazy?"

"Whaddya mean? Like what?"

"Like blow his brains out."

"Shit. Don't say that."

"Yeah, don't say that. That's horrible."

"Why not? It's a possibility. He might have a gun. You never know."

And with this possibility ripe in everyone's mind, they pressed closer to the rain-spotted glass to see better—to see, perhaps, the flash of a handgun, or some act of desperation. But it didn't come. There was no gun flash or act of desperation. At least not here and not now. Instead, Roy backed up, swung his car out, and drove away.

"And that, folks, is the end of that," said Chad.

This epitaph drew nods and murmurs of agreement. A few of the women, like Mary and Letty, kept their heads down and didn't say anything. To break the somber mood, Larry cheerfully reminded everyone that they had Roy and Dora to thank for their upcoming luncheon at The Cheesecake Factory. There was a quick discussion amongst some in the group as to what day they should have the luncheon. Next Friday was agreed upon. After that, the group broke up and everybody went back to their cubicle.

When the following Thursday rolled around, there was a small group of engineers lined up along the window to see if Roy and Dora would reappear. Mary pointed to the white sedan when it entered the parking lot. It parked in its regular spot. Larry suddenly appeared and asked if Roy and Dora had returned.

"Just Roy," said Mary.

"No way," replied Larry as he stepped up to the window and looked out. "Whaddya know? There he is. You know she won't show. He's gotta know she won't show."

And she didn't show. Five minutes passed, then ten, and the blue minivan did not appear. The man remained seated in his car. A few of the engineers got bored and wandered back to their cubicles. Mary kept vigil. Larry left saying, "Let me know if he offs himself," but returned fifteen minutes later to find Mary and a few others still keeping watch on the parked sedan.

"Someone go down there and tell him it's over," said Larry.

"Go ahead."

"I mean, come on," he added. "It's finito, kaput. Get over it." He stepped up to the glass and rapped his knuckles on it. "Hey, Roy!" he called loudly. "It's over. Time to call it quits. She's not coming back." Larry stepped back and shook his head.

"Go back to your boring life," chimed in Sandy.

"Get back to molesting little boys at your church," quipped Leon.

"Shut-up!" snapped Mary.

"YOU shut up!" Leon shot back. "I'm just telling the truth."

"The hell you are," replied Mary angrily. "You don't know any-thing about that man. Not a damn thing. So keep your dirty jokes to yourself."

"Whoa!" laughed Leon. "What got your panties in a bunch? I'm just kidding. Chill, sister, chill."

"YOU chill!"

But before this disagreement could get worse, Larry pointed down to the parking lot and called out, "There he goes!" Everyone's head snapped back to attention. They watched in dead silence as the white sedan backed out, swung around, and drove out of the parking lot. The show was over.

"Don't forget about lunch tomorrow," said Sandy, throwing a mischievous wink at Leon. He winked back. Everyone else returned to their cubicles without further comments.

The next day, twelve of the engineers, along with Teri Wentz, enjoyed lunch at The Cheesecake Factory compliments of Roy and Dora. The lunch lasted over an hour and there was lively conversation and more than enough good cheer to go around. The whole event seemed to put a proper punctuation point on the saga of Roy and Dora, like grabbing a cold one and pushing back in a recliner after the completion of some unpleasant chore.

The following week, everyone's attention on the fourth floor was tuned in to rumors that were flying around about consolidation and a potential move down to Santa Clara. Thursday came and went and only a couple people noticed that Roy and Dora's parking spots were permanently empty. Talk about Roy and Dora gave way to more pressing matters and the whole topic would have evaporated into the past if it hadn't been for Chad. A couple weeks after the luncheon, when rumors of the consolidation were at their strongest, Chad shared a link to an on-line news article with the other engineers. The article reported a suicide jump off the Golden Gate Bridge, which added to a total of over 1600 leaps since 1937, and noted that the latest jumper was a white, middle-aged male. He remained unidentified but his white Toyota had been found abandoned at the Fort Point parking lot.

This article triggered a flurry of conjectures and speculations amongst the engineers on the fourth floor. Some suspected it was Roy. Others were sure it wasn't Roy, pointing out that middle-aged men jumped off the bridge all the time and white Toyotas were a dime a dozen. There was an ongoing email discussion and Chad hit "Reply All" to say that the authorities undoubtedly knew who the jumper was (since they found his car), but were not going to release the details out of respect for the family. He further pointed out, in his condescending way, that none of them would ever know who the jumper was, so there was no way they could tie the jumper back to *their* Roy. But the debate continued for a couple days as a sidelight to the looming possibility of a consolidation. Was it Roy or just a weird coincidence? There was no way to know for sure. The debate terminated when an announcement was made that, yes, they were going to relocate the engineering office at Twin Dolphin down to Santa Clara. The move would come after the holidays.

In January, after the holidays, Mary was busy in her cubicle packing for the move. It was Friday and the movers were due that evening. She had only a couple more boxes to pack. She stuffed her stapler and rolodex into a box, closed it, taped it, and placed a packing slip on it that provided her new cubicle number to the movers. Theoretically, everything would be in her new cubicle when she walked in Monday morning, but she'd been through enough of these moves before to know that something always went wrong. A box would be misplaced or her phone or LAN connection would be missing—it was always something like that—but she didn't really mind it. She was rather pleased about the move since her commute would now be ten miles shorter.

Mary finished up her last box and stepped out of her cubicle. Most everyone was done packing and the fourth floor was nearly empty. She stopped in front of the large window and looked out at the foothills. She was going to miss this view—she had no view in the new offices, just walls and ceiling—and her eyes gazed out across the expansive parking lot, passed over Roy and Dora's empty spots, and rested on her own car. It was one of the last cars left in the parking lot and it reminded her that it was time to go home.

Molimo

They each had their space, which they both respected, but she knew his space was bigger than hers especially when his genius began to play and find expression. And when it found expression, it invariably led him into the depths of hard work—dedicated, obsessive work—where he stayed until his labors bore fruit of some kind. It was a process she was very familiar with, and the result of the process was usually something special. Like the software company he started and then sold to McAfee for $10 million. And after that was a chat box creator which used artificial intelligence to start online chats with customers. That was another big pay day.

By the time they were thirty-three, she and Toby were retired. But the word "retired" was a relative term to Maya. It was true that they didn't have to get up in the morning and go to work, attend board meetings, or meet and greet potential investors, but their life was filled with hobbies and adventures, ranging from wine-making to excursions into the rainforest. Their small family was in perpetual motion. Most days Maya had to hustle to keep up with her self-imposed schedule. Besides home-schooling their twelve year old son, she was involved with a number of charities and was writing a children's book. As for her husband, he was a bundle of unpredictable energy and she knew when to keep her distance. Over the last year she had watched him get deeply into anthropology ("applied anthropology," he called it), which included investing capital in a start-up company in Menlo Park. The company called themselves "High-Tech Anthropologists" and planned to use extensive, in-the-field research to improve work performance.

She, her husband, and their son Toby Jr. lived in a house in Saratoga. Back in 2007, with their first $10 million in the bank, she had found the house, made a cash offer, and successfully turned it into the kind of home—part utilitarian, part amusement park—they could all be happy with. This included a sound-proof workroom for Toby Sr. (painted his favorite shade of green) that was equipped with a fiber-fed Ethernet LAN arrayed with multiple hard drives, soft switches, routers, and seven TV and computer screens. There was also a game room with a state-of-the-art gaming console, surround sound, and adult-sized toys like a five foot Jenga game. In their large and wooded backyard they had built an elaborate tree house in a giant oak tree complete with internet, TV, and HVAC. Toby and Toby Jr. would have slept out there all the time if she had let them.

She was happy with where Toby and Toby Jr. were now as father and son. She had grown concerned the first eight years of her son's upbringing, what with Toby Sr. consumed with his projects and start-up ventures, and she had gently prodded her husband to spend more time with their son. But that was like trying to get a hummingbird to stand still. Not that he'd been a bad father; he played with Toby Jr. when he was home, for short stretches, and always showed interest in Toby Junior's achievements, but he didn't "know" his son and his son didn't "know" him. But that had all changed a few years ago, and she was pleased to see they had grown closer. In the last year, especially, they had become almost inseparable.

Now they were like two kids together. They played video games, rode motor bikes around the backyard, went hiking together, and had developed an easy-going rapport reminiscent of childhood buddies. A large part of this rapport, she was sure, had to do with her husband's child-like nature. She had recognized it immediately when she first met him at Stanford. Yes, there was the apparent genius of his intellect, but what had drawn her to him was his wide-eyed curiosity and a kind of goofiness that she found charming. As they dated and became closer, she realized that in some ways he had never grown up, and whether this was an asset or a detriment to a life together as husband and wife she was willing to find out. She enjoyed the challenge.

She had her own theories when it came to genius, and she wasn't really convinced that Toby was a genius—not, say, like Da Vinci or Einstein—but he was undeniably brilliant and brilliant people, in her opinion, came with a travel bag filled with quirks and eccentricities. Toby was no different. For instance, crackling wrappers or paper set him off (which was why she never wrapped Christmas presents), he'd make four right turns before he'd make a left (which was why she always drove), and he could talk back-wards, whole sentences in fact, when he got stressed out. But there was one other thing he shared with brilliant people, people like Paul Allen (whom she had met more than once), and that was this: he was relentless, and once he glommed on to an inter-esting idea he didn't let go of it until he had dissected it, turned it inside out, and exhausted its potential.

Ideas came into his head like dandelion seeds where they sometimes took root and blossomed. She got a kick out of some of his flights of fancy. The latest, of course, was cultural anthro-pology. It had become his idée fixe and he was always watching documentaries and reading books having to do with primitive cultures. He seemed most interested in rites of passage and she and Toby Jr. got swept up in his passion. This included a trip to Newfoundland to attend a feast celebrating a young Inuit man's first kill—a caribou—marking his transition into man-hood. From there Toby tried to get them into Kenya to witness a Maasai youth killing a lion as part of his rite of passage but they were informed that lion-killing no longer took place. Instead they went to the Democratic Republic of the Congo to visit the Bambuti, a tribe of pygmies still living in the rainforest.

She never ceased to be amazed at how her husband always got what he went after. Through intelligence, powerful contacts, and money, he was usually able to orchestrate the outcome he was after and the DROC was no different. There they discovered the Bambuti were either civilized in towns or scattered in the rainforest and hard to find, but Toby hired a pygmy tribesman who guided them in their land cruiser to a small forest village of about forty pygmies. Out of pure luck or gifted planning (she wasn't sure which) they happened to alight on the village just as it was in the middle of their nkumbi initiation festival, and Toby was able to buy himself in as a spectator with the food and wine they had brought in the jeep. Maya had never seen her husband so excited. As for her, she had no intention of witnessing a ritual that included circumcision, but it was all a moot point since women were forbidden to participate in the ritual anyhow.

Three days were left of the festival and on the first night she stayed hidden in a hut with four other women pretending to cower at the man-made animal noises in the forest, including an eerie-sounding musical instrument she knew to be called a molimo. By the second day she'd had enough of the hut, the mosquitoes, the forest critters, and all things Bambuti and returned to one of the large towns to wait for her husband and son.

When they returned, they were both pumped-up and full of stories about their adventure. They had also brought with them a long cylindrical object wrapped up tightly in blankets which they clumsily tried to hide from her. When she asked what it was they glanced at one another, smiling mischievously, and either ignored her or changed the subject. She stopped pressing; she knew what it was. Somehow they had managed to bring a molimo—a long trumpet-like instrument—back with them and were treating it the same way the pygmy men treated it, like a sacred object that had to be hidden from women. She let them play their game and watched with some amusement as Toby finagled a way to get the fifteen foot object shipped back to the states.

Back home in the Bay Area, Toby and Toby Jr. had taken receipt of the molimo off a UPS truck and somehow managed to sneak it into his work room without Maya seeing. She only knew about it because she heard a strange noise, almost like an elephant's call, from behind his work room door one day. She knocked, heard the noise immediately stop, and pressed her ear to the door as she waited for him to open up. It took a while, and when he finally opened up she asked him about the noise but he feigned ignorance. No bother; she had put two and two together: he had the molimo in his room, was learning to play it, and, true to form, was not going to mess with its "magical" powers by telling her about it. What his purpose was she had no clue, but she knew she would find out when the time was right.

She turned right onto the dirt road that led to their cabin in the woods. Their drive up to the Sierras had been long due to heavy traffic and she was looking forward to laying down and taking a nap. As they approached the main cabin, her son yelled out, "Dad! They left it on the porch!" She glanced up at the porch and saw a long box leaning against the door—no doubt the molimo—and she guessed at once that Toby had had it shipped to the cabin.

"Stop here," ordered Toby some twenty yards short of the cabin.

"Yeah, Mom, stop here," added her son excitedly. "And you can't look."

"Yes, you can't look, dear. Promise you won't look."

She stopped the car to let them get out. "*Alll riiight*," she said. "I won't look."

"Promise?"

"I promise."

Satisfied with her promise, the two jumped out of the car and ran up to the porch. But of course she looked. Pretending to keep her head down, she watched as they picked up the package, Toby Sr. at one end and Toby Jr. at the other, and carried it over to the detached cottage where they opened the door, set it in, locked the door, and went back to the main cabin where they signaled her that it was okay to come up.

She got out of the car, shaking her head. They both looked like two kids who had just been caught stealing candy. "What are you two up to?" she asked with a smile.

"Can't tell you, Mom. Maybe later."

"Definitely later."

"Okay," she said with a shrug of her shoulders. "So help me unload the car."

They finished unloading the car and got settled in their cabin. It was a log cabin replica situated remotely in an evergreen forest. It had three bedrooms, an upstairs, and a large fireplace along with a back-up generator. They used it primarily for skiing in the winter. The fact they were here in mid-August struck Maya as slightly odd, but her husband had told her that he wanted to come up here and spend a few days working on "a special project" and she went along with it as she always did when she saw he was fired up about an idea. She wondered what it was all about given the fact that the cabin had no internet service, and cell phone service was spotty at best. For some reason he wanted the seclusion—he and Toby Jr., so they could work on their "special project"—which was all right with her since it gave her quiet time to work on her children's book.

After dinner her husband and son went out to the cottage. The cottage was small and they used it primarily to store ski and snowboard equipment. It also had no electricity, and when she glanced out there after dark she saw the window aglow with the soft light of a Coleman lantern.

At eleven she went out on the porch and stood there debating whether she should go over and interrupt them. Then she heard something in the forest—a deep, gentle, lowing sound—and she stopped and listened intently. First it was in one part of the forest, then it was in another, and the lowing sound sometimes broke into a falsetto before stopping and then starting again at a different spot in the woods. At one point it was very near and sounded just like a growling animal, and it frightened her for a moment (there were mountain lions in these hills) until it changed suddenly to a trumpet sound. She knew that trumpet sound immediately—it was the elephant call—and understood it all. Her husband and son were in the forest playing the molimo. She chuckled to herself and went back inside.

It was after midnight when her husband came to bed. She had been reading and she set her book down to quiz him. What was he up to? What was this "special project" he was working on? How did their son fit into his project? But he side-stepped her questions and assured her that she would know everything in time.

She gave up for the moment and waited for him to get into bed. Once he was in, she turned out the light and slipped out of bed. She knew how to get him to talk and, yeah, it was kind of devious but she didn't really feel guilty about it. She took off her nightgown and slipped back into bed naked, snuggling up next to him. After they were done making love, he rolled onto his back and she softly stroked his chest with her hand. In this relaxed state, his mind clear, he would talk now. That was the way it always went—he became dreamily talkative afterwards and she could ask him anything and he would answer. Just like a truth serum.

"Babe."

"Hmmm."

"Tell me what's going on. What are you and Toby up to?"

"Huh? Oh…" And he sighed evenly before continuing in a slow, languid manner. "Rite of Passage… It's a video game experience I'm working on—but more than that—more than just a video game—an event creator, a catalyst… Boys don't have a ritual to mark their change into manhood anymore, so they get stuck like me—or struggle and get into trouble…"

(This last statement surprised her; it was a small gem of self-realization she hadn't thought her husband capable of, and it triggered a quick succession of thoughts—he was an only child, his mother was on her fourth marriage, she treated him like a child, there had never been a strong male influence in his life—but she let those thoughts play out in her head without interrupting him.)

"It's like being stuck in a time warp," he continued. "But in the video game, you start out playing at age eight and go maybe until you're eighteen, or even farther, I haven't decided, and you create an avatar for yourself that takes you from childhood, through puberty, and into manhood… You create a village and the people in it are your family, friends, and teachers—we'll use voice and facial re-creation—and they grow up with you as you age… You can choose to be like a child of the Maasai or of the Inuit or the Plains Indians or any number of primary peoples, even ancient Greeks or Hebrews… In the early levels of the game you learn your tribe's myths from a shaman or wise man. Later you learn to ride and hunt and go on adventures, and then in puberty you experience a rite of passage that takes you into manhood— something like killing a lion or a caribou—and it's permanent and indisputable... And when you get older you become a chieftain and lead your warriors into battle, get married, have children... in parallel with your own life."

He stopped and arched his back and yawned. "I'm tired... Let's go to sleep," he said drowsily.

"Okay, dear... But what's Toby doing? What's his role in this?"

"Huh, oh... we're just acting out one of the levels of the game and he's helping me."

"I see," she said and lifted up on her elbow and kissed him on the cheek. "Thanks for telling me. Now get some sleep. I love you."

"Love you, too."

This all made sense to her; it was consistent; it was all part of his ideation and creation process she was so familiar with. First there was the idea he fixed on, the immersion, the diligent work, role-playing and human factors testing, and it usually ended up in a software program that made them lots of money. With that comforting thought, she rolled over and went to sleep.

The next night, flush with insight into the meaning of their game, Maya stood hidden in the shadows of the porch and listened to her men play. The molimo started up again, a beautiful haunting sound that moved from one spot in the forest to the next. But this time it was answered by singing. It was her son singing but she couldn't make out the song. It wasn't a Bambuti song; it was a different language altogether, and she guessed that they had probably made up a language and song to go with their role-playing. She found the whole thing dearly touching, this deep bonding between father and son, and she recognized some of the father-like traits that were beginning to emerge in her son. He wasn't the genius his father was, she was sure of that, but he was a smart kid and this role-playing, this total immersion in an idea, was very much like his father and would serve Toby Jr. well later in life.

She listened a little while longer to their song until it got too chilly and she went inside.

On the third day, their last day at the cabin, Toby and Toby Jr. jumped up from the lunch table and went out to the cottage together. Obviously, today, they had decided to start work on their project early, but that was okay with her and she went over to her desk, opened her laptop, and started working on her children's book. It was slow going and after a couple hours she leaned back and rubbed her temples.

She heard a scream.

She recoiled at the sound and turned her head, her whole body on alert. It came again, a pain-filled scream—her son's scream—and she lept up and bounded out of the cabin. She came to the cottage door and found it locked. Inside she could hear her son sobbing in pain.

"Open up!" she screamed, yanking on the doorknob. "Toby! Open up! What happened?! Toby! Goddammit, open up!" She yanked frantically at the doorknob, yelling for Toby to open up. Finally she felt the doorknob unlock and she burst into the room.

A number of things registered in quick succession—*her husband standing, his face white with fear, holding a small knife in his hands. There's blood on the knife. Her son is in a chair, bent over, crying loudly. A sickening scent fills the room—the smell of butane mixed with copper and salt—and it hangs in the room like a foul-smelling cloud.*

"What have you done?!" she cried at her husband, but he remained frozen, the knife still in his hand. Panic-stricken, she approached her son slowly. From behind she heard her husband say, "*Flinchedhe.*" She knelt down next to her son and put her arms around him and with caresses and comforting words tried to calm him down. "What's wrong, baby. Tell, mom. It's okay now. Tell mom what happened?"

"*Flinchedhe,*" repeated her husband.

"What are you saying?" she shot back angrily. "'Flinchedhe.'" What the hell does that mean?" But she paused for a moment, her mind racing, and unraveled the word. "He flinched. Is that what you're saying? He flinched? What the hell does that mean? Are you fucking crazy!" And she turned her attention back to her son.

After a few minutes she was able to soften his hard cry and relax his shoulders, but he still resisted her attempts to straighten up. She kissed his cheek and stroked his hair, filling his ear with soothing words. Finally, hesitantly, he began to come up out of his cocoon of pain.

"Show me what hurts," she said calmly. "Show mom what hurts." His hands gripped his crotch and she gently pulled them apart and saw the white towel. It was soaked with blood.

Her husband was charged with child abuse, specifically corporal injury on a child, along with child endangerment, child neglect, and assault and battery. The entire weight of the California legal system came crashing down on top of him. He was denied bail and remanded to a psychiatric hospital in San Jose to await trial. Within a few days of his committal she was called in to meet with the psychiatrist and found out that Toby had been diagnosed with OCD and a dissociative disorder which included thoughts of suicide. They had put him on anti-depressants and started cognitive behavioral therapy.

Weeks passed and, as they did, her rage began to slowly dissipate since that night in the forest. But she was still hurt and angry with him. Nevertheless, she was relieved when she learned there would be no trial. His lawyers struck a deal, and as part of the arrangement he pleaded guilty to child endangerment. All other charges were dropped, and he was sentenced to time served and two years' probation. His hospital stay came to an end, and as part of the plea bargain he was going to be allowed to return home under the stern eye of Child Protection Services— but only if she and her son agreed to it.

Her nights had been long and sleepless, and her stress level was not improved by this decision she had to make. She'd gotten plenty advice from people as to what to do, including a divorce lawyer, but none of it made her decision any easier. Irreparable damage had been done to her and her son, both emotionally and physically, and a reconciliation that brought her husband back home seemed a remote possibility to her. She had a difficult time imagining them picking up where they had left off. For one, their social life was shot to hell. His case had not been headline news (sinful millionaires were a dime a dozen in Silicon Valley) but their colleagues, business partners, friends and family—their entire community—all knew that Toby had been convicted of what amounted to child abuse. That made him a pariah.

And that smell was still branded in her brain, that butane-copper-salty smell, and she couldn't shake it. The foul odor filled her nostrils when she tried to sleep; it seeped into her nose when she was trying to work on her book, and she didn't think she would ever get rid of it.

But despite the debacle, despite the shame and hurt and that smell that wouldn't go away, she still had her hopes. Hope was ingrained in her nature, and she knew better than anyone that if she dug deep enough into the ashes she would find some glowing embers. For one thing—and this wasn't a hard thing to admit to herself—her husband was not a cruel individual. Far from it. What he had done was the result of his social ineptitude, of his unbridled enthusiasm (as misguided as it was) and not an act of wanton cruelty. Therefore she couldn't bring herself to condemn him, which, at the end of the day, left her no closer to making this tough decision.

She decided to sit down with her son and talk it through. Afterall, this decision affected him, probably more so than anyone. The botched circumcision had been corrected and Toby Jr. had healed up just fine, but since that night in the forest he had not said much, not even to his therapist, and had kept pretty much to himself. This was perfectly understandable to her, since emotional wounds took longer to heal, and she approached their conversation with great care.

After dinner, they remained at the dinner table and she laid out the situation as matter-of-factly as she could. When she was done, she asked him what he thought—what he felt about it all—and waited for his response. He had listened intently without asking questions, and now he gathered himself and gave her his answer.

His response was forceful and, at first, the forcefulness of his words astonished her. He loved his dad, he said, and he wanted him home. He wanted them all to be a family again. She shouldn't blame just dad for what happened; he had gone along with it and knew what he was doing. (Here she objected. Dad was the adult and should have known better.) Yes, he understood that, but dad had given him numerous chances to back out and he didn't. He wanted to go through with the ancient ritual, and he was old enough to know what he wanted. Anyhow, he had flinched, and a boy was not supposed to flinch.

She wanted to interrupt him and point out that his whole premise—this ancient ritual performed in modern times—was absurd and preposterous, but he ignored her and pressed on. He didn't care about the past, about what happened, only about the future, only about what could be, and this simple equation invigorated him in a way that reminded her of her husband. Finally he reached across the table and took her hand.

"Do you still love dad?" he asked her.

She glanced away as tears came to her eyes. He remained silent, awaiting her reply. "I'm not sure," was the best answer she could give him.

"Well, then maybe you still do, and maybe we can still be a family. It's worth a try. Don't you think it's worth a try?"

He stopped and looked into her eyes. She admired him at this moment more than she had ever done in her life. Even the fact that his voice was changing and, at times, had cracked during his talk hadn't detracted from its forcefulness. She smiled lovingly at him.

"Can we give it a try?" he asked. "Whaddya say, Mom?"

"She nodded and answered, "Okay."

Toby Jr. got up (he was getting so tall, she thought) and walked around the table to her. He cradled her head in his hands and kissed her on the forehead. "Thanks, Maya," he said.

THE TWENTY-TENS

If you've got a business – you didn't build that. Somebody else made that happen.

Barack Obama

The ideas within this philosophy are certainly not exclusive to any writer.

Nic Pizzolatto

The inscription placed by Dumbledore on his family's headstone:
"*Where your treasure is, there your heart will be also.*"

Matthew 6:21

The Box Factory

"I would prefer not to."
Bartleby the Scribner

Gerald Maddox needed to hire a new employee to work the corrugator and help out in shipping. His former employee Joe Moreno had decided to pick up and move to Nevada, leaving him in the lurch. This abrupt exit had forced Gerald—or Gerry, as most folks called him—to work the corrugator himself while he quickly posted the job opening on-line and waited for responses. After a week, he had winnowed through a number of applicants, narrowing his list down to three, and called each one to set up an interview.

Gerry owned Allied Packaging in San Jose, California. Technically, his wife owned the business, a move he had made fifteen years ago in order to take advantage of the tax break and regulatory relief that came with a woman-owned business. But it was Gerry who ran the business. He had founded Allied Packaging back in 1982 and had grown his small business into a successful enterprise that grossed $1.5 million in annual revenue. Back in '82, they had just manufactured standard corrugated boxes but today they supplied Bay Area customers with all their shipping and packaging needs, from bag sealers to bin boxes, poly bags to bubble foam, and from wine shippers to corrugated mailers. He employed twelve people and was fully incorporated.

He was proud of his business and considered himself a good boss and someone easy to get along with. Confrontation was not a part of his management style. In fact, he would pretend to ignore infractions, joke his way through acts of insubordination, and just plain walk away from conflict if the alternative meant going toe to toe with someone and raising his voice. He was a peace-loving man and it manifested itself through his management style. Over the years, he had taken a number of management classes, and he strongly identified with the Democratic and Affiliative styles of management as opposed to the Authoritative or Results-driven styles. But it wasn't the classes that had instilled these characteristics of trust and helpfulness into his management style; it was simply that these management styles aligned nicely with his already peace-loving nature.

Some folks might have taken this broad-mindedness as a weakness, as a Laissez-Faire style of management ripe for abuse, but that wasn't the case with the employees at Allied Packaging. For the most part, they liked Gerry and considered him a "cool boss" who paid over the minimum wage, cared or at least pretended to care about their personal problems, and patted them on the back when they did well. He appeared to have their best interests at heart and they appreciated it. Not that they weren't above making fun of "the old hippie" or playfully mocking some of his sayings like "Individually we're one box; together we're a case," or "It takes a village to make a box." But these digs were usually in jest and just a part of the banter that goes on between employees on the factory floor.

Gerry believed he had a strong team, and he was convinced that diversity was the key. His employees covered all major ethnic groups. Unfortunately, the ratio of male employees to female was still 80/20 despite his efforts over the years to hire more women. But overall, he was pleased. His team showed up to work on time, did their job with little complaining, and had twice rewarded his kind-heartedness by voting not to unionize.

But, of course, like any diverse workforce, he had a couple trouble-makers, though "trouble-makers" was probably too harsh a word in his mind. Rambunctious was more like it. Maurice Brown, nicknamed "Mo," and Dave Torres, nicknamed "Chato," were in their twenties and best buddies. More than once they had showed up to work hung over from the night before, and they had a habit of calling in sick on Mondays. When they worked next to each other on the factory floor they continually goofed around and played grab-ass, but Gerry usually solved that problem by reassigning them work stations farther apart from one another. But once they beared down they were good workers, and Gerry looked past their antics and chalked it up to youthful vigor.

One other employee was a bit of a pain in the ass and Gerry was always on his guard when he interacted with her. Vicky Berlin was a heavy-set woman with a spiked hair-do and multiple piercings. She drove a Harley and was a charter member of Dykes on Bikes, and her daily attire usually consisted of an ironed, collared shirt and Dockers, topped off with a leather vest and studded leather bracelets. Gerry paid no never-mind to all that show; it was her in-your-face aggressiveness that made him uncomfortable. Vicky wanted a promotion in the worst way, and was not above hounding him on that fact or in pointing out employee infractions in order to raise her stock. Gerry partially solved this problem by creating a new job title, Area Floor Manager, and "promoting" her into it with a slight raise. Her job didn't change, but the new job title pleased her and curtailed her restlessness for the time being.

It was from within this milieu that Gerry went into his job interviews. Once again, there had been no female job applicants, but the three male applicants looked strong on paper and Gerry was eager to make a decision. The first applicant was Hispanic who spoke broken English and was, Gerry guessed, an undocumented immigrant. But he had only shipping experience. The second applicant was a thin white man who was in his late thirties with a thick scrub of gray hair. He had both shipping and packaging experience but fidgeted throughout the interview while talking a mile a minute. Gerry figured him for a tweaker and crossed him off his list. The third applicant was African-American and had recently worked at Crown Packaging in Hayward. He had experience on the corrugator, the rotary-die cutter, and knew how to drive a forklift. His name was Rodney Toombs.

Job experience was on Rodney's side, but it was his job interview that sealed the deal for Gerry. He found Rodney to be soft-spoken, humble, and sedate in his manner—all qualities that Gerry strongly related to—and he hired him on the spot despite the fact that Rodney's urban drawl was a bit hard to understand. Gerry saw multiple benefits to hiring Rodney; besides the short learning curve there was Rodney's quiet demeanor, which he hoped would act as a calming tonic on some of his other employees like Mo and Chato, and perhaps even Vicky.

Gerry gave Rodney a tour of the factory and introduced him to everyone. He preferred to be called Rodney—not Rod—and wasn't much of a talker. When greeting a new co-worker, he extended only a few fingers in a handshake and refrained from small talk. Nevertheless the tour went well. Gerry showed him the corrugator (where Rodney would be starting out) along with the cutting and scoring machine, the bailer, converter, and rotary die-cutter. They finished off in shipping where 6000lb rolls of paper sat waiting the production line, the large rolls casting a shadow over multiple-sized packages awaiting shipment out of the loading dock. Back in his office, Gerry sat him down for a tutorial on their product line and reviewed all the Cal-OSHA and other safety rules of the plant. Rodney seemed a quick study.

The first two weeks Rodney worked the corrugator, and on the third week Gerry moved him over to the rotary die-cutter. He picked up the work quickly, and after another week on the die-cutter, Gerry was pleased to see that Rodney fit right in. He allowed himself a pat on the back; he'd made a wise choice in hiring Rodney.

It wasn't until the fourth week that the trouble began. Rodney was working the die-cutter, which he seemed to enjoy, when Gerry came by on a Monday morning to ask him to run the forklift in shipping. Chato had called in sick and Gerry needed to juggle things around to make up for the man shortage.

"I don' wanna," said Rodney.

"Huh?" replied Gerry, not sure if he had heard right. "What was that?"

"I don' wanna."

Gerry stood still, slightly flabbergasted, running all the reasons someone would say that to him through his brain. Was Rodney not feeling well? Was it a training issue? Maybe Rodney had lied on his application about knowing how to run a forklift. That was probably it, he decided. But no biggie, folks lied on their job applications all the time. He'd train Rodney on the forklift. Problem solved.

"Is it the forklift?" he asked. "Are you not comfortable operating the forklift?" Gerry waited for a response but Rodney remained quiet, working the die-cutter, and just shrugged his shoulders. This slightly irritated Gerry. "Your résumé says you know how to operate a forklift," he pressed, wanting to get to the bottom of this. "Can you?"

"Yeah."

"Well then," said Gerry, rather relieved, "I could use your help today in shipping, running the forklift. What'cha say?"

"I don' wanna."

"What do you mean, 'you don't want to'?" shot back Gerry. He found he was getting angry and had to check himself. Anger was counter-productive, he knew, and he paused a moment to calm himself down. He tried again in a more affable manner: "Help me understand. What don't you want to do? What's the issue we need to work out?"

No answer came from Rodney. He continued to work the die-cutter and ignored Gerry's question.

After standing and waiting a good thirty seconds for an answer, Gerry decided to let it go for the time being, deciding that Rodney was just having a bad day. It wasn't worth the confrontation and he'd address this with Rodney at another time. "Okay, Rodney," he said. "We'll talk about this later." And with that, Gerry went off to shipping to work the forklift on his own.

The next day, Chato returned to work and everything went back to normal. Gerry did not address Rodney's insubordination and instead, in a conscious and strategic decision, resolved to ignore it. Some folks didn't like change; they preferred the same routine day after day, and Gerry figured Rodney was one of those people. What was the big deal, afterall? Rodney did a good job on the die-cutter and he was low maintenance. He didn't make demands and kept a low profile. It was true that he had very little interaction with his fellow employees, preferring to keep to himself, but there were worst things in the world than being a loner. He did interact with Mo at least once a day. Mo brought Rodney a big bag of Skittles after lunch each day and Rodney paid him, opened the bag, and munched on the Skittles the rest of the day as he worked the die-cutter.

In Gerry's view of it, what was a little odd behavior in the grand scheme of things? Not much.

Vicky approached him a week later, demanding to know why tasks on the factory floor weren't being rotated as usual. Gerry had a long-standing policy of what he termed "rotation education," which ensured that employees moved from station to station so they didn't get bogged down in one task. It kept folks out of a rut and increased employee versatility.

"What do you mean?" he replied. "We're still rotating." But he knew where this was going.

"Not the die-cutter," she retorted. "Rodney's been on it for a month. I'd like to work the die-cutter for a change. When can I?"

Gerry tried to explain the situation as best he could but he knew he was on weak ground. Rodney liked working the die-cutter, he explained. He was good at it and didn't want to move, and Gerry preferred to let status quo alone for now. Vicky tore into him, telling him in no uncertain terms that it was unfair for someone to hog a machine. "Tell him to move," she demanded. "Make him move. Who runs this company, you or him?"

Gerry sympathized with her viewpoint and promised to look into it.

Later that day Gerry approached Rodney, who sat working the die-cutter and munching Skittles. "Rodney, how's it going?" asked Gerry cheerfully. He waited for a response, didn't get one, and pressed on. "You're doing a great job here. Keep up the great work... Also, and I think I already covered you on this, we have a rotation policy here in the plant. What that means is you'll eventually need to rotate to another task. Actually, pretty soon."

"I don' wanna."

Gerry half-expected that response but frowned at it anyhow. "It's not a matter of wanting to, or not," he explained. "It's company policy. Other folks look forward to working the die-cutter. In fact, I've already gotten complaints about you being on it too long, and they have a point. So, we're going to have to move you. But your choice. What would you like to do? The corrugator again? The converting machine? Or how about quality checker?"

"No."

"No won't cut it, Rodney. You'll have to rotate—but I'm giving you a choice."

"I don' wanna."

Gerry sighed to himself. What was he going to do about this? If this had been any other employee he would have met this obstinance, this disobedience, with a firm hand, but there was something about Rodney that disarmed him. He couldn't bring himself to discipline or even reproach Rodney. To do so would have made him feel, somehow, narrow-minded as though he were disciplining a special needs student. It felt wrong. And Gerry was someone who trusted his feelings.

After a moment in which Gerry digested Rodney's response, weighing his different options, he decided to let it go and return to his office where he shut the door and waited. Inevitably, Vicky knocked on his door, demanding to know the outcome of his "talk" with Rodney. He tried his best to explain the nuances of the situation to her but she wasn't buying it. Finally he shrugged in resignation, noting that "it is what it is," and asked her as one professional to another what she thought of Rodney.

"The guy's looney-tunes," she responded. Gerry forced a laugh at that, but Vicky wasn't done. "The guy never moves from that chair," she added. "I never see him take lunch or even a break. Isn't there a state law that says he's gotta take a break? Pretty sure there is."

Gerry admitted that there was such a law. Regardless, he needed time to address this issue, to dig into it and find out what was behind Rodney's stubbornness. Perhaps it was a learning disability, or some form of autism; all he could do right now was be patient with him and try to get to the bottom of it. Would she let him do that, he asked her. Would she give him some time to work this out?

This appeal caught Vicky off-guard—she could sympathize with it—and she backed off. Sure, they'd give him more time, she said, acting as spokesperson for all the other employees. Just as long as it didn't take forever. Gerry thanked her for her understanding.

In less than a week, Gerry had a growing concern on his hands. Someone, and he wasn't sure who, had overheard Rodney's response of "I don' wanna," and spread it across the factory floor. Now it had become a running joke. He first heard it in shipping when a UPS driver asked Chato to sign for a package. Chato's immediate reply was "I don' wanna," eliciting a sarcastic laugh from others nearby. He heard it again later at the coffee machine when one of his employees replied "I don' wanna" to a request to make a fresh pot of coffee. Again there was more sarcastic laughter. Each time it happened, those laughing shot a glance at him to gauge his reaction.

He had approached Rodney a couple more times about rotating but had made no headway. Rodney did not want to move, would not consider moving, and brushed off Gerry's attempts to reason with him by shrugging his shoulders. Instead of being upset with Rodney's single-mindedness, Gerry was intrigued by the problem, and like any complex problem that came his way he was determined to sort it out and solve it. He spent a few days observing Rodney and found out that Vicky was right: Rodney never left his seat in front of the die-cutter other than to go to the restroom. He didn't appear to eat, other than Skittles, and never joked around with the other employees. He took the bus to work and back. Gerry also called Rodney's previous employer, Crown Packaging. They confirmed his past employment but were vague about his work performance, telling him that Rodney hadn't worked there long enough for them to make a fair assessment.

After piecing all this information together, Gerry was more convinced than ever that Rodney was a special needs case; he was someone who needed to be sympathized with and accommodated rather than harassed. Rodney's tasks needed to remain narrow, his life made simpler, and to that end Gerry decided to leave Rodney alone. He had been content with that decision until now.

But the whole "I don' wanna" craze had changed his mind. And what worried him about it was not a drop-off in production—his employees were still working hard—but rather the spirit behind the mocking phrase of "I don' wanna." It was not so much a dig at Rodney as it was ridicule of his management style. And that, he knew, could be infectious and dangerous to a business. He would have to do something about it. He would have to confront it whether he liked it or not.

The confrontation came soon enough. Mo tracked him down a day later in the front lobby and put his hand on Gerry's shoulder to get his attention. "You betta' check it out," he said. Gerry followed him back into the factory. Chato quickly joined them and had a mischievous grin on his face.

"What's up?" asked Gerry.

"You'll see," answered Mo. Chato added an "Ah huh," for emphasis.

As they approached the die-cutter, they came to a halt and witnessed the scene. Vicky was sitting at the die-cutter working the machine while Rodney stood five feet behind her watching. He was frozen in place.

"How long's he been standing there?"

"'Bout twenty minutes," replied Mo. "He got up ta-go to the john and Vicky jumped in."

"He hasn't moved?"

"No. He don' wanna." Both Mo and Chato snickered at this joke.

"All right," said Gerry with authority. "You guys go back to work. I'll take care of this." As they turned to leave, he suddenly called Mo back. "I see you selling Skittles to Rodney. You ever talk to him?"

"Not really."

"What's your take on him?"

Mo raised his chin up in thought and took a deep breath. "You askin' me 'cause we're both black—just kidding... I'd say he's one stone cold brotha'."

"How do you mean?"

"Ya know, *stone cold.* Chilled out. Like an ex-con."

"Is he an ex-con?"

"How do I know? Just sayin'. Could be... He's black, so yeah he probably is." When Gerry moved to object to this, Mo cut him off by saying, "Just kidding," and Chato laughed at the joke.

"All right, I get it," said Gerry, ignoring the joke. "You guys go on, I'll take it from here." He waited until they were out of ear-shot before approaching Rodney.

The man looked downright eerie just standing there, immovable, like some statue in the cemetery. Gerry came up next to him and looked at his eyes. He seemed to be staring at the back of Vicky's neck.

"Hey, boss!" chirped Vicky from her seat.

Gerry gave her a short wave as he attempted to gain Rodney's attention. He stepped into Rodney's line of sight and made eye contact with him, and Gerry asked him politely to follow him into his office. With some gentle coaxing and elbow tugging, Gerry was able to move Rodney off his spot and get him to follow. As they walked to his office, Gerry could hear the sound of feet shuffling behind him, and when he glanced back he caught a glimpse of Rodney, slouching with his head down, hobbling across the floor as though he were in chains. An image of a slave following his master popped into Gerry's head. He found the image unsettling.

Gerry closed the door to his office and sat on the edge of his desk while Rodney remained standing. Gerry studied the young man for a moment. He was over six foot in height, slightly overweight, and wore his hair in a buzz cut. He was clean shaven. According to his résumé, Rodney was thirty-two and he looked his age, though his eyes had an older kind of somberness to them. As usual, his attire consisted of a hoodie sweatshirt, baggy pants, and high-top tennis shoes. In Gerry's mind, he was non-descript, someone you could pass on the street in the city and not take any special notice of.

Would he take a seat, Gerry asked him. No. Well then, what happened today was bound to happen. Gerry had given him fair warning. Everybody rotated jobs, and his refusal to do so had led to this impasse. Surely he could see that? Given the circumstances, would he now move over to the corrugator or operate the forklift in shipping?

"I don' wanna."

Gerry sighed and looked the young man up and down once more. A path forward was forming in Gerry's head and he took a moment to flush it out before putting it into words. He knew he'd have to be tactful and choose his words carefully, but he was satisfied with himself that it was the best way to solve his problem.

Maybe this job was not the right match for him, suggested Gerry. Perhaps he was better suited for a job elsewhere? Another packaging company? Maybe even a totally different line of work? Something more fulfilling. Gerry would even help him out. Yes, he knew Rodney had only worked here a little over a month but Gerry would give him a month's severance pay to help him in his job search. What did he think about that?

"No."

That "No" rattled Gerry a bit. It wasn't hostile or impertinent-sounding; instead it was simple, to the point, and irrevocable. As he digested the finality of that "No," he recognized for the first time that Rodney intimidated him and maybe always had. He couldn't explain the reason for that, but it was true, and he struggled a moment with that realization. Was he afraid of Rodney? Yes, maybe a little, but he couldn't let that fear cloud his judgement. He decided to take a different approach.

"You're a smart guy," he said. "If I remember right, your résumé said you spent a year at Chabot College... What did you enjoy studying?"

"Whaddya mean?"

"I don't know, like Sociology or Psychology. What was your favorite?"

"I dunno."

"Maybe Political Science. That was my favorite."

"Hmm."

Gerry took that "Hmm" as a yes. *Political Science.* There you go," he replied optimistically, but as he said this and looked back into Rodney's eyes, those eyes that seemed to hold no interest in anything, he lost his train of thought. The image of Rodney shuffling behind him like a chained slave popped back into his head and with it came an epiphany. Gerry saw it clearly now: Rodney wasn't some special needs case; he was something much more than that. And all the piece parts came together now and coalesced; the quiet disdain, the premeditated silence, the passive aggression, it all fit together like a hand in a glove. Rodney was in rebellion against the world; he was in rebellion against four hundred years of oppression and persecution. And his rebellion wasn't violent or threatening; it was more profound than that. It seemed almost an enlightened rejection. Rodney wasn't going to do what he was told to do any longer, especially by a white man. His choices were the only ones that mattered.

The sheer audacity of this revelation nearly staggered Gerry and he had to stand up and walk over to the window to regain his composure. He was sure now that he'd hit upon the truth of the matter, but what to do about it was a whole other question. It wasn't as though he could go out and eradicate all the triggers for Rodney's behavior. If anything, federal and state law, along with his own sensibility, had created a safe work environment free from overt discrimination. But he was progressive enough to know that racism couldn't be litigated away; it ran deeper than that; it was more subtle and sinister than that. Gerry was keenly aware that subconsciously he was guilty of small racisms every day, in just the way he talked or acted or took certain things for granted. He had learned that this kind of racism was born out of his privileged upbringing and was engrained in his psyche.

But he was at a loss over what to do about it.

Rodney stood motionless while Gerry thought it through. The only thing to do, he finally decided, was to break the construct. He'd leave the choice to Rodney. There would be no more cajoling, tugs of the shoulder, or manipulative suggestions on his part. These were only hidden slights anyhow and he would stop them here and now. Rodney was free to decide his own fate. The novelty of this approach, with its streak of radicalness, appealed to Gerry and he smiled to himself.

"Okay, Rodney," he said. "You're your own man, so I'm leaving it up to you. I'll respect whatever decision you make...Take your time. You can have my office." And with that, Gerry stepped past Rodney and left his office.

An hour later, Rodney was still standing in the same spot. Gerry could see his image through the blinds. As closing time approached, nothing had changed, but Gerry was committed to his course. He let Rodney be. At five o'clock the factory began to empty and Gerry, realizing the young man still occupied his office, faced a dilemma. He'd have to go back into his office to get his car keys and brief case, then close up, and that meant confronting Rodney. He meandered around his empty factory for a while trying to decide what to do. He could still see Rodney's image through the blinds, standing, immobile, like some haunting specter.

The whole ridiculousness of the situation finally began to sink in and Gerry, fully resolved now, re-entered his office and nonchalantly picked up his things. He'd come to another bold decision—he would let Rodney close the factory up—and he wrote the door code on a piece of paper and laid it on the edge of his desk. "There's the door code," he told Rodney. "Lock up when you're done and I'll see you in the morning." There was no reaction from Rodney. "Well then," added Gerry in parting, and he left his office and went home convinced that this show of trust on his part would reap dividends in the morning.

When Gerry arrived the next morning he was pleased to find the door lock engaged. His trust in Rodney had not been misplaced. He turned on the lights and walked to his office, noticing as he did that the blinds were shut and the door closed. He found the door locked, but before he fished out his key to unlock it a sixth sense told him to put his ear to the door. He knocked and listened. There came a yawning groan.

"What?" came a groggy voice.

"Who is that?" replied Gerry in disbelief. He knocked harder and rattled the door knob. "Rodney, is that you? Open up." There was no answer, only the sound of slow and languorous movements. "Rodney, open up."

"Hold."

"What?—okay." At the moment, he was at a loss, so he just stood still outside the door and listened. There was a small bathroom in his office and he could hear the water running. After a good ten minutes, all of which Gerry spent standing like an idiot outside his own office, Rodney came and unlocked the door. Gerry quickly turned on the lights but left the blinds drawn. He watched as Rodney walked away from him and sat on the sofa against the wall. It was obvious the young man had slept here the night.

Gerry peppered him with questions. Why was he still here? Did he sleep the night here? His office wasn't a hotel room. Did he understand that? But there was no response to his questions; Rodney merely sat on the sofa looking past Gerry. A mix of emotions swirled through Gerry's breast; he was at once outraged, confused, and disappointed. But most of all he was troubled, and it was a kind of feeling that cut to the core of his being and made him second guess his assumptions. He didn't like that feeling one bit, and he pulled back from it.

From a practical standpoint, there was only one thing to do. Make Rodney leave.

"You're gonna have to go," he said. "You can't stay here. We have work to do. Come on, let's go."

"I don' wanna."

"Don't give me that crap. Out. Get out... or I'll call the police." But he regretted saying this as soon as it came out of his mouth. It just reinforced the whole white/black construct he'd sought to tear down the day before.

Rodney laid down on the sofa, putting his head on a pillow, and turned his back to Gerry.

Checkmate, thought Gerry. At least for now. He went through the motions of opening up his office, got a cup of coffee, and went around to greet his employees. He let them know they'd be a man short today, and he made adjustments to the work assignments to compensate. At the end of the day Rodney was still camped out in his office.

Three days passed with no change. Rodney remained in his office rooted to the sofa, either standing next to it looking out through the blinds, sitting on it, or lying down. He hadn't changed his clothes and the stubble of a beard was forming on his chin. Gerry hadn't seen him eat either. If he snuck out at night to get something to eat he left no evidence of it in the office. It worried Gerry. Was the guy homeless? He didn't appear to have a cell phone either. Didn't everybody have a cell phone these days? Had there been some upheaval in his personal life to put him over the edge? Would Gerry come in one morning and find Rodney hanging from the rafters? There were no getting answers out of him, and so for the time being Gerry was content to let him be. Rodney was like a tree stump in the backyard that was too difficult to move. You just learned to live with it and worked around it.

The employees at Allied Packaging knew of the situation, and to Gerry's surprise it had not become a subject of scorn and ridicule. Their attitude seemed to be one of amused curiosity. If anyone came into his office to talk or drop something off, they would glance over at the stationary figure, grin as though they'd just seen the geek at the carnival, and carry on with their business. On the factory floor they could see his image through the blinds, standing immobile, but the weirdness of it wore off after a few days and they went about their business.

But soon the whole state of affairs became intolerable to Gerry. He couldn't work in his office. There—always there—was Rodney, looming over him like a menacing ghost. He couldn't concentrate. He tried putting a partition up between them but that didn't work; he could still *feel* him there, breathing, being.

His office had become a tomb; he couldn't conduct private business or bring clients into it any more. He had hoped that Rodney would eventually tire of it all and leave, that he would come in one morning and find Rodney gone, but the likelihood of that happening diminished with each passing day. Something had to be done.

"Hey, boss, how's it going?" It was Vicky.

"Okay, I guess."

"You don't look okay."

"No? I guess I'm worried about Rodney. Something needs to be done... Any ideas?"

"I told you, the guy's looney tunes. Everyone here knows he's looney tunes. You need to go in there and fire him, and if he doesn't leave, call the cops and have him dragged out. That's what I'd do."

"Well... yeah, I've been thinking about it."

"Stop thinking about it. Grow a pair, dude. Go in there and kick him out."

Gerry nodded weakly while pretending to take her advice to heart. Funny thing was, his wife had given him the same advice: fire Rodney and remove him from the premises. Of course, his wife's advice had been more diplomatic; she had used terms such as "take control" and "be forceful" which weren't that much different than "grow a pair." And what was worse, his wife had accused him of being paralyzed by "white guilt." That didn't sit well with him.

"I know, and I will. But it's complicated... I'm going to talk to HR today."

"'Bout time," replied Vicky.

In the afternoon, Gerry went out to his car and called HR from his cell phone. As a small business, Allied Packaging didn't warrant their own Human Resources Department and instead paid a small monthly fee to have it outsourced. Gerry got a consultant on the line and explained the situation to him. The consultant listened to him, asked a couple clarifying questions, and then asked him if the whole thing was political. Gerry wasn't sure what he meant. Was it political in nature, repeated the consultant—the whole occupation of his office—was it a sit-in or some kind of protest against a perceived insult or racial discrimination? Gerry wasn't sure, but he didn't think so.

Well, that made all the difference, explained the consultant. If it was political, then terminating his employment would probably lead to an EEOC complaint. That meant an investigation, mediation, and possible fines if he didn't have his case well-documented. On the other hand, if this guy Rodney was just being a nuisance who refused to work or take orders then, yes, Gerry was well within his rights to fire him. And if this Rodney guy, African-American or not, refused to vacate his place of business then that constituted trespassing and Gerry could call the police and have him removed. In fact, if the latter was the case, the sooner he fired him the better. If this Rodney guy hurt anybody or "went postal" Gerry might be held liable for having ignored the problem for so long.

After Gerry hung up with the HR consultant, he sat in his car lost in thought. He knew he needed to act, but he didn't want to. He felt sorry for Rodney; the young man was obviously troubled. Who knew what would happen if he threw him out in the real world? Rodney seemed so horribly vulnerable; he might be taken advantage of, get hurt or worse, and all that would be on Gerry's head. It was a riddle wrapped in a mystery, and Gerry felt boxed in from all sides.

After sitting in his car for a half hour struggling with a path forward, he finally reached a decision. As unpleasant as it was, Rodney would have to go. In the end, it came down to good business. Allied Packaging was Gerry's baby, his heart and soul, and this sad immovable object was impacting his bottom line. He was paying an employee who didn't work. Employee morale was at stake. He had no choice but to act.

Gerry waited until after the factory closed up to confront Rodney. He thought it worth one more try to convince Rodney to take a month's severance pay and quit. He pleaded with him to do so but all he got in return was silence. The young man just stood there without acknowledging Gerry's existence. Rodney had lost weight; his clothes were wrinkled from constant wear, and the stubble on his chin had turned into a beard. Gerry studied him for a while, fighting back a wave of compassion to let it all go, to just let it be, but he stifled the emotion and stayed focused on his mission. The time had come.

"Rodney, you're fired. You'll need to gather up your things and leave."

Silence.

"You hear me? You need to leave. Now."

"I don' wanna."

"And I don't want you to stay. So I'll give you five minutes to clear out or I'm calling the police." Gerry looked for a reaction to this but got none. He sighed, flipped off the lights, and left to walk around his factory for eight minutes before returning to his office. Rodney was still there, standing in the shadows, calm and unshakable. "Okay," replied Gerry, sitting down at his desk and picking up the phone. "Sorry for this." He dialed 911.

Two San Jose police officers arrived in fifteen minutes and Gerry led them back to his office, explaining the situation as they went. They understood and were clear on their duty; this guy Rodney had been fired and refused to leave. He was now trespassing. They would politely ask him to leave and if he didn't they would arrest him and remove him forcibly. Was there anything else they needed to know? Did he have any weapons? Gerry answered them with an emphatic no.

Once in his office, Gerry flipped the lights back on and stepped aside. In short order, the two officers attempted to talk to Rodney, got no response, handcuffed him, and led him out the door. Gerry followed them, watching as the two armed policemen, one of either side of Rodney, nearly dragged him across the floor. The sight of it struck a chord deep inside Gerry's sensibility. There it was in a nutshell, the sum of his fears, everything he had tried to avoid and transcend—the symbol of white America's treatment of the black man—and he was an accomplice to it. A sick feeling of failure welled up inside him.

When they reached the exit one of the officers pushed open the door. The sunlight seemed to catch Rodney off guard and he stopped and looked away. The second officer gave him a shove to get him out the door.

"There's no need for that," said Gerry.

"Don't tell us how to do our job."

"Yes, sir."

Gerry stood in the doorway and watched as they placed Rodney in the back seat of their squad car and drove away. He shut the door, keyed in the combination to lock it, and walked back to his office. There he shut the door, sat down at his desk, and cried.

With the office to himself and things back to normal, Gerry should have felt a light-hearted sense of relief, but instead he felt guilt. After a few days, he decided to call the police to find out what had happened to Rodney. He wanted to drop all charges. When he reached the front desk, they informed him that Mr. Toombs had been booked and then subsequently tagged as "fifty-one-fifty" and transferred to Emergency Psychiatric Services on Enborg Lane. The officer gave him the number to EPS but Gerry held off a day before calling. At first EPS wouldn't give him any information, but once Gerry explained that he was Rodney's former employer and was concerned about his welfare, they told him that Rodney had been transferred to the hospital due to malnutrition. He refused to eat and was in a weakened state.

It took a day for a doctor at the hospital to call him back. He answered the call on his cell phone and stepped outside to talk in private. The doctor was keen on gathering information on Rodney and Gerry did his best to answer his questions. No, he wasn't a family member, just an ex-employer concerned about his welfare. No, he wasn't aware of family members they could contact; Rodney's job application listed no emergency contact information. No, he wasn't aware of any trauma or past history that might explain Rodney's condition. And what exactly was Rodney's condition, asked Gerry. Severe malnutrition, exacerbated by a refusal to eat, explained the doctor. They had him hooked up to feeding tubes for the time being but the prognosis was not good if they couldn't break him out of his malaise. It was a "strange case." The doctor agreed to call Gerry if there was any change in the young man's condition.

Gerry consoled himself that Rodney was being helped, that is was beneficial for him to be in a hospital and under a doctor's care. Maybe that had been the young man's fate all along. Perhaps some deep-seated disorder had finally broken out and taken over, and it was simply Gerry's misfortune to have been there when it happened. He could stop his worrying; the state had him now.

A couple months went by and Gerry, wholly engrossed in running his factory, found himself thinking less and less about Rodney's fate, and it caught him a bit off guard when the doctor finally called him back again. The doctor was sorry to inform him that Rodney had passed away. Strangely, the news did not shock Gerry. The doctor told him that they had failed to track down any family and wanted to know if Gerry wished to claim the body? No, he said. He'd only known him briefly. Thank you for the call.

As the days and weeks passed, Gerry continued to reflect back on his time with Rodney. He was past recriminations, of what he should or could have done better, and really found himself trying to put a final definition on the young man. The old explanations—special needs case, eccentric genius, black activist, mental patient— they no longer satisfied him. There had been something more at work with Rodney. He was convinced of it. There had been something, in a way, transcendent about Rodney Toombs that he couldn't put into words.

It finally came to him early one morning as he sat down at this desk with a fresh cup of coffee and began his daily routine. He glanced over at the sofa. There, suddenly, in his mind's eye he saw Rodney standing as before, serene and aloof, unperturbed by the noise of the world, and at that moment Gerry understood it all. Rodney had not revolted against the world; he had renounced it. Like some Hindu yogi or otherworldly Brahmin, Rodney had rejected the push and pull of human existence and taken his own path. All the evidence was there: the abstinence, the profound apathy for worldly things, and the unshakable resolve. Look how he spoke only to answer, never showed anger or arrogance, and humbly disdained the rules of civilization. "I don' wanna" was his mantra. And when Gerry imagined Rodney's death, it wasn't in the fetal position emaciated by hunger but rather as a soul freed from its shell and bathed in the warmth of enlightenment.

Gerry nodded to himself and smiled. He was sure that explanation was the true one, and it comforted him.

He could hear his employees starting up work and his factory coming alive, and he picked up his coffee cup and walked out of his office. He was feeling good. Vicky Berlin came in and banged her helmet against a table. She looked pissed about something and Gerry avoided her. He said good morning to Mo and Chato, who looked a little hung over, greeted a few others, and then walked over to the rotary die-cutter. Gerry had filled the opening left by Rodney some weeks ago, and he stopped and studied the back of his new employee. The sight filled him with a sense of accomplishment. He had finally been able to hire another woman.

Serum 114

W e're in the living room of an apartment. It's sparsely fur-
nished with a flat screen TV on a credenza, a well-worn
couch, a coffee table, and one other chair. The walls are an
off-white and punctuated with framed movie posters, mostly
film noir stuff like *The Killing* and *The Asphalt Jungle.* The lone
exception is a poster of the movie *Singin' in the Rain* from 1952.
Numerous Post-it notes and sheets of lined paper, scribbled with
ideas and reminders, are stuck to the wall, giving the place the
look of a dorm room during finals week.

Two men in their late thirties occupy the room. Both men
are screenplay writers. Seth Gould is wearing pajama bottoms
and a grungy-looking UCLA sweatshirt and sits on the couch
with his laptop. He's slightly over-weight, his dark hair is thin-
ning on top, and he looks a bit like a pudgy, balding version
of Jeff Goldblum. This is his apartment and he looks comfortable on the couch. The other man is Vince Peyton, also a screen
writer, and he's in blue jeans wearing a black t-shirt emblazoned
with the logo for the punk band The Misfits. He is thinner than
Seth with shaggy blonde hair that's styled purposely to resemble
Owen Wilson, but the resemblance is slight. He sits then stands,
chain smokes, and paces the room with a nervous energy.

Seth and Vince are in the middle of a brain-storming ses-
sion. They are in desperate need of a winning concept that will
put them over the top. Something ground-breaking, something
along the lines of *The Sopranos* or *Breaking Bad,* a killer pitch
and pilot for a mini-series that will break the door down, deliver

the goods, and give them the artistic control of a David Chase or a Nic Pizzolatto. Neither writer has had much luck lately and teeters on the brink of inconsequence. The last real work for Seth was punching up scripts for *Inhumans*, which was critically panned and cancelled after eight episodes. The same with Vince. His last gig was *Criminal Minds: Beyond Borders,* which managed to last two seasons before going belly-up. Neither of them has worked since or sold a story or script. In the parlance of the industry, "They can't get arrested."

The two met in college and are buddies. On the surface is an easy-going rapport but underneath we can sense a tension—a tension that occasionally bubbles up in the form of one-up-man-ship and snarky exchanges. Neither friend wants the other to succeed before he does, but neither friend desires the other to fail, and it's this very paradox that has brought the two together in collaboration. Like the Coen Brothers or Zemeckis and Gale, they have decided to join forces and leverage off each other's strengths. Seth's talents are story ideas and character development; Vince's are scene-setting and gritty dialogue.

It could be day or night. A black sheet is tacked up over the lone window and the only light in the apartment comes from an overhead lamp. The bright, artificial light throws out odd shadows. The coffee table is strewn with empty beer bottles, candy wrappers, a half-eaten bag of chips, a large porcelain ash tray, packages of cigarettes, and a mirror that's being used to cut up lines of coke.

The two writers throw out ideas, go off on tangents, and prime the engine with puns and movie trivia as they wait impatiently for some kind of hyper-creative fever to kick in. It's a higher state of consciousness they seek, akin to religious fervor, and they expect its gift-giving ascension at any moment.

"I thought we said no anthologies," says Vince. "The airways are saturated with them—*True Detective, Black Mirror, Channel Zero, American Horror Story.* And especially horror anthologies. Oversaturated, man. Like westerns in the fifties. Didn't we say that?"

"We did," replies Seth.

"Then what?"

"But I'm just saying. It doesn't have to be horror. Think of it as 'Kick-ass Playhouse' where we air an action-packed story each week. Not horror or comedy or drama. We mix elements of each into every episode. Martial arts or special ops stuff in the jungle. Home invasions gone wrong. Bad-ass dudes out for revenge like *Wick*. You know, *Punisher* stuff, but not superhero shit."

"'Home invasions,' huh? Like your movie script—what's it called?"

"*A Spoonful of Blood.* Exactly. I can easily skinny it down to an hour episode. That way we can leverage some of our stuff in the bank."

"I don't have anything like that. Just two scripts that are horror sci-fi, and we said no horror sci-fi. Anyhow, I thought you're still pitching that script."

"I am."

"What's the logline?"

"*Mary Poppins* meets *Straw Dogs.* A young nanny, home alone with young children, turns killer to protect her precious babies from the threat of ruthless home invaders."

"Nice. I like the 'precious babies' bit. Who'd you pitch it to so far?"

"The usual suspects. Productions companies. I couldn't get in to Netflix or HBO so I tried AMC and FX but no bites. Even tried AT&T Entertainment Services. Someone told me they were desperate for material. Dark stuff—and Woke."

"What could be more Dark and Woke than a nanny with a meat cleaver?"

"Exactly, but they turned me down after a week of leading me on. Fuckers."

"Keep pitching, dude. Meanwhile, no anthologies, kick-ass or not. You were on the right track before with the dysfunctional family saga thing. *The Sopranos* thing."

"Best line from *The Sopranos*."

"'Hi, my name is J.T., I'm an alcoholic and an addict. I'm also a TV writer, which by default makes me a douchebag.'"

(Laughs) "Right. Perfect… I also love that line by Chris, the one about Lou Gehrig—"

"'You ever think what a coincidence it is that Lou Gehrig died of Lou Gehrig's disease?'"

(Laughs) "Exactly. Too good. David Chase is a god. You know there was no improvisation allowed on his sets. All script changes had to be approved by him."

"I heard that. How about another line?"

"From the Sopranos?"

"No, of coke."

"Dude, I only got an eight-ball and we gotta make it last."

"We need a charge."

"All right, okay, two short ones then." Seth sets his laptop aside and leans over the coffee table where he opens up a small envelope and taps out the white powder onto the mirror. He picks up a razor blade and goes to work. Vince watches intently while he continues to talk to Seth.

"You know who's a god? Nic Pizzolatto, dude. *True Detective,* season one. It's all him, man. Complete creative control. His vision from start to finish. No producer bullshit to put up with. No network wonks to dick with. He just gets free rein, and the results speak for themselves. Absorbing, darkly twisted poetry. You know, his favorite philosopher is Emil Cioran—he even said so—and Cioran's world view permeates his writing. I think I told you about him. He was like this Romanian philosopher who died back in the nineties—this deep pessimist who writes about suffering and decay. An existentialist. Well, maybe more a stylish nihilist. He says things like 'Chaos is rejecting all you have learned, chaos is being yourself' and stuff like 'Darkness itself glows in me.' He's got this book. *On the Heights of Despair* it's called. Read it. You'll want to cut your throat after. But anyhow, his world view permeates throughout True Detective and Pizzolatto stays true to it, except for maybe right at the end where McConaughey's character says, 'Well, once there was only dark. If you ask me, the light's winning.' It's a bit of a cop-out. I mean, he paints this whole world without hope, so it's a bit of a cop-out. Maybe McConaughey put it in there. I think he's some kind of born-again Christian, so that would explain it. But otherwise, ninety-nine point nine percent of *True Detective* is Pizzolatto, and that's impressive. The man's a god."

"To the gods," says Seth as he snorts a line of coke and offers the rolled up dollar bill to Vince.

"To the gods."

"That's the model, for sure. A single vision. That way you can blend genres and tone and not get locked into a formula. You can be more experimental."

"Hmm, yeah." (*Sniffs*) "Exactly. Just look at *Channel Zero*.

"You're obsessed with that show."

"I know, but it's everything we're talking about. Single vision. Experimentation. It's like a deeply disturbing nightmare brought to the screen."

"That nobody watched."

"Cause it was way ahead of its time. Like Van Gogh.

"Best line from *Channel Zero*."

"Ahh, let's see… 'One dog moves out, another moves in. It's the circle of life.'"

"Wait, isn't that from American Horror Story. Jessica Lange, right? Fiona."

"Shit, you're right, dude. How'd that happen?"

"Must be a glitch in the Matrix."

"Hold on… hold on. Here we go. 'Mmmm. Give me parfait and ear wafer. My favorite. Bring it on.'"

"There you go. Good come-back."

"It's too many horror anthologies. Just what we were talking about."

"Which reminds me. What were we talking about? Let's get re-grounded. Where were we?"

"Dysfunctional family sagas."

"Right. So here's the idea I've been playing with. The Russian mob. We follow a Russian mob family from its inception, say 1989 with the fall of the Berlin Wall, all the way up to present time. A Russian Sopranos, only spanning an entire generation, so more like *The Irishman,* but we'll go from the beginning and stay linear."

"Okay, I can see it. But I don't know anything about the Russian mob."

"Just Google it. You'll find a ton of stuff on Wikipedia."

"I mean, I've seen *Eastern Promises* and *John Wick*, so I get the gist of it. But I don't know the history behind it. What source material are we using?"

"There's books out there like *Red Mafiya* you can read but I got the history stuff covered for now. I got relatives—Soviet Jews—who came here and settled in Brooklyn, in Little Odessa, and are connected to the Russian mob. I've heard all sorts of stories—plus my grandfather speaks fluent Russian, so we can use him as a dialogue consultant."

"That'll help. Mob talk and street talk's just straight dialogue colored over. *The Wire* did that all the time. We just need to Russianize it, and I can do that."

"Right on, and we got all the ingredients. Organized crime, drug cartels, human trafficking, the evils of capitalism. We got ex-KGB, hitmen, power struggles, all the ingredients of a dark and twisted world ruled by greed and violence. And there's the dysfunctional family—in this case a Russian crime lord who rules over a collection of psychopaths and degenerates."

"The key is to make them into real people, like you and me. Complex, multi-faceted. No hard lines between good and bad."

"We can even set this thing in LA. There's a Russian mob presence in LA right now, though it might be Armenian. But it doesn't matter. We make it Russian. And here's the other thing I'm thinking—when we pitch this we put in a teaser. We say it's a series that spans over twenty years but culminates with them rigging the 2016 election for Trump, maybe as a payback to Putin for favors rendered."

"HBO will love that."

"That's what I'm thinking."

"I like it, dude. I think we got something here—who do you keep texting?"

"Todd. He's going to swing by later. Told him to pick up a pizza."

"Round Table?"

"Yeah."

"So where do you want to go from here? Sketch out a story? Start building characters? Like how do you see the patriarch? Is he a Tony character or more like a Vito Corleone?"

"He's anti-Tony. Not fat and neurotic but focused, in control. Probably ex-KGB. We'll call him Leonid for now."

"Leonid. Nah, how about Boris?"

"And his wife Natasha? Come on, dude. It's Leonid—Leo for short. Anyhow, he's smart and ruthless, more like Michael Corleone, but the perfect family man, protecting and nurturing, but someone who can torture and murder without blinking an eye."

"Are we talking Liam Neeson with a dash of Charles Bronson?"

"More like Bronson with a dash of Sean Penn. Someone like Jon Bernthal or the dude who plays Hannibal Lector now.

"Mads Mikkelsen."

"Right, so what I think we do now is start flushing out the main characters, then sketch out the overall story, then start working on the pilot. Should take a few days."

"I'm in. And I got this idea for a character. Something radical I've been thinking about for a while. We introduce a pedophile. Maybe Leo's brother Boris, but we don't demonize him. We make him interesting."

"Ehh, I don't know. There's still some taboos out there and that might be one of them."

"Seriously? Chappelle's telling pedophile jokes and everyone's laughing. The boundary's already been crossed. So stay with me here, I'm just thinking out loud. We make the brother a pedophile. Leo loves the guy—it's his little brother—and trusts him with his life, but Boris's got this sickness. And maybe we just drop hints about it in the first season, but in the second season Leo finds out about it and implodes. On the one hand he's revolted by it but on the other he loves his little brother. Should he whack him or forgive him? It's a classic dilemma ripe with possibilities. I even have a line of dialogue: Leo says, 'How could you have done this to me, little brother?' To which Boris answers, 'I didn't do it to you, I did it unto others.'"

"Nice line... All right, maybe. But we probably have to whack him in the end."

"Yeah, probably. But let's see where it takes us first."

"All righty, let's get into this. We'll work on the nuclear family first."

"What's our working title? Something like the Romanoffs or the Zhivagos?"

"I was thinking *LA East.*"

"Okay, I get it. L.A. here and Russia from the East. That works for now."

(Time elapses) In a brief montage we see the two writers working. Seth sits on the couch and types on his laptop. Sometimes he nods in agreement, other times he shakes his head and looks up at the ceiling in thought. Vince paces the room, gesturing as he speaks, lighting cigarettes and chewing up the scenery. Occasionally he claps in approval like a quarterback after a pass completion. *Church of the Poison Mind* by Culture Club plays over this montage.

"Make him a big Michael Bublé fan," says Vince.

"I was thinking more like Neil Diamond," replies Seth.

"Nah, not Neil Diamond. We could go with some off the wall eighties band, like Culture Club."

(Buzzing sound)

"That's Todd. Buzz him in."

Vince walks over to the door and buzzes Todd in. He leaves the door ajar and goes back to pacing.

"We could even go with Springsteen," says Vince. "It would show he's got a poetic side."

"No, we want Leonid's taste in music to be a bit schmaltzy. Springsteen's not schmaltzy. Neil Diamond is schmaltzy."

"But we made him an art collector, so why would his taste in music be—Hey, Todd."

"Hey, guys," says Todd. "Shit, it smells like a smoke shop in here. How can you breathe? Anyone hungry?"

"Famished."

Their friend comes in and places an extra-large pizza on the coffee table. Todd Graves is an aspiring actor. He's in his early thirties with dark hair and a stubble beard. He lacks Hollywood good looks but with his mournful eyes and slightly gaunt face he comes off as rather ghoulishly handsome—like Kylo Ren in *The Force Awakens*. This look helped him score a role as a zombie in *The Walking Dead*, though he was killed off after three episodes.

"Wow," says Vince, "that dinner smells good. Let me guess, meat?"

"Combo with everything."

"What we owe you?"

"Ten bucks a piece."

"A Lannister always pays his debts."

"There's beer in the fridge."

"You guys need one?"

"Yeah."

"I'm good."

"I'm surprised your landlord lets you smoke in your apartment."

"He doesn't give a shit. He's a Marlboro man himself."

"Haven't you seen that commercial where the cigarette smoke enters the heating vents in an apartment then creeps along and comes out and descends on baby cribs and innocent toddlers like some poisonous gas?"

"Screw 'em."

"That's the spirit, Vince."

Todd returns from the fridge, hands Seth a beer, and sits down in the other chair while Vince remains standing. They all dig into the pizza.

"How's it going?" asks Todd. "You guys come up with a killer concept yet?"

"Working on it," replies Seth. "I think we got something. We're flushing out the characters."

"What is it?"

"Can't tell you yet. It'd jinx it."

"Come on."

"Nope. Not yet."

"At least give me a clue. Is it post-apocalyptic? Dystopian? An Antifa comedy, or a dysfunctional family? Are we chasing after serial killers? Come on, it's got to be one of the above. Just gimme a clue."

"Dysfunctional family."

"Okay, 'dysfunctional family.' Doesn't give me much to work on. Is it a make-fun-of-rich-people thing like *Arrested Development*, or a fucked-up-mother-daughter thing like *Sharp Objects?*"

"None of the above."

"Hmm, 'none of the above.' Intriguing."

"Just eat your pizza, dude, and stop being so nosey."

"Just gimme one more clue. Are we talking real-life stuff like *Shameless*, or something else?"

"Something else. You want a line of coke?"

"Nah. I'll pass. I took out the *trash* before I left the house, so I'm not even that hungry. I gotta split in a bit to go to a Death Dinner. I just came by to give you two idiots some sustenance."

"A Death Dinner?"

"Yeah, the cast of *The Walking Dead* always throws a party when somebody gets knocked off the show. They call it a Death Dinner. Since I was in three episodes, I get invited."

"Awesome. Do producers show up?"

"Usually."

"If they're looking for writers, talk us up."

"I might. Give me another clue in exchange."

Seth and Vince look at one another and nod in unison.

"Organized crime," says Vince.

"Ahh, okay. 'Organized crime.' So let me think this through…"

"Don't hurt yourself."

"Organized crime and dysfunctional family. Let's see, the mafia's been done. White guy turned meth dealer—done. Black drug lords—done. Cartels—done… My guess is the Russian mob."

"Unbelievable."

"Lucky-ass guess."

"Ha, I got it—and only two clues. Bazinga."

"And keep it to yourself, dude. We're still in the ideation, working out the storyline. We don't even have a series bible yet. So don't jinx it for us."

"Have no fear. I ain't gonna say nuthin'. My word's my bond. It wouldn't matter anyhow. Everybody's working something on the Russian mob, so who would listen?"

"The hell you say. Who's working a series about the Russian mob? Where'd you hear that? Who is it?"

"There are top men working on it now."

"Who?"

"Top. Men."

"Funny."

"He's just messing with you, Vince. Don't take the bait."

"Seth's right. I'm just messin' with you."

"Fuckin' guy."

"I mean, who cares how many writers out there are doing the Russian mob thing. It really comes down to formula. Whoever delivers on the formula the best is the one who gets the deal. And I'm sure you guys got it down pat."

"We have no formula. We're transcending formula."

"Really?"

"Really. We're merely displaying the human condition. And you can't call the human condition a 'formula.'"

"Exactly. Seth's right. Just look at season one of True Detective. It's mesmerizing. It's compelling and sickening at the same time because it's the human condition. It shifts paradigms. And it's because Pizzolatto transcends formulas."

"Vince, Vince, Vince. I know Pizzolatto's your god, but True Detective is everything you say it is because it delivers on the formula."

"Bullshit."

"Just listen to me for a second. Eat your pizza and listen. Now... if you want to be critically acclaimed, if you want to 'shift paradigms' and be ground-breaking, you gotta go dark. Am I wrong? I mean, when you guys started brain-storming today, one of you used the term 'dark and twisted.' Right? 'Dark and twisted.' One of you said it, right?—I'll take that as a yes. So here's the formula for dark and twisted: you lament mankind's depravity while reveling in it on-screen. Mayhem, madness, erotic violence—it's all gotta be there. First you dismantle the idea of family and replace it with social decay and dysfunction. Then come your characters—they're what? 'Complicated,' right? Neither good or bad. Mostly selfish assholes with some redeeming qualities. You strip them down to their basic primal nature, pull back the curtain, and let 'em cum and shit and puke and have carnal knowledge with a pig on stage, and voilà, there's your formula for success."

"Again, you're talking about a world view. A view of the human condition. That's not a formula. That's just holding a mirror up to humanity"

"Come on, Seth. It's cause and effect. Take Hallmark. They have a view of the human condition. It's definitely not your view of the human condition, but they got a formula to deliver that world view every Christmas with a never-ending stream of syrupy movies."

In a silent interlude, Seth appears to counter Todd's point, which segues into a brief montage showing the three men talking around the coffee table. (*Time elapses*) Todd monopolizes the conversation, and we see both Seth and Vince begin to grow impatient with Todd's non-stop diatribe. The song *A Forest* by The Cure plays over this montage.

"Don't you have a death dinner to go to?" asks Seth, as the sound returns.

"I do, I do," replies Todd. "But I wanna help here. Instead of the Russian mob—and I came up with this idea just the other day, so you're the first to hear it—instead of the Russian mob how about a reality show about the homeless? Wait, wait—hear me out. I just read this article about this homeless guy in Frisco who goes out each morning into this upscale neighborhood where all the rich techies live, and once he gets there he dives their dumpsters and finds all this incredible stuff like TVs and unused laptops then hocks it for a small fortune. And that could be your pilot. Call it Dumpsters of the Rich and Famous. Then each week you follow—"

"No reality shows—"

"Well, wait, let me finish—"

"No," replies Seth. "I've got the talking pillow now, okay. We're not doing a reality show. You have to be a filmmaker to do reality shows, and that's not our thing. No reality shows."

"Jeez, got it. Just trying to help... The Russian mob it is then. So how about this—and it's the little things that count—make sure to throw a token into your story. One of those puzzles or recurring symbols to keep your audience alert. Like the log lady in Twin Peaks. Tarantino uses them all the time—the band aid on the back of Marsellus' neck. Or CRM-114."

"What's CRM-114?"

"You're killing me, Smalls. Tell him, Seth. You're the Kubrick geek."

"CRM-114 or just CRM pops up in a bunch of his movies. It first pops up in *Dr. Strangelove* as a decoding machine in the cockpit of the bomber. In *A Clockwork Orange* he uses the homophone 'Serum 114,' which they inject into Alex to program out his violent nature. It's a fictional device and nobody really knows what it means."

"Right. And the weirder the better—keep 'em guessing."

Todd checks his phone, stands up, and gets ready to leave.

"Leaving?" asks Seth. "Don't forget to take your formula with you."

(Laughs) "Just put it in some Tupperware and I'll take it with me—and, hey, I'm not arguing with you—about your world view and all. I probably agree with you. It makes my work easier. Right, Vince? You've been awful quiet there, bro. What's on your mind besides another cigarette, your next line of coke, and a killer line of dialogue?"

"Amigo, you just wrote my epitaph."

"What's that from? Some old western, right? Okay, I'm outta here."

Todd walks to the door where he stops and points to the movie poster for *The Killing*.

"Vince, give me a line."

"'What's the difference?'"

There's a moment of silence as Todd ponders the response.

"Hmm. Is that a line of dialogue or are you just telling me to shove it?"

"Probably both," replies Seth. "But he quoted the last line of the movie. 'What's the difference?'"

"Got it. Very clever, dude. And hey now—if you sell this pilot, don't forget about me. I do a great Russian accent. 'Dat fuckin' nobody ees John Wick. He once vas associate of ours. Dey call hem Baba Yaga.'"

"Not bad. We'll keep you in mind."

"I'll have my people call your people, and all that. Dos vadanya... Oh, one more thing. Just curious, Vince. Would you sell your soul to the devil to be like Nic Pizzolatto?"

"Yep."

"Good to know. See you guys."

Todd exits. Vince makes sure the door is closed and then locks it.

"That guy's a bummer," says Vince.

"Yeah, I know. When he's on meth he talks crazy. Good pizza though."

"He sapped my energy. Like some vampire. We need a charge to get things going again."

"I think you're right."

Seth sets aside his laptop and begins to cut up and lay out two lines of coke while Vince tries to pick up their thought process before they were interrupted by Todd.

"So I was thinking while Todd was yakking away, maybe Neil Diamond works afterall. We got Leo running his crew out of a nightclub in downtown L.A. He's ex-KGB, a cold-blooded killer, and a ruthless bastard. At the same time, he's a loving family man, doesn't cheat on his wife, and dotes on his five kids. We made him a precious art collector—which, by the way, works for us by having him pull off an art heist later on, maybe for a Jackson Pollack, which he ends up hanging in his basement."

(*Sniffs*) I like that idea. Here." He hands Vince the rolled up dollar bill. "Let me get that down."

Vince quickly snorts his line, licks the remains with his finger, and stands back up. Seth is back on his laptop and typing away.

"How old did we say he was?" asks Vince.

"Just a sec," replies Seth… "He's in his sixties."

"Right, sixties. So that puts his music in the seventies—which means Neil Diamond works. *Solitary Man.* That can be like his theme song." (*Sings*) "'I'll be what I am. A solitary man. Solitary man.'"

"I was thinking *America.*" (*Sings*) "'They're coming to America. Never looking back again. They're coming to America.' I forget all the words, but it's got that irony thing going for it."

"We need to get into the whole soundtrack. It's creates the milieu and sets the mood. David Chase used his whole record collection for *The Sopranos*, from oldies rock to hip hop. We gotta do the same. For the pilot, I was thinking gothic rock, like Nick Cave. Something dark and—shit! Todd ruined that phrase for me. I can't even say it anymore."

"Just go with D and T. I'll know what you mean."

(*Laughs*) "Something D and T."

"Nick Cave's already been covered. *Peaky Blinders.*"

"That was just one song. Then we'll go with the Cure or Alice Cooper."

"I don't want to get into the soundtrack yet. We still have too much work to do on our characters. Leo's pretty much done, so we gotta move on to the rest of the family. Okay? You with me?"

"Sure. Let's work on Boris."

In Tribute To Granddaughters

"**R**eady there, little girl?"

"She's coming," replied my wife. "She's puttin' her shoes on. Wait till you see her outfit. It's *sooo* cute."

"We ain't goin' to the mall," I said. "We're goin' fishin'."

"She knows that."

"Then what's takin' so long? She just needs blue jeans and a t-shirt. No make-up. No earrings. You hear me in there, little girl. Put on some get-dirty clothes and let's go." I had this image of her coming out in one of those striped jumpsuits of hers, sporting Minnie Mouse earrings and a polka-dot purse. And that just wouldn't do.

"*She knows that.* Cool your jets."

Just then she appeared from out of the bedroom. "Yeah, cool your jets there, Poppa-doodle," she said cheerily. "How do I look?" She raised her arms out, dropped them, and then stood at attention as though waiting inspection.

"You look *sooo* cute," said my wife.

I gave my granddaughter the once over and nodded in approval. She was camouflaged-out. She had on a dark-green, camouflaged t-shirt with matching shorts that went to her knees, along with flip flops and one of those baseball caps that are frayed around the edges to make them seem old and worn. She looked like she was ready to go on jungle maneuvers.

"That'll work," I said. "Where'd you get all the camouflage clothes?"

"Didn't you know," replied my wife. "That's her new thing. We got that at Target along with a blue set."

"Yeah, I got this one and a blue one, and I gotta pink one at home."

"Pink camouflage? Seriously?"

"Get with it, Papa."

"Yeah, *get with it,* Papa."

"I'm getting with it," I said and looked her over once more. Here was my granddaughter, a ten-year old whirling dervish, all decked out in camouflage-chic and ready to go fishing with her grandfather. Her name was Minerva, after the Roman goddess, but everyone called her Minnie, though on occasion I liked to call her Minnie-me. And Minnie-me now spun around to give me the full fashion statement. Despite my protests, she had recently cut her long, beautiful hair into—I guess you would call it—a bob with short bangs, and now with it stuck under a baseball cap, along with her camouflage shirt and shorts, she looked every bit the tomboy. Just like her mom at that age.

"Now, you got everything?" I asked her, checking my own pockets to make sure I had my keys, my wallet, and my knife and snips.

"I'm ready, freddy."

"'Kay, then we're outta here. Give your grandma a kiss goodbye."

"Got your fishing poles?" asked my wife.

"Don't need 'em. They supply everything."

"Really? That's convenient. Give me a kiss, sweetie." My wife corralled Minnie in her arms and gave her a kiss on the forehead along with a big hug. "Mind your Papa."

"I will."

I kissed my wife goodbye and said, "We'll be back around one," and ushered Minnie out the front door while my wife called after us to "have fun" and "catch lots of fish." We jumped in my truck and I made sure her seatbelt was tight before I pulled out and drove off.

The trout pond was about a half hour drive up into the foothills of Oregon City. This wasn't going to be lake fishing in a boat, or fly-fishing along a river—not *real* fishing at all, but rather a kind of carnival game where you fished from the bank of a man-made pond stocked with trout. It was like shooting fish in a barrel and you were sure to get one. But it was close-by and you didn't need a fishing license, and it was perfect for kids who'd never been fishing before.

Minnie was here with us for two and a half weeks during summer vacation. Most of that time had been intricately planned out by grandma and included arcades, amusement parks, trips to the beach and the zoo, assorted forays to clothes stores and toy stores, and swimming in the local pool. But with only three days left before she headed back home, the excursion list had dwindled down to nothing and Minnie was confronted with staying indoors. That meant a whole day with her eager, active mind peeling back the wallpaper, demanding attention, and arguing with her grandmother over sound volumes and data usage. I avoided this little crisis by suggesting she go fishing with me and she jumped at the chance.

Within minutes we were on a winding road with woods on each side. The woods became broken up, here and there, by large estates and horse ranches, and we passed hay farms where rectangular bales of hay sat in rows on the harvested land. Black cows grazed in open pastures. Occasionally, around a bend or on the side of a hill, there appeared a nursery or Christmas tree farm. Traveling through this kind of country on the way to go fishing always reminded me of my dad. He loved fishing.

I remembered the last time we'd gone fishing. It was on a lake in Minnesota. He was weak from the chemotherapy so he sat up front and leaned against the bow of the boat while I operated the outboard motor. He pointed to a spot across the lake and I steered in that direction. And leaning forward like that, with the wind in his face and the smell of the lake in his nose, he glanced back at me and smiled. Being on a lake always made him happy. It was too bad the rest of his life hadn't been like that, but then he only had himself to blame for that. He'd been a good dad at times, fun to be around, but over time he'd gone bad, real bad, and done some unforgivable things before he ran off. But I dearly loved him all the same. And now, out on the lake, he seemed to rally and catch his second wind, smiling happily back at me, and we fished all day and had a great time. The next day I had to fly back home and he died six months later.

I turned on the radio and glanced over at my granddaughter. She was on her iPhone.

"Where'd that come from?" I asked her. She was engrossed in something and ignored me. "Hey you. Minnie-me. Wake up. Where'd that phone come from?"

She appeared irritated at the interruption. "I brought it with me. Duuuh," she replied.

"Well, put it away. We're goin' fishin'. And you're missing all the sights. Look, there's some horses. Now put it away."

"Just a sec."

"No, now... Hear me? What's so fascinating anyhow? Are you texting someone?" She ignored me and continued to play with her phone. "Did you hear me?" I repeated more loudly.

"Sip your tea," she said without glancing away from her phone.

"'Sip your tea.' What does that mean?" I waited for an answer but got none, so I raised the volume level a little higher. "Minnie! I'm talkin' to you. Get off your phone. And what does 'Sip your tea" mean?"

"Means mind your own beeswax." She spoke this without taking her eyes off her screen, like an air traffic controller guiding in a plane.

"That's what I thought." I watched her out of the corner of my eye as I drove along the country road. She had no intention of minding me. Her concentration was locked onto the little screen of her iPhone, which she kept slightly tilted away from me so I couldn't see what she was doing, and that concentration, as I knew so well, could become a kind of rebelliousness at times.

"Put the phone away. I won't tell you again," I said in my bad cop voice. "Hear me, little girl? Whatever it is you're doing—texting or playing a game—wrap it up... Now!"

The angry "Now!" got her attention and she glanced up at me with a look of alarm mixed with oh-woe-is-me. She had bright, expressive eyes that she used to full effect, and I called this her silent screen face because it packed all sorts of emotion into one look. And now would come the negotiation.

"Jeez, Papa. Don't get mad at me," she replied in a hurt voice. "Just let me finish this one thing. Five minutes. Just let me finish."

"What is it?"

"A game. Roblox. We're almost done."

"All right. Five minutes then," I replied in my good cop voice. "But no more."

She smiled, satisfied with the outcome of the negotiation, and returned to her game. I turned the radio up on the Van Morrison song *Domino* and checked the clock. I knew that in five minutes the negotiations would start again.

Minnie was like that sometimes. Obstinate. But that was my granddaughter; she was a horn-of-plenty full of talents and emotions. For one, she was ahead of the curve in most everything, and I mean everything. For example, she won her school's spelling bee in the fourth grade, and I'm talking the *whole school* here. She was also artistic. She was an accomplished drawer, musically inclined with a beautiful singing voice, and had proved herself a master engineer of Lego-built housing. But balanced against this precocious little intellect was a junior black belt in Karate and a wizard skateboarder. Bundled all together, along with her loud commanding voice and a natural leadership style, she had all the makings of a philosopher king. I was quite convinced she would be the first female president of the United States. Either that or a ruthless and powerful drug lord.

It remained a mystery to me why some people, born and bred in difficult circumstances, thrive and blossom while others wither and die. It had to be something in-born, and Minnie was a perfect example of that. She was the oldest of three kids, all from different fathers, and what with the constant moving, rotating father-figures, and a home life littered with the flotsam and jetsam of domestic disputes, it was a wonder she hadn't withdrawn into a cocoon or been diagnosed with ADHD and put on meds. Instead, what we had was this neon sign in the desert, inviting in all weary travelers.

That was my Minnie-me. There was something there I could relate to, which probably explained the peculiar bond we shared. We had a similar way of looking at the world and, like me, she had a whimsical and goofy sense of humor which I enjoyed triggering whenever possible. When we were together hanging out and having fun, the rest of the family tended to view us as two aliens from a distant planet. Not that we always got along together, and I chalked that up to her artistic, temperamental side. She could be a butthead. Like now.

Five minutes came and went, and I gave her an extra two to make it seven. "Time's up," I said.

She ignored me again and I got loud again and we came to an impasse. So I upped the ante.

"I'm pretty sure mom gave you rules about your phone and you're breaking them. I can call her now and ask her—but I won't. Instead I'm gonna pull over and take your phone away because I'm bigger and stronger than you and feed it to the cows."

"Cows don't eat iPhones."

"These cows do."

I caught a slight grin on her lips but she still held on tight to her phone, so I slowed the truck down and pretended I was pulling over. This called her bluff.

"Oh, my god! Okay. Fine," she exclaimed in self-righteous indignation. She turned off her phone and shoved it into the big pocket of her camouflaged shorts. "There. Happy? I bet you wouldn't care if I was reading a book instead."

"Read one and find out."

"I didn't bring one."

"So what you reading these days?"

I could tell she wanted to stay angry with me, but questions like this, questions that appealed to her tastes in music and literature, tended to captivate her despite her efforts to resist.

"Harry Potter," she replied.

"Just like your mom... Who's your favorite character?"

"Dumbledore. But I also like Sirius Black."

"Sirius Black. Which one is he?"

"He's Harry's godfather. He got blamed for the murder of Harry's mom and dad and gets sent to prison, but he escapes by turning into a black dog. Later on he gets murdered."

"What! Don't tell me that. I may wanna read the books."

"Haven't you seen the movies?"

"Just the first one, so don't throw out any more spoilers."

"I can't believe you never read the Harry Potter books. They're like the most famous books in the whole wide world. I thought you read everything."

"Obviously not."

"What kind of books did you read when you were my age?"

"I always liked Ray Bradbury—oh, here we are." I almost missed the entrance to the trout farm but caught it in time and made a sharp left turn. A gravel road took us to the side of a building where we parked and looked around. There was only one other vehicle parked nearby, a beat-up truck, and there was someone sitting in it.

"Hmm, let's check it out," I said a little skeptically. There was no one fishing around the pond and, by the looks of things, I wasn't sure they were open. We walked over to entrance where we found the door open and a bunch of posted signs that explained rules and prices. A man got out of the truck and came over and greeted us.

"Howdy folks." he said.

"Hi. You guys open?"

"Yep." He stuck out his hand in greeting. "Name's Dwayne."

"Tim. Nice to meet you."

 He was dressed in overalls and carried a tobacco-stained plastic bottle that he spit his dip into. I explained that we were here to fish and also needed fishing poles. He quickly explained the set-up: there was a small flat fee, which included poles and bait, but otherwise you paid for the fish you caught and you could catch as many as you wanted. He pointed to a shed that housed the fishing poles, all hanging from racks, and there must have been fifty of them. Minnie and I picked out two poles. They were already set up with bobbers, sinkers, and hooks, and Minnie chose a purple one. When we came out, the man handed me a bucket along with a Styrofoam cup filled with night crawlers and wished us good luck.

The trout pond was oval-shaped and smaller than a football field. It was surrounded by a manicured lawn, trees, and a number of picnic tables. We found a good spot under the shade of a pine tree that was right next to a picnic table and close to the water. I leaned the poles up against the tree then walked over to the pond where I dipped the bucket in and filled it halfway with water. Minnie squatted down and inspected the cup full of night crawlers.

"I'm not touching those," she declared while pinching up her nose. "No way. They're gross."

"What? Why not?" I asked playfully as I kneeled down next to her. I pulled out a night crawler like a fat piece of spaghetti and waved it in her face.

"Eewww, get it away from me," she yelped, jumping back, but there was a smile on her face.

"Don't worry, little girl. I'll bait your hook." I grabbed her purple fishing rod. "Remember what I showed you about casting and reeling? Good. Let's practice a couple casts before I bait your hook."

We walked to the edge of the pond where I showed her the button to push for casting, explaining that you had to let go of the button right before you tossed your line out. I showed her how it was done by casting the empty hook out into the water. I waited for the bobber to settle before reeling it back, reminding her to go easy and not too fast. She was eager to try it herself, saying ""Let me try," and "I can do it," and I handed her the rod. Minnie spread her feet and swung the rod back like I'd showed her. She hesitated there for a moment and then flung it forward toward the water, forgetting to let go of the button. The line snapped back and twisted itself around the end of her pole.

"Whaa! What happened?" she shouted in surprise. "I did it right. W-T-F."

"No, you didn't. You forgot to let go of the button—and don't say W-T-F. I know what that means. Here, hand me the pole." I took the pole from her and unwound the line. "Now watch. You press the button..."

"But I did."

"I know, but you gotta let go of it when you're here. Watch again." I cast out the line and handed her back the fishing pole. "Reel it in... There you go. Nice and easy. Just reel it up to the bobber—good. Now try again."

She tried again with the same result. She threw out more exclamations, this time claiming there was something wrong with the fishing pole. I assured her there wasn't. "Listen," I said calmly, "I'll bait your hook and cast out the first couple times until you get the hang of it." This plan met with her approval.

I took out my snips and cut an inch-long piece of night crawler and threaded it onto the hook while Minnie watched intently over my shoulder. We walked back to the water's edge where I cast out the line, let some line out, and handed the pole over to Minnie. "Now watch the bobber," I told her. "If it goes under water that means you gotta fish. Then you set the hook and reel it in. Got it?"

"Got it, Poppa-doodle."

I started to walk back to the tree to attend to my own fishing rod when I caught her bobber moving out of the corner of my eye. It hadn't been in the water more than five seconds.

"What's that?" she cried excitedly. "Do I have a fish?"

"Hold. Not yet. Something's playing with it." I watched her bobber closely. It shivered slightly, inched left then right, and suddenly went under water. "You got one! Reel it in."

In her great excitement, Minnie yanked up on her pole and backpedaled. I yelled at her to stand still and reel the fish in but it was useless, she was too excited. Within seconds she had pulled the trout out of the water and up onto the bank where it flopped about. "I got one! I got one! I got a fish!" she screamed happily.

"Good girl. Now calm down. Start reeling it in. Walk slowly towards it and reel your line in. Good. There you go."

"Don't let it get away."

I assured her it wasn't going anywhere and waited until she had reeled in her line. She held her pole up with the trout dangling on the end of it as though she were displaying a prize. I reached for the trout but Minnie backed up and I missed it. She laughed at that, and we performed this silly dance until I got her to stand still so I could grab the fish and remove the hook. I cleaned it off in the bucket of water and held it in my hand for her to look at. It was only about ten inches long, your basic farm trout, olive green in color with black spotting and a pinkish stripe from gills to tail. I dropped it into the bucket and Minnie squatted next to it, watching it swim around.

"Are we going to eat it?" she asked.

"That's the plan. Ever had trout before?"

"I don't know. Don't think so. Are they good?"

"If you cook 'em right, they're delicious. But these are kinda' small, so we need to get a few more. Are you ready to catch another fish?"

"I'm ready!" she shouted, jumping up. "That was lit. Let's do it again."

"Grab your pole and let's get it baited up."

She retrieved her pole and I put a new worm on it, cast it out for her, and within seconds she had another bite. Within forty-five minutes, she caught seven fish, but most of that time was spent untangling her line while teaching her to cast and reel. I got a kick out of watching her. Each time her bobber went under she shrieked in excitement and yanked her pole back yelling, "Let's goooo!" Sometimes she remembered to reel in, other times she forgot, but inevitably the trout would appear on land flipping and flopping in protest, and she would cheer in delight. After each triumph she would squat down next to the bucket and marvel at her growing catch of fish.

I never did get a chance to fish on my own.

We stopped at seven fish, not that Minnie was happy about that, but you paid by the fish here and I figured seven was a big enough investment. The trout ranged from ten to twelve inches long, and I laid them out on the grass and had Minnie kneel next to them with her pole so I could take a picture with my cell phone. She had a big smile on her face.

I tossed the trout back in the bucket and we walked up to the entrance. As we approached, Dwayne got out of his office-truck and greeted us. "How'd he do?" he asked, squinting first at Minnie and then at me. Minnie snickered at that.

"She's my granddaughter," I replied politely. "She did great. She caught seven."

"Seven? Wow—here, let me have that." He took the bucket of fish from me and walked over to a long, outdoor sink that was set up for cleaning fish. "You can put the poles back in there," he added. I put the poles back in the shed and returned to find him cleaning the fish, which was a pleasant surprise. First he measured the fish then placed it under running water, snipped around the gills, slit it open with his knife, and deftly removed the guts. He placed the finished product in a large plastic bag. Minnie watched the whole process with a clinical fascination, like a first-year med student watching an autopsy.

He removed something from the next fish and placed it on the edge of the sink next to us. It was tiny and white with a speck of red to it, and it looked like something you'd pick out of your teeth. "It's a trout heart," he said. "Is this your first time fishing?" he asked Minnie. Yes, it was, she told him. "Well then, the tradition is you have to eat a trout heart."

Minnie looked at him with suspicion, as though he were trying to pull a fast one, and backed away from the sink. "No way. Gross."

"There's nothing to it," he said. "Watch." He picked up the tiny heart with his finger, placed it on his tongue like a baby aspirin, and washed it down with the water out of the running spigot. "See, nothing to it." He pulled another heart out of the next trout and placed it on the edge of the sink as before while he playfully dared her to gulp it down. You have to uphold tradition, he told her. Everybody ate a heart their first time. He'd even take twenty dollars off her grandpa's bill if she ate it.

She parried his attempts to talk her into it with smirks and funny faces, but I could tell that the whole idea was beginning to intrigue her. She looked to me for advice.

"It's up to you," I said. "You don't have to if you don't want. No big deal."

"You eat one, Papa."

"All right. You got it." Without hesitating, I picked up the heart, placed it on my tongue, and washed it down with the water bottle I carried with me.

"Whoa, ha, ha," she laughed, impressed at my boldness.

Dwayne quickly placed another heart on the edge of the sink. "That's the last one," he said. "It's now or never."

Now her struggle began in earnest. She stepped towards the sink, danced back, said "I don't know," stepped forward again saying, "I'm going to do it," then danced away again. She was both repulsed and attracted at the same time, and I watched in amusement as she tried to psych herself up. The fish were all cleaned and bagged and it was time to pay up and go, but she resisted the urge to call it quits.

"Okay, okay," I'm gonna do it," she declared loudly. "Put it in my hand." I picked up the heart and placed it in her open palm. She examined it closely. I opened up my water bottle and handed it to her as well. She held the heart in one hand and the bottle of water in the other, weighing them up and down as though they were the scales of justice. After some hesitation her face turned serious and I knew then she would do it. This small rite of passage, this act of daring-do, had become fixed it her head and she wasn't going to back down now. She popped the heart in her mouth and washed it down."

Her shoulders shivered as it went down but the deed was done. "Nothing to it," she sang out in triumph.

"Didn't think you'd do it," said Dwayne with a tobacco-stained smile.

"Impressive," I added.

I settled up with Dwayne and gave him a tip. Minnie and I walked back to my truck with our bag of fish. She was talking a mile a minute about how she had eaten a fish heart and that she'd have to tell her mom and grandma and everybody at school. Nobody would believe it. I should have taken a video of it. Oh well.

I started up the truck and pulled out. "Did you have fun?" I asked her.

"That was hella fresh," she replied with a big, wonderful smile.

"Guess that means yes."

She wanted to do all the talking and I let her talk. She was still excited and I got a kick out of listening to her. At one point she laughed and said, "Can you believe it? That guy thought I was a boy."

"He's an idiot."

"Well, I kinda' look like a boy with my hair short and these camouflage clothes... Anyhow, my teacher says there's no such thing as gender."

"Really? She said that?"

"She says there's no such thing as 'he' and 'she.' It's all neutral."

"Imagine that. And all this time I thought men and women made babies."

"Jeez, Poppa-doodle. Get with it."

"I'm getting with it. But that means I can't call you 'little girl' anymore. Right? I'll have to call you something else, like 'little thing' or 'little it.' So you have your choice. Which will it be—'it' or 'thing'?"

"I like 'it'. Call me 'Little-it' and I'll call you Poppa-thing."

"Perfect."

That settled, Minnie decided to play a game as we drove through the countryside. "I spy with my little eye something that begins with "W," she said. I looked around and immediately answered, "Wires."

"Dang. That was too easy. Your turn."

I spied a yellow warning sign and she guessed it right away. She spied a barn with a red roof and I pretended to take a while but finally got it. It was my turn again.

"Here's a hard one. You'll never get it. I spy with my little eye a C-E-A-I."

"You can't say it that way. That's too many letters. You can only say one letter."

"I can do what I want. C-E-A-I. Do you give up?"

She filed a formal protest, claiming I was changing the rules and it wasn't fair, but I ignored her with a sly grin and repeated, "C-E-A-I. If you give up I win."

"Just hold on a sec. Give me a chance," she replied as she sat up and scanned the road and countryside. I could see her mind racing to solve the puzzle. "C-E-A-I," she said to herself. "Hmm... C-E-A-I... I got it! A Car Entering An Intersection. C-E-A-I. Right? I got it, right?"

"Nope. But good guess." She sat back in her seat in exaggerated dejection and said, "Then I give up. What is it?"

"Easy. A Cow Eating an iPhone."

She laughed. "Where? Show me," she demanded. I pointed to imaginary spot up on a green pasture and said, "Right there. Don't you see it?" She pretended to see it and laughed again.

"You're sooo weird," she said.

"You're weirder."

"You're the weirdest of the weird."

"And you're the weirdest of the weirdest."

"You're the weirdest of the weirdest, infinity plus one. End of story."

I conceded the point. There was probably something better than infinity plus one but I couldn't think of what it was, so I told her she won, and she smiled happily. She asked if she could listen to some better music than Classic Rock. I raised an eyebrow at that remark but went ahead and scanned the radio stations using a button on my steering wheel until I hit a song and she yelled "Stop!" It was a Shawn Mendes' song—her favorite—and she immediately started singing along with it. When it ended, another song came on but she didn't like it so I kept scanning. After a minute of that I got a better idea. I hit another button on my steering wheel and said, "Siri, play *Everybody* by the Backstreet Boys."

"I *luuuve* that song," she breathed out with emotion. "Me and Mom sing it all the time."

"I know." The song came on and we sang it together while we passed the horse ranches and hay farms along the road, and when it was over we sang some other songs we both knew. I took her to DQ for lunch and she ordered her usual, a plain hamburger with fries and a chocolate shake. We sat and ate and made fun of people, and in the middle of lunch she suddenly got up, walked around to me, hugged me, and gave me a kiss on the cheek. "I love you, Poppa-thing. Thanks for taking me fishing."

"You're welcome, Little-it. Love you, too."

Satisfied with her world and everything in it, she sat back down to finish her lunch. And it was this moment for me—not the shrieks of joy at catching a fish or bravely eating a trout heart or even the sing-along—but this moment and this moment alone that was the very best part of my day. But I kept this joy to myself and quietly ate my lunch.

When we got home, Minnie replayed the whole adventure for her grandmother. She called her mom and gave her a full report. Yes, she had eaten a trout heart. She *really* had. Pictures of her kneeling next to her fish were texted to friends and family and posted on Facebook. But somehow Fox News missed the story.

That night I sat in my chair and drank a glass of red wine. Minnie appeared in her pajamas and came over to get her good-night kiss. She leaned forward so I could kiss her on the forehead, and she thanked me again for the great day. She started off for bed but I stopped her.

"Hey, Minnie-me," I whispered. "I got a secret for you."

"What is it?" she asked as she sneaked back over to me and leaned her ear in to hear my secret.

I whispered to her, "Den som sover syndar icke."

"What's that mean?"

"It's Swedish. My grandmother used to say it to me before I went to bed. It means 'He who sleeps does not sin.'"

"I don't get it."

"Me neither... That's cause it really means 'Sleep tight and don't let the bed bugs bite.'"

She sniffed a short laugh through her nose at this, said "Nite, Poppa-doodle," and ran off to bed.

I picked up my glass of wine and called after her, "Nite, little girl."

CPSIA information can be obtained
at www.ICGtesting.com
Printed in the USA
LVHW020709260121
677443LV00019B/3821